Written on the Wind

Books by Judith Pella

Beloved Stranger
Blind Faith
Texas Angel

DAUGHTERS OF FORTUNE
Written on the Wind

LONE STAR LEGACY
Frontier Lady   *Stoner's Crossing*
Warrior's Song

RIBBONS OF STEEL†
Distant Dreams   *A Hope Beyond*
A Promise for Tomorrow

RIBBONS WEST†
Westward the Dream   *Separate Roads*
Ties That Bind

THE RUSSIANS
The Crown and the Crucible*   *Heirs of the Motherland*
A House Divided*   *Dawning of Deliverance*
Travail and Triumph*   *White Nights, Red Morning*
Passage Into Light

THE STONEWYCKE TRILOGY*
The Heather Hills of Stonewycke   *Flight From Stonewycke*
Lady of Stonewycke

THE STONEWYCKE LEGACY*
Stranger at Stonewycke   *Shadows Over Stonewycke*
Treasure of Stonewycke

THE JOURNALS OF CORRIE BELLE HOLLISTER
My Father's World*   *Daughter of Grace**

*with Michael Phillips   †with Tracie Peterson

JUDITH PELLA

Written on the Wind

BETHANYHOUSE
PUBLISHERS

MINNEAPOLIS, MINNESOTA

Published by Bethany House Publishers
A Ministry of Bethany Fellowship International
11400 Hampshire Avenue South
Bloomington, Minnesota 55438

Printed in the United States of America

ISBN 0-7642-2608-8

ABOUT THE AUTHOR

Judith Pella is the author of several historical fiction series, both on her own and in collaboration with Michael Phillips and Tracie Peterson. The extraordinary seven-book series THE RUSSIANS, the first three written with Phillips, showcases her creativity and skill as a historian as well as a fiction writer. A Bachelor of Arts degree in social studies, along with a career in nursing and teaching, lends depth to her storytelling abilities, providing readers with memorable novels in a variety of genres. She and her husband make their home in Oregon.

Visit Judith's Web sites:
www.judithpella.com
http://members.aol.com/Pellabooks

PART I

"And while I am talking to you mothers and fathers, I give you one more assurance . . . I say it again and again and again: Your boys are not going to be sent into any foreign wars."

FRANKLIN ROOSEVELT
Election Eve, October 1940

1

THE ORCHESTRA played a mellow rendition of "Moonlight Serenade" as Cameron Hayes drew in a deep breath and made her move. Seated several tables away from where she stood by the refreshment table, industrialist Donald Farr looked like a benevolent grandfather. The perfectly styled graying hair, the aquiline features, even the crows-feet at the corners of his pale blue eyes made him seem harmless indeed.

Farr, however, had been in a lot of hot water lately over some dubiously acquired government contracts. He'd testified before a Senate investigative committee, and his smooth-talking, high-priced lawyers had reprieved him. But Cameron was not as easily swayed as a few senators. She'd broken the story in the first place—the kind of journalistic coup that had six months ago finally propelled her into a position as a hard-news reporter at the *Los Angeles Journal*'s city desk. Not an easy feat, even at the beginning of the fourth decade of the twentieth century, for a mere woman who was also only twenty-four.

She hadn't been enthusiastic about attending her father's fiftieth birthday party until now. But seeing the infamous industrialist had dramatically changed her attitude. Here was Farr, completely at her mercy. He would never know of the butterflies in her stomach or of her mild trepidation at defying her father's wishes. She would approach him with the cool aplomb of a seasoned veteran—even if it killed her.

Not that she would wage a frontal attack on the unwitting party guest. She could be subtle, despite what many of the "victims" of her incisive style might say. Allowing a smile to slip across her face, she

9

began to cross the expansive lawn of her family's Beverly Hills home, now dotted with tables where many of the two hundred guests reposed. Farr would not know what hit him.

Seated with Farr was his wife, an attractive blonde easily twenty years his junior. Also at the table were four other guests, including the Los Angeles police commissioner. There were no vacant chairs at the table. Undeterred, Cameron reached the table, broadened her smile, and greeted the industrialist and his companions.

"A lovely day for a party, don't you think?" She thought that sounded very subtle.

"Your father is lucky to have been blessed with such a balmy day for February," said Mrs. Farr.

"Even Mother Nature does obeisance to dear old Dad." Cameron grabbed a vacant chair from an adjacent table and squeezed it into a small open space next to Farr. Smiling sweetly, she added offhandedly, "You don't mind if I join you for a minute?"

"Well—" Farr began.

"It was so kind of you to come to Daddy's party, Mr. Farr," Cameron hurried on, ignoring Farr's attempt at a protest. "I know you've been busy lately. Haven't you just returned from Washington?"

"Yes, a few days ago."

"I am so glad to be back," added Mrs. Farr. "It snowed while we were there."

"Then it must be quite a relief to be home—in more ways than one. I trust your trip was successful?"

Farr smiled. His gray hair might give him a grandfatherly air, but his eyes, even when he smiled, were hard. "Indeed it was; nevertheless, I am glad to be away from there."

"Surely you weren't nervous about appearing before the Senate."

"I had nothing to be nervous about—"

"There you are, Cameron!" interrupted a feminine voice. "Daddy sent me to fetch you."

Cameron turned and saw her youngest sister, Jackie. "What could he want?" She was not at all pleased at the interruption.

"Come along with me, and you can find out," Jackie replied.

"But we were just having such a nice conversation here—"

Farr hurried to his feet. "Please, don't let us keep you, Miss Hayes. It's your father's birthday, after all."

Cameron hesitated, but her sister gently tugged at her arm. "He's waiting."

As she rose Cameron said to Farr, "Perhaps we can finish our conversation later."

"I'd love to." But Farr's steely gaze indicated he'd sooner see the Los Angeles basin freeze over than do such a thing.

When Cameron and her sister were several paces from the Farr table, Cameron stopped. "What's this all about? Dad is over there." She jerked her head in the opposite direction from where they were heading.

A bit sheepishly, Jackie answered, "He sent me to rescue you—or rather poor Mr. Farr. Told me to tell you *no work*."

"Who said I was working? I was just having—"

"I know, 'a nice conversation.' I'm just doing what I'm told, Cameron."

"Oh, little Jackie, when are you going to wise up?"

"It is his birthday. Can't you do what you're told just for today?"

"Well, I guess I owe him at least one day of the doting daughter routine."

Jackie smiled. At barely twenty, she was a sweet child, so pretty and innocent in appearance that she did not look the least bit silly in the lavender frock of organza with its ruffled décolletage. Her wavy light brown hair, pinned with lavender bows on each side of her head, fell to her shoulders. She was the very picture of the college co-ed that she was—wide-eyed, eager to please, enthusiastic, not to mention naïve about her future.

The only obvious similarity between the two sisters was the wide-set eyes inherited from their mother. But where Jackie's were a pure brown, Cameron's were green, or hazel, or dark brown, depending upon many factors, such as her clothing, her surroundings, her moods. But Cameron was attractive, no question about that. The auburn hair framing a heart-shaped face could have been as feminine and ingenuous as Jackie's, especially when she let it hang in loose waves, as it was now, but Cameron tried hard to camouflage those features. When working, she usually wore plain wool suits and crammed her hair under a simple matching hat. Today was the exception, and in a dark burgundy crepe dress with a draped neckline and a trim, belted skirt, she proved she could look stunning. But her looks were of little importance to her. All she wanted to prove was her ability as a journalist and so allowed herself little time for social pleasures.

The two sisters began walking once more, but in a few moments, Jackie nudged Cameron to a stop, scanning the crowd.

"I wonder where Blair is," she said.

"Don't tell me you are going to ruin her day, too," Cameron said with a slight groan.

"Daddy's going to make a speech, and there will be some pictures taken. He wants us there."

Blair was the middle sister, and they found her, not surprisingly, in the midst of a small herd of young men, looking every bit like Scarlett O'Hara in the scene at the Twelve Oaks barbecue in the movie *Gone With the Wind*. Of course, Cameron did not usually go to movies—she found real life far more stimulating. But she had been assigned to cover the Hollywood premiere—not even the star-studded Atlanta premiere. Regardless, it galled her to no end that she was still shuffled off to the society beat when the paper was shorthanded. No one would dare throw a society story at Johnny Shanahan—but that was another matter entirely.

Cameron half expected to hear Blair utter a simpering "Fiddledee-dee!" when she and Jackie penetrated the circle of her male admirers. Instead, she had a sip of champagne, as if to fortify herself, then said, "My, I think the competition has arrived!"

"We could never compete with you, Blair, love," Cameron said snidely. She loved her sister but had a difficult time understanding her.

Blair lived for the social pleasures Cameron so pointedly eschewed. She seemed to have no greater ambition in life than to shop for the latest styles and to wear her purchases to beguile men. Her mother, in a desperate attempt to get her to settle down, nagged her often about marriage, but Blair liked men too much to limit herself to just one. In fact, she often said she had no intention of marrying at all in the near future. She thought she might like to be an actress or a singer and spent a lot of her time with the Hollywood crowd toward that end. But it wasn't a burning ambition—nothing, in fact, was. Her time as a wealthy society girl was spent partying, drinking way too much, and building on her already notorious reputation with men. Her lifestyle shocked her parents—an achievement that might well have been her highest ambition in life.

Blair drained her glass of Dom Pérignon and held it out to one of the men. "Do be a dear and fetch me another."

Cameron caught the glass before it reached a proffered hand. "Later, Blair. Daddy wants us."

"Oh, pooh on him! I'm busy." Blair's full red lips puckered into a coy pout.

"Now, now, Blair, don't be stubborn. Daddy calls."

"And since when are you the obedient daughter?"

It was a rather uncharacteristic position for Cameron to take, but she understood the value of expediency better than her sister. "Just for the time being, Blair. It won't kill either of us."

Blair glanced at the bevy of handsome young men, then shrugged. "Duty calls, boys. But I'll be back."

She swung her lithe body into line with her sisters', and with arms linked, they turned in the direction of the head table.

2

CAMERON LOVED her father, but she had a nagging suspicion that she did so largely out of duty. Not that she hated him exactly; it was just that Keagan Hayes was simply not the kind of man anyone could really love. In fact, Hayes himself would no doubt sneer at such sentimental hogwash.

He was instead a man for whom the words "tough" and "no nonsense" might have been coined to describe him. He looked more like a scrappy Irish laborer than the publisher of one of California's most prestigious newspapers. At fifty, his once muscular six-foot frame had gone a bit to paunch, but he still bore an imposing figure, heightened by a thick thatch of graying red hair, a prominent nose with a bump at the top where it had been broken in a fistfight, and the most penetrating, flashing green eyes imaginable. The idea of a young daughter snuggling in his lap was preposterous. At least Cameron could not remember a time when she had done so. There were times when she had longed to feel her father's arms around her, but not anymore. The waiting had hurt too much to long for the impossible, and she would not let herself be hurt like that by any man again.

Perhaps he did not encourage such behavior because he simply could not accept that he'd been cursed with daughters instead of sons—and everyone knew sons did not cuddle with their fathers. By the time Jackie had been born, their mother, Cecilia, had developed enough strength of will to insist that this daughter be accepted for what she was—a girl. She selected a feminine name—well, as much so as she dared. And even now she adamantly called her youngest Jacqueline, not the more masculine name that Keagan, and everyone else, used.

It had been different with Cameron's birth. Keagan had been so positive his first child would be a son to name after his father that when he realized the baby was only a daughter, instead of admitting defeat, he named her for Cameron Hayes, his Irish father. A year later, he was certain he would finally have a son to make up for the disappointment of Cameron. He planned on naming this son Blair after the brother who had traveled with him from Ireland but had died before arriving in the "Promised Land."

Keagan would never forgive his daughters their curls and ruffles, their giggles or tears. The girls had their scars because of that, but Cameron was certain Keagan was also a lesser man for it.

But that certainly didn't keep this crowd from honoring him on this milestone birthday. The people raising glasses of champagne in a hearty toast to him, representing the most affluent and influential California had to offer, seemed rather sincere. Many of them no doubt respected and admired him. But just as many probably hated him. All doubtlessly feared him to some degree because he controlled the kind of power that could make or break them.

"Speech!" cried one of the guests, as if that wasn't going to happen anyway on this auspicious day.

Hayes rose with surprising grace, considering his size and coarse appearance. He took a long swallow of champagne, then handed the fluted crystal glass to his wife and grinned.

"No sense letting the champagne get warm, now, is there?" Born in

Ireland, he had retained only a hint of brogue in his deep voice. "I'm almost speechless by this turnout. And I am touched that with the war in Europe, so many journalists and others found the time to come. To tell the truth, I didn't think I had this many friends left in the state." He paused for the responding laughter. "But I never got into the newspaper business to make friends, and I'm sure none of you are here to apple-polish the publisher of the *Los Angeles Journal*. We value truth, and that's what I like to think this day is all about. In other words, let's forget the birthday part. I'm too old for birthday parties anyway, even though my family thought it was time I had one. But what can a man do with a bunch of women but give in to their whims now and then. Thanks again, all of you!"

Hayes reached out his hand, and his wife replaced the glass, then he took her hand and pulled her up next to him.

"Come on, Cecilia! You ought to be honored here, too. After all, you've had to put up with me for well over half of these fifty years."

Cecilia's lips twitched into a demure smile. Trim at five and a half feet, she looked almost swanlike in her pale pink filmy chiffon frock. Years of finishing-school training were clearly evident in her elegance and poise, but a discerning observer would have noted a tenseness in her eyes that indicated she'd rather be anywhere else than in front of two hundred attentive faces.

Just then a photographer scurried forward and snapped a shot of the couple. "Mr. Hayes, how about one of the whole family," he stated.

"Splendid idea!" Hayes said. "Where are those girls?"

In a few moments his three daughters were shuttled forward, and the photographer arranged them so as to flank their father. When the photo was taken, Hayes gave each daughter a brief hug and kiss for the benefit of the photographer.

"They may not be sons," boomed Hayes, "but at least they're pretty!"

"Can I quote you on that, Dad?" rejoined Cameron.

"That's my girl, always working!" Hayes chuckled and didn't notice his daughter's stiff smile in response. "All right, folks, there's a half ton of food waiting to be eaten, so go to it. But save room for cake!"

A general migration followed to tables generously laden with prime rib, roast turkey, ham, dozens of different kinds of salads and breads and pastries, bowls of caviar, and more champagne to wash it all down. It was a feast such as Keagan Hayes had only dreamed of years before when he was hawking newspapers back in New York City. And he remained incredulous at his astonishing advancement in life—and he never let others forget, especially his family.

They'd heard the story until they could repeat it verbatim, how at fifteen his parents told him he had to leave his home in Ireland or starve. With ten living siblings all under the age of fifteen, it stood to reason that he, the oldest, and the next eldest brother be the ones sacrificed. At least they had some chance of surviving, however slim, on their own. They went to Belfast and hired out as cabin boys on the first freighter they could find going to America. Keagan's brother died en route, washed overboard in a storm. Keagan jumped ship in New York and ever after nursed a serious hatred of water.

In the States he suffered the usual hard knocks of the immigrant life, including persecution and poverty. But, a born scrapper, he seemed to thrive on adversity, never turning away from a fight and never having qualms about starting one for a cause he deemed worthy. After he caught a growth spurt and put some muscle behind his cocky nature, he was not a man to be challenged lightly.

By eighteen he'd saved enough money from a variety of odd jobs to travel west. He got a job with the *Los Angeles Journal* selling advertising—actually treading the streets of L.A. wearing a sandwich sign. But that was his foot in the door. He made utmost use of the opportunity by selling more advertising than any of his predecessors. He was not above any trick, devious or dirty, to meet and surpass his quotas. In short order he came to the attention of his superiors. Before he was twenty he had been promoted to head the advertising department. At this time the *Journal* was far from being one of the most prestigious papers in California, or even in L.A. for that matter. It was merely plodding along and probably would have folded altogether had Hayes not rejuvenated the advertising department.

But he was more interested in writing news than selling it. He got his opportunity when he stumbled onto a vice scandal involving fake shares in oil and sugar companies. The trail of cover-up and laundered money led to the mayor's office, prompting the L.A. mayor to be recalled. This not only raised the level of respect for the paper but also propelled Keagan into the editorial department, where he discovered his true niche. And it was at a party for the editorial staff, given by the publisher, that he met Cecilia Atkins, the daughter of the *Journal*'s publisher.

Within a year he had won her heart and they were married. Amos Atkins wasn't thrilled to have his only daughter marry the immigrant, even if he secretly admired the young man's moxie. But he capitulated when Keagan agreed to convert to Protestantism. That was proof enough to Atkins that Keagan was committed to his daughter.

Despite what Keagan's detractors might say, he insisted his subsequent rise within the paper was the result of pure hard work and skill, not nepotism. But even Hayes admitted he probably wouldn't have attained the position of publisher except for his marriage, though he staunchly denied that was the reason he married Cecilia. As it was, when Atkins retired in 1932, it made perfect sense to pass the paper on to Hayes, since Cecilia was an only child. Keagan had been acting in the capacity of publisher for years, anyway, because of his father-in-law's declining health.

Whatever the *Journal* now was—and it had been called everything from a slanderous rag to a beacon of truth and righteousness—Hayes was largely responsible. He'd found the *Journal* a decaying second-rate paper and remade it into one of the most powerful political and social forces in the state. No wonder the Atkins name was all but forgotten. The Hayes publishing empire had become synonymous with the *Los Angeles Journal*.

Cameron well knew what her name meant in the city of Los Angeles. And she usually wanted to forget. Like her father, she hadn't attained her job as a reporter for the *Journal* through her family contacts. In fact, her father had often appeared to be her biggest obstacle as she had pushed and shoved her way into the predominantly male world of journalism. From clean-up girl—literally with a broom and dustpan—to copy girl, to gossip and fashion columnist, to "sob sister," she had slaved at every demeaning task the paper had to offer before her father grudgingly accepted her first news story. And he still begrudged her every inch of space in his paper, despite the fact that she had gained the praise and respect of many of her colleagues.

Yes, she did indeed have a curious relationship with her father. It seemed she was always battling against him for stories or for simple respect as a reporter. But beneath all the friction, there was one clear motivation in her heart. She wanted to please him.

"I NEED a drink!" Blair said, sidling up to her sisters as they retreated from the front table.

There were many reasons why Blair did not care to celebrate her father's birthday, the least of which was that she'd be forced to behave as if she cared. However, she was an aspiring actress, and this was a prime opportunity to hone her acting skills. When she smiled before the camera recording the event, she was certain she looked like a daughter who was proud of her dear daddy. The pose was no doubt perfect. The camera would never capture the fact that her smile did not extend into her heart.

"Goodness, what a lot of hot air! But then Daddy always could spin the blarney, couldn't he?" Blair added wryly.

"What do you thespians say?" Cameron replied. "The show must go on."

"And what a show! I wonder if there's a patent on all those manufactured smiles."

Cameron laughed, not something she did often, but when she did, the sound contained a quality of real enjoyment. Jackie's smile was far less enthusiastic. She was no doubt taking this party entirely too seriously.

It had always been Blair and Cameron of the sisters who had more in common. Well, truth was, they probably had only one thing in common—a certain cynicism about life that expressed itself most noticeably in their similar love-hate relationship with their father. For some reason they, more than their younger sister, had borne the brunt of

Keagan's overbearing, demanding nature. And more than anything, they carried the stigma of their worst failure—having been born female. Their father confronted them constantly with this shortcoming. It had a differing effect on each girl. For Cameron, it made her strive to show him she was just as good as any son, not that she truly believed she had hope of ever winning her father's approval. But it had driven her into the newspaper business, and though it turned out she loved it, she always knew why she had followed her father's path. Jackie was probably too young to display her true motivations, but thus far she showed no inclination toward rebellion. She behaved herself, excelled in her studies, and generally made no waves.

Blair, on the other hand, had gone to the other extreme. She saw the hopelessness of pleasing Keagan Hayes and chose to do just the opposite. She wore her womanliness, her femininity, as if it were both protective armor and a lethal weapon. And she made all the waves she possibly could.

"Well, it will be over soon," Cameron encouraged, "and we can all go back to being the beloved miserable family we know so well."

Yes, it was that easy, at least for her sister Cameron. But then Cameron was strong, the kind of woman who confronted life on her own terms. Because she was steel inside—at least she appeared so to Blair—Cameron did not bend under the weight of their father's rejection. She met him eye to eye, nose to nose, at his own game—and, by heaven, she had beat him, or at least she had proven she could succeed by his rules. And she had garnered much respect in the male-dominated newspaper world.

Blair herself had never dared look her father straight in the eye. Whatever there was inside her, it was not steel. She supposed, if anything, she was more like a movie set, appearing quite glamorous and pretty and well constructed, but in reality made of nothing more than clapboard and paper-mache, ready to collapse with the slightest breeze. Luckily, her father didn't care enough to test her mettle. In his mind, she was only a girl, hardly worth the effort.

But Blair pointedly shook these thoughts from her mind. She hated introspection, especially when there was a party going on, and even more she hated to face the realities of her screwball family. Instead, she noted some familiar faces in the crowd of party guests.

"Well, at least there are some interesting people here," she said to her sisters. "Producers Sam Katz and Darryl Zanuck—I've talked to both of them! And Errol Flynn! It's almost as good as a Hollywood party."

"Well, Daddy is good for something."

Blair added, no doubt in a futile attempt to garner her older sister's envy, if not admiration, "Errol was sure there might be a part for me in his next movie. . . ." Blair's eyes had been idly scanning the crowd as they spoke and now they paused. "Who is that gorgeous man over there?"

She didn't recognize him from her Hollywood circle. He certainly was good-looking enough to be an actor. But he was wearing an army uniform. Had he come directly to the party from a studio set? He was with another man, a far less attractive man but also in uniform.

Cameron turned and, following her sister's gaze, said, "I recognize the sandy-haired one. Walter something. His father is a designer at Douglas Aircraft. Never saw the other one."

"No, you'd remember him if you saw him. At least I would. He must have just arrived. I've got to meet him."

"Why, Blair, I would never have guessed a military man would be your type."

"Neither would I, but it might be a rather amusing change of pace."

Cameron rolled her eyes. "My, you are wicked." And the slight touch of admiration in her voice made Blair forgive her sister all else.

"Come on, let's go meet them."

"I'm not interested."

"Oh, I forgot," Blair intoned with annoying superiority, "you're stuck on that awful Johnny Shanahan, though I can't imagine what you see in him. You certainly can do better than a scruffy newspaper hack—"

"Watch it, Blair!" Cameron warned, only partly with good nature. "Say what you will about Shanahan, but please don't malign my chosen profession."

Blair laughed with good humor. "I would never do that, even if it is Dad's profession, too. How about you, Jackie?"

"No, I think I'd better check on the kitchen help," Jackie said. "I don't want Mom to have to worry about anything today."

Blair just rolled her eyes in derision at her sister's typically conscientious gesture. "Come on, Cameron. Let's go meet those men before someone else snags them. Besides, I want someone to distract Walter

Whoever while I make my move on Handsome."

She strode away, and shrugging, Cameron joined her, mumbling something about the usefulness of culling a relationship with someone at Douglas.

Blair never used a straightforward approach with men. If she were a psychoanalyst, she might interpret that as a protective device. Having been rejected by her father, she feared the same from all men and thus felt safer taking them by surprise. It only mattered to her that this ploy usually worked. Few men had ever resisted her charms.

As they neared the two army officers, Blair cocked her head toward her sister and said in a conspiratorial tone loud enough for the men to hear, "These gentlemen don't look familiar. Do you suppose they are gate crashers?" She then turned her gaze, full of sparkling charm, upon the two guileless men.

The tall, strikingly handsome officer apparently caught on quickly, for he answered in mock dismay, "I guess we're found out! But actually, only I am the gate crasher."

"Wonderful!" said Blair, lifting her eyes to meet his. Their gazes held for a long, entrancing moment. An electric-like thrill shot through Blair at the intense, almost mesmerizing, quality of his dark eyes. Her voice cracked slightly as she added, "I like you more every minute."

"I hadn't expected such a welcome," he said, a wry smile bending his lips.

The smile was stunning, bringing all the angles of his face into an appealing relief. Blair had been around many handsome men—goodness, many were bona fide movie stars! But this man was a cut above most of them. His muscular body was only enhanced by his uniform, but the package would have been amazing in any wrapping. Jet black hair and deep-set eyes, just as dark, gave him the appearance of mystery, but there was also an oddly contrasting boyishness about him. The perfect blend of Clark Gable and Gary Cooper. And indeed, Blair was almost certain now he must be an actor. She could not picture his wonderful looks tainted by the grime of a real battlefield.

She barely heard the new voice intrude upon her frank admiration of this man.

"I brought him along as my guest," the other fellow was saying. "Hope no one minds. I didn't want to be the only man in uniform here."

"We'll forgive you if you introduce yourselves," Blair said, not taking her eyes off the tall, dark and . . . well, handsome stranger.

"I'm Walt Davenport," responded the sandy-haired man.

"Your father is at Douglas Aircraft, isn't he?" asked Cameron.

Drat her with her questions, Blair fumed inwardly. Didn't she realize this wasn't about the nondescript light-haired fellow?

"Yes, he is. He designs the planes and I fly them. In fact, I will be leaving next week to join up with the RAF. Britain is in desperate need of good fliers."

"What an admirable thing to do," said Cameron. "Things have settled down a bit in London so far this year, but only the most optimistic think it will last. They lost so many good pilots during the Blitz."

"And do you fly also?" Blair asked the dark-haired officer, realizing he was indeed a military man, not an actor.

"No, nothing that glamorous, just regular army. Lieutenant Gary Hobart." He held out his hand and Blair took it, gazing deeply into his mesmerizing eyes as she did so.

"I'm—"

"I know who you are, and your sister also. I'm glad I got a chance to meet you . . . ah, you both." But even as he said the word "both," his eyes were glued to Blair. And for a rare moment in her life, she was flustered by the attention of a man.

"It looks as though the lines at the food tables have shortened," Cameron said. "I wonder, Walt, if you would like to accompany me? I'm starved."

Always practical, isn't she? thought Blair. But perhaps it was just her way of letting Blair get alone with Lieutenant Hobart.

"Don't mind if I do. How about you, Gary?"

Gary glanced at Blair. "Would you care for a bite?"

"Why, Lieutenant Hobart! What an invitation!"

The innuendo in Blair's tone was nothing more than the usual kind of banter that flowed at the parties she frequented. But Gary actually reddened, obviously not having caught the implications of his words until then. Blair began to feel foolish for her glib words. What a stupid thing to say!

"I mean . . . food . . . luncheon . . . ah . . ." he stammered.

She hurriedly tried to rescue him and redeem herself. Giggling pleasantly but not demeaningly, she said, "I couldn't eat a thing just now. Maybe later."

"I'll be along later," Gary said to his friend.

As Cameron and Walt strode away, Blair linked her arm around Gary's and said, "Do you dance, Lieutenant?"

The orchestra began playing "Falling in Love With Love," and not waiting for his response, Blair took Gary's hand and led him to the dance area. In a matter of moments he was holding her close, and as she laid her head against his shoulder, she could hear his heartbeat— strong and sure—and somehow soothing. She began to hum the tune, then without thinking, she softly sang the words.

"Falling in love with love is falling for make-believe. . . ."

Yes, this was like a scene from a movie, and as with a movie, Blair let herself be transported . . . to where, she didn't quite know, just anywhere besides the reality of her life.

"You have a lovely voice," he murmured, his words only gently admitting a little reality.

"Thank you," she breathed.

"What do you do when you are not being the daughter of a newspaper publisher?"

"I'm an actress, or I hope to be." Part of her didn't want to talk, yet she wanted to know everything about this man. "And you, Gary? When you are not being a soldier?"

"I sometimes feel as if I eat, sleep, and breathe the army. It's only been a year since I graduated from West Point, which dominated my life. Still does, I suppose."

"Hummm . . . West Point . . . is your family from the East Coast, then? I'm not familiar with the Hobart name here on the West Coast."

"There's no reason you should know the name." His tone was soft and matter-of-fact. "I was born here in Southern California. My parents have lived in Van Nuys all their lives."

"Van Nuys. . . ?" Few society families came from there.

He chuckled as if reading her thoughts. "My dad drives a truck for a freight company. My mom is a housewife in our three-bedroom bungalow."

"Oh." Her cheeks pinked. He must think her a terrible snob.

Stepping a few inches from her, he fingered her chin, tipping it upward. "Are you disappointed?" His tone conveyed more concern with setting her at ease than with any embarrassment he might be feeling. Fact was, he did not seem embarrassed at all.

"No, of course not," she said quickly. Then she added apologetically, "I have nothing against truck drivers' sons. Honestly. It's just that we don't get many here at Beverly Hills functions."

"Believe me, I don't get to Beverly Hills often!"

His disarming laughter made her relax, and she laughed as well. "But West Point . . ." She paused. "I thought only the rich and well connected got in there."

"So do very annoying young men who hound their congressmen until they must hand out an appointment or go crazy. Being first in my high school graduating class helped."

"Why the army?"

"My grandfather was a career army man, a noncom. He was a master sergeant when he retired. He was in the Great War, so I grew up hearing his military stories. When my dad didn't follow that path, my grandfather hoped I would. I can't remember a time when I didn't want to be a soldier."

"For him?"

"Maybe partly, but I don't think I would have made it through the Point if it hadn't been my dream, as well."

"It works out quite well that you also happen to look spectacular in uniform," she cooed.

He chuckled. "If I didn't think you were joking, I'd be embarrassed."

"You have no reason to be embarrassed," she replied and left it at that.

They danced for several more minutes. The afternoon air was warm for February, and soon Gary took off his coat and tossed it, along with his hat, onto an empty chair. This was oddly reassuring to Blair, taking it to mean he planned to stay awhile. When the band took a break, Blair and Gary wandered across the lawn and strolled in the garden. Blair had never much appreciated her mother's beautiful flower garden, especially her prize roses, but now it lent the perfect romantic backdrop. Gary commented that his mother had a penchant for gardening, as well. It pleased Blair that they had something so ordinary in common. They talked for a time, mostly about him, for Blair had an almost uncanny knack of talking while revealing little about herself. Gary spoke much about his family, and church figured a lot into his conversation. Oddly, that didn't put Blair off, because he was in no way heavy-handed about it. In fact, she found herself often nodding as if she understood all about family camaraderie and church picnics. She even tossed in an appropriate comment or two, gleaned from hearing her mother and Jackie speak of such things. Blair was an expert at being "all things to all men." A true chameleon. By the time they were interrupted with an announcement over the loudspeaker that it was time for the birthday cake, she was quite enjoying this role.

Blair didn't give a fig about cake and would have ignored the announcement, but just then she saw her mother waving to her across the lawn.

"I'd better go," Blair said resignedly.

"Of course."

Later, when the guests began dispersing, Walt Davenport caught Gary's gaze, and in the silent exchange between them it was clear Davenport was ready to leave.

"He's driving," Gary explained to Blair, "so I have to go."

She could have offered to give him a ride. She could have easily enticed him to stay. She was ready to do just that, but something held her back. Gary Hobart was different from all the men she had ever been with. He played by different rules—in fact, he didn't seem to be "playing" at all. In a way, he was quite guileless, almost naïve. Yet there was a strength about him, a confidence that unnerved her.

Maybe it was just that she wasn't used to this boy-next-door type. He was a stunningly good-looking Andy Hardy. A most disconcerting combination.

He took his jacket and hat from where he had laid them earlier. He seemed to hesitate as he slipped on the coat. Was he going to ask her out? What would she say? He wasn't her kind of man. And it had nothing to do with where he came from, but *Van Nuys!* For goodness' sake! Well, she wasn't a snob. But . . . Van Nuys!

"Can I call you sometime?" he asked finally.

"Of course." She knew she sounded as if she was doing him a great favor. He'd hate her for that.

But he smiled instead. "Great! I'll call you soon. I guess I'd better go, then. I really enjoyed meeting you."

Andy Hardy, or even Gary Cooper, couldn't have been more pie-eyed than this soldier appeared at that moment. Why, then, did Blair feel as if it were Clark Gable sweeping her off her feet?

4

JACKIE WATCHED her sisters stroll away arm in arm. She never used to feel this disconnected from them. True, the three of them had never been truly close, at least in the way that common bonds permit. They were each one as different from the other as fish are from bunnies and cows from algae. They had few similar interests, goals, or even peeves.

Yet lately, Jackie felt even more the "odd man out" with them. She knew it had to do with her faith in God and the fact that both Cameron and Blair had little interest at all in spiritual matters. But as her sisters had become less inclined toward God, Jackie had grown stronger in her faith. Perhaps it had to do with getting older, at least on Jackie's part. She had begun to find a faith of her own, not linked to her parents', especially her mother's, as when she had been a little girl. Christ had become real to *her* now, and it was a marvelous relationship, even if it did place a bit of a wedge between her and her sisters at times.

She was around them so seldom—Cameron had her own apartment in downtown L.A., and Blair was at parties and such nearly every night—that the gap between them wasn't usually so pronounced. But today she felt it keenly, especially in that it was combined with their differing attitudes toward their father. Cameron and Blair were cynical and aloof where Dad was concerned. Jackie could understand that. Keagan was definitely a hard man, and even she had a difficult time with him. But she felt strongly that God wanted her to respect him no matter what, and she refused to slight him now before his friends. She believed if she kept confronting him with kindness and Christian love, he would eventually soften and perhaps even turn to God himself.

"Jacqueline."

As Jackie neared the back door leading into the kitchen, she paused upon hearing her name called softly. "Mom," she replied before even turning. She knew it was her mother, because only she used her given name instead of the nickname everyone else used.

"What are you going to do in the kitchen, dear?" Cecilia asked, her tone only good-naturedly scolding.

"I'm just going to make sure all is in order and they're not low on anything."

"The housekeeper will let us know if anything is amiss."

"Then why are you here, Mom?" Jackie grinned wryly.

Cecilia smiled sheepishly. "The same reason you are, I suppose. But I'm the hostess. You should be out having a good time like your sisters." She sighed and reached out a slim, delicate hand, gently fingering one of Jackie's curls. "You are truly a gift, Jacqueline. I don't know what I'd do without you."

"Mom, why don't you go enjoy the party and let me take care of all these behind-the-scene matters. I really don't mind. And I know Daddy would rather you be at his side."

Cecilia's brow twitched and her expression became rather enigmatic. Jackie knew the look well, though she'd never been able to figure out the cause of it. She was far closer to her mother than to her sisters, but in the moments that Cecilia wore this guise, Jackie felt leagues distant from her. It was odd to think her mother had secrets, perhaps private hurts, but that look made Jackie acutely aware of the fact.

"All right." Cecilia patted her daughter's arm. "But don't get lost in the kitchen. I'm sure the servants have everything in hand."

Cecilia walked away, a reluctance in her step. She was as out of sorts at an event like this as Jackie was. Cecilia's awkwardness came mostly because of her near painful shyness. Jackie's was because—actually, she could not quite define her own sense of detachment that certainly went beyond her isolation from her sisters. She wasn't even certain it was entirely due to her faith. She liked simplicity, she supposed. She would have been better off as the child of a common laborer than that of a wealthy, powerful newspaper publisher.

She shrugged as she opened the kitchen door. Wasn't there a Scripture verse about being content with what one had? Though she supposed the apostle Paul never intended it to mean that one should be content with wealth and riches and not keep longing for poverty!

Jackie spent a few minutes in the kitchen but was really not needed, so she returned to the party. Cameron was busy eating luncheon and chatting with a man in an army uniform. She had her small notebook and a pencil in hand and had obviously found someone to interview. Blair was strolling in the garden with another man in uniform.

Jackie realized she knew no one else at the party. None of her college friends were in attendance—she had told her mother not to invite them unless their parents were also invited. They would have been bored silly at a function such as this was. The music was sedate, as was the dancing. No jitterbugging allowed!

But Jackie reminded herself about being content. And she wasn't going to be glum, either. That would be her gift to her father. So she walked toward the dance platform, stepped up to one of the younger male guests, and tapped him on the shoulder.

"Jeffrey Meade, I thought that was you," she smiled. "I am dying to dance. Would you care to accompany me?"

He grinned in response. "I'd love to."

———

Most of the guests were gone. Cameron surveyed the broad lawns of the Hayes home, more littered now than festive. Passing a vacant table, the very one Donald Farr had occupied, Cameron picked up a fallen empty bottle of champagne and set it on the table. Servants were already threading through the rubble cleaning up.

"What a day!" Cameron murmured to herself.

"Indeed it was."

Cameron hadn't noticed her father's approach. She looked up and smiled. "So it was all you hoped it would be?"

Keagan shrugged. "I hope for nothing. I want and I get—you should know that."

"I nearly forgot," she answered wryly. "But, Dad, surely when you stepped off that boat thirty-five years ago, you hoped it would end up like this. The American dream, and all that."

"End up? Good heavens! If I thought this was the end, I'd slit my throat. I'm just getting started."

"Where else is there for you to go?"

"That's youth for you. No vision. You see a successful man at fifty who has conquered all. I see only the next challenge. There are no pinnacles, Cameron. You just go from one mountaintop to the next. If you plan to take over the *Journal* one day, you'd better broaden your vision. I'll have no shortsighted wimps sitting in my office."

"Of course you are right, Dad." And he was, though she hated to admit it.

"Now, I didn't come after you to chat," Keagan continued. "I had a call I thought you might be interested in. Congress has approved FDR's Lend-Lease Act. This should raise the ante quite a bit in the European war."

"That's good news, then."

"Let's hope it hasn't come too late."

Since 1939 Hitler had been steadily taking one country after another in Europe. Now all of western Europe and Poland had fallen, leaving Britain standing alone. The Axis powers of Germany and Italy were threatening the Balkans, and England had begun to send troops to aid Greece. But Churchill had been pleading with Roosevelt to send more assistance. Britain was running out of money to buy supplies from the U.S., and they desperately needed another solution to the matériel problem. Lend-Lease was Roosevelt's way of circumventing the kind of war-debt problems that had loomed after the Great War.

"During the election last fall, Roosevelt was firm that he intended to send only matériel to England, not men. Do you think this will keep us out of the fray?" Cameron asked.

Though Cameron worked the city beat, she tried to be well versed in national and international news because, despite her father's assessment of her, she did have a wide vision, at least for herself.

"We'll get into this war yet," Keagan predicted, with a gleam in his eyes.

A staunch Roosevelt supporter, Keagan had been a strong proponent of the lend-lease proposal, touting it often in editorials. At least Cameron liked to think this was the reason for his enthusiasm for American involvement rather than a mere lust for headline glory.

"Well, Dad, how does it feel to have gotten a birthday present from the president himself?"

"Good! Almost as good as when I predicted the Russo-German Nonaggression Pact in '39 to a chorus of naysayers. But I could see that was the only way Stalin could protect the USSR from German aggression, at least until Russia could arm itself." He grinned. "It's these kinds of coups that make it all worthwhile."

"Yes, but you had a bit of an edge where Russia was concerned. Your years as a correspondent in Russia helped, don't you think?"

"But I had the brains to take my experience and use it to judge world events logically and correctly! And I'll tell you, as I've told others, still to everyone's denial, Germany is going to turn on Russia, mark my words. I'm sure Hitler is already worried over Russia's expansion into Finland and the Balkans since the Pact was made. The enmities between those two countries aren't going to fade with a measly pact."

"I hope you are not right about that, Dad. That would up the scope of the war in Europe tremendously." Cameron meant the words, yet the journalist in her could not keep from hoping she could somehow find herself in the middle of it all. "Dad, have you decided who you'll send as a replacement for Tom George in Rome?" Cameron felt bad for the *Journal*'s Rome correspondent whose sick wife was forcing him to leave his post just as things were getting interesting. Yet Cameron still eyed his post covetously.

"No, and even if I had, I sure wouldn't tell you before I told my managing editor."

"You know I turned in an application for the job."

"You don't have a prayer, Cameron, so get it out of your head right now. I tore up your application the minute I laid eyes on it. You know I won't send a woman to a foreign station. And now that Italy has declared war against the Allies, there is no way I will put a second-rate correspondent there."

Cameron bristled. "Is that comment against me personally or women in general?"

"I don't have to explain myself. You aren't going, so forget it."

"But, Dad—"

"Don't ruin my birthday, Cameron. The issue is closed." He glanced up at a passing servant. "Hey, you, is there some good whiskey floating around here? I'm sick to death of champagne."

"I'll get you some, sir."

"On the rocks."

"Yes, sir."

"Anyway, Dad," Cameron persisted, "you know what I really want is to be posted to Moscow."

"I can't afford to keep even one man there these days," he replied. "There are only two correspondents in the entire country, both from the wire services. There is no news in the Soviet Union."

"But, Dad, you've mentioned sending a journalist to Russia to update the progress of the Pact. You know I'd be the perfect candidate. I spent some time in Russia, too, as you well know."

She could tell this caught him momentarily off guard. He wouldn't need to have a bureau in Moscow to send someone on a short-term jaunt. But there was something else in his expression just then. Was he impressed that she had been on her toes? She hated the surge of pride rising within her. But there it was. Just maybe she had pleased him, though she'd never hear him say so.

"I still want to do that, but at the moment the budget won't permit it," he replied.

"You'll have to send someone if what you say is true about the war spreading there—"

"When the time comes, I'll send a man."

"But you know I am the most qualified. I spent most of six years there—"

"When you were a child."

"You know very well I didn't have my head in the sand. Unlike Blair and Jackie, I didn't spend my time playing with dolls."

Keagan rolled his eyes. "I well know! At seven you were hounding officials for interviews. At thirteen, you were trying to bribe Cheka agents—"

"I didn't bribe—"

"Nearly got us expelled from the country." For a brief, very fleeting moment, Cameron was certain she detected a tiny hint of pride lurking behind her father's ire. "At any rate, I won't field a female correspondent—especially to Russia with war impending."

"Listen here, Dad," Cameron said, undaunted by her father's rebuff, "you can't write me off just because I am a woman. Look at Dorothy Thompson in Berlin. She's won a Pulitzer."

"A complete rarity. But you are no Dorothy Thompson."

Keagan knew the famous columnist and former Berlin correspondent was Cameron's hero. He must know his words hurt, but she didn't let it show. She just continued her argument. "That's not good enough—"

..., you want more reasons? Okay, come to my office in the
...rning—"

"Tomorrow's Saturday."

"Then get yourself in there Monday, like every other employee, and
I'll give you a whole list of reasons. And the first is that I'll never hire
anyone who bothers me on my birthday!" He spun around and stalked
away.

Cameron knew she should have kept her mouth shut or at least
waited until after that whiskey had arrived. But patience was a virtue
she seriously lacked. In any case, she certainly wasn't ready to bow to
her father's pronouncement. She *would* show up in his office on Monday, and she would continue to browbeat him even if she received
nothing more than the satisfaction of driving him to distraction. With
war escalating daily in Europe, she did not plan to miss all the excitement and journalistic glory.

5

ON MONDAY MORNING Cameron did not get in to see her father because she was sent to cover a breaking story in Santa Monica. It involved an East Coast mobster, gambling, and the crusading mayor of
Los Angeles. Cameron was certain this was front-page stuff, so her
dreams of going to Europe could wait. And she did manage to get a
great story, but while trying to get in closer to the mobster on his gambling ship, she fell into the water of Santa Monica Bay.

After sloshing into the *Journal's* offices in downtown Los Angeles,
Cameron found the spare clothes she kept in her locker, which was
located in an alcove off the main corridor, and went to the ladies' room

to change. This wasn't the first time she had ruined a suit while pursuing a story.

She dressed quickly because there was an article to write to go with the photos taken in Santa Monica Bay. Gathering up her discarded wet clothes, she headed back to the lockers and hung them up to dry. She was bent over checking the seams of her stockings when hands grabbed her from behind. Spinning around, her knee poised to do damage, a voice stopped her.

"So, the sailor is home from the sea," he said, full of sarcastic glee.

"Johnny Shanahan!" Cameron exclaimed. "You don't know how close you came to becoming a permanent soprano."

"Neither of us would have liked that." He locked his arms around her and pulled her tightly to him.

And before she could respond, his lips pressed against hers, an act that drew a full, impassioned response from her. But quickly pulling away, she said, "I've got work to do."

Johnny ignored her words, and putting an arm around her waist, he gently pinned her up against the wall. Cameron glanced quickly around, but they were alone in a secluded area. She found it hard to act upon her claims of work to be done. His fedora pushed back rakishly on his head, his sleeves rolled up, and his necktie loosened at the collar all gave the man a disheveled but disconcertingly enticing look.

"How can you think of work when our hearts are so full of love?" He lowered his mouth to hers again.

"What has gotten into you, Shanahan?" He wasn't a man to speak of sentimental things like love, even if he did so, as he was now, in a tone dripping with sarcasm.

"I've missed you, sweetheart."

"This isn't about love, now, is it?" That would have shocked her more than his surprise appearance.

He shrugged and his lips bent into a sheepish grin. "You know me too well, Hayes. But if I could love anybody, it would be you. Why, I'd even marry you . . . if I ever married anyone."

"Dear me . . ." she simpered mockingly, "such words do make a girl's head spin." She then ducked under his arm that was braced against the wall. "You are forgetting one thing, *sweetheart*," she added in her normal voice. "*I'm* not the marrying kind."

He burst out laughing at that. "That's why I love you, Hayes—and

...ep I think I do love you. You are the only woman I know who ...n truly respect."

"Probably because I am too much like you."

"Probably."

She turned back toward him and smiled at the playful glint in his eye as he breathed that final word. Johnny Shanahan was no brawny stud. Only a few inches taller than Cameron and weighing in, fully clothed and probably soaking wet, at no more than one hundred fifty pounds, he nonetheless emanated a strong appeal that went beyond physical appearance. He wasn't even that good-looking. His close-set eyes were framed by a prominent scar over his right brow, where one of the disgruntled objects of his reporting, an ex-prizefighter, Johnny found out later, had swung a chair at him. His thin lips could be as sensuous as a queen's courtesan's or as sharp as that same courtesan's saber. Square cheekbones and a cleft in his chin completed the picture of a man who should not have had such power over women. But he did.

Call it charm, call it charisma—Shanahan had it. Cameron hated to think of the women he had been with. Married, single, divorced, debutantes, actresses, and girls from the secretarial pool. They flocked to him. Cameron held no illusions even now that when he and she had been "seeing" each other regularly he was completely faithful to her. In a way, she didn't mind. It was her safety net. She, every bit as much as he, didn't want to admit how deep their feelings might be for each other. She had her career to think about. Or so she wanted to think. In truth, a man like Shanahan made it quite easy to maintain her protective wall against intimacy.

"I have got to get to work." She tore her eyes away from his nearly magnetic persona. "I think my piece on the gambling ships will make the front page in the morning edition."

"Did Landis tell you that?"

"Not in so many words, but it is front-page material."

"This lend-lease business might just upstage you."

"Old news." Her smirk exuded confidence.

"I hope you're right, baby."

"I better be. I nearly got drowned getting that gambling story, and I refuse to watch it shunted off to an inside page because of some stupid war way over in Europe. Americans don't care about what happens thousands of miles away." Taking a breath, she noted a grin on

Shanahan's face. "What's so funny? You know how I hate being patronized!"

"Believe me, I know!" He made an effort at solemnity. "But just a few days ago you were spouting off about how the world is shrinking and 'no man is an island.' "

"Yeah, well, that was before I found out I don't have a prayer for Tom George's job."

He put a hand on her shoulder, a truly compassionate act that rather surprised her. "I'm sorry, Cameron."

"You knew all along, didn't you?"

"I couldn't *know*, of course, but I guess I saw the typeset on the wall, as it were. I didn't want to be the one to burst your bubble." His tone was still gentle. And Cameron glimpsed another facet of his appeal, a side he too often suppressed, but which he revealed when he deemed it beneficial, or profitable. Still, even if it was calculated, even if Cameron wasn't exactly certain it was real compassion, she was comforted because he made it seem genuine.

"I thought just this once my father would give me a break."

Shanahan barked a dry laugh. "Hayes, I didn't think you could be naïve."

"Yeah, pretty stupid of me. He tore up my application. I'm going up to see him later—"

"Why put yourself through that? He'll never send a woman to Europe, especially with a war there."

"I wish I could be like you, Shanahan, satisfied with the city beat. Many women would kill for what I've achieved, but ... I don't know ... I'm just not satisfied."

He looked at her as if seeing her afresh. She thought he might kiss her again and wished he would. But instead he said, "As long as there is a taller mountain to be climbed, you are never gonna be satisfied."

She thought of her father's words the other day and realized anew how much like the old man she was. "Don't you want more, Shanahan?"

"I had a taste of it. I covered the Spanish Civil War for a stint."

"And?"

"Hey, let's not beat a dead horse, okay? You and I are darn good right where we are. I've got a Pulitzer Prize under my belt because I am one of the best journalists around—"

"And the most modest." She smiled, then did what she was dying to do. She put her arms around him and pressed her lips to his.

"Let's get out of here. . . ." he murmured around the kiss.

"I have to work," she said with reluctance as she slipped away from the temptation of his arms and moved into the main hall.

They reached the elevator, and she paused, still wavering, when a voice from behind forced them to turn.

"Cameron, you got that piece on the gambling ships done yet?" It was the city editor, Harry Landis. Cameron could hardly ignore him.

With an inward and perhaps even an outward groan, Cameron turned. "I'm working on it, boss."

Landis cocked a skeptical brow at the elevator and then at Shanahan. "Oh yeah?"

"I was just going to check at the photo lab to see how the art is coming."

"The lab's that way." Landis pointed his thumb in the opposite direction.

"Oh, well, uh . . ."

"Give the girl a break, Harry," Shanahan put in. "We were just going for a cup of joe."

Cameron choked down ire at Shanahan's interference, even if she had been caught off guard and *had* needed to be rescued. Accepting help from anyone never came easily for her.

"Okay, but I want that piece in an hour. When I go to the department meeting, I want something concrete to show when I insist it goes on the front page."

"The front page?" Cameron hated the little-girl awe in her tone.

"If it's good enough."

"I'll get right to it, Harry," Cameron replied obediently. As Landis stalked away, she started to turn back toward the city room.

"Hey," Shanahan grabbed her arm. "What about us?"

"This can't wait, Johnny. You understand."

She started to go, then as an afterthought turned back to smile sympathetically and make a date for dinner. But Shanahan was boarding the elevator. The car was full, and by the time he had made his way inside and turned, the doors were closing. There wasn't even a chance for a wave good-bye. But he ought to understand. They both well knew each other's priorities. Work first, everything else second.

CAMERON HEARD the news about the Rome correspondent before she left the city room for the evening. It was seven o'clock. Shanahan was already gone. She had heard about it only from one of the copyboys and so maintained a hope it wasn't official. Still, it struck her like a fist to the stomach. She wanted to be professional about it, but she knew the blow was personal—and it hurt more than she ever thought it would.

She and Shanahan had managed to make plans for dinner earlier, and now Cameron saw no reason not to go. She had been a bit perturbed when he'd told her to meet him for dinner at the Steak Pit, a nearby eatery where many of the local newspaper hacks gathered. She'd thought it was terribly unimaginative of him, not to mention that it clearly showed how he took her for granted. Now, however, she didn't mind at all, for it would have been a shame to waste a fancy restaurant on this evening.

She wanted to give Shanahan the benefit of the doubt. After all, oddly enough, newspapers were the worst breeding grounds for rumors. She'd tried to verify the copyboy's tale with Landis, but he'd already left. Hadn't Johnny just hours before gone on about how content he was with the city beat? He had all but said he had no interest in working as a foreign correspondent.

Surely, then, there must be a mistake.

She tried to calm herself as she walked around the corner to the Steak Pit. It was crowded inside for a Monday night. The noise level was as high as the perpetual cloud of smoke lingering near the ceiling.

Though Cameron was only one of a handful of female reporters in town, she had earned a welcome in this conclave of reporters. Even if the rules still prohibited her from the Press Club, her male associates had accepted her here. In fact, they often forgot completely her femininity and smoked, drank, and cursed quite freely in front of her.

Johnny may have made their date at their usual spot, but at least he had secured a secluded booth. She approached it with a smile plastered on her face. He lifted his martini in greeting.

"What'll you have, doll?" he asked, grinning. He looked as if he'd already had a few himself. Was he celebrating?

"You know I hate it when you call me doll, or other such demeaning names." She signaled a waitress as she slid into the booth facing Johnny. "I'll have a cup of coffee," she told the waitress.

"Okay, Hayes . . . my dear," he sneered. "You're late."

"I'm always late."

"Late but beautiful. Who could want more?"

"You're in an exceptionally chipper mood, Shanahan."

He took a pack of Lucky Strikes from his inside jacket pocket. "You're not complaining, are you?"

He offered her one and she shook her head. He knew very well she didn't smoke. She'd seen too many people become dependent on cigarettes, and she guarded her independence too selfishly to let anything or anyone control her. Besides, her mother had soundly drummed it into her that smoking was unladylike, and this was at least one area where Cameron could curry her mother's good graces.

As Shanahan lit his cigarette, the waitress brought Cameron's coffee. She had a long gulp. She thought that perhaps she should have ordered something stronger so she could catch up with Johnny before she confronted him. But when he finished his martini and ordered another, she saw the impossibility of gaining on him without ending up flat on her face. Best to face him sober anyway—at least one of them should be.

"I heard the funniest rumor just before I left the office this evening," she began.

"When aren't there rumors at that paper?" he said vaguely.

"That is so true, Johnny. That's why I simply can't take this one with more than a grain of salt." Sipping her drink, she told herself once more he couldn't be so low as to have lied about Rome.

"Best way to take rumors—with salt, ya know." He craned his

head around. "Where's that waitress?"

"Shanahan, did you get offered that job in Rome?" There, it was out in the open.

"Well . . ." A waitress passed just then, and he snagged her. "Hey, doll, I ordered a martini 'bout an hour ago. . . ."

"I'll check on it, Johnny," the woman said, adding, "Can I take your dinner order while I'm here?"

Shanahan waved her away. "Martini first; food later."

"So, Shanahan, what about Rome?" Cameron persisted. She was not interested in dinner, either.

"Come on, Hayes. Can't you at least wait until I get my drink?"

"Punctuality may not be one of my virtues, but neither is patience." She ground out the words between clenched teeth. She smelled guilt all over him. It was stronger than the odor of vermouth.

"What'd ya want from me, Hayes?"

"The truth."

"Now, that's asking too much!" he growled, then burst out laughing. "Come on, let me see you smile. You got a beautiful—"

"You make me sick, you lying, cheating, low-down—" She gasped in a breath, then searched her mind for worse adjectives. She was a writer after all; she ought to be able to come up with some good ones. But something made her stop. Maybe because she knew she would have given criminals and politicians more of a chance to vindicate themselves. Shanahan was her boyfriend, if not more.

"You forgot traitorous, sniveling, lying snake," he taunted.

"I said 'lying,'" she replied dryly. "But don't know how I forgot 'snake.'" Pausing, she glanced at her cup, but her stomach was in too many knots to want it. "Why'd you do it? Why did you apply for that job, then lie about it?"

"I didn't apply—" He stopped abruptly and rubbed his hands over his face. Twisting his head around, he shouted, "Cora, I need that drink!"

The waitress had been on her way and now came to the table with Shanahan's martini. He grabbed it like a drowning man grasps a passing branch. But then he didn't immediately drink. Instead, he stared into the glass, fingering the toothpick that impaled the olive. He lifted it out, staring at it with bleary eyes. Suddenly he looked very drunk.

"I hate these things. Why do they insist on putting them in?" He dropped the olive on the table, and now Cameron saw a lineup of the things, like tin soldiers or the body count on a battlefield. He lifted his eyes to her. They had become almost as green and pathetic looking as the discarded olives. "You didn't have a chance of getting that job, Cameron," he said rather plaintively. "I didn't take anything from you."

"But why you . . . if you didn't apply?"

"Sometimes you are like a dog with a bone—you just can't let go." Shaking his head, he lifted his glass to his lips and gulped his drink.

"That's my nature."

"Fine for journalism. Terrible for life."

"Please don't get philosophical on me, Johnny."

"I do that when I get drunk."

"It's not one of your finer qualities."

"We both have our faults."

The conversation stopped with the suddenness of an object slamming against a brick wall. The silence that hung in the air between them was as palpable as a throbbing bruise. Cameron knew she should have dropped the subject right then. The weary, resigned quality to Johnny's voice hinted that she was probably going to be better off not knowing any more about that correspondent's job. He had been right when he said she would never have gotten it. So what did it matter who was hired? She should be happy for her friend and let it go at that. But she smelled something rotten in the matter, and when she sniffed such an odor, there was no way she could back off until she ferreted out the cause.

It was her nature.

"You may as well tell me, Johnny," she said, her soft tone in no way masking the sharp edge of her intent. "I know you're hiding something."

"Holy smoke, woman! Quit while you are ahead."

"Why did my father give you this job?"

He rolled his eyes and in one swift gulp finished his martini. "Did it ever occur to you that maybe it's because I'm the best man for the job?"

"Yeah, and you *are* the best man. But after Spain you were lucky to keep your city beat," Cameron replied. Shanahan didn't often talk about Spain, but rumor had it that he had been kicked out of the country for dallying with a general's daughter. The *Journal* had lost the accreditation money—ten thousand dollars!—they put up guaranteeing a correspondent's behavior. Cameron added, "And you have further lost favor at the *Journal* because of seeing me. Let's face it, you are not my father's favorite person."

Cameron could not count the times she and her father had argued over her relationship with Johnny. Though Keagan admired Johnny as a reporter, he believed that where Cameron was concerned, Johnny was little more than a male gold digger. Cameron knew that was not true. It simply wasn't Johnny's style.

Nevertheless, she should have been pleased that her father cared enough to meddle in her life, but it did not strike her in that way just now. He wanted someone better for Cameron, not because he cared about her, but because he cared about the newspaper she would inherit.

"What better way to deal with a despised employee than to send him thousands of miles away?" Shanahan asked dryly.

"It doesn't make sense. Why not just fire—?" Suddenly the truth of the matter hit her. Dazed, as if she truly had been hit, she could not speak for a moment. The explanation that hovered before her was leagues beyond stunning. It mocked everything she was, everything she had fought so hard to become. And the worst of it was that the mockers were the two men she should have been able to trust above all others—her father and her lover.

Gaping at Shanahan, her stomach twisted. She opened her mouth to speak, but still nothing came out.

"I'm sorry, Cameron," Shanahan said quietly, even contritely, if he were capable of such an emotion.

"You swine!"

"I—"

She cut him off. "He dangled a carrot before your eyes, and you bit it off like a starving man." Finally words came in a dizzying rush. "And I'll bet he didn't even have to ask twice. You must have fallen all over yourself grabbing his twisted offer. What's a little thing like friendship—or whatever in blazes it is we had—when it comes to ambition, huh, Shanahan? You are lower than I ever imagined."

"Get off it!" Shanahan retorted, all his momentary guilt and remorse gone. "Quit acting like the wronged woman. You would have dumped me in a minute to go to Rome or anywhere else. So what's the difference if it's me?"

"The difference is, you made a deal with my father. Just for the record, that's what happened, isn't it?" Glaring at him, she still harbored a small hope that he would deny it. "He said he'd send you to Rome if you would forget about me, right?"

"You want it between the eyes, Cameron?" he spat. "Okay, that's what happened. And I jumped at the chance. All that hogwash about being content where I am was just that—pure bunk. I was born to that job, and with a war in Europe I would have sold out my own mother for it. But don't give me that righteous indignation act. You would have done the same."

"It isn't what you did, Shanahan, it's *how* you did it. Do you know how it makes me feel to have my father and you scheming behind my back to manipulate my future? I'm not some witless, helpless woman that you can play me like that." But tears sprang to her eyes and mocked her words. She swiped at them angrily, then hurriedly slid from the booth.

"Come on, Hayes," he said in a conciliatory tone.

"Forget it." That was all she could manage to get past her trembling lips. There was no way she would betray any further emotion. She spun around and strode from the restaurant.

Outside, the night air was crisp and sharp after the stifling air of the restaurant. Cameron walked a block before hailing a taxi. As the cab pulled up she was ready to go to Beverly Hills and do battle with her father. But when she climbed in and leaned back against the worn leather seat, she suddenly felt very tired.

"Where to, ma'am?" the cabby asked.

She rattled off the address of her west L.A. apartment. She told herself she wasn't buckling under. But to confront her father at his home after business hours was simply not the professional thing to do. It was more the act of an angry daughter—and that was the last thing she wanted to resemble at the moment, even if his actions were far more against a daughter than an employee.

Still fuming and trembling when the taxi pulled up in front of her building, she paid the cabby, then marched up to the door and went in. With every movement she tried to make her anger supersede her hurt. She picked up the mail from her box, then climbed to her second-floor studio. Inside she was greeted by the rather sterile atmosphere of her home. She spent little time here except to sleep, and she had a constitution that could manage on very little of that. There was a bed, a big easy chair, a coffee table in front of that with a pole lamp next to the chair, and a radio on the kitchen table. The kitchenette contained only a coffeepot and a couple pieces of crockery she'd pilfered from her mother's kitchen. The little icebox, she knew, was empty. She never cooked, always eating out, usually merely grabbing a hot dog or some such thing from a street vendor or cheap diner. The only items of any personal nature in the apartment were a stack of reference books that she had not even bothered to get shelves for and, of course, her portable Underwood typewriter.

She switched on the radio after a few minutes because the silence of the place was oppressive. A Tommy Dorsey tune wafted through the speakers. She kicked off her shoes, plopped down in the big easy chair, and looked through the mail. Finding nothing of interest she tossed it aside and sighed. This was her life, but why it should suddenly depress her, she could not guess.

Maybe because it was eight o'clock in the evening and she could not remember when was the last time she had been home at such an early hour. What was she doing? Sitting here like some scorned lover? Wallowing in . . . what? Self-pity?

This was utterly ridiculous. She jumped up, slipped her shoes back on, grabbed her handbag, and headed out. Surely there was something going on in this city to better occupy her time. If nothing else, she'd head over to her favorite police precinct and sniff out something to report.

Cameron did not return home that night until two in the morning. Much to her delight she happened upon a nice little homicide and managed to be in the right place at the right time to scoop the story and make the morning edition.

AFTER ONLY FOUR hours of sleep, Cameron was up at six. She had her usual half pot of coffee while she dressed and read the morning paper. Much to her delight, the gambling article had a nice place on the front page with the fabulous photo of the gambling boss standing on the deck of his ship.

Heading to the office that morning, she was glad she had waited to confront her father. She had cooled off, or so she thought. She'd be able to approach him rationally, like a . . . well, like a man. At least she would not give her father any cause to label her an emotional woman.

She knew he'd be in his office by seven. As she waited for the elevator, Shanahan sidled up to her.

"Hi'ya, Hayes." His tone was cheerful even if his eyes were red rimmed and glassy. "Those ruffled feathers of yours smooth down yet?"

She glared at him in response, and suddenly all her ire returned in full force.

"Oh . . . I see we're still a bit touchy," he went on. "I knew I should have sent you candy and flowers."

"Why you . . . you . . ." she sputtered, unable to find suitable words to vent what she thought of his purposefully demeaning words.

Then the elevator arrived, and as she pushed her way in, she wasn't certain who had been reprieved. At least Shanahan knew enough to wait for the next car.

She tried to calm herself as she entered her father's office.

"Good morning, Cameron," greeted Molly, his secretary, in her usual bright but businesslike manner.

"I'd like to see Mr. Hayes," Cameron replied tightly.

"Oh, he can't be disturbed now. He's on a very important long-distance telephone call."

"You mean it would upset him if he was interrupted right now?"

"Yes, I am afraid so."

Cameron strode toward the inner office door.

"Cameron!" Molly called.

Ignoring the secretary, Cameron flung open the door so hard it hit the wall with a loud crack. Keagan Hayes, phone receiver pressed to his ear, looked up sharply. Cameron caught the corner of the door with the heel of her shoe and slammed it shut.

Keagan spoke into the receiver, "Ah . . . Senator, do you mind if I call you back? Something has come up." He hung up the phone, but when he looked back at Cameron, his expression was stony cold. "What is the meaning of this?"

Cameron hated her emotion, silently cursing it, but there it was, seething from her. And here before her was the cause, and she simply could not restrain it, even though some more rational part of her seemed to whisper she was about to make a fool of herself.

"You tell me, Daddy dear, what the meaning is of what you did yesterday," she challenged.

"I assume you are talking about the Rome post? Well, I told you I would not give it to you."

"This has nothing to do with my getting that position, though I deserved it, and you well know it." She gasped a breath, knowing she should never have mentioned that. "I resent your trying to manipulate me. That's what this is about."

"So you are upset that I wish to send away an unsuitable suitor—"

She snorted a dry laugh. "Rest assured that doesn't bother me, either. John Shanahan isn't my lover or my fiancé or any other thing to me. You can send him to Timbuktu, for all I care. You can send him straight to—"

"Calm yourself, Cameron!"

"Don't fool yourself, Dad. I may be angry, but I am calm." She knew she was lying, but no way would she admit anything less to him. "You cannot control my life like that. Do you understand? I refuse to allow you to keep me under your thumb. If I do decide to marry, it will be to whomever I please. Neither you nor anyone else is going to maneuver my future. I am my own woman—"

His laugh cut her off. "Come now, Cameron! You are not so naïve as to truly think that? Your daddy pays your salary, after all. Your daddy got you a cushy job. Your daddy made sure yesterday that cheesy article of yours about the gambling ships made it to the front page. How else do you think a twenty-four-year-old piece of merchandise has achieved anything in this business?"

The words hit her like a bomb. Yes, they had always been implied, if not by her father, then by others. But she had never believed the implications. She still didn't. She had talent. She was a natural. She was good. Wasn't she?

"You know I'm telling the truth," Keagan said coldly.

Cameron's lips trembled so that she could not make them work to form words. Then moisture filled her eyes. She glanced up at the ceiling, trying desperately to keep emotion at bay.

Finally she muttered, "And it's all about truth, isn't it, Daddy?"

"Yes, it is."

Choking back ire, choking back tears, which she refused to let escape beyond the rims of her eyes, she swallowed and tried to affect the same cold glare she saw on her father's face.

"You are wrong, Dad, so very wrong." Somehow a calm came over her, and it became clear what she had to do. "But even if there might be a grain of truth to what you say, I am through letting you manipulate and crush me. I don't know why I didn't do something about it a long time ago. I am resigning from the *Journal* as of this minute. You will receive a formal written resignation within the hour." She could not believe how absolutely good the words felt.

"Fine," he said evenly. "I won't even require a two-week notice. But you realize, of course, that the only place you'll be able to find a job now will be in a diner or a department store. No newspaper will have you—"

"You'll see to that, will you?"

"I won't have to. If you couldn't even make it at your daddy's newspaper, what other paper will have you? You are finished in this business, Cameron."

"We'll see about that."

"What we will see is you crawling back to me." His lips twitched into a humorless smile. "You will eat your words."

46

"You don't know me very well if you think that. But I'm not surprised, because you only let yourself see what you want to see." She forced a smile to her lips, a smile, she would have been surprised to note, that was hauntingly similar to his. "It will be you who will regret your words, you who will regret my leaving. I will have no regrets. I already feel as if heavy chains have fallen from my back."

The trembling began when she reached the elevator. But the reality of what she had done did not really strike her until she stepped out on the editorial floor, completely on reflex, and ran into Harry Landis.

"Why aren't you at your desk?" He accosted her without preamble. "I've got assignments for you, and the day is wasting away."

"Sorry—" she began, then it hit her. "I won't be doing any more assignments for the *Journal*, Harry."

"What're you talking about?"

"I no longer work here."

He blinked once at this bombshell, then still in his crisp editorial tone asked, "What is going on?" He glanced at his watch. "Make it fast. I have a meeting in five minutes, and you have to be at city hall—"

"I've just resigned. The publisher and I have had a difference of, shall we say, opinion."

"Did he fire you?"

"I said I resigned."

"You can't do that! I won't allow it. I need you. Does he know you are one of my best men—ah, reporters? I'm gonna go up to talk to him—"

His words, spoken with obvious candor—he'd hardly had time to spit out false flattery—stunned Cameron and made her feel almost giddy with pleasure.

But she replied with matter-of-fact restraint, just as a newsman should, "Don't do that, Harry. The only thing I'm going to miss about this paper is working for you. I've felt nothing but respect from you, and that means a lot to me. But it is time I move on, preferably to someplace where the Hayes name means only five letters of the alphabet."

"I never saw the Hayes name, Cameron," Landis said with uncharacteristic earnestness. "And I sure don't think your father ever gave you an inch because of it."

"That's not what he said, but it doesn't matter. I hate to leave you high and dry, Harry, but I have been left with no other choice." Something caught in the back of her throat. Times like these she cursed being a woman. A man would not be getting choked up and teary-eyed at a time like this. Johnny Shanahan would simply thumb his nose, shake the dust off his shoes, and leave. "I'll see you later, Harry." She spun around and fairly bolted, forgetting the elevator and heading to the stairwell.

———

During the rest of that day Cameron learned something rather revealing about herself. She had absolutely no life outside the newspaper. No hobbies, no friends, no . . . well, no distractions. The day lay before her like the gaping mouth of a beast. She wandered around the city for a while, got bored trying to shop, and finally bought a sandwich and went home, there to find her cold, empty apartment and nothing else.

She spent the rest of the afternoon writing a résumé on her Underwood. She typed ten copies, then found the addresses for her top ten choices of newspapers. These ranged from the *Christian Science Monitor* to the *New York Times*. Some she chose because she'd heard rumors of upcoming openings, others . . . well, there was no need to explain the *New York Times*—that would be an out-and-out coup. She was reeling the last résumé from the typewriter when a knock at her door stopped her.

For a moment she didn't respond. She never had visitors. Then it occurred to her it might be Shanahan or—an even more farfetched notion—her father. It was neither.

"Mom! Jackie! What in the world—" Her mother had never been to her place, and Jackie had only come once to pick her up for dinner.

"Can't we just come for a friendly visit?" asked Cecilia in her naturally soft voice.

"Mom, Cameron's too smart for a smoke screen," Jackie said. "We heard what happened, and we've come to cheer you up."

"Why would I need cheering up?"

"Cameron dear," Cecilia said, "why don't you invite us in so we can talk?"

Cameron stepped aside; then, after closing the door and remembering her place was hardly set up for receiving guests, she hurried to the chair, swept up the wrapper from her sandwich and other trash her work had left, and moved over the low table on which her typewriter sat.

"There you go, Mom," she said, gesturing her mother to the chair. She and Jackie sat on the edge of the bed.

"I don't know why you won't let me do some decorating here for you," said Cecilia. "I would love doing it, and this could be such a cute little room."

"Well . . ." Cameron gazed about the cold room, realizing something else that should have occurred to her while she was writing her résumés. "I doubt I'll be here much longer."

"What do you mean?"

Cameron picked up the stack of envelopes. Shuffling through them, she said, "Kansas City, Chicago, New York—"

"You can't be applying for jobs in New York," Jackie exclaimed. "Not so far away."

"Why would you want to work in New York when there are plenty of newspapers right here in L.A.?" Cecilia lifted her eyes, wide and serene as always, to beseech her daughter. "The *Times* is nearly as good as the *Journal*. Even . . . well, the *Globe* wouldn't so bad."

"I'm trying to be open to anything."

"This whole thing is so distressing. Your father isn't the easiest man to get along with, I will admit, but Cameron, to throw away a promising career—"

"I haven't gone that far, Mother. I still have a career. I've only been out of work for a few hours." Yes, it already felt like years, but that was a private matter. "There are tons of fish in the sea, and I have great qualifications. I'm not worried."

"Have you considered a new career?" Cameron's mother had never fully accepted her daughter's job. Even though newspapers had been Cecilia's livelihood since birth, to her it would never be appropriate for a lady to actually *work* for one, especially as a reporter, a hack. "You could finish your college—" That, too, had been hard for Cecilia when Cameron had quit college after only a year to work for the paper. "Wouldn't it be fun, you and Jacqueline attending UCLA together?" But Cameron knew her mother's main objective in encouraging college was the opportunity it afforded in finding a proper husband.

"I don't want a new career, Mom," Cameron replied through slightly clenched teeth. When she had quit the *Journal*, she had not considered the act would involve the entire family and dredge up every old wound.

"Maybe I could talk to your father. He might take you back if handled . . . well, carefully."

"No, Mom. I don't think I'd want to go back under any circumstances. I'll never advance there. It is bad enough Dad refused me the correspondent's job in Rome. Maybe that was asking too much from him, but there is no reason why he shouldn't send me to Moscow for a specific one-time article. I am familiar with the place and have some contacts."

"I don't know why you are so intent on going there of all places!" Cecilia's tone was uncharacteristically emphatic.

"It's always been my dream to go back."

"Such a backward, repressive country. No one here cares about what goes on there."

"If that is truly the case, then it is more imperative than ever for American journalists to be there. We are foolish to discount the power of the Soviet Union so easily. We—"

"I am glad you are not going there."

"So you side with Dad?" Cameron asked, surprised at the challenging tone she leveled at her mother.

"It's not a matter of sides—"

"Say, I have an idea," Jackie put in brightly. "Why don't we get some lunch? I'm starved."

Dear Jackie, the family mediator. Mature beyond her years, she somehow found a way, at least usually, to hold things together. She was like a very nice glue.

But Cecilia wasn't going to go for that now. "It's four in the afternoon," she pointed out petulantly.

"Dinner, then? By the time we get to a restaurant, it would be perfect timing."

"I suppose that would be okay," Cameron said. "But, Mom, you must promise not to nag me anymore."

Cecilia's eyes darted between her daughters, perhaps gauging how successful she would be against them both. Obviously aware of her weaknesses, she shrugged. "All right. But I do want to pray for you, Cameron. Nothing wrong with that, is there?"

"Right now. . . ?" Cameron could not help squirming a bit. "You know how uncomfortable that makes me."

"I guess I will just have to do so to myself, then." Cecilia rose. "Now let's go eat. And we will all be good girls, won't we?"

LESS THAN TWO weeks had passed since Cameron's departure from the *Journal*, but it felt like a year. And still she was unemployed. There had been some responses to her résumés. Basically what she'd heard was "We don't think one with your specific qualifications would fit into our editorial staff at this time." Read: "Our all-male club is closed." One paper even implied that her references were not "glowing." She had the distinct impression her father had gotten to them.

Shanahan departed for Europe. Neither made any attempt to see the other before he left. It was better that way. Even Cameron knew she had become far too involved with the man, especially for a woman with no intention of marrying. And one thing was all but certain to her—even if she did one day capitulate to the idea of marriage, she could not imagine Johnny being the man with whom she'd take the plunge. Yes, he held a strong, sometimes overpowering, appeal to her, but even she could tell there was something missing in him. She couldn't define it, didn't even know what it was, but she'd felt at times he lacked some one nebulous thing she desired in a man. But that didn't keep her stomach from churning when she thought she'd never see him again.

The snake! The swine! The rat!

Yet despite what he might lack, there was still something incredible about him. She could close her eyes and even now see that devilish grin with the glint in his tobacco brown eyes that spelled danger—enticingly delightful danger. At times she wondered what he'd really done that was so bad. Her anger should have been directed entirely at her father instead of at him. Shanahan had merely jumped at an opportunity that even a better man would have been unable to refuse. A despised streak of honesty in Cameron made her wonder if her anger had, after all, stemmed from the fact he'd been so ready to take a job thousands of miles from her. She hated to think she cared that much. So she forced herself not to think about Johnny at all.

She had in fact received one job offer—at least she assumed it was an offer, though she ignored it. Max Arnett's secretary had called Cameron requesting that she join Mr. Arnett for lunch. Cameron said she'd call and set something up as soon as her busy schedule permitted. She knew it was the height of arrogance to brush off the publisher of the *Los Angeles Globe*, but she just was not ready to stoop to working for the third-rated newspaper. If she must work for a third-rate outfit, let it be out of town where her failure was not so evident to everyone she knew.

After two weeks of idleness, however, a kind of desperation set in. A gnawing fear gripped her insides, hitting her especially hard when she was walking past a restaurant and saw a Help Wanted sign in the window and nearly went in to apply. If nothing else, money was quickly becoming a problem. She supported herself, unlike her sisters who lived at home. She had done so since the day she quit college and had never regretted it. She had a little savings set aside, but it wasn't going to last long. She needed a job.

When her mother called to invite her to dinner—"Just to see if you and your father can talk and work things out"—she accepted. And regretted it.

"So is this something in the way of the Prodigal returning?" her father asked, greeting her as she arrived at the Beverly Hills house. He was gloating.

"Don't worry, Dad, I hate fatted calf." She tried to match his glib attitude but knew she fell short. If she was some sort of twisted Prodigal, she was pretty certain she wasn't in for the kind of welcoming the guy in the Bible had received.

Cecilia put an arm around Cameron. "Now, you two be nice. We don't mix business with family."

Cameron looked askance at her mother's naïveté. She had been around the Hayes family dynamics for a couple of decades, yet Cecilia always seemed so oblivious.

Jackie and Blair were also present that evening, and as usual when their father presided over the family, there was a certain charge to the air. The women in the family, who could be fairly relaxed and warm with one another when alone, were now very much on their guard. Keagan's presence dominated all.

Cameron wondered why she had come. To placate her mother? Or was she just as naïve as Cecilia? Cameron could be only so tough, then . . . well, her life was proof of how far that went. How she wanted to wrest a small drop of respect from her father! She hid it well most of the time, but the desperate need was there—buried deeply, perhaps, but there nonetheless.

As they sat at the dinner table, Keagan mentioned casually, "Got a call from my old buddy Hal Bigalow—you know, he's now the editor of the *Kansas City Herald*. You remember him, don't you, Cecilia? He was in Moscow with us."

"The name is familiar," Cecilia answered vaguely. She was always uncomfortable when talk turned to the family's sojourn in Moscow. Cameron never knew why.

"Kind of like 'old home' week, 'cause out of the blue I also heard from Don Schults at the *New York Times*." Keagan was smirking. He added, "All us old newspaper hacks got to stick together."

"Why is that, Dad?" Cameron asked, a small inkling of what it all meant dawning upon her.

"We just do. That's the way it is in the newspaper business."

"And I always thought it was high competition."

Keagan shrugged and asked for the green beans.

Cameron added, "Funny thing, but I turned in résumés at both the *Herald* and the *Times*."

Keagan just laughed, spooning beans onto his plate.

"What did you do, Dad?" Cameron's voice was soft, because had it been louder, it would have shook.

"I made dessert tonight," said Jackie cheerily. "Angel food cake. Turned out perfectly—"

"Forget that, Jackie," Cameron cut in. Then, eyes focused on her father, she asked again, "What did you do?"

"I talked with some old friends," Keagan replied smugly.

"Why don't we finish dinner instead—" Jackie unwisely tried again to deflect disaster.

Cameron turned on her. "Shut up, Jackie!" she raged. "I'm so sick of your diplomacy. Don't you know it's a waste of time?"

When Cameron saw her sister practically melt with dejection, she felt terrible, but her rage now had a life of its own. She'd deal with Jackie's hurt feelings later.

"Apologize to your sister," Keagan demanded.

"What? Are you suddenly concerned for your children's feelings?" Cameron jumped up. "What about my feelings at finding out my own father has been sabotaging me?" she all but shouted.

"Someone had to put you in your place," he shouted back.

"So, you admit it!"

"No one I spoke to would have hired you anyway," he replied. "You think you are some hotshot reporter, but I have seen cubs better than you. You just had to learn the hard way."

"Thanks, Dad, I appreciate the lesson," she said dryly, then turned and left.

She got as far as her Hudson coupe. She slipped behind the wheel, but when she tried to put the key in the ignition, her hand started trembling so much that the key fell to the floor. That seemed to loose something within her. Tears she hadn't even known were close suddenly flooded from her eyes. With a harsh brush of her fist, she tried to wipe them away, but they kept coming.

"Why. . . ?" she murmured over and over, hardly even knowing what she really wanted to know. "Why. . . ?"

What a shock when she realized her lament didn't mean "Why did my father do this to me?" but rather "Why do I love him and want him to love me?"

How pathetic of her! Yet she knew it was a very basic desire of any child. It really wasn't asking so much, was it? She just wanted him to love her. Her mother had always told Cameron that her father just had a hard time showing his feelings, that he did love his children. But it was becoming almost impossible to believe that. Still . . . was he sabotaging her out of love? Oh, how she wanted to believe that he was doing this just to keep her at his side because he enjoyed her company, not because he wanted to control her.

But a sick knot in her stomach told her she was only trying to fool herself. Perhaps the best thing was to accept it and forget all the sentimental tripe about love.

Accept it. But the ache in her heart didn't stop that easily.

"Cameron."

She hadn't heard anyone approach, but when she looked up, she saw both Blair and Jackie standing by the car. She rolled down the window but couldn't speak.

"I didn't hear your car leave, so I hoped we'd find you still here," Jackie said. "Have you been crying?" she added with concern.

"No . . . no," Cameron replied, but the lie was obvious.

"Of course you haven't," said Blair, not placating, but rather with tender support. She understood how galling it was to be caught shedding tears over their relationship with their father.

"I thought you might want to go get some ice cream," Jackie said. "I know of a new place not far from here."

"I don't know . . ." Cameron hated to be in such a needy place. She was the big sister, after all.

"Every girl can use an ice-cream cone now and then," said Blair.

Cameron realized then how very glad she was that her sisters had come. She smiled weakly. "Sure, why not?"

"I'll drive," offered Jackie.

Cameron scooted over as Jackie climbed in behind the wheel. Blair got in back.

"For the record," Jackie said, starting up the engine, "Mom encouraged us to go after you."

Blair added with a touch of cynicism, "Well, she got Jackie's attention and jerked her head toward the door."

"Still, I'm sure she was upset at Dad for what he did," Jackie said.

"I suppose it wouldn't have mattered even if she had said something." Cameron had long ago come not to expect too much from their mother. Cecilia meant well but . . . what was it Keagan always said? The road to nowhere was paved with good intentions. Then she remembered something else. "Jackie, will you forgive me for snapping at you during dinner? I wasn't thinking straight."

Jackie gave a reassuring smile. "I know you didn't mean it."

"I vote we forget all about what happened in there and just have a good time," Blair said in characteristic fashion.

Later, at the ice-cream parlor, they tried to follow Blair's advice. Instead of mere cones, they each had a huge banana split with mounds of whipped cream on top. Cameron made an attempt to join the sisterly banter, but at one point her attention slipped away as a stab of worry over her future assailed her.

"You okay, Cameron?" Jackie asked.

"Yeah . . . sure. Great ice cream."

"If you want to talk about it . . ."

Blair made a little sound of disgust at Jackie's spoiling the mood with seriousness.

Cameron just sighed. "I guess I am just a little worried about what I'm going to do now. What if I can't get another newspaper job?"

"You will. I'm sure of it!" encouraged Jackie. "Despite what Dad says, you are talented."

Cameron looked at both her sisters. A sense of loss suddenly flooded over her. Change was coming, she knew. The world was on the brink of war, and her personal life was headed in an unknown direction. She felt very certain that whatever happened, she and her sisters might never again enjoy ice cream together. Or, if they did, they would be very different people when it happened.

9

MAX ARNETT called again, himself this time. "Come to my office in the morning, Cameron, and let's talk. I used to bounce you on my knee when you were little, and I'd like to get reacquainted."

Cameron agreed but not because of his hogwash about her bouncing on his knobby knees. Max and Keagan had been rivals for as long as Cameron could remember. There was even some rumor that Keagan had stolen the affections of Cecilia from the man. For years Arnett had his teeth nipping at the *Journal*'s heels like that of an ill-tempered puppy. There was a time when the *Globe* had enjoyed a preeminence over the *Journal*, and the two had traded places frequently over the years, though now the *Journal* was in the number two spot behind the *Times*. Yet the *Globe* was close enough to the *Journal* that the carrot was ever there, as was the hope to grasp it.

Cameron wouldn't want to work for the *Globe*, but she did think that considering them would prick at her father. He would never show it, of course, but it would not sit well with him in the esteem of his colleagues that his daughter worked for a rival paper. In fact, the more she thought about that, the more enticing the idea was. When she entered Arnett's office the next day, she was not completely close-minded.

"I am so glad we could finally get together," Arnett said, offering Cameron a chair—an expensive leather one—in front of his desk. He sat in an adjacent chair rather than behind his desk. "It has been far too long. When was the last time? Unfortunately, I could not make it to your father's party."

Cameron wondered if he'd even been invited.

"Well," he went on, "whenever it was, you have since truly come into your own as a fine young woman, Cameron, and as a journalist."

Besides the rivalry of the newspapers, Cameron now remembered why her father disliked this man. He was all Keagan was not. Patrician, even elegant, well-spoken, refined. The Arnett family had been in the newspaper business since the gold rush days. Max had been groomed for his job all his life, and not just as a publisher, but as a society scion. No wonder Keagan scorned him.

Cameron, however, was willing to form her own opinion of the man, unclouded by his rather benign, self-effacing manner. A short, slightly built man with thinning blond hair, clean-shaven soft skin, and rather vague gray eyes, he seemed as if he couldn't harm a fly. Yet she knew he could be tough. A few years back when there had been some union trouble, he had personally confronted union leaders and kicked them out of his building.

"Shall we have some refreshments?" he asked.

"No, thank you. I would, however, like to know the purpose of this meeting," Cameron said.

"You get right down to it, don't you? That's what makes you a fine newspaperwoman." He paused as if needing to prepare himself for a discussion uncluttered by social niceties. "I have followed your work, and I want to say I am quite impressed. Your recent piece on the gambling ships was incisive and insightful."

"That was the last article I did for the *Journal*."

"Ah . . . a terrible matter, that. I won't lie, though, and say I did not think it was the best thing for you. I could not see your career advancing far there."

Cameron cocked a brow. "No?"

"Was not the stigma of nepotism hanging over you?"

"I suppose so, but believe me, my father did not give me special favors. That would have killed him." Yet she thought of what he'd said about the gambling ship story. But she could not let her thoughts take that direction.

"Please, don't take me wrong. You have fine talent. I have recently read nearly everything you wrote for the *Journal*, and it was exceptional. I heard why you quit."

"You did?"

"Yes. You'd been turned down for a correspondent's position—on the mere grounds that you are a woman. Is that how it was?"

"Basically, yes. But I don't want you to get the idea I am some temperamental prima donna. There were some personal issues involved that I wish not to discuss."

"I'm sure there were." He tapped his lips with his forefinger and looked over the top of his wire-rimmed glasses at her. He reeked of venerability and kindness. Cameron steeled herself against this persona. "And that is exactly why I believe you have done yourself a favor by leaving the *Journal*. I sense you are a journalist who wishes to work without the weight of personal issues. And I, Cameron, would like to offer you just such an opportunity."

"A job at the *Globe*?"

"Yes."

"On the city desk?"

"That would be my second choice for you."

"Second choice?" Awful visions of fashion shows and movie premieres darkened her thoughts.

He smiled, a bland lifting of the corners of his thin lips. "My first choice would be to offer you a correspondent position."

"Really?" She tried to keep from wondering what the catch was.

"Does this interest you?"

"Where?"

"Would it matter?"

"I am not so desperate, Mr. Arnett, that I would go anywhere."

He smiled benignly and leaned back. "Tell me, just for interest's sake, where would you like to go?"

"Europe, naturally. I want to cover the war. I do have some small knowledge of the Soviet Union from years spent there when my father was Moscow bureau chief. I've always dreamed of returning there."

"Not many correspondents care to be sent there. These days most would consider it a hardship post and a poor career move."

"That may be true at the moment, but sooner or later the Soviet Union is going to be a key player in the war in Europe. My father correctly predicted the Russo-German Nonaggression Pact, and he also predicts that Germany will turn on Russia. I don't agree with my father on many things, but his political astuteness is quite sharp, especially regarding Russia." She added, "My own stay in Russia was quite enlightening. I would suggest, Mr. Arnett, that an update on the Russo-German Nonaggression Pact at this time would be a most effective use of a correspondent."

Again that smile bent Arnett's lips, so warm and at the same time so cool. "If I ever do send a correspondent there, I will definitely consider you. Unfortunately, the *Globe*'s resources cannot support an agent there at this time, and I would be loathe to waste your talents there. But how does Rome sound to you?"

She had expected to hear anything but that. "Rome?"

"I have an opening there at this time. The *Globe* cannot finance a large foreign correspondent department. We don't even have an office in Rome. Our man there works out of his hotel room, as would you— ahem, your own room, of course. Our foreign department isn't flashy, but I think you can change that for us."

"Why?" she finally managed, her tone a bare squeak. At first she'd thought this entire conversation was merely academic, now, it seemed, she was truly being offered a position, one that seemed far too good to be true.

"There is a war in Europe, and I believe that war will be the *Globe*'s ticket to the front of the competition. I have been beefing up all our foreign bureaus, at least those within the direct orbit of the war. But I imagine you are wondering, why *you* specifically? Being the good reporter that you are, you won't accept surface reasons. And I won't rest on them either—however, your abilities are a big part of my choice. The fact that you are a woman, I believe, unlike many short-sighted men out there, will be a wonderful asset, lending a new perspective to the news." Suddenly he leaned forward, gray eyes sharp now with purpose. "All right, now I will tell you my final reason. I want to use you, Cameron, to beat out every man over there, and especially every *Journal* correspondent. Tell me honestly that you wouldn't like to do that?"

"I can't, not honestly."

"I thought that might appeal to you. I merely want to use that hunger of yours to further the *Globe*. I think we can do it together."

Cameron leaned back, mainly to get out from under the scrutiny of Arnett's eyes. She knew now what his power was—an uncanny ability to lure the unsuspecting in by kindness, then to snare them with melting charisma.

For two weeks she'd tried to think of how to show up her father; now Arnett was giving her the chance to do just that. Yet suddenly she felt a twinge of loyalty toward her father. Was this man before her some evil entity goading her into—what? Taking a job with a rival paper? Her father had given her no other choice. Why not give the *Journal* a run for its money? She could do it, too. Toss in the added benefit of competing against Shanahan, and well, it was just too tempting. And she had no doubt Arnett had thought of that, as well. Yet still something held her in check. And she knew exactly what it was.

"Listen, Mr. Arnett, you are right about my uneasiness over the years of working for my father. I know I am qualified, but there has, nonetheless, always been a small nagging doubt. Would I have succeeded without him? Now you offer me the job of a lifetime. But why? Essentially *because* of my father. Because you want to use me against him. I just don't know what to make of it. Should I despise you, along with him, for wanting to use me as a pawn? Or should I thank you for the opportunity and leave it at that?"

"Don't mistake me, Cameron. I care too much for my paper to hire someone for any reason except that he or she truly qualifies. You take a close look at my editorial staff. You won't find a goldbricker among them. I take complete responsibility for the fact that the *Globe* remains third in the city. You are qualified. I believe it like I believe nothing else!" His gaze was steady. Cameron could not doubt him. "I just think that luck has finally smiled upon me—to put before me a qualified journalist at the right time to send to the right place. I wouldn't do it otherwise. I don't know how else to convince you."

Cameron was silent for a long while, weighing all she had just heard. In the end she was convinced to follow her own instincts. She knew her abilities better than anyone, and she knew she had what it took to go to Europe. Let these men think what they would. She knew what she knew.

She thrust out her hand to the publisher. "All right, Mr. Arnett, I accept the job, but with one proviso." She paused, and even she realized the gall of her next statement. "I don't want to be locked into Rome. Should the *Globe* open a bureau in the Soviet Union, I want to be assigned to it. Also, if I front part of the expenses, I'd like the *Globe* to send me to Moscow in the near future to do an in-depth article on the progress of the Pact."

"It's a deal, Cameron." Arnett grasped her hand in his. "Let's get you settled into Rome first. That will be your base. Then I will get the proper papers in order for a jaunt to Russia. I believe I can have all in order in a month or so."

Fleetingly Cameron thought he had agreed far too easily to her Moscow proviso. She should have been worried. But what did she have to lose? She was still going to Rome, and that was a huge coup in itself.

10

IT SURPRISED CAMERON when two days later her mother telephoned and asked if she could take her out to lunch. It was not exceptionally unusual for them to lunch together, but to Cameron the timing was rather suspicious. She had told no one of her talk with Arnett. She wasn't exactly trying to keep it a secret, but she had simply been avoiding the repercussions sure to come when the news reached her parents. Had her mother heard? What would be her reaction to her daughter working for the *Journal*'s fiercest competitor?

They met at a little French bistro just off Hollywood Boulevard. It was one of Cecilia's favorite places to dine with her daughters. The furnishings were frilly French Provincial, the curtains on the windows were ruffled lace, and the tablecloths were pink. Cameron felt as comfortable here as her mother would have felt in the *Journal*'s smoke-filled newsroom.

Cecilia, never one to come easily to any point, engaged Cameron in casual chitchat while they ordered and waited for their food. Cameron felt on touchy enough ground with her mother that she wisely opted not to push the woman. She endured a discussion of clothes and society news and was relieved when her salad arrived as a distraction.

They were halfway through their entrée, a tasty beef burgundy, when it seemed Cecilia was ready to declare her intent.

"Cameron, I am just the tiniest bit disappointed with you."

"Why is that, Mom?"

"You are going away, aren't you?"

The food no longer tasted good. Cameron set down her fork as she prepared to take her knocks. "I was going to tell you."

"When was that, dear?" Cecilia's tone was sweetly innocuous, but Cameron knew such a tone coming from her mother usually concealed a huge bite. "We are nearly finished with lunch."

"Well . . ." Now Cameron knew what the objects of her interviews felt like. She'd always thought she'd inherited her style from her father, but now she wondered. "I didn't want to ruin our meal," she added lamely.

Cecilia sighed, shaking her head. "Oh, Cameron, how can you go so far away? And with a war on."

"So you spoke with Max Arnett?"

"We are friends from way back. He called me, I believe, hoping the news of your defection would sit better coming directly from him." With another frustrated shake of her head, she added, "Oh, I'm not expressing this properly at all. I knew from the moment you had applied for the *Journal*'s Rome bureau that I needed to let go of you. I knew you would never be a homebody like Jackie, or even Blair. I knew you would never be happy unless you were in the middle of the 'action,' as you are fond of putting it."

"Then why do I sense displeasure from you?"

"My feelings are very mixed-up at the moment. I'm upset that you still hadn't told me after two days. I'm upset because Max is going to send you to Russia. I'm also confused because I can't stop from wondering if this is all God's will. That somehow He is telling me—" She stopped with a little gasp, her hand grasping her throat. "I don't know if I can say more—or even if I should. I just don't know what to do." Her eyes filled with moisture.

"Mom . . ." Cameron said softly, reaching across the table and taking her mother's slim, delicate hand. Cameron's own hand was rough by comparison, the nails not manicured. The tips of a couple of fingers were darkened with ink from when she had changed her typewriter ribbon. With an encouraging smile, she gently suggested, "Let's get out of here, perhaps go for a walk. This sunshine can't last, so we had best take advantage of it."

"That's a good idea."

Cecilia paid the bill, and they left. Indeed, it was sunny for February. The temperature had to be seventy. The streets were busy with pedestrians and vehicles. Cameron led them toward a little neighborhood park she knew of. Her mother loved flowers and nature, so a park might help soothe her frayed nerves.

At the park Cameron breathed in the clean, sweet air, fragrant with the scent of roses.

"I will miss these Southern California winters," she commented.

"There will be no roses in February in Moscow."

"But, Mom, can't you understand just a little why I want to go?"

"I never could, not really."

"They were good years for me." Cameron had always known the reason Russia held such appeal for her, though usually she tried not to think about it. Now she knew she must for her mother's sake. "It was the best time I ever had with Dad. He was . . . I don't know, different there. I know he worked all the time, and you couldn't have liked that, but he let *me* go with him. And it was heavenly. I can truly say they were the best years of my life."

An ironic smile slanted Cecilia's lips. "They were the worst years of *my* life."

"Why, Mom?"

Cecilia paused by a beautiful pink camellia and bent down, plucking some weeds from the rich brown earth. "Goodness! What am I doing? Reflex, I suppose." She shrugged. "But I don't mind weeding even in someone else's garden. I find it relaxing."

"Max should have my travel documents worked out in a couple weeks," Cameron commented, thinking it best to ease her mother into reality. "Mom, please try to understand. This is an important job both in Rome and hopefully later in the Soviet Union. I know that's where I belong."

"I understand." Cecilia straightened and brushed soil from her hands.

They walked a short distance before Cecilia paused by a bush of yellow roses. "Cameron, it's not that . . ." She paused with uncertainty. Shaking her head, she appeared to force herself to continue. "I fear your going to Russia mostly. It is a dangerous place. An unhappy place."

Cecilia's sudden tenacity regarding Russia surprised Cameron. Her mother hardly ever talked about Russia, much less voiced such a strong opinion on anything regarding the country. If Cameron hadn't been in Russia with her mother years ago, she would have wondered if Cecilia had ever been there at all, if the place had ever been a part of her life. This reaction of hers now was completely inconsistent.

"Mother," she said, "what is this all about?"

Cecilia looked away, seeming to focus on one of the rosebuds that was about to open. She reached out, fingering the satin petals.

"I knew I would have to tell you sooner or later," she said, her voice as soft as the yellow bud. "That's partly why I have so opposed your going to Russia, hoping perhaps that I could avoid this discussion forever. Now I am torn and confused. I have prayed about this and have still been confused—until this moment. I suddenly know this is inevitable. I must tell you, Cameron, but you are the only one I can discuss this with. Blair would never understand, and Jackie . . . she is so young." Pausing, she took Cameron's hand. "Come, let's sit down. This may take a while."

They found a bench and sat as a gentle breeze wafted over them. It brought the scent of flowers, but Cameron hardly noticed anything beyond the strain in her mother's voice. What was coming now? It could not be anything good.

"God forgive me, but I thought my secret would never have to be told. I thought I could easily take it with me to my grave. Perhaps that would be best, yet . . . I know I can't do that. It cries out to be re-vealed, and I long to have another help me carry my burden. Will you be that person?"

"I will try, Mother. What secret is it?" Cameron tried to be properly solemn. This was a great thing her mother was asking. But on the other hand, what earth-shattering secret could a mild, unworldly woman like her mother possibly have?

"It happened in Russia long ago, before you were born." Cecilia hesitated, moving her finger through the fine layer of dust on the edge of the wrought-iron bench. "Your father calls that time his 'glory days.' He was covering the Great War and was based in St. Petersburg. I came along with him. We were young, newly married, and we thought we were invincible. But what was glory for him quickly turned into misery for me. He was gone all the time, and I felt stranded in a place I did not know and where I could not even speak the language. When he wasn't at the Front, he was—well, he was everywhere but with me. I was left entirely to my own devices, you see. There were a few other foreign wives at the embassy and such, but I was always painfully shy, far more so back then than I am now. I never felt that I fit in with them. The luncheons, the parties—how I dreaded them. I would usually find myself standing alone in a crowd, and your father, if he was in attendance, was always off talking with someone else."

"It must have been awful, Mom."

"I soon began avoiding the social gatherings unless your father ab-solutely required me to be there. And I often avoided even those by pleading a headache or some other malady." She lifted her eyes to meet Cameron's gaze, and in them Cameron saw pain that seemed as fresh as it had been twenty-seven years ago. "But even in spite of that, I was so lonely. Your father said my misery was of my own making, and I suppose he was right. But it didn't make it better. Of course I spoke no Russian, so I was isolated from the Russian people, as well. However, even in Tsarist times there was an invisible barrier between foreigners and citizens—not as strong as later, but still difficult to break through. I escaped into books, and when I exhausted the supply we had in the flat, I began to prowl in bookstores. There was an English bookstore I frequented." Pausing, she jumped up, obviously agitated. She strode a few steps away, pausing beside a potted fuchsia next to the bench. She picked off a couple dead leaves. "I haven't spoken of him for nearly all of these last twenty-seven years."

"Him?" Cameron asked, her throat tightening.

"His name was Yakov Luban. He was a Russian Jew. He owned the bookstore, but more importantly, he spoke English. He would recommend books to me, and sometimes when a book came in that he thought I would enjoy, he would send me a note. I'd drop by to pick it up, and we would discuss what we had been reading. He was a young man, only a year or so older than I, but he was a widower, and I suppose he was as lonely as I."

"Oh, Mom . . ." Cameron sensed where this was going, and she didn't mean to sound reproving. Yet this was her mother, her dear, sweet, and yes, saintly mother!

Cecilia turned to face her daughter. "I'm sorry, Cameron. I told you I was weak."

"I'm the last person to judge you," Cameron quickly added apologetically. "It's just a shock, that's all."

"Would it sound awful if I told you it was nothing sordid or dirty?" She shrugged as if the question didn't really require an answer. "He was a sweet, tender man, and he never purposely seduced me. It just happened. I can't even now say if we actually loved each other, but we desperately needed each other. We filled something in the other that was empty, missing. He knew I wouldn't—couldn't—leave my husband. Even after I learned I was . . . in trouble—"

"What!" Cameron's head snapped up as she gaped at her mother.

Cecilia nodded. "And before you question if the child could have been Keagan's, I will say that it positively was not. At that time your father had been gone for about three months to the Front. So I knew it was Yakov's."

Cameron tried to moisten her dry lips but with no success, since her mouth was dry, as well. "But . . ." Her mind spun with questions, even denials. Foremost was how her mother could have kept this a secret. "Did you have an abortion?" she asked bluntly.

"Yakov had no other children, and despite the circumstances he was thrilled at the prospect of having a child. I could have done what other women have done in similar straits, that is, deceive my husband into thinking the child was his. It might have worked, and after what ended up happening, I wish now I had. But Yakov was so dear to me that I was miserable at the prospect of denying him his child. And I believed that if I kept the child and deceived your father, there would be such a pall of guilt and doubt over our lives that neither we nor the child would ever know happiness. That's when I hit upon a plan that I thought could somewhat solve my horrible dilemma. I told Keagan that I had a girlfriend from college who was living in Stockholm and that she wanted me to visit for a few weeks. I had been able to hide my condition because it was winter and I wore many layers of clothing. And when your father and I were intimate, which was seldom anyway . . . well, women were far more modest in those situations than they are today. He just thought I was gaining weight. I managed to get to my fifth month before I raised the Stockholm trip. I was so miserable he was probably relieved to be rid of me."

"Mother, this is unbelievable," Cameron breathed. "To have been able to keep such a thing from your own husband . . ."

"We didn't have much of a relationship," Cecilia admitted with a sigh. "He denies it now, but I know he married me only for the newspaper. I didn't mind that much. He was a handsome, exciting man. But he had other women, even in Russia. That's partly why I was so miserable. Believe me, he saw little of me in *every* way."

"So you went to Stockholm?" Cameron prompted. She was uncomfortable with that particular direction of the conversation.

"I stayed there until the baby was born. I feigned one excuse after the other to prolong my stay, such as telling Keagan my friend's sister was getting married and I must stay for the wedding, or that I had a touch of the flu. I was able to play that illness along quite well, and it provided a reason for my 'weight loss' when we saw each other again."

"What happened to the baby?"

Cecilia dropped back onto the bench. She was very pale. "Yakov came to Stockholm for the birth. We agreed that he would raise the child." She blinked several times, and Cameron saw the tears welling in her mother's eyes. "It was the hardest thing I ever did."

Cameron grasped her mother's hand between both of hers, her own eyes filling with moisture.

"I knew it was the best thing for him. . . ." Cecilia began.

"Him?" Cameron breathed. Did she have a brother somewhere? Was it possible?

"Yes . . . we had a son. We named him Semyon—it was Yakov's father's name. Afterward I returned to Russia for a short time, but I was so depressed knowing my child was so close, but I could not have him. I finally returned to the States alone. I had some wild fantasies about telling Keagan about a poor orphan baby we could adopt. But

Semyon wasn't an orphan. He had a father who loved him dearly. Anyway, I knew your father could never accept a son that was not his own. And I doubt I could have carried off a deception. . . ." She paused, smiling ironically. "I guess in the end, I did after all, didn't I? For your father still knows nothing of this. At the time, however, I certainly did not believe I could. I thought I was doing the best thing for the child. I could not have known that in two short years the country in which I had left my child was going to explode."

"The Revolution!" Cameron exclaimed. "Were they—?" She could not finish the sentence.

Cecilia did not answer directly. It seemed she must say her piece in a certain order for fear she'd not say it at all. "After I returned home, my father saw how miserable I was and naturally assumed it was because of the separation from Keagan. So through a little intimidation and a little bribery, my father convinced Keagan to return home, as well. Not long after, I gave birth to you." Cecilia smiled, squeezing Cameron's hand. "You saved my life, dear! You gave me joy when I'd thought I would never know joy again. Now it was your father's turn to be miserable, for not only was his firstborn not a son, but he was missing one of the greatest news stories in history—the Russian Revolution. Part of my father's bribery was that he would make Keagan managing editor of the paper if he would commit to staying in Los Angeles for ten years. Again, it was the newspaper that kept us together."

"What happened to . . . the child?"

"I kept in touch with Yakov through an intermediary here in the States. As you well know, communications between here and Russia are never perfect. They were abominable during those uncertain times. Then it all ended. The last letter was in 1920. I tried to make discreet inquiries, but getting information was next to impossible. It was tortuous not knowing, but I soon realized that for my own sanity, I had to give them up. And that's what I did. I know it sounds cold, but what else could I do?"

"I understand, Mom. You don't have to defend yourself to me."

"Of course I am defensive. My relationship with Yakov was wrong. It hurt and had the capacity to hurt so many lives. I guess guilt is the reason I have always been so weak around your father."

"He was no angel, either."

"Yes, but I pretended to be so good. I think that's what made it worse. It wasn't all pretense, though. The experience did strengthen my relationship with God. I knew a forgiveness from God for my actions that truly gave me humility. Keeping it a secret all these years is another matter I have laid before God. I still don't know if keeping it secret was right or wrong. But I believe it was the best thing to do at the time for all concerned."

"I think so, too, Mom." In a way Cameron wished her mother had continued to keep her secret. But it touched her, that her mother had chosen her to be the one to hear the truth. "Do you still not know what became of them, Mom?"

"In 1924, three years shy of his ten-year agreement, my father assigned Keagan to head the Moscow bureau," Cecilia began again.

"That was when Lenin opened up the country to U.S. reporters in order to get grain for the famine?" Cameron clarified.

Nodding, Cecilia replied, "Even my father realized Keagan was the most qualified man for that momentous job. And believe me, your father was again in his glory. He dragged us all along with him. I desperately didn't want to go and reopen wounds that were just healing, but our marriage had begun to strengthen, and I could not deny him." She smiled faintly. "Your father is a good man, Cameron, for all his bluster. Do you remember the awful scare we had when we thought Jackie had polio?"

Cameron nodded. "Even I started praying then."

"As did your father. He went with me to the hospital chapel every night while she was hospitalized. He actually knelt next to me, and we prayed. I knew it cost your father dearly to humble himself so before anyone, even God. But he did it because he knew how important it was for me."

"I never knew that."

"So the problems in Russia, I'm sure, were as much my fault as his. Maybe he worked all the time because I was such a depressing character to be around."

"I do remember your being awfully moody and withdrawn when we were there. I was having a ball and couldn't understand why you were always so sad."

A faint smile teased Cecilia's lips. "Now you know . . . you know everything."

Cameron leaned back, completely drained. How had her mother lived with such a secret for so long? Why had she chosen now to reveal it to Cameron? But though many more questions were assailing her, she could not find the will to ask a single one. She and her mother just sat silently for a very long time. The sun moved high overhead, but the warmth of it did not penetrate Cameron's chilled insides.

One thought kept echoing in her head. *I have a brother.* Or did she? He might well have died during the chaos of the Revolution, civil war, and famine. Or if he was alive, he was surely lost to her forever. She had a brother . . . a big brother. Part of her could only think of him as a *child*, her mother's illegitimate *baby*. But if he was alive, he'd be a little more than a year older than Cameron. He'd be a twenty-five-year-old man now. She glanced at her mother and knew Cecilia was thinking the same exact thing. A sob escaped Cecilia's lips. Cameron reached out and embraced her mother. She did not know this boy named Semyon Luban. How could she feel such a deep loss, then? How could she empathize so with her mother's grief?

Grief for something she'd never had. It was a strange sensation, to say the least.

All of a sudden she heard herself utter the last words she imagined saying, but which she knew must be said. "You can never tell Dad."

"I know that. It might well kill him."

"But I'm glad you told me, Mom."

"So am I. It seems so right that you should know."

"What of Blair and Jackie?"

"I fear that if too many know, it could get back to your father."

Cameron nodded. Neither of her sisters shared many confidences with Keagan, but there could be a slip. She thought of Blair using information like this to hurt their father in a fit of anger during one of their many shouting matches.

"Cameron, now you know why I am so conflicted," Cecilia said. "Since I learned you might be going to Russia soon, I could only think of having you there—you, who never gives up until you get your story and reach your goals. You could find him."

"Yes . . . I could . . ." Fingering her lip pensively, Cameron's mind raced with the various approaches she might take in such a search. She could find her brother. She knew it!

"Am I being selfish?" questioned Cecilia. "It would devastate Keagan. And the boy . . . if he is alive, how might this affect him? And if you found him, could he leave Russia? I have heard things—"

"We'd find a way," said Cameron, full of confidence. "As for Dad,

I just don't know. We could take things one step at a time. First, I'd have to get to Russia, and that's still not a certainty."

"Max said you had offered to pay your own expenses."

"Yes."

"Well, don't worry about money. I have some of my own. I also have various contacts, some of whom even your father knows nothing about. Not in Russia but here in the States. I might be able to help."

"You must be careful, Mom. Dad must not find out."

"We will put it in God's hands. If Keagan does find out . . . well, that also God will deal with. We'll have to pray God will work it out."

"I don't know . . . maybe you could do the praying. I doubt God would listen much to me, anyway."

"You'd be surprised, dear."

Cameron sighed. "You know what? I'm starved. French food never did stick with me much. I know a great place for homemade pie."

"Lead the way, dear."

11

THE EUROPEAN TRAVEL documents came amazingly fast. Cameron already had a passport—she had always kept it current, just in case. But Arnett must have worked some other magic to push through everything else. She wondered how much her mother had to do with this. Nevertheless, she was scheduled to fly out of Los Angeles on the tenth of March.

Max told her he was also getting together a Russian visa, but that would take some time. She hoped to be able to travel to the Soviet Union by the beginning of April. He said he liked more and more the idea of an in-depth report on the Russo-German Nonaggression Pact. Cameron thought he liked far more the idea of stealing the idea from Keagan and beating him to Moscow. With Cameron paying her own way, he did not have to worry about budgetary constraints, as would Keagan.

The day before her departure, Cameron's little apartment was a shambles. The closet was emptied out, the contents strewn all over the bed, chair, and even on the floor, as were the contents of her dresser. She could take only two suitcases with her on the plane, and she had a weight limit of forty-four pounds. She had three coats, including a raincoat, draped over the back of the chair. It got cold even in Rome in the winter, but the third, the heaviest coat, was designed specifically for the Arctic cold of Moscow. She planned to wear all three onto the plane so they would not be included in the luggage weigh-in. But nonetheless she was baffled at how to pack a life into such limited space. She was no clotheshorse, but still there were things a woman must have. She had already discarded two evening dresses and their accessories. She now held up her third and final evening dress, then tossed it aside. If she managed to get into a formal Italian soirée to interview some big mucky-muck, she would just make do. Her navy serge suit, a Paris original she had splurged on to interview the governor last year, was stunning and, though not exactly evening wear, would not look shabby no matter where she was.

"Goodness! Looks like a bomb has gone off in here," came a voice from the doorway.

Cameron glanced up to see her sister Blair had let herself in.

"I have a plane to catch at six in the morning, and my suitcases are still nearly empty," Cameron said, showing rare helplessness. She was actually glad to see her sister. "You've been to Europe, Blair. Help me."

"So have you."

"When I was fourteen!"

Blair came and looked into the suitcases on the bed. One was empty, the other was half filled with several books, notebooks, pencils, and a couple of reams of typewriter paper.

"This stuff must weigh a ton," Blair said. "Won't those cheapskates at the *Globe* provide you with supplies once you get there?"

"I just want to be prepared. And these things will be in even scarcer supply in the Soviet Union."

"So, you really are going back to that awful place?"

"If I am lucky and Max can arrange it."

With a shrug, Blair picked her way around a pile of clothes on the floor, then stopped, bent over, and lifted one of the evening gowns. "Why is this on the floor? Cameron, don't tell me you are not going to bring evening clothes."

"The weight. Not only the dresses but the shoes, handbags, and hats to match. I just can't do it."

"You must have at least one evening ensemble." Blair rolled her eyes. "It may only be Rome, hardly Paris, but still there are social conventions to follow!"

"I'll get something there if I need to."

"With a war on? Who knows what you'll be able to find." She dropped the dress she was holding and picked up another, a lavender evening suit of crepe de chine with a straight, draped skirt, beaded blouse of a much paler shade of lavender, and a short, simply lined jacket. "This is you, Cameron, and very versatile. You must take it. Now where are the shoes—"

"All those beads weigh a ton," Cameron protested as Blair laid the dress in the empty case.

"Then something else must go." Blair reached into the other suitcase and plucked up a book, tossing it onto the bed with relish.

"That's my dictionary!"

"With this evening gown on, no one will care how you spell anything!" Blair grinned that annoyingly infectious grin of hers.

Cameron smiled. "I guess it is Italy."

Together they managed to fill both suitcases. There were more wool sweaters and skirts than Blair wanted, but more scarves than Cameron would have packed. "They will just add a bit of sparkle to whatever you are wearing. And believe me, even the Italians will like you better for it."

Cameron did manage to squeeze in the dictionary. And Blair nearly had a fit when Cameron eschewed a hatbox in order to make room for her fifteen-pound Underwood. Then she snapped the suitcase clasps, put the luggage on the floor, and hefted each.

"What do you think? Will I make it?"

"Just give 'em a sweet smile, and you won't have a problem."

"That may work for you, Blair, but I doubt I'd get away with it." Cameron plopped down on the bed. Blair joined her. "I'm glad you came by. I am sure I would have still been here at five-thirty tomorrow fighting this thing."

"Always happy to help."

Cameron glanced at the clock. "Goodness! It is one in the morning. What are you doing out so late, Blair?"

"I got bored with Jack Warner's party and left. I decided to come here on a hunch you might be going crazy getting ready."

"When I talked to you yesterday, you were leaving for another party. How do you do it? I would find them all boring."

Blair shrugged. "I love it! And it looks like I might get a movie role out of it all. Looks like we are both living our dreams."

Cameron sensed a hollowness in her sister's words and knew she should give Blair a chance to say more, but she was exhausted and, as it was, would only get three hours of sleep before she had to leave.

She did ask, "You're going to be okay, then?"

"Heavens, yes! I'm a cat—always landing on my feet. You better be okay, too."

"I will miss you. And everyone," Cameron said, satisfied to accept her sister's glib response. "It was nice of Mom to take me out to dinner last night."

"I still can't believe Dad didn't show up."

"I'm not surprised. I'm working for the enemy now."

"I admire you, Cameron." Blair's tone was suddenly solemn. "You broke free—really free. It must feel good."

"I don't think we'll ever be free of our father. I have this wonderful job, but his shadow still lurks over me, if only in thinking I'm with the enemy." She sighed. "But that doesn't mean we can't make it in spite of our chains." Cameron wondered what her sister would think if she knew what had happened to their mother in Russia. But she did not want to think of it, lest even a stray look might clue her sister and pique her curiosity.

Blair was saying, "That's exactly what you are doing. Breaking the chains. Sometimes I think . . ." Blair paused, ran a hand through her silky platinum hair. "Oh, I think lots of junk that is pure silliness. Don't mind me. You are going to Rome! Even with a war on, it will be wonderful. The Eternal City."

Cameron reached an arm around her sister and hugged her close. "I'll miss you, sis." Sudden tears sprang into her eyes, and she didn't know why. She had not even cried at dinner with her mother. Maybe it was because Blair was so hard and glib and yet so vulnerable. Maybe it was because they needed each other more than they had ever realized. Maybe because Blair would now be a lone warrior in the wars with Keagan Hayes. Or perhaps it was because Cameron felt she was about to head into the very eye of that war, doing battle with the man in a more overt way than she ever had before.

She blinked back her tears. "Blair, can I tell you a secret? I . . . I'm a little scared."

"You?" But, bless her heart, she did not laugh. "Oh, Cameron, everyone's scared, but I know of no one better suited than you to laugh at her fears and be successful anyway."

Cameron walked her sister to the door and hugged her one final time before she left. Alone, she looked around the apartment. There was a lot more to do before she could sleep. She was going to keep the apartment just until she was certain things were going to work out. But she wanted to clean it up. She doubted she'd get any sleep anyway.

She was scared but excited, too. She wanted to be the cool, level-headed journalist, but her fluttering stomach reminded her she was a woman, as well—a woman embarking upon, she was certain, a journey of great discovery.

PART II

Somewhere over the rainbow way up high,
There's a land that I heard of once in a lullaby.
Somewhere over the rainbow skies are blue,
And the dreams that you dare to dream really
do come true.

E.Y. HARBURG
The Wizard of Oz, 1939

12

"TAKE FIVE!" the director yelled.

And Blair, totally exhausted, had never been so glad to hear two words. She was rehearsing for a new musical extravaganza motion picture. Something called *Three on a Match*, a musical set during the Great War. It was about three doughboys on leave in Paris who, of course, meet three French girls and find romance. Blair was only in the chorus line, but she was working in a real movie, so she wasn't complaining. Well, it was only a low-budget picture. Busby Berkeley had nothing to worry about; neither did Fred and Ginger. No one had ever heard of the director or the lead actors in this movie.

No matter. Blair was still thrilled. Errol Flynn had come through for her—and so quickly! Less than a week after seeing him at her father's birthday. It wasn't his new picture, but he told her if she worked out, and if he ever did a musical, there was no telling what might come. She did not mind at all that as payment for his favor he'd requested she accompany him to Sardi's for an evening.

But weeks of rehearsal were showing Blair that being a musical actress was no lark. She was taking the place of a chorus girl who had quit—no one was saying the cause, but Blair thought the poor thing had probably dropped from exhaustion.

Blair grabbed a towel to dry her perspiration, but the makeup gal immediately took her to task.

"Watch your foundation!" the woman scolded as she fussed over the star's lipstick.

"What does it matter?" countered Blair. "We're not even shooting."

"Who knew you would need extra rehearsal? Otto wants to shoot later today, and I don't want to do my work twice."

"Ya'd think this was a real picture," said one of the other chorus girls sidling up to Blair.

"An actress has to start someplace," Blair responded.

"We're not all *starting*, honey. Pretty soon I'll be too old for anything but character parts." She was one of the taller girls, and she looked down on Blair, who at five-seven was not exactly petite. "I've made a half dozen two-bit movies like this, and every time someone tells me it could be *the one*." She gave a derisive snort. "I should have gone home years ago. Topeka is starting to look better and better."

"I know it's not easy—I'm sorry. I forgot your name."

"Story of my life! What am I doing in this business, anyway? Name's Cynthia Bell, and a fine name it is, too. I made it up myself, but even I forget it sometimes."

Cynthia was tall, shapely, and pretty. She might be only thirty, but in Hollywood that was indeed ancient. Blair, at twenty-two, was a child by comparison.

"Have you been in any big movies, Cynthia?" Blair asked as she helped herself to a glass of water from the pitcher that had been put out for the performers.

"I was in the chorus of *Gold Diggers of 1935*. Never a lead role—hey, there's Fred Banister."

Blair glanced across the set, and sure enough, the studio's biggest producer was there talking to the director, Otto Feinstein. Banister owned a share of Olympic Pictures and was married to the studio president's daughter. He, therefore, was quite powerful. Whatever could he want with a two-bit director like Otto?

Blair quickly forgot her curiosity as the chorus was called back to work. Otto was determined to get the number they were doing on film before the end of the day. This was one of the last takes of the movie, and Otto wanted it in the "can" before the week was over. Banister remained on the set observing. After running through the number two more times, the director deemed them ready for a "take." The entire time Blair had the feeling Mr. Banister was looking only at her. She had to be imagining it, but nevertheless, she made an extra effort to punch up her enthusiasm. She was no true dancer but one had to be versatile in order to get jobs in Hollywood, and she had spent money on several dance classes as well as acting classes. She knew the right moves, even if she wasn't as skilled as Ginger Rogers. They got the number in only two takes, and Blair felt she'd had a lot to do with the success.

Apparently Fred Banister did also. As he lifted a cigarette, fitted neatly into an ebony holder, to his lips, he gave her a definite "once-over." The coy tilt of his lips indicated he liked what he saw.

"Miss Hayes," Otto called, "Mr. Banister wants to see you."

Blair strode over to the two men, wearing confidence as she wore the skimpy, sequined costume—quite well on both counts. Her acting teacher had told her she could act. And she knew how to handle men, even big-time producers. It helped, of course, that her next meal didn't depend on this job. Still, it was a dream of hers to make it in show business. It had nothing to do with money. It was . . . she didn't know why she wanted it. Perhaps it was just a means for her to shine in her own right, to prove to her father that she had value, not that he valued show business much. Maybe that was part of it, too. He thought acting was among the lowest and most demeaning things a woman could do. So, if it was impossible to please him, it was almost as good to drive him mad with her unladylike behavior.

"Mr. Banister," Blair said, coming up to the two men. "What a treat to have you watch our performance! I think this will be a wonderful picture." She batted her lashes and even threw a coy side-look at Otto—may as well use the opportunity to butter him up, too.

"A musical won't hurt our budget," Banister replied. "But these costumes look expensive." He fingered the beaded shoulder strap of Blair's outfit. His fingers brushed her bare shoulder, lingering a moment longer than was necessary.

"All the costumes are leftovers from last season," said Otto quickly. "Except for minor tailor expenses, they cost nothing."

Banister's eyes roved over Blair's costume. She did not flinch under the almost lecherous scrutiny. She had no reason to feel embarrassed. She looked good from the length of her fishnet-stockinged legs, up the curve of the swimsuitlike outfit of a glimmering mix of royal blue and silver. Her platinum hair shone under the jauntily tilted blue top hat glittering with sequins.

"Feinstein, why don't you find something else to do," Banister said dismissively.

"Yes, sir, of course, sir," groveled Otto.

Then Banister said to Blair—he had not taken his eyes off her,

"Errol was right about you, that you'd be worth a trip down to the set. But you are not a dancer, are you?"

Blair hadn't expected that, but she answered quickly, "Well, a girl does what she has to do."

"I like that attitude."

"I am a much better singer," Blair added, "but I have also been honing my acting skills. I've been taking classes—"

"The best acting isn't learned; it comes from within."

Banister must know what he was talking about. Two of his pictures had been nominated for Academy Awards. Despite the slightly sleazy leer in his eyes, he was a skilled producer and a man whose attentions any aspiring actress would do well to cultivate.

"Yes, you are quite right," said Blair.

"I am starting to cast a new production, a drama. I'm having a difficult time finding a girl for a certain supporting role. This will be a major motion picture. I cannot reveal names at this time, but I have all but signed an Oscar winner for the male lead. Would a picture such as this interest you, Blair?"

What kind of answer did he expect? Any actress in her right mind would cut off an arm for such a part. But despite her inner desire to jump up and scream "Yes!" she just smiled—a part enigmatic, part ingenuous, tilting of her lips.

"I could hardly turn down a role like that," she said.

"I didn't think so. Why don't we go up to my office and discuss the details?"

"All right." But when Banister turned to lead the way, Blair gently laid a restraining hand on his arm. "Would it be okay if I get out of this costume first?"

He gave her *that* look again, and a less experienced woman would have squirmed. Blair just grinned as if such looks didn't bother her at all.

"I'll expect you up in my office in ten minutes, then."

He walked away. Blair hurried to the dressing room. The other girls were in various stages of shedding their costumes. Apparently Otto wouldn't need the chorus again until tomorrow. Blair told the others her good fortune.

"Banister doesn't give away parts in his pictures," Cynthia said.

"No, I don't suppose he does," Blair answered vaguely.

"So how far are you gonna go to get the part?" asked another dancer.

"What a question!" Blair said glibly as she tossed aside the sequined suit and slipped into her dress. Too bad she had only this simple rayon floral frock to wear. But, then, it might show her versatility if she looked just as good in rayon as in sequins.

She took off the costume hat and fluffed her silky shoulder-length tresses, which had been pinned up under the hat. There wasn't time for a new style so she pinned it up again, this time under the little straw hat adorned with feathers and netting at the back that went with the dress. She touched up her makeup, then stood back to scan her image in the mirror. It would have to do. How she wished she'd worn her stunning new Chanel wool jersey. But she hadn't wanted to show up her co-workers who, for the most part, lived on shoestring budgets, not that of a wealthy newspaper publisher.

It was nearer to twenty minutes before Blair was ushered into Fred Banister's plush office. He did not seem in the least perturbed by her tardiness. He'd used the time to also change out of his suit coat into a silk smoking jacket. He looked quite debonair. Indeed, he was rather handsome for a middle-aged man. His husky build had not yet gone to flab, though he was forty-one years old. Blair heard he had played football in college. But his athletic appearance was offset by thinning, graying hair, and a deeply lined, though quite tan, face.

Blair hardly realized she was sizing the man up until he spoke.

"So do you like what you see?" His tone was wry. He knew he presented a formidable and enticing sight.

"How could I not?" she hedged, not forgetting he was a married man.

He put his cigarette, in its holder, to his lips, took a slow, languorous draw from it, then blew out the smoke in two vaporous rings.

"That's impressive," she said.

"Care for one?" He held open a gold cigarette case.

"Thank you, no. My mother taught me it is an unladylike habit."

"A drink, then?"

"Okay."

He went to the wet bar and filled two glasses from a pitcher of already mixed liquid.

Handing her a glass, he told her to sit, which she did, on a French Provincial satin-covered settee.

"Blair . . . that's an unusual name," he said as he took the vacant place beside her. He was very close.

"I'm named for my uncle."

"A man's name. How odd." He cocked his head and gave her a frank appraisal. That same look was in his eyes, and now she began to identify it as a look of possession. "That will never work in this business. I see you with something very feminine. Jennifer, perhaps. And of course you must change Hayes so as not to confuse you with Helen."

"That wouldn't be so bad, would it? She's a great actress."

"I see you more as the next Jean Harlow."

"Such an untimely death . . ."

"But I see *your* future as bright and long." He alternated a sip of his martini with a puff from his cigarette. He blew a stream of smoke into her face.

Her gaze remained steady, though she was growing more and more uncomfortable. She did not feel in control, and she always made sure she was in control where men were concerned. Fred Banister exuded power on so many levels that Blair found herself unbalanced.

"I-I hope so," she replied, hating herself for the small crack in her voice.

"Very bright." He set aside his now empty glass and crushed out his cigarette in a nearby ashtray. He lifted his open palm, holding it a mere inch from her face. "Your future." He held out his hand as if offering a gift. The implication was clear. He held her future in his hands. With a gleam of definite ownership in his eyes, he leaned close to her.

She tried not to retreat, though his act was clearly aggressive. On one level she'd had much experience with men. She had wooed and cajoled them, flirted and flaunted herself before them. She gave them everything . . . and nothing. Everyone assumed she had done it all, and, of course, the men she dated weren't about to correct the misconception. But for all her posturing with men, Blair was still a virgin.

She could not help flinching slightly when he brought his finger to her cheek and traced a line down her jaw and neck, lingering at the décolletage of her dress. If there had been any doubt in her mind before, it was clear now what this man—this powerful man—wanted. Her throat went dry, and she tried to swallow.

"Are you nervous, Blair?"

"No," she replied in an obvious lie.

"I ask so little, don't you think?" His lips brushed hers, and his breath was warm and not entirely offensive with a hint of peppermint mingled with alcohol. "I offer much."

"It sounds like a wonderful movie." She hoped to stall what was appearing more and more to be the inevitable. "The role you spoke of, how . . . small is it?"

"I'm sure you have heard it said that there are no small roles—"

"Only small actors," she finished with a weak smile.

His brow arched gamely and he went on, "This particular role is quite juicy, really. The dying kid sister of a man who is forced to choose a life of crime to pay her medical bills. A small but pivotal part, with a supporting actress Oscar written all over it."

Blair licked her lips, now as dry as her throat. Visions of the glittering Academy Awards ceremony flickered before her eyes. Her father would have to take notice then, when she held the coveted statue in her hands. Perhaps she would even throw the old man kudos. *I thank the Academy and I especially thank my parents, my father who taught me—*

But the fantasy drew to a grinding halt there. Her father had never taught her anything, except perhaps to believe she could never succeed on her own merits and that if she ever did "make it," it would only be due to her exchanging her body for success. And as usual, Keagan Hayes was no doubt right. The only way she could ever grasp her dreams was through submission to a man like Fred Banister.

But she wouldn't be the first woman to take such a path. How else was a woman going to make it in a man's world? Cameron was certainly the exception—yet even Cameron could not deny that having a father who was a newspaper publisher had helped.

Nevertheless, everyone knew that in show business the "casting couch" was a woman's biggest ally. She might need talent to get further, but for that first break some concessions must be made. And as Blair looked at the "concession" seated before her, she told herself it wasn't such a horrible thing to do. He was not a disgusting man. Rather charming, really. What had she to lose? Her morality? Her reputation? Most people thought she'd lost all that long ago.

There was so much more to gain. Stardom. Well, maybe.

The knock at the door startled him more than Blair, but it was then as she blew out a puff of air that she realized she'd been holding her breath.

"I told my secretary not to disturb me," Banister mumbled, disgruntled.

But the tap came again. "Mr. Banister, sir, I am so sorry, but there is an urgent call."

"I told you—!" he yelled.

"It's Mr. Eisenburg."

Blair knew that Eisenburg was Banister's father-in-law, the president of Olympic Pictures.

Banister growled under his breath, jerked away from Blair, and rose. "Finish your drink, dear," he said as he strode to his desk. "I'll be with you shortly."

There was an ominous conversation on the phone that lasted only a few moments. When Banister put down the receiver, he headed to the door, pausing only as he opened the door.

"I have to go. There has been a fire on one of the sets," he told her.

"Is anyone hurt?"

"I don't think so, but there could be major financial damage. You'd better not wait for me."

The relief that washed over Blair surprised her. "All right," she said.

"We'll finish our conversation later. Call me."

She nodded.

But when he was gone, she could not get out of his office fast enough.

THE NEXT DAY Blair met Jackie for lunch at their favorite Italian restaurant on Sepulveda Boulevard. Jackie waved as Blair approached. Blair was glad to see her sister. They might live in the same house, but because of Blair's working and social schedules they hardly ever saw each other. Jackie had to be the farthest pole from the Hollywood scene as possible. A twenty-year-old college co-ed, she was wearing a blue-and-cream-striped rayon dress with pleated skirt and a bow tie at the neck. She was the very image of Deanna Durbin and Judy Garland, except she was real, not a pretend image on a screen.

"I went ahead and ordered breadsticks and coffee," said Jackie as a waiter seated Blair.

"Good. I'm starved." Blair plucked a breadstick from the basket and bit off the tip. "I have never worked this hard in my life. Don't ever let anyone tell you acting is a lark. It is hard work." She didn't mention that she had started the day off with a blinding hangover from the previous night's party and a sharp reprimand from her director for being late to the set.

"But it is exciting, isn't it?" Jackie said. "I can't wait to see you up on the theater screen."

"I thought that would be a thrill, too, but to tell the truth, I will be glad when I finish my part in a week and can move on. I don't care if I never see *Three on a Match*."

"Your first movie and you are disillusioned already?"

Blair gave a noncommittal shrug. "I don't know. . . ."

"Was acting really that much of a dream of yours, Blair?"

"Of course it was!"

"Last year you wanted to be a singer and the year before that a fashion designer."

Blair put cream and sugar into her coffee. She'd forgotten that sweet little Jackie could be annoyingly forthright.

"I think I am going to change my hairstyle," Blair hedged. "I saw a darling short bobbed coif that I think would be fabulous with my hair color." She put a hand on her medium-length hair, shoving it behind her neck to give the effect of a shorter length.

"You have wonderful hair. Don't cut it," Jackie said. "Besides, you can do so much more with it when it's longer."

"It seems so old-fashioned."

"What's wrong with that?"

Jackie didn't understand, and now Blair realized why she had nearly canceled the lunch date. Part of her wanted to get away from the Hollywood scene, yet there were pitfalls outside that world, as well. Especially now when, after a night of debating, Blair had all but decided to see Fred Banister and take that part, regardless of what she had to do. Maybe her words about being disillusioned were an attempt to coax her sister into playing devil's advocate against an acting career. Blair had to deal with the matter in such a covert way because she could never directly tell her sister what she was actually planning to do. If Jackie didn't understand about rebellious hairdos, she definitely would never even begin to fathom the twisted world of getting ahead in show business.

Cameron might understand, if only she wasn't traipsing around Europe. However, even Cameron would never encourage Blair's decision—not necessarily on moral grounds, as would Jackie, but more because she could never accept that a woman was that helpless. Cameron would lose all respect for Blair if she did this thing.

Blair couldn't understand why it mattered what her sisters thought anyway. She had worked hard to flaunt her family's approval.

Blair sipped her coffee, then decided she needed something stronger. She waved to the waiter.

"A gin fizz, please," she ordered.

Jackie got that disapproving look on her face but said nothing. The waiter brought the drink and took their luncheon order. The sisters chatted about trivial things, a mild tension hanging over them, which grew when Blair ordered her second drink.

"Tell me about that beau of yours, sis?" Blair asked, thinking it a safe subject.

"Jeffrey?"

"You have more than one?" Blair laughed, making sure the sound was full of innuendo, just to annoy Jackie.

"There's only one, if you can call him a beau."

"Mom said it was getting serious."

"Jeffrey is getting serious. I don't know about me." Jackie's cheeks actually turned pink.

"Men! They are impossible, aren't they?" Blair's drink arrived and she had a long swallow before adding, "I'm glad to hear you are not getting tied down. Play the field, girl. Why should men have all the fun, huh? I've been with more than a dozen men this year, Jackie dear. What a ride!"

"That doesn't really appeal to me, either."

"You gotta live a little, sis!"

"Does that make you happy?" Jackie's doe eyes lifted and all but penetrated Blair's gaze.

Blair resisted the urge to squirm. She finished her drink instead. "Happy? Of course I am happy—deliriously so!"

"You don't seem happy with your work."

"That's not everything, you know." Blair was almost drunk enough not to notice the defensiveness in her tone.

Jackie toyed with the handle of her coffee cup, then said, "I know we don't have exactly the same values in life, but . . . well, it seems that since we were raised the same, we really shouldn't be so different. I guess I've always thought that down deep, because of how we were raised, we are more alike than it appears on the surface. Blair, doesn't some small part of you want a husband and children and a little house and some peace?"

Blair laughed, a hard sound that she knew came off as mocking her sister. However, she knew it was as much a jeer of herself. "I can't imagine anything so boring!"

"So you truly want to flit from man to man, partying every night, drinking until you are numb—"

"Jackie, don't start preaching at me!"

"I'm not!"

"But you are dying to, aren't you?" Blair paused, took a breath, and added more coolly, "Oh, let's not ruin this time together. I hardly ever see you. Can't we just chat about . . . well, clothes and movies and such?"

Jackie did not answer for a long moment. Her eyes glittered with a sadness that Blair found hard to define.

"We got a letter from Cameron today," Jackie finally said, her tone resigned.

"I kind of miss that old girl," Blair said as she scanned the room for the waiter, lifting her empty glass in a signal when she caught his eye. "I suppose she is taking Rome by storm. What an adventure!"

"I don't know if it's exactly that," Jackie replied. "I mean, there is a war going on over there."

"You certainly don't believe all that propaganda Daddy prints in his paper, do you?" Blair tittered with superiority, loving the chance to denigrate anything to do with their father. "They are just trying to sell newspapers, so they build up the foreign situation far more than it really warrants."

"Cameron has written some of those articles, in the *Globe*, at least."

"Oh, she'd be the worst one to glorify it all. She used to talk about Russia as if it were some fairyland. She is still talking about how she wants to go back. I personally had more than enough when Dad was stationed there. It was cold, dirty, backward, and the clothes were simply awful!"

"You were just a child." Jackie smiled, shaking her head. "You couldn't have cared about clothes *then*!"

"Even when I was a baby, I preferred designer diapers."

Jackie chuckled, then became serious again. "Anyway, I think the war in Europe is pretty serious," she said earnestly. "They say England has barely survived the Blitz. If Hitler starts bombing England again, it could really fall, and that would be the end of a free Europe."

"And *they* say that to try to get us involved in their little skirmish."

"I didn't know you read any newspapers, Blair." Jackie chuckled good-naturedly, but there was still tension in her gaze.

"I've read a headline or two. And no matter how you look at it, what's happening in Europe is their problem."

Jackie lifted a brow. "I also didn't know you were such an isolationist."

Blair's third drink arrived, and she sipped it before responding. "I'm nothing, really. I couldn't care one way or the other. It simply isn't any of our business. They are always fighting over there. But I will be upset if we are dragged into it and all the young men go to war. Who will I date then?" She grinned.

Jackie shook her head dourly. "Despite what you think, Blair, there is a very real chance we will become involved. And Mom is worried Cameron is in the middle of it."

"Mom worries about everything, but I'll wager that even if Cameron is being shot at by those Germans, she is not complaining."

"Well, I guess I can't really argue with that. She's had assignments all over southeastern Europe. She doesn't say if she has been in any actual danger, but she has covered a lot of the political battling. Truth be told, she is happier than—" Jackie stopped, her gaze flickering up at Blair momentarily, then quickly away.

"We're all happy, then!" Blair added merrily. "Isn't it simply wonderful?" She smiled, but only because a fresh drink had arrived.

"Blair, I wish—"

But Blair cut in. "What do you wish, Jackie dear?" she asked caustically.

"Only that . . ."

But their meal arrived just then, and Jackie never got to finish her sentiment. Blair certainly did not give her the chance. Her words probably would have only been sentimental drivel anyway. Jackie had no concept of reality. Her world was way too saccharine, too pat, too . . . well, too much like the movies.

And Blair did love the movies. But she knew she'd never have her own fairy-tale life, even if she wanted it, which she didn't.

She didn't at all.

No . . . not at all.

She gulped down her drink and began to forget just how much she envied her little sister's simplistic, genteel view of life.

When they finished their lunch, Blair was almost as glad to get away from her sister as she had been to get away from Fred Banister. What was wrong with her? Would she ever fit in anywhere?

She loved the Hollywood life. Yet even she could not deny that some of the things Jackie wanted had a draw for her, as well. Perhaps that had been the appeal of Gary Hobart, the army officer she had met at her father's birthday party.

That day . . . she still thought about it, about the man who could have made it a turning point in her life—if only she would have let him. But she had been scared. What would Jackie think about that? But then she might not be surprised at all that a decent, regular guy like Gary had so completely shaken Blair.

14

AFTER THE LUNCH with Jackie, Blair felt defiant and didn't know why. Being around Jackie had for some reason made her angry. She supposed she hated that tiny thorn of envy that always pricked her when she was around her sister. It was a totally ridiculous emotion, because she did not want her sister's staid, normal life. But she was especially angry because of how it had caused her to dredge up all the memories of meeting Gary. She didn't want him, either.

She wanted Hollywood's glitter and glamour.

She did!

And that's exactly why she sucked in a breath—a steadying breath because her knees were trembling a bit—and marched up to Fred Banister's office. She was ready to do whatever she had to do in order to make it in her chosen profession. She would not be put off by her sister's silly sense of morality. People like Jackie simply did not understand the realities of life.

But despite her firm resolve, her heart was pounding as she stepped from the elevator onto Banister's floor.

At that moment cursed thoughts of Gary Hobart plagued her again. Why now did he have to come to mind, except that she had been in a similar situation with him in that she'd been unable to suppress her self-doubts and fears when he had called her the next day after the birthday party to ask her out to dinner. It was a memorable occasion when she couldn't quell her conscience. They had talked on the phone for fifteen minutes, and once again she quickly sized up Gary as a very normal boy. He was ordinary in an almost beguiling way. He had spoken of his life as if she would understand things like mowing the lawn, feeding the dog, or helping to fix his dad's Ford. His mother was working on a church bazaar, and he had to go help her carry boxes.

A church bazaar. Goodness!

But as during the party, Blair did nothing to dispel any illusions Gary might have about her. She still wasn't certain why she'd done that. She rejected the only reason that came to her—that in view of Gary's decency, she had been ashamed of who she was.

"But you know what that is like, I guess," he had assumed. "I might be tied up for several hours."

"Oh yes," she lied. "I do that sort of thing all the time."

"But I'll be done by dinner. Would you have dinner with me?"

The question had panicked her. He certainly had no intention of taking her to the Coconut Grove or Sardi's. No, it would be some quaint little Italian place or, if he wanted to impress her, perhaps an upscale hotel. There would be no celebrities where he took her, no glitz, no bevy of reporters trying to photograph famous people. After dinner they might go for a walk in a nearby park. Perhaps he would hold her hand. He might take her home to meet the folks—Mama Church Bazaar and Papa, owner of a sturdy old Ford.

Yes, she had utterly panicked. How could she want those things yet scorn them, as well? Her upbringing was to blame. Just as her sister had said at lunch, "I've always thought that down deep, because of how we were raised, we are more alike than it appears on the surface."

Those words conjured in Blair's mind visions of her mother teaching her to be a lady, teaching her to be a good girl, warning her against the evils of sin. Then Blair reminded herself that she'd already broken so many of the commandments that there was no turning back.

That's what had made her flee from Gary Hobart. She had told Lieutenant Hobart, "I'm so sorry, but I have a previous commitment."

She was committed to a way of life that was as much her choice as it was her *sentence*. She was as far removed from church bazaars as Gary was removed from women who placed their virtue on the open market.

She still thought of Gary every now and then because, now that she thought of it, that encounter had indeed marked a kind of turning point in her life. It was then that she had turned her attention fully toward her acting career. She had once and for all shunned the last vestiges of her moral upbringing. Or so she had thought. But, curse it, she was still haunted by it, despite the clear knowledge that she would never be able to measure up to the standard set by her parents. She'd known long ago she could never please them, especially her father.

Well, then, perhaps this day would be another turning point. After she did what she planned to do, she truly would never be able to turn back. Everyone would know what it meant for a girl like Blair to get a part from Banister. Her parents would know. Her father knew Banister and surely must know the kind of man he was. Once and for all, Blair could shed the chains of her *upbringing*.

Nevertheless, she trembled all over, and there was a knot in her stomach. Her mother's genteel face and her sister's questioning doe eyes continued to invade her thoughts. But she forced herself to keep moving. Her mind a lead wall, she arrived at Banister's office. But as she reached for the knob, the door swung open.

"Blair darling! What a surprise seeing you here!" Darla Brooks grinned. Her lipstick was smeared and the bow at the neck of her blouse was askew. Darla was an up-and-coming young starlet, already way beyond anything Blair had achieved. Darla had been in some important pictures, not in starring roles but big enough to receive critical recognition.

"I could say the same thing." They had sat together only last night at the Coconut Grove. Darla had been quite chummy, and Blair, who didn't have many female friends, had begun to wonder if Darla could fill that void. Blair had confided to the more experienced actress about Fred Banister, and Darla had encouraged her to do whatever it took to get the part.

Now Blair felt immediately uneasy. Darla worked for MGM. She had never made a movie for Olympic Pictures.

"The oddest thing happened this morning," Darla want on airily. "I happened by the studio to see Tom—he's in the new Flynn picture. Anyway, I ran into Fred. I'm going to be in his new picture. I'll play the dying kid sister. Isn't that thrilling?"

"That was the part he offered me," Blair responded woodenly.

"Really? Well, I'll be!" Darla wore a look of such innocence that it could only be a performance. She knew very well she was stealing the part from Blair. Most likely she had come specifically to get the part.

Blair could say no more. Her head swimming from the gin at lunch and from the sudden emotions swirling in her head, she pushed past Darla.

"I want to see Mr. Banister," she said to the secretary, forcing the words past a lump of bile in her throat. She had just made a momentous decision. She had been prepared to sell herself to Fred Banister. Now everything had been flung back into her face. She was shaking even more now than earlier.

She did not hear the secretary speak into the intercom, nor did she hear Banister come from his office.

"Ah, Blair, my dear . . ." came his smooth, now loathsome voice.

"I-I just saw Darla . . ." She couldn't think of what to say, whom to accuse. She felt betrayed, but by whom? Banister, Darla . . . or herself?

"I expected to see you last night," he said. "When I didn't, I assumed—"

"Or maybe you just thought a warm body in hand was better—" she began, her voice shrill.

"Please, let's be adult about this," he cut in.

"Why, you—!" But she could get no more coherent words out of her mouth. Instead, she spun around and fled the room.

————

Blair didn't care what it looked like—a single young woman sitting in a bar alone. She reminded herself that she was indeed just the kind of woman who drank alone at bars. She might not have in fact sold herself to the producer, but she still felt dirty because of her intentions. But that sensation was mixed liberally into her confusion, anger, and even disappointment.

At least if she had done that loathsome thing, she would have had the satisfaction of a premier part in a big movie. Now she had nothing, and she still had to live with the fact that she had been *willing* to do it. She hated Banister for what he had done.

But she hated herself even more.

She was well on the way to being good and drunk when she heard her name.

"Is that you, Blair Hayes?"

For a moment she thought she was reliving the scene in Banister's office, except it was a male voice greeting her. She turned and saw that he was familiar, but she could not remember his name. Her brow wrinkled as she tried to place him.

He was average height, heavyset with a balding pate and horn-rimmed glasses covering small, classically beady eyes. With his slightly reddened bulbous nose, he was an altogether unattractive man. His clothes were expensive, but the way they fit him so poorly, they might as well have been bought at a thrift store.

He chuckled pleasantly. "I don't expect that you would remember me."

Yes, she supposed few beautiful women ever remembered him. "I'm so sorry. Where did we meet?"

"Peter Marquet's party last month. I'm Claude Fleischer." He held out his hand, still smiling.

She offered her own hand, and he took it and brought it to his lips. "I'm a fool for not remembering you," she said, rather enchanted by his charm, which shone through his homely features. "I believe that night I'd had a bit too much champagne."

"We all did, as I recall."

"Do sit down, Mr. Fleischer." She motioned to the empty barstool next to her.

"I don't want to intrude," he said. Obviously he assumed she was with someone.

"I was to meet a friend," she lied, "but he just sent a message that he couldn't make it." It was more difficult than she thought to shed her Puritanical past.

He took the seat, wiggling a bit this way and that to fit into the tight space. "One other thing I recall about that evening was your lovely voice," he said once he settled into place. "You sang that Judy Garland tune from *The Wizard of Oz*."

" 'Over the Rainbow.' "

"Yes. I was impressed."

"Thank you."

The bartender approached and refilled Blair's martini. Fleischer ordered a glass of sherry.

"I hear you are working on a movie these days," said Fleischer.

"A little musical. Nothing important."

"So you are singing?"

"Only in a chorus."

"A waste. You have a fine talent." Fleischer looked at her over the rim of his sherry glass as he sipped the drink. "I'm surprised you haven't made it further in this business. Have you a good agent?"

"That's right!" said Blair, the light finally dawning. "You own a theatrical agency."

"I did, but I sold it a few weeks ago to embark upon a new venture. I bought a nightclub—a dream I've had for years. I'll never know how I got into the agent business. It just happened and the money came in, and I simply accepted it all. I was never happy. But now . . . ah, I am in my element. I've never enjoyed myself more."

"I'm glad for you, Claude." She smiled when he seemed to enjoy her using his given name.

"And you, Blair, are you content with what you are doing?"

She initially rankled at his nerve in getting so personal, then she shrugged, sensing immediately that he was the kind of man you just got personal with in a fatherly or brotherly sort of way. She could easily see him flitting about his nightclub, friends with everyone.

"Show business is a vicious place, Claude," she said.

"I was an agent. I know." He chuckled. "Some would say agents are the most vicious animals in the show biz jungle."

She laughed. "I like you, Claude."

"And I like you, Blair." Pausing, he seemed to consider something before speaking. "When I heard you sing at Peter's party, I sensed a level of passion I seldom see from performers. I thought you were happy, not in a ha-ha way but viscerally, if you know what I mean. You were in your element."

"I like singing," she said lightly. Viscerally? She'd feel silly claiming that much.

"Maybe you are in the wrong segment of show business."

"You think I should make records?"

"Perhaps eventually. But you have to begin performing on stage first."

"On stage?"

"Like in a nightclub."

"Your nightclub, perhaps?"

He smiled. "It is not the Coconut Grove."

"Well, I'm not Judy Garland."

"You would truly consider working at my club?" He seemed suddenly quite sober, as if he was asking far too much of her. "I'm not even on the Sunset Strip."

"I am a nobody, Claude. I'm rather surprised you'd want me."

"But you know people. Your father is the publisher of one of the biggest newspapers in the state. What you could do for my club"—he shook his head—"I dare not even imagine."

"Perhaps we could have a mutually beneficial relationship, then." The sudden excitement welling up inside her took her by surprise. Not ten minutes ago she hated herself. But this chubby, ugly man had turned that around with a few words. Maybe she wasn't as wretched as she thought. Maybe she had some value after all. Maybe acting in movies hadn't been a true dream. Perhaps this was it instead.

She thrust out her hand. "Let's shake on it, Claude."

He grasped her hand eagerly. "As they say in the movies, 'This could be the start of something good.'"

15

Belgrade, Yugoslavia
April 1941

THE DOOR BURST open. The sound wrenched Cameron from a deep sleep. For one frightening moment total disorientation consumed her.

"What're you doing sleeping at a time like this?" came a vaguely familiar male voice.

"Huh? What time is it?"

"Two A.M."

She groped her way to a sitting position, then rubbed her eyes. "Shanahan?" She reached for the switch to the lamp at her bedside.

Johnny grabbed her hand to stop her. "No lights. There's a black-out. Come on. Up and at 'em. Time to go."

Her mind cleared by slow degrees. She remembered she was in a cheap Belgrade hotel. She'd been sent there to cover the news of the government coup. But what remained fuzzy was why Johnny Shanahan looked amazingly chipper for this hour in the morning. Further, they worked for competing newspapers, so why was he—what *was* he doing, anyway?

"Go? Where? Why?" she asked, trying hard to shake the cobwebs from her mind so she could match his vigor.

"Holy cow, woman! Would you just once not ask questions?"

She swung her feet out of bed, then knuckled her eyes once again. She didn't usually sleep so deeply, but she'd been traveling around the Balkans for the last week, following the capricious schedules of planes and trains, surviving on little sleep, and that on station benches or hard train seats. When she had arrived in Belgrade to cover the military coup against the prince regent, she'd been exhausted, and the hotel bed, lumpy as it was, had lured her into somnolence.

"Where's your suitcases?" Shanahan asked as he pulled open a closet door and found them. "I'll get you packed while you get dressed."

"I don't want you pawing through my stuff. What's going on? I'm not going to budge until you at least answer that question."

He hauled out one of the cases and plopped it on the bed next to her. "Okay. That's fair. I have it on the best authority that Germany is about to bomb Belgrade. Any more questions?"

"Yes, a million."

"Later."

"Why are you letting me in on this?" Cameron asked as she went to the closet and took out a skirt and sweater.

"*Letting you in on this?*" he repeated incredulously, for a brief moment ceasing his frenzied activities and just staring at her. "I am not letting you in on a scoop, Hayes. I am trying to get your carcass to safety."

"I can take care of my own carcass."

"Oh yeah? I pounded on your door for five minutes before I finally got the concierge to let me in. Even a bomb wasn't likely to wake you."

"I haven't slept in two days," she replied defensively. Neither had Shanahan, but here he was.

They had been dogging each other all over southeastern Europe since her arrival in Rome two weeks ago. It had been both exhilarating and frustrating. Just as she began to feel she was giving the man a real run for his money, he'd somehow get the best of her, just like now.

The *Globe*'s budget was such that the Rome office was expected to cover all of southeastern Europe. Jim Prichard, the *Globe* correspondent in Rome, loved the idea of having an assistant to do all his footwork. At first Cameron tried to tell him she wasn't an assistant, which in Prichard's mind meant one step up, if that, above a secretary. But soon Cameron realized the footwork was the meat of the job.

"Okay . . ." Johnny's voice softened with rare sympathy. "You can't always be on top of things. We've been keeping a pretty grueling schedule. And the Serbs have been playing games with the Germans for so long it was easy to believe the political posturing might go on forever."

"I should have known it was going to happen," she said. "The Germans weren't going to stand for losing a hold on their puppet, the prince regent. They need Yugoslavia to get to Greece."

"Let's analyze it all later. Get dressed."

"I suppose it's too much to ask for some privacy?"

He rolled his eyes. "Okay. I'll head over to the British legation to make sure they don't leave without us. They've got a fleet of vehicles waiting for a fast getaway. Be there in fifteen minutes."

"I guess we've no choice. I hate running, though. But I just got a wire from Max saying that my Soviet visa came. He's sending it on to Athens, where I was supposed to be in a couple of days."

"If we can get out of here."

"I know why I want to leave, Johnny, but don't you want to be here for the action?"

"I don't fancy getting caught in a German-occupied zone. We may technically represent a neutral country, but the Nazis can still find ways to make our lives miserable. I know of a couple of American correspondents arrested by the Gestapo in Czechoslovakia, and they were nearly shot as spies. At any rate, we'll see some action with the Serb army in the south."

"What correspondents? How did they get away?"

He just shook his head as he opened the door to leave. "I'll tell you all about it later, Hayes. Now just get moving. Fifteen minutes."

Some time later, two British diplomats, their driver, UP correspondent Carl Levinson, Shanahan, and Cameron squeezed into a sedan packed also with food, luggage, and spare gasoline. It had been somewhat longer than fifteen minutes before they finally got off, no fault of Cameron's. The two Brits were leaving ahead of their colleagues with important papers, and it took some time for them to decide what papers must be taken.

They reached Mitrovica, about one hundred fifty miles south of Belgrade, shortly before noon that same Sunday morning. There they learned from the commander of the Serb Ibar Division that the capital had been heavily bombed that morning not long after Cameron's hasty departure, and twenty-seven of two hundred German bombers had been shot down.

Cameron spied the telephone on the adjutant's desk, and while Shanahan and Levinson were in deep conversation with the commander, she sidled up to the adjutant.

"I need to make a very important call," she said. "Might I use your phone?"

"I must keep the line open for emergencies," the man replied. He was no more than twenty-five and a good-looking fellow with a broad Slavic face.

"Of course, I understand. But I won't take long. I must inform my boss in Rome that I am all right. He will be concerned."

The fellow smiled apologetically and shrugged his helplessness.

"I will also be able to get through a report on what is happening here, and that will go far in garnering much-needed public support for your country." She flashed what she felt was her most charming smile.

"I . . . don't know . . ." He glanced toward the commander, then called to him. Much to Cameron's dismay, this also drew the attention of Shanahan and Levinson.

The adjutant spoke in his own language to his commander. They conversed back and forth for a few moments before the commander said to Cameron, "You wish to call Rome?"

"I assure you it would be nothing subversive."

"You will do so quickly."

"As a wink." When the commander gave her a quizzical frown, she added, "Yes, very fast."

"Hey, this is great," said Shanahan. "I need to call my bureau, too—"

"Only one call," the commander said firmly.

"But—"

"I am sorry. We cannot say how long we will have service."

"Listen, Shanahan," Cameron said, "I owe you for what you did this morning. You can get a message through my office."

"Aw, Hayes, that is very generous of you."

"What about me?" asked Levinson.

"Of course—" Cameron began only to be interrupted by the commander.

"It must be quick call," he said.

"Yes, yes. Very quick," she replied.

The adjutant rang the operator, but it was ten minutes before the call finally got through. Cameron was relieved Prichard was in his room.

"Jim, I haven't much time," Cameron said into the receiver. "You'll have to flesh out the story." The commander listened closely as she spoke, stopping her once when she gave some sensitive material. She reported the facts she had of the bombing and gave a couple brief descriptions of conditions she'd encountered on her trek from the capital. The line crackled several times, and she had to repeat herself often. "Did you get all that?"

"Cameron, hurry up," urged Shanahan.

She nodded at him while listening intently to Prichard's voice, which was breaking up considerably. "Jim, I want you to take some messages for Shanahan and Levinson—Jim? Can you hear me?" She flicked the button on the phone set. "Jim? I have—Jim?" With a grimace, she turned to her associates. "The line's gone dead."

"What? Are you sure?" Shanahan stepped toward the desk.

But the commander took the receiver instead and clicked the button several times. Looking relieved, he held the receiver out so that a dial tone could be clearly heard.

"See. Okay!" he said. Shanahan reached for the receiver, but the commander flinched away. "Only one call, I said."

"Yeah, and I just want to finish *that* call," argued Shanahan.

"Party disconnected."

Shanahan and Levinson protested loudly at the commander, then they turned their wrath upon Cameron.

"You cut that call off intentionally," accused Levinson.

"I did not!"

"You gotta admit, Hayes," said Shanahan, "it was rather good timing that the call got cut off *after* you finished your report."

"How dare you!" She looked to the commander. "Tell them it went dead for a minute."

But of course the commander had no way of supporting her. He held a working phone in his hand.

"We're in the middle of a war, for heaven's sake! Phones go dead." She may have done a few underhanded things in the past to get the better of the competition, but this time she was innocent.

They wouldn't believe her.

"And after I saved your neck today," lamented Shanahan.

"I could have gotten out of Belgrade without any of your help," she raved. "Why, probably the only reason you dragged me out of the city was because you didn't have the nerve yourself to weather a bombing and you didn't want me scooping you."

"You always did have an active imagination, Hayes," Shanahan said.

Cameron was forced to endure Shanahan's company for quite a while longer as they continued to trek through Yugoslavia one step ahead of the Germans. The tensions from L.A. had followed Cameron to Europe. While she and Johnny had been professionally civil to each other, Cameron had tried to maintain an emotional distance from him. In a way Cameron knew he had done nothing in L.A. to warrant her eternal punishment. But in view of everything, she thought it safe to keep aloof. Still, she wasn't around him long before she realized his friendship was important to her, perhaps much more than any romantic liaison. However, she was uncertain how to navigate the fine line between the two. The safest approach seemed to be their competitive banter. They both were most comfortable with that.

But all this was overshadowed by the thrill of their adventurous romp through southeastern Europe. They were arrested once at Stara Kachanik by Serb gendarmes who had been told to be on the lookout for German spies traveling in an automobile bearing diplomatic plates. They were held for a couple hours before the authorities determined their papers were in order and allowed them to continue on their way. They interviewed fleeing refugees and encountered soldiers along the way, and Cameron gathered significant material. But there was no more phone communication, and she had to sit on her stories until she could find a way to send them. Her only consolation was that Shanahan had to do the same.

The next morning after leaving Belgrade, they headed to Skoplje, one of the larger population centers in the south. On the road were more refugees, folks with carts and bundles trying to flee the inevitable. German bombers winged overhead, and Cameron doubted she would find their destination in one piece. One Messerschmitt flew low, an unnerving sight as it "buzzed" their car's windshield.

"I don't like that," Shanahan muttered.

Then came the sharp rat-a-tat of artillery. Their driver swerved as shells struck the dirt on the road only a few feet ahead of them. Amidst the screeching of brakes, the car thudded and bounced off the side of the road, finally coming to a stop in a ditch.

"Everyone all right?" the driver asked in a shaky voice.

The passengers all assured him there were no injuries, then they tumbled from the vehicle. It was pitched nose down into a rather steep crevice. Two tires were flat.

"Now what?" asked Levinson.

"Nothing for it but to join the refugees," said Shanahan. "Skoplje can't be too far."

The Brits opted to remain with their disabled vehicle in hopes that other diplomatic vehicles would be along soon. Levinson decided to do the same. Cameron didn't fancy sitting in a ditch while Germans were strafing the road. If another diplomatic car did come, they could always hitch a ride when it caught up to them. So she joined Shanahan and the flow of refugees on foot. They left their baggage in the car, hoping to catch up to it later in Skoplje.

"Just can't let me out of your sight, eh, sweetheart?" Johnny taunted as they walked.

Cameron only snorted derisively in response. She certainly wasn't going to admit that had played into her choice.

Looking around, Cameron wondered where all these refugees would go. They probably hoped Skoplje would offer shelter, but now it appeared as if it would soon become another German target. These people appeared to be mostly peasants. They had probably lost everything already and had little hope for the future, a hope that would be even dimmer under German occupation.

More bombers dotted the sky, and soon bursts of light could be seen exploding in the direction of the city. A Messerschmitt, probably patrolling the road, buzzed the refugees once again. Women and children screamed in fear and ran for cover. Along with a few civilian vehicles, there were some military trucks on the road, which no doubt the pilots considered a danger and therefore appropriate targets. What other reason for the sudden strafing?

Now the travelers were screaming and running in earnest. Vehicles slammed on brakes. One old truck burst into flame as it toppled over the edge of the road. Shanahan grabbed Cameron's shoulders and shoved her over the edge on the other side of the road. Shells ate up the dirt, sending sprays of debris into Cameron's face. She was nearly blinded by the grit and felt, rather than saw, when something slammed into her. It made a muffled thud against her body, and she knew what it was without having to see.

"Oh . . . d-dear God! Johnny!" she cried.

"I'm here, Cameron," he said gently.

His voice had never had a more reassuring ring. Then, of course, she realized it couldn't have been Johnny who had bounced into her. That was only a little comfort. As her vision cleared she saw a body sprawled out beside her. It was a woman. Blood oozed from her head.

"Tanya!" a man yelled. He was standing above them on the road.

A plane roared overhead, and Shanahan leaped up to the road, grabbed the man, who was obviously in a daze, and pulled him into the ditch just as shots sprayed the road again.

"Tanya!" the man wept, reaching toward the body of the woman. He bent over her, murmuring words of misery in his own language.

The woman stirred, her eyes fluttering open. Weeping, her husband spoke words of great relief in his own language.

Cameron moved close to Shanahan. She was trembling all over and didn't care if he saw. She needed to be close to someone just then.

"That was a pretty brave thing to do," she said to him.

He merely shrugged, as if pulling the man to safety had been nothing. "I was afraid he'd get shot, fall on me, and break my neck," he replied, clearly uncomfortable in being caught in any heroic act.

"Uh-huh," she said dubiously.

After stanching the woman's wound with a handkerchief, the man lifted Tanya into his arms and stood. Cameron was about to stop him, for clearly he was attempting the impossible if he intended to carry the injured woman all the way to shelter. Then Cameron saw a cart at the top of the bank that was packed with carpetbags and such. She watched the man tenderly lay his wife among all their worldly possessions. Though his wife had been spared, there was still a grim aspect to the man's expression. For them, it would still be a long, perilous road to safety.

Cameron snuggled closer to Shanahan, and he stretched his arm around her.

"The glory of war," he said dryly.

"Johnny, I have a confession to make if you promise not to tell anyone."

He laughed, the sharp, clear sound discordant with their surroundings. "Hayes, I'm a reporter. It's my job to tell people's secrets."

"Well, I'll tell you anyway. I was really scared a moment ago. I still am a little."

Though he restrained further laughter, it continued to linger about the corners of his lips. "So you are not made of steel after all?"

"Not completely, I guess."

"Are you afraid to die, Hayes?"

"That might be it. I don't know. I really never thought much about dying. I've never seen a dead person before except a couple of bodies on slabs in the morgue, and once I saw a body covered with a sheet at a crime scene. Seeing that woman made me realize how close we all are to it . . . death, I mean."

"We're in a war, Cameron. There's gonna be bodies. I'm glad you were spared this time, though." His dark eyes gave her face an intense appraisal. "You up for this, Hayes?" His tone was more entreaty than challenge, and that oddly comforted her.

"Aren't you afraid even a little, Shanahan?" she asked. "Or don't you worry about death?"

" 'Course I'm afraid, but there's one thing that scares me more than dying and that is getting wounded just enough so I have to lie there and watch someone else scoop me on the story. I just pray if I am gonna eat a bullet, it kills me outright."

"Goodness! That's pretty grim, Shanahan, even for you."

"Just practical, sweetheart, that's all." He looked up. The sky directly overhead was quiet now. Around them, people scrambled back up to the road to continue their seemingly hopeless trek. "Guess it's safe to move again," Shanahan said and started to stand.

Cameron laid a restraining hand on his arm. "I'm glad I was with you for this. It helped having you with me."

He smiled, then suddenly pulled her close and covered her lips with his in a passionate kiss. She didn't fight him, didn't even think to do so. Her lips responded to his, and the kiss drew out until they were alone in the ditch and refugees were streaming past them up on the road once again.

"I've missed you, Hayes," he murmured.

"Me too, Johnny."

He brushed a smudge of dirt from her nose. "What do ya say to our dropping this crazy feud between us?"

"The fact remains we work for competing newspapers," she said logically enough, though everything inside told her to forget work *just this once.*

"Doesn't mean we have to be at each other's throats, does it?"

"No, it doesn't."

"Good. Come on." He scrambled to his feet and reached out a hand to her.

Almost as a gesture of goodwill, she let him help her to her feet and back up to the road. As they began walking, she suddenly asked, "Was I starting to get to you, Johnny?"

"What d'ya mean?"

"You know. Was I giving you a run for your money?"

Cursing, he rolled his eyes. "You just can't let it go, can you?"

She cursed herself, as well, realizing he was right. There was some combative streak in her that just had to win, or maybe the idea of peaceful coexistence with Johnny sounded boring. It had felt good to be close to him again, to have him hold her as he had. Yet, did she truly prefer the competition?

"I'm sorry, Shanahan" was all she could think to say.

"Yeah, like you were sorry about cutting off that call to Rome."

"I did not cut it off!"

"I ain't buying, Hayes."

"Well, I did not cut off that call, and if you meant a word of what you said a minute ago about not being at each other's throats, you'd believe me."

"You know I never mean anything I say!" He grinned. "Any more than you are telling the truth about not cutting off that call."

"You're impossible!"

"Battle stations again, Hayes?"

"You bet!"

They arrived in Skoplje in time for another air raid. They found shelter along with dozens of others in the dungeon of an old castle. Afterward they had their papers approved at the divisional headquarters and then toured the city. The bombing had been uncannily accurate, but because the bombs had been of small caliber, the damage was not devastating. However, all services had been disrupted. There was no electricity, no telephone service, and all radio communication had been knocked out. Dead bodies were still lying untended. Early casualty reports counted thirty dead and over a hundred wounded in the first raid, but no figures had surfaced for the most recent attacks. They also learned that the bombings in Belgrade had left seventeen thousand dead.

16

Greece
April 1941

WITH THE GERMANS literally nipping at their heels, Cameron and Shanahan raced into Greece from Yugoslavia. But it was more than German might that drove Cameron. Her Soviet visa was waiting for her in Athens. Yes, she was a little torn about leaving this exciting war zone, but she could feel in her bones that events soon were going to explode in the Soviet Union. The day before leaving Belgrade, Cameron had interviewed a government official who had let slip a rumor that Hitler had specific plans for the invasion of the Soviet Union. Cameron had heard such rumors before, but the German invasion of the Balkans clearly showed a pattern evolving that supported the validity of those rumors. Germany was clearing the way for an invasion of Russia by gaining control of the Balkan states and thereby leaving the Soviets with no buffer against attack.

Cameron needed to get to Russia, but the war was stopping her at every turn. They had barely made it out of Yugoslavia without getting trapped. Now it looked as though they might not be so lucky in Greece. German bombers had started their now famous blitzkrieg style of attack on Greece, almost in tandem with that in Yugoslavia. Greece had no illusions they could stand against German force, despite the fact that the previous autumn they had repelled the Italian invasion attempt. It appeared that Greece would likely fall.

Trying to avoid advancing German troops, Cameron and her traveling companions were forced to take a circuitous route toward Athens. It was now the twenty-third of April, and less than a week earlier, Yugoslavia had surrendered to the Nazis. There was a strong resistance movement already rising in that country, but with so many ethnic divisions among the Yugoslavians, it remained questionable how effective they could be.

Cameron was still traveling with Shanahan and Levinson. The Brits had taken leave of them upon arriving in Patras on the Pelopennese. The journalists were now trying to get transportation east. Though only about a hundred fifty miles lay between Patras and Athens along the gulf coast, it was too dangerous to travel the highways by automobile. The trio was becoming anxious about making it to Athens, not only because of the advancing Germans, but also, and perhaps more importantly, because the capital appeared to be the only communications center remaining in Greece. They all had several weeks' worth of dispatches they wanted to get to the States. Cameron, of course, had her own reasons for wanting to get there.

In Patras, Cameron had managed to get an interview with the British commander. She felt a slight twinge of guilt in having taken advantage of the situation while Shanahan and Levinson were out scouring the city for transportation for them. Though the trio each represented competing news agencies, they were forced by circumstances to work together. In Athens there would no doubt be a mad race to beat one another to the nearest cable office, but for now they were comrades.

"Colonel, how far have the Germans pushed into Greece?" Cameron asked, pad and pencil in hand.

"We have strong positions north of here," the officer answered tightly, an attitude Cameron attributed to both military censorship and the man's natural British reserve. "I have every confidence we will turn the Germans back at Thermopylae."

"That can't be more than fifty miles across the gulf."

"That is correct."

"What about casualties?"

"There are casualties," the man acknowledged.

Of course he wasn't going to admit the extent of British losses, but Cameron had heard they were nearly double that of the Germans. This invasion was becoming rather humiliating for the British, who had sent an expeditionary force of some fifty-eight thousand to Greece at the beginning of the year. But the humiliation of defeat was nothing compared to the prospect of Britain losing its strategic position in the Mediterranean, threatening its forces in Egypt and the Middle East.

At that moment Shanahan burst into the office. The colonel looked relieved.

"Hayes, I managed to get us tickets on the afternoon train to Athens. We haven't much time."

With the fighting drawing close and the action heating up, Cameron was reluctant to leave. The heat of war had an appeal that almost overwhelmed her desire for Russia.

The colonel noted her hesitation and said, "You had best take advantage of this opportunity. It could well be the last train out of here."

With a resolute sigh, Cameron grabbed her suitcase and typewriter case. She was down to one suitcase now, having pared down her belongings shortly after leaving Yugoslavia. She'd gotten rid of all her books—a painful parting—her evening clothes, and anything else that wasn't absolutely necessary. Though the temperature was in the seventies in Greece, she still kept her coats; her heavy wool one was now packed in her suitcase, but she had to wear her raincoat, despite the fact that she was sweating by the time she and Shanahan raced to the train station. Shanahan, knowing her reasons for this wardrobe choice, taunted her behavior, saying that Moscow was still a long way off.

The platform at the station was mobbed with people trying to escape the town ahead of the invaders. It was a small miracle they found Levinson in the crush. They were not happy when it was announced the train had been canceled.

Shanahan cursed and kicked his suitcase before grabbing it and his typewriter case and stalking from the station. Cameron followed, while Levinson went in the opposite direction to check out another lead he had on transportation.

An air raid forced Cameron and Johnny to duck into a shelter for an hour. They were crammed into the small space so tightly there was barely room to breathe. Cameron had noted a sign written in both English and Greek over the entrance of the shelter: "Built with funds contributed from America."

"Couldn't they have contributed a few more dollars for a bigger shelter?" Cameron groaned as someone's elbow jabbed her ribs and a large foot ground down on her toe.

After the air raid they found a café, one they had frequented since coming to Patras. There was no food to be bought, but they managed to get a cup of tea, very weak tea at that. Cameron plunked her Underwood on the table and opened the case.

"What're you doing?" Shanahan asked.

"What does it look like? I'm going to write something, even if it never has a chance of getting back home."

"Forget that," he said. "We have to think of a way out of here."

"I can think and write at the same time." She cranked a sheet of paper into the Underwood, then set her fingers on the keys and began to set down the contents of her recent interview with the colonel. Pausing, she said, "What about a military truck? I bet if we go back to that colonel and tell him our plight, he'd accommodate. He seemed anxious to be rid of us."

"Of you, you mean," Shanahan replied dryly.

Cameron rolled her eyes and kept typing. A few moments later a woman entered the café. She was tall and willowy and quite attractive, with jet black hair and eyes and creamy skin. Very Grecian in appearance.

"There you are, Johnny dear!" She spoke English with a thick accent.

"Filia," said Shanahan. He gave her a casual, unreadable smile.

"Are you still seeking to leave town?" she asked.

"Yes, but the train's been canceled and there probably won't be another."

"I may have a way . . ." she paused, turning dark, exotic eyes upon Cameron. "Perhaps we should speak privately?"

"Oh, don't worry about her," Shanahan said with a quick look toward Cameron. "She's nobody . . . a colleague, you know. You can trust her."

Cameron bit back a retort at his casual dismissal of her. "Nobody" indeed! But if this little Greek tart could get them to Athens, then a bit of restraint wouldn't kill Cameron.

"You want to sit down?" Shanahan asked his friend, gesturing toward a vacant chair.

"No, thank you. I have an appointment I must keep. But I wanted to tell you I just remembered a friend I have who works for the railroad. I'm sure he will have information not available to the general public. Sometimes they say trains are canceled, but there are always military trains no one is told about."

"It's worth a try. How do I find this man?"

"I must introduce you. Meet me at the Adonis Hotel in an hour."

"Thanks, honey," Shanahan said with a grin that was now very readable and clearly said he was willing to express his appreciation in more than words. "You're a real pip, Filia!"

She reached out her hand and brushed his jaw with great familiarity. "I hope we'll have time to say a proper good-bye before you go."

"Count on it, honey!"

With that, the Greek beauty exited the café.

Shanahan glanced at his wristwatch. "I hope Levinson turns up before we have to leave."

"You don't really think that woman is going to help us." It was obvious to Cameron the gal was just giving Johnny a big come-on.

"Why wouldn't she?" Then the light seemed to dawn, and he shook his head. "I get it. You're jealous."

"Ha! Not in the least. I'm just not going to pin my hopes on a common streetwalker."

"You don't know anything, Hayes, especially about her." He appeared truly offended, almost as if he really cared about this woman he could not have met more than two days ago. It wasn't like him at all.

"Well, given your history—"

"Unlike you, Hayes, I'm not afraid to get involved with the real people in places I cover—to get to know them, get on their level."

"Please, don't try to ennoble some tawdry liaison."

He shrugged coolly. "You can't understand, Hayes, because since you've come to Europe you have been afraid to get beneath the hard facts of the news—"

"Just because I am not willing to sleep with anyone on the street just for a story—"

"I don't claim to be a saint, but I do know how to cover my assignments with heart. Cameron, I've read some of your stuff and—"

"You have been snooping in my things?"

"Simmer down, sweetheart! For the last few weeks we've been practically sleeping together. It's hard not to look over your shoulder occasionally." He paused, fingering the cleft in his chin. The fact that he looked more sage at the moment than offended at her words rather irked her. "I'm gonna give you some free advice."

"You are, are you?" Her tone dared him to try.

"Cameron, you've got a problem with intimacy."

"Me!" she burst out. It was the last thing she expected to hear from him. "That's rich coming from a man who has never had more than two dates with a woman."

"I had more than two with you."

"We'd better not get into that."

A hint of a smile twitched his lips before he spoke. "Back in L.A. you were coming along nicely in your writing. Maybe being thrown into this new environment made you regress. You are relying too much on the facts and figures of war. Your material's been cold, devoid of passion. I've seen you in some pretty hairy situations, and I've seen you react with emotion, but it hasn't translated onto paper."

She had wanted to interrupt him, and when he finished, she wanted to shove his words back into his face. Then she remembered there was a time when Johnny Shanahan had been her mentor whom she had greatly admired. And though she didn't want to admit it now, she knew he was still the best there was, and she'd be a fool to let her personal feelings cloud the truth of his words. If they were true, she wanted to fix it. She wanted to be as good as he.

"Is it really that bad, Johnny?" she said, suddenly feeling very vulnerable.

"You remember that strafing in Yugoslavia and that woman, Tanya, who was wounded?"

"You remembered her name!" She didn't know why it should surprise her. It was so unlike him. Yet, on the other hand . . .

"Of course I do. It's part of my job to remember details like that. Anyway, I saw what you wrote after that. It was a great account of the types of bombers the Germans used, the tonnage of bombs, even a very accurate numbering of casualties gleaned from officials. You even had some good descriptions of the destruction. But I never sensed the fear and horror of being caught in such a situation. I never glimpsed the pathos of Tanya's husband carrying her up to his cart, though I know it got to you on a deep level.

"You got talent, Hayes," he added and was so sincere it scared her. It must mean things were worse than she imagined. "But, shoot, you're green. You've only been in the business a few years, and only a few weeks as a correspondent. You're afraid of showing your ignorance by asking for help, and you're afraid of opening up your heart and soul when you report."

"But we're writing news, not human interest."

"Go ahead and write the facts, but you can't forget this is a war and, more than facts, it's about people suffering. It's about scars on land and on people's souls. If you can't communicate that, then why are you over here in the middle of it? You may as well sit stateside in Washington and regurgitate official communiqués." Pausing, he glanced toward the door. "That dame that was just here is a perfect example. I met her because I wasn't satisfied with merely interviewing commanders and such." He reached into his pocket and withdrew a paper. "Here, have a look at this."

Cameron took the paper, unfolded it, and read:

Patras is a town devastated by war. Once a quaint Grecian fishing village, you cannot now look around anywhere without seeing rubble and debris. In fact, hardly a building has been left unscathed. The streets are packed with the homeless and displaced, with people whose lives will never be the same even after this war ends.

This reporter recently met one such person, a young woman whom I saw walking down the street weeping. I thought she might be one of many searching the rubble unsuccessfully for missing loved ones. She was that, and more. She had just received the news that both of her brothers had been killed in the fighting near Thermopylae. Her father, also in the military, could not be found to be told the terrible news. This girl was now left with two equally loathsome fears: first, that she would see her father before the authorities found him and be forced to be the one to tell him his only sons were dead. Or second, that he, too, had been killed in the fighting.

This reporter was helpless to ease that woman's grief. I let her cry on my shoulder for a time—

Cameron lifted her eyes from the paper and said skeptically, "Cry on your shoulder, Shanahan?"

He gave a sheepish laugh. "Okay, maybe I let her do more than that, but there are limits to the emotions that can be exposed on the page, you know."

She smiled, then more sincerely said, "This is really good, Johnny."

"It's why I'm over here," he replied with a hint of modesty, then added with his old arrogance, "and why I own a Pulitzer."

"Boy, I almost thought you were going to get through an entire day without mentioning your Pulitzer!"

He laughed, and at that moment Levinson came in. Before exchanging information with him, Cameron gave a final thought to Shanahan. He could be a cold, arrogant piece of work, yet his written words had touched her, and she was left wondering just who the real Johnny Shanahan was. Had he reached out to the weeping girl on the street because of real concern, or because he smelled a story? Or simply because he was feeling lustful? Was he a man of deep complexities? Or a better actor than a Barrymore?

In so many ways he was a stranger to her. He spoke of intimacy, wrote with passion, yet he was an expert in holding at arm's length the woman he probably knew best in the world. And the irony was, he could do this while kissing Cameron and physically embracing her. She told herself, as she had often, that it was better this way. In fact, she applauded him. She'd like to learn how to do the same.

FILIA'S FRIEND at the railroad told them about a military train that would depart just before dawn the next morning. He assured them they would blend in enough not to be noticed sneaking aboard the train—all except Cameron. He looked her up and down, leering and disapproving at the same time.

"No women on military train," he said. "You'll stand out like— how you Americans say?—sore toe."

"Sore thumb," Cameron corrected, then added, "Don't worry about me, I'll blend in."

Filia, who had many soldier acquaintances, managed to scrounge up some army fatigues for Cameron and a couple of camouflage jackets for the men. Cameron put on the fatigues and found them so comfortable and practical she wondered why she hadn't found some sooner. Of course women in slacks were looked down upon in these Mediterranean countries, and she hadn't wanted to offend those she was depending upon for news material by wearing slacks. Now, of course, there were other priorities.

But looking in Filia's mirror, she couldn't help a twinge of vanity— she who usually gave little thought to her appearance. The fatigues were stained and wrinkled and hung on her slim figure horribly. Yes, they were comfortable, but they made her look like an old sack of potatoes. She had a fleeting thought of her sister. Blair would be appalled at the sight in the mirror.

"I've come a long way from choosing evening gowns," she murmured.

For the first time in a long while, she gave thought to just how far she had distanced herself from her life in California. She'd been dodging armies and bombs, scrounging for clothes and food, sleeping on floors or in the backs of cars or under the stars. By comparison, her life in the States had been that of a pampered socialite. Oddly, she didn't miss it at all. She missed her family, of course, and was frustrated that she couldn't communicate with them. She wondered if Blair had landed that movie part she dreamed of. How was Jackie faring in college? Was her mother too awfully worried about Cameron? And her father. . . ? What was he doing now that he couldn't make her life miserable?

Yes, it all seemed so far removed from the reality of the present.

Cameron hitched her belt tighter around her waist so the jacket wouldn't balloon out, then turned to join her colleagues, who were waiting in a café next door to Filia's apartment. Shanahan gave her a wolf whistle as she approached. Laughing, she gave a model twirl.

They returned to their hotel rooms and spent their last night in Patras. Cameron slept little and woke easily at four o'clock. She donned her fatigues, packed her suitcase, and met the others in the lobby. There was nothing but an ersatz coffee for breakfast. Filia gave them a loaf of bread for the journey. Cameron would have been more effusive with her thanks, for indeed the girl had been a great help to them, but she was just a bit irked seeing the girl with Shanahan so early in the morning.

Again they found the train station mobbed.

"Some secret train!" Cameron muttered.

But the crowds shouldn't have come as a surprise, because Shanahan had greeted them that morning with the dismal information that the Germans had broken through the British defense at Thermopylae. The enemy was now in control of the shore across the narrow gulf. Everyone, civilians and military alike, was more desperate than ever to get away.

The train pulled in with only ten cars. It was a battle to get aboard. In the frenzy Cameron forgot that she and her companions had less right than any to travel on the train, for they were not only not military, but they were foreigners as well. But she elbowed, pushed, and shoved her way through the mob until she reached the door of a car. A big Greek private got there at the same moment. He jabbed her in the eye with his elbow and then howled with laughter when she winced and nearly let go of her hold on the doorframe. Her eye stung with pain and tears, but she held fast as the man tried to shove her away. Incensed at the private's behavior, Cameron lost control and instinctively kneed him. Yelping in agony, the fellow fell away from the door, and Cameron, seizing the advantage, squeezed into the car.

Shanahan and Levinson were already inside and miraculously had found two vacant seats. They took turns sitting and standing. Cameron did not argue when the men let her have the first shift in one of the seats. Sometimes it paid to be a lady, even one in army fatigues.

By the time the train pulled out of the station, hundreds of passengers had been crammed inside, with many more riding on the roof of the cars. Cameron thought about what an idyllic journey this would have been in peacetime along the picturesque Grecian coast. The cliffs towering over the sea fell a hundred feet to the sparkling blue water of the gulf. It was hard to imagine an invading army poised dangerously just on the other side of that gulf.

At least it was hard to imagine until the tangy sea air was disturbed by the sound of a Messerschmitt engine.

The sun was fully up and they had been traveling several hours. The conductor had informed them it would be a fifteen-hour trip to Corinth, only a hundred twenty miles away! Cameron could not believe this possible until she realized the train stopped at every station along the way—not by design but because soldiers and refugees would get on the tracks and force the train to stop so they could board.

The roar of the approaching airplane engine was immediately followed by sharp bursts from its machine gun. The train passengers all reacted instantly and simultaneously to the deadly sound. They dove for the aisles. Those already standing in the aisles just dropped. It turned into a giant dog pile. Cameron couldn't decide if it was a blessing or a curse to have ended up on top of the pile. At least she wasn't getting crushed by smelly, sweaty bodies, but when the plane fired again, she realized she was a perfect target, since she was about level with the windows of the car. She tried not to think of the poor men riding on the roof. But the screams and shouts outside, along with the sight of bodies falling to the ground, made that difficult.

The plane ceased firing, and through the window Cameron saw it circle wide as it prepared for another pass. This time, however, it dropped a bomb, destroying the track behind the train and a good portion of the last car. This was definitely going to be the last train to

Athens, from the looks of the demolished track and the crater left in the wake of the bombing. The train screeched to a halt. Cameron couldn't understand why. Maybe the engineer had been hit or perhaps he just thought their best chance to avoid more bombs would be to debark and run for the cover of the woods. At any rate, once the train stopped, that's what everyone who was able did.

The Messerschmitt was making its third pass just as Cameron and her cohorts had reached the car door. They only had time to jump down and roll under the car for cover. An instant later machine-gun lead shattered what was left of the windows of the car and a good portion of the door.

"Dear God in heaven!" Levinson screamed in a shaky voice as he pointed up at the sky.

Looking up they saw the plane circle yet again. If it decided to drop another bomb, they would be finished, for they could never get to the woods in time, and if they risked leaving the cover of the car, they'd be sitting ducks to machine-gun fire.

"It's a little late for prayer, Carl," muttered Shanahan.

"My mama always said it's never too late for prayer," Cameron said. She'd always disdained such statements from her pious mother and couldn't imagine why they spilled from her lips now. Perhaps it was true what she'd heard that there were no atheists in foxholes—or under a firing Messerschmitt.

"Your mother said that, Hayes?" asked Shanahan, and amazingly, with them all mere seconds from death, his tone held its usual wry humor.

"Yeah." She simply could not think of a snappy comeback.

"The wife of that old so-and-so, Keagan Hayes? Well, I'll be! But on second thought, I guess she must need a lot of prayer with him for a husband and you for a daughter."

"Why, of all the—" Cameron began but stopped as the plane approached, spitting more lead.

When it finished and retreated—apparently not to return, for it did not circle this time but rather turned and headed straight north—the reporters rolled from their cover.

Levinson grabbed Cameron's arm. "Wait a minute!" he said. "What was Shanahan saying? You're not that Hayes, are you?"

"Some reporter you are," taunted Cameron. "It only took you three weeks to figure it out."

"That explains a lot—"

"What d'ya mean by that?" Cameron challenged.

"Why a greenhorn gal—"

"Clam up, Carl," Shanahan broke in sharply. "Hayes is here because she deserves to be here. She isn't even working for her father."

"If you don't mind, I can fight my own battles," Cameron snapped, not knowing which of her colleagues to be more angry with.

Johnny scowled at her, and she could see she had chosen a poor time to argue feminism. Why couldn't she just say thanks and leave it at that? Maybe he would have defended anyone, man or woman, in the same way.

"Let's get out of here before that plane comes back," Johnny growled.

They saw smoke rising from the train engine and noted for the first time it had been shot up pretty bad. The engineer was dead. They got their luggage. Shanahan's suitcase had a row of bullet holes on the side. There were dead and wounded lying outside all along the train. Medics were circulating among them. There was nothing more to be done.

The three journalists hiked for several miles, keeping within sight of the tracks but staying as close as possible within the cover of the woods. Realizing they couldn't walk all the way to Athens, which couldn't be less than sixty miles away, they finally opted to risk the highway. But there was no traffic going either way. They walked until late afternoon. Cameron's feet ached in the boots, obtained by Filia along with the fatigues, but which were too big even with a couple pairs of socks.

The three refugees were beginning to discuss camping possibilities when, seemingly out of nowhere, an RAF truck rumbled down the road. They flagged it down, and though it was packed with wounded from the train, all three managed to squeeze into the cab with the driver and a medic.

"Yes, we're bound for Athens," said the driver in response to their first question. "Hopefully we'll get there in time."

"In time for what?" Cameron asked.

"The country will be evacuated soon."

"Is it that bad?" asked Shanahan.

"The country's been all but overrun with Jerries, I'm afraid. We got out of Patras just before it fell this morning. You're very fortunate to have made it out."

Somehow Cameron didn't feel lucky. She thought of all the dead along the railroad tracks. She thought of the people left behind in Patras and the other villages along the way. She even thought about Filia. After losing two brothers and perhaps her father, she was now forced to face the prospect of living as a virtual captive of the enemy. If she had survived at all. Who knew what kind of desperate defense had been staged by the citizens of that town?

Cameron glanced over at Shanahan. He was staring rather stoically straight ahead, but the muscles of his jaw were twitching violently. Was he thinking of the Greek beauty he had befriended and the grim fate before her?

Impulsively, Cameron reached over and laid her hand on his arm. He glanced down at her hand, then up into her eyes. A sad smile flickered around the corners of his lips. She knew he didn't feel very lucky, either.

———

The evacuation began two days after they arrived in Athens. For many it brought back memories of Dunkirk the year before. Cameron wondered if Adolf Hitler would indeed have his way in Europe. In fact, he *was* having his way. Besides Britain, there was only one other "fly in the ointment," Hitler's supposed ally, the Soviet Union. But would the German leader really be so crazy as to attack Russia when Britain still remained a viable enemy? Creating a two-front war would be lunacy. Hitler's previous failure in his attempts to cross the English Channel certainly could not drive him to such an extreme. One of the first laws of warfare was "Never attack Russia." And despite rumors to the contrary and her own father's predictions, Cameron could not believe any leader would be so stupid as to make the attempt.

But what galled her as much as anything was that she might well miss it all. Her visa had not arrived in Athens. Prichard had sent it, so it was to be assumed it had become lost en route. To start the process over or even to get copies could take weeks. If war did erupt in Russia, the last thing anyone would care about was an American reporter's visa.

Cameron considered these things while heading for Egypt on a British ship. It was now the middle of May. She had been forced to spend some time on Crete where the British forces had evacuated after being forced from Greece. As their position there began to crumble, she decided to take advantage of an evacuation ship, along with Shanahan and Levinson. The real action of the war was now in the Middle East, and if she was smart, she'd consider herself quite fortunate she was heading there. Besides, Egypt put her that much closer to Russia should anything break there.

It was hard to shake a dream she'd fostered for years. Yet more than that drew her now. If Hitler was going to attack Russia, he had to do it soon so his troops would get a foothold before winter set in. Added to that was the ever looming presence of the United States and its uncertain position. America's entry into the war would dramatically alter Hitler's chances of victory. It would, however, be another matter entirely if he could subdue the Soviet Union. Therefore, Hitler had to make his move, and soon, if he was going to make it at all.

And, heaven help her, all Cameron could think of was what a coup it would be for her to be in Russia when that happened.

Leaning against the ship's rail and breathing in the damp, salty air, she wondered if she was doing the right thing. What if she got to Russia and Hitler showed he had some sense after all and didn't attack? Then she might be stuck there away from all the action. Of course, with America coming closer and closer to entering the war, she also had to consider the possibility that if she remained on the European mainland, she'd end up a hostile and likely a German captive. She might do well to stay in Egypt. With Europe now in Germany's hands, the war in the Middle East was going to heat up. A German offensive in March, just prior to the invasion of the Balkans, had pushed the British back to Egypt. There was sure to be enough action here to satisfy any journalist.

"I didn't think you liked the water," said Shanahan coming up beside her.

"I don't, but breathing fresh air on deck seems to quiet my rebelling stomach."

He chuckled. "Nice to have a little bit of peace for a change."

"Really, Johnny? I thought you were an addict for action and adventure. As for myself, I am starting to get bored."

"There'll be some good battles in the desert."

"Uh-huh . . ." she replied noncommittally.

"You've got something else up your sleeve, don't you?"

"I just want to keep my options open."

"I asked your father to get me accredited to the Eighth Army. A stint as a combat correspondent ought to be a nice change. In the trenches with the troops, I'll get some good material."

"That should be exciting."

"You're still not holding out hope for Moscow, are you?"

"I guess I won't know anything until Arnett contacts me in Cairo."

"Holy cow! You are being evasive."

"Not intentionally." She gazed out at the frothy wake left by the ship, wondering if that was true. She couldn't think why it would matter, but Shanahan was such a cagey beast he was sure to make something of it. Arnett had purposely set her and Johnny at odds, but now was her chance to break away from the game, to truly be on her own. It seemed prudent to do nothing to jeopardize that chance.

18

Cairo, Egypt
May 1941

"EGYPT!" CAMERON muttered as she looked down at the cable in her hand.

She cursed as she crushed the sheet in her fist. Arnett had informed her in the cable that he was arranging to get her accredited to the Eighth Army. Less than a week ago Shanahan had requested that he be assigned to the Eighth Army. Cameron did not have to be a genius to figure out that Arnett had heard about this, and it had prompted his decision regarding Cameron's assignment. He was still determined to keep up the cat-and-mouse game between her and Shanahan. He had said that the lost visa was perhaps a "blessing in disguise." Her talents would be put to far better use where she was . . . "Where," he said, "fate has put you."

"Fate! Bah!" she intoned through clenched teeth. She had shot back a cable that let him know in no uncertain terms what she thought of that and how she didn't appreciate his reneging on his promise. It would probably just get her fired.

She spun around to leave the operator's office and nearly slammed into Shanahan.

"Bad news?" he asked, no doubt taking note of the fire in her eyes. A cigarette dangled between his lips, and there was an amused gleam in his eyes.

"What do you want?" she asked gruffly.

"I want to send a cable."

"Oh." She decided she was getting paranoid. "Well, good luck. You'll need it here today."

She brushed past him and headed for the hotel, which was close to the cable office. Even in wartime, Cairo offered some fairly decent accommodations. Nothing four-star, but tolerable. She entered the second-rate hotel, decorated in the once opulent but now rather shabby décor of circa the Great War. As in most countries, journalists tended to congregate together, staying in the same hotels, drinking at the same bars. Cameron wasn't certain if that was for the camaraderie it afforded or for keeping tabs on one another. The Cairo Arms was no different.

Entering the hotel's public lounge, she was greeted by several fellow journalists—English, French, American, and others. She sat at a table with a small group and listened to them gossip about the war. A ceiling fan turned lazily overhead, barely disturbing the late afternoon air of that warm desert day in May.

Though distracted, she forced herself to pay attention to the conversation. If this was to be her assignment, she needed to be apprised of the "lay of the land." Besides, this was no assignment to be sneered upon. North Africa was the most important theater of war now. Since the fall of France, Britain had committed most of its troops here and to the defense of the Suez Canal. She might have more of an emotional commitment to the Soviet Union because of her father's connection and what her mother had told her, but if Arnett could get her attached to a combat division in Africa . . . well, that would be quite a coup for a woman.

"Our Tommies practically hold the man in awe," the *London Times* correspondent was saying.

"He's a brilliant tactician," said Don Mayfield, the Cairo correspondent from the *Journal*. "He proved that in France."

"Who are you talking about?" Cameron asked.

"Rommel, of course."

"The German field marshal?" Cameron had heard of his exploits in France, how, during the invasion last year, his was the first panzer division to reach the Channel.

"He's been in Africa only a couple of months, but he is already making a name for himself."

"At our expense, unfortunately," lamented the Brit.

"That will change now that you don't have to commit troops to Greece," offered Cameron.

"Righto! We can only hope," said the Brit, raising a glass of warm ale to his lips. "Of course, we would have more than a hope if you Yanks would get into the fight."

"FDR promised during the election last fall that he would not commit our boys to a foreign war," said Levinson, the UP correspondent.

"Poppycock! Pure electioneering. He would have said anything to be the first man in your history to win a third term as president. Everyone knows he wants to enter the war. A mere month after the election he declared that the best defense of Great Britain is the best defense of the United States."

"Making America—how did he put it?—'the arsenal of democracy,'" said Cameron. "He used the analogy of lending a garden hose to a neighbor whose house was on fire. But even with such fine posturing, he was lucky to get Lend-Lease approved," Cameron added, "and I am sure that was only passed to salve our collective conscience about the war. But the isolationists are still furious over it."

"Oh, we'll get into the war!" Shanahan had come into the lounge, but his cheerful visage of earlier was decidedly absent. "And I'll be stuck in the USSR." He grabbed a chair from another table, wedged it in among the group, then glared at Cameron. "What's this crazy obsession your father has with Russia?"

"What's going on, Shanahan?" asked Mayfield.

Johnny waved a piece of paper—very like the one Cameron had crumbled in her hands a half hour earlier. "I'm in the middle of this war's hottest spot, and that moron wants to send me to Russia. Says an update on the progress of the Nonaggression Pact is due. I can tell him everything there is to know right here and now. Germany is blasting its way through Europe while Russia sits on its haunches thanking whatever gods those atheist idiots worship that it isn't them getting blasted through."

"Everyone but Stalin knows they're next," offered Cameron, swallowing back her ire at Johnny's good fortune.

"Well, I don't know it," shot back Shanahan. "And it would be insanity for Hitler to strike now, if at all. He'd have but four months to succeed before winter set in. Even Hitler can't be so arrogant to think he can overrun a country like Russia in that amount of time. If he attacks, it can't be until next spring, and in the meantime, I'll be wallowing around trying to make news out of nothing."

"That is tough luck," offered the Associated Press man. "As I've heard, there are only two full-time journalists in the entire country right now from the AP and from the UP. I know the AP man, Henry Cassidy, and his job lately hasn't exactly been a hotbed of news gathering."

"This is your fault, Hayes!" Johnny said.

"My fault!"

"Your old man knows you've been following me all over Europe—"

"Following you!" she blurted, feeling a bit like a parrot, but she had no immediate riposte. She shoved back her chair. "Never mind!" was all she could say before she stalked away.

She strode across the worn Persian carpet of the hotel lobby and then out the door. A blast of heat greeted her, a reminder that the hotel was cooler than she'd realized. Well, she didn't care if she shriveled up in the heat, she was not going to sit for another moment of Shanahan's abuse. What a thing to say! And in front of all their colleagues! She could kill him for that alone.

Cameron tried to focus on the sights and sounds of the city, easily the most foreign of all she had seen thus far in her travels as a foreign correspondent. The Cairo Arms was on the edge of the European section of the city where the streets were broader and of a more modern appearance. The British presence was acute, especially with the profusion of military vehicles. Rumor had it that King Farouk was a bit too ambivalent about his British overlords. He was far too friendly with the Italians, Hitler's allies. The Egyptians didn't support the war, but they heartily supported making money off it. However, after years of being under the British thumb, they secretly enjoyed watching British defeats and humiliations. But those same ones who might smile at a Limey retreat were also apt to shake in their sandals if the Germans came too close. One could almost feel sorry for these poor people caught so in the middle, that is, until one happened to glimpse that opportunistic gleam in a cunning Arab entrepreneur's eye.

This place was rife with possibilities, a newsman's dream. Cameron could live with it even if it wasn't her dream. If only Johnny wasn't about to go off and live *her* dream. That's what made it stick in her throat like desert sand.

"Hey, you! Hold up!"

Johnny's voice cut through her thoughts like an unwelcome wind. Was he going to rub it in further? She was about to hasten her steps when she suddenly realized the childishness of the act. She stopped but did not turn.

He was panting as he hurried up to her. "You're gonna kill me yet, Hayes!" he gasped.

"If only . . ." she replied through gritted teeth. "What do you want now?"

"To apologize."

"Huh?" She stared at this shocking statement.

"I was out of line back at the hotel." He shook his head with what seemed almost like true regret. "I aimed my anger at you when it should have been directed at your father—kind of impossible, though, with him thousands of miles away. I forgot you are as much at odds with the man as I am."

"All right. Apology accepted," she answered tightly. She hated it when he capitulated before she was ready to let go of her own emotions.

"Come on back to the hotel, and I'll buy you a drink."

"I don't feel like it right now, Johnny. I think I'll just walk a bit."

"Mind some company?"

"It's a free country."

"It's more of a monarchy occupied by foreign oppressors," he replied glibly.

"I know how they feel." She started walking and he joined her. "I'm not following you, Johnny. I want to make that clear. But Max Arnett has it in his mind that you give me some sort of edge."

"Maybe he's right. You make me awfully edgy, too."

She rolled her eyes. "You are impossible."

"Well, look at it this way, I might just be your ticket to Russia, then." He arched his brow slyly. "When Arnett finds out where I'm headed—"

"I hadn't thought of that." Her tone rose hopefully, then spiraled downward again as the full implication of Johnny's words occurred to her. "You don't get it, Johnny. True, I got this job fully aware of his intent, but I don't want to be used anymore. I'm sick of it. I've wanted to go to Russia as a journalist for years. I am more qualified than anyone. It galls me that the only way I can get there is as a pawn. I hate it. This would not be happening if I were a man—"

A grunt made her stop and glance at Johnny. He grinned ruefully. "That's right, doll, I'm a pawn, too—me, a man last time I looked! I wouldn't be here either if it wasn't for you. You know what I say to it? Blast 'em all! We've got the last laugh because we are here experiencing what only a select few civilians will ever experience in this war. And I plan to ride it for all it's worth—even if I have to do it in the frozen wastes of Russia."

Shocked as usual at his ability to make her forget her anger toward him, she was forced to smile. "You do have a way of looking at things, John Shanahan."

"So everything's jake, doll?"

"Only if you stop calling me doll."

"Oh . . . well, er . . . Miss Cameron Hayes."

She wanted to hug him then and might have if they hadn't been in the middle of the crowded city. The turbaned Muslim men and the veiled women would have been scandalized, and for all Cameron knew, there might even be laws against such public behavior in this Arab country. She walked faster instead. They were getting into the Egyptian sector now. The streets were narrower, more uneven, and in disrepair. Automobiles were crowded among ox-drawn carts, donkeys, and camels, all bearing piles of exotic merchandise. Smudge-faced children darted in and out between carts and kiosks while veiled women robed in sweltering black haggled with vendors over prices. Cameron was vaguely conscious of disapproving glances from the Arab men. She stood out quite a bit in this sector in her knee-length linen skirt and cotton blouse. The colors were plain brown and white, but she suddenly felt like a peacock.

"You hungry?" Johnny asked as they passed a kiosk of fragrant pastries. Without waiting for an answer, he paused and bought two, handing her one. As they continued walking, he said, "You never had a chance to answer my question. What is it with Russia and your father? You, too, for that matter."

"Well, it's not an obsession," she said, a trifle defensive, then she gave it another moment's thought and added, "An interest, I suppose . . . no, it's more than that." She took a bite of the sticky pastry. After another pause, she continued, "Russia just gets under your skin. It's hard to explain. A Russian proverb says, 'Russia is not a state, but a world.' That's part of its magic."

"Your father spent several years there, didn't he?"

"Yes, broken up around my mother's tolerance." She thought about her talk with her mother. No need to get into all that with Shanahan. But she now knew why those years in Russia had been so mixed with equal parts of joy and strife—not unlike that enigmatic country itself. "My father first went during the Great War—"

"I've read some of his work from then," Johnny interrupted, with a hint of rare admiration in his tone. "I sometimes forget he was quite a journalist in his own right."

"Yes, I've read it all, too. It helps remind me of the man he was before . . ." Before what? Cameron wasn't quite certain what had happened to the idealistic, passionate man who had written so eloquently about the Russian war effort in the Great War. Whatever it was it seemed too personal to discuss with Johnny just now. But Cameron believed something had happened to Keagan Hayes after that first stint in Russia. It was almost as if he had known of his wife's secret anguish. He couldn't have known, of course, but perhaps her unhappiness apart from all that had touched him more than he let on. In any case, it was then that his idealism first began to get a bit tarnished. Cameron had always suspected it had something to do with her mother and even the arrival of her and her sisters. With a shrug, she went on, "My mother was with him for nearly a year, but she grew ill . . . plain homesickness, probably because he left her alone so much. Anyway, she returned home. He followed soon after, before the end of the war, before the Revolution. He was not happy about that, to say the least. Then I came along. . . ."

"That must have lifted his spirits!" Johnny said with a teasing smirk.

"Made the man absolutely hysterical for his firstborn to be a daughter instead of a son." She rolled her eyes dismissively. "And his joy was further enhanced by the arrival of two more daughters. But I digress—actually, I'm sure he saw us as little more than digressions. He used the time at home to turn himself into a Russian scholar. But by then foreign correspondents were strictly forbidden in the country. It didn't change until 1921 when, after years of war, revolution, and civil war, a terrible famine ravaged the land. Lenin had to seek foreign aid. The U.S. was willing to help with one stipulation: that correspondents be allowed into the country to report on the results of the aid. Lenin had no choice but to agree."

"That's when Hayes returned?"

"No, that's when my youngest sister was born." She smiled, almost as if she enjoyed thinking of her father's dismay at the delay. Yet from her present perspective, for the first time in her life she could almost sympathize with him. She felt a little bad for being responsible for interfering with his dream. "No one has ever said anything, but I've always believed he struck a deal with his father-in-law. If he stuck around until Jackie was old enough to handle the trip, Grandpa Atkins would appoint him as Moscow bureau chief and let him go to Russia with his blessing. It finally happened in the fall of '23, just months before Lenin's death. For the next eight years that's where my father was, except for a couple of dutiful trips home."

"What of the rest of the family?"

"At first my mother was rather enthusiastic about the trip, but gradually a depression began to loom over her. I suppose it had a lot to do with the fact that Dad was hardly ever home again. Mom is extremely shy, and she never could get in with the social scene—you know, with the wives of other journalists and foreign diplomats and such. I loved it. I was six years old and thought I had just fallen into a white fairyland. I was old enough not to be a complete nuisance to my father, and sometimes he'd let me tag along with him to meetings. I had tea with Trotsky before he was exiled. Molotov gave me candy. A couple men who are now hard-bitten generals bounced me on their knees. I had incredible freedom in those days. Too young to be a concern to the secret police but old enough that my parents let me wander about a lot on my own. When I was ten . . ." She paused suddenly and cast an apologetic glance at Johnny. "You didn't want to hear all of that, did you?"

"Are you kidding? In all the time I've known you, I never heard your life story." He grinned. "Please continue. This is very enlighten-ing."

"I don't talk about it much." This was perhaps the first time she truly realized that fact. "It was wonderful and difficult all at once. It was really hard on my mother. She went home a couple of times—luckily she had a father who could afford the travel expenses. Finally, when I was ten, she'd had it. She said my sisters and I needed an Amer-ican education. That was her excuse, anyway. It was better than saying she was leaving my father. But I didn't make it easy on her—" Shana-han made a sound, clearly understanding how that could be so. Smirk-ing, Cameron continued, "I resented being taken from my little fairy world and being shuttled off to boarding school. I got into so much trouble at school that finally my father was summoned back to the country. My 'punishment' was to be taken back to Moscow with him. I was in heaven. I was thirteen by then, and the next two years were among the best in my life. The only thing I regret about them was that I never learned the Russian language. I have no head for languages, but the cutest boy was assigned to me as an interpreter, so I had no desire to learn and risk losing his dreamy attentions. And that's it. When I was fifteen, we returned to the States for good."

Shanahan screwed up his face, bringing his fingers into play as well, and did some quick ciphering. "That would be about '32 when your father took over as publisher."

"My mother and her family prevailed upon Dad to come home. I think another deal was struck. I never before gave it much thought, but I believe my father reconciled with my mother in order to become publisher." If this story was enlightening to Johnny, it was even more so to her. Thinking about it from an adult perspective shed light on so much of it—and she wasn't sure that was a good thing. Now there was also the new aspect of her mother's story. No wonder she seldom spoke of these things. With a sigh, she added, "Good old Dad."

"Ambition makes people do . . . things," Johnny said.

"You know all about that, don't you?"

"We both do."

She nodded. "It's still hard not to resent the man for it. I think that's when he changed once and for all. We had such a good relation-ship in Moscow—maybe that's why I love the place so much. It was the only time in my life that Dad and I had any common ground. There is the newspaper, but—"

"You and your father are in too much competition there for it to be pleasant."

"I wonder why that is?" She gave her head a frustrated toss. "Goodness, what a twisted family I have."

"You ain't alone there."

"So, are you going to tell me your life story, Shanahan? I'm dying to hear."

"I've had enough history for one day. Another time."

The afternoon was wearing on. From the top of a nearby mosque the call to prayer was sounding.

"Well, Johnny, now what?" Cameron said after a long silence.

"You want to go pray or something?" he said in snide reference to the Muslim ritual.

"Hardly. I was just wondering about the irony of our situation. I'm here where you want to stay, and you are going where I want to go."

"A raw deal," he mused.

"I guess we'll just have to make the best of it," she said. "I'm sure I'll be up to my elbows in news before long."

"And I'll be up to my elbows in snow."

"Don't underestimate the Russians. To quote another Russian saying, a poem actually, 'Russia cannot be understood by wit alone. Common measures cannot be applied to her. She has a special character. One must simply believe in Russia.' If you view her with the right attitude, she won't let you down."

"I will keep that in mind. Any other sage wisdom, Miss Hayes?" He smiled with a warmth that made Cameron's skin tingle.

She shook her head as disappointment settled back over her. "Oh, Johnny, I wish I was going with you." And she knew she meant that in more ways than one. She was going to miss him, too. He aggravated her to death, but he was a good friend, if nothing else.

"I am surprised, Hayes, that you just don't go. Why wait for Arnett's permission?"

"I need papers, for one thing."

"Surely you have contacts through your father in the State Department. A couple of well-placed cables ought to produce some results. You had a visa once. It just got lost."

Shanahan's idea was not a new one to her. She'd already given it much thought and had already realized why it wouldn't work. "I can't risk it," she said gloomily. "If Arnett fires me, it could ruin me in the business. My father has already undermined me to several papers. If his rival also lets me go . . . well, it wouldn't look good. I'm stuck here. But I will see if my mother can apply some pressure."

"Your mother? Why her?"

"Oh . . . well . . . she has contacts, too, and my father sure isn't going to help."

"Don't give up hope. In the meantime you still have this little war here to occupy you."

Nodding, she said no more, letting him believe this had less to do with him than with Russia.

19

CAMERON SAW the Pyramids and was duly impressed. But she was more impressed with Charles de Gaulle and the Free French whom she encountered as they began to gather in North Africa for the fight against Hitler. When after three weeks there had been no word of her accreditation to a combat unit, she made the most of her desert sojourn by interviewing dignitaries and diplomats. Apparently it wasn't going to be as easy as Max thought to get her in with a combat unit—and that might just force him to pursue Russia again.

She contrived a trip to the Suez Canal, over which so much of the fighting here was about. That vital waterway appeared narrow and insubstantial, really, for all the stir it was causing. The Germans could easily bomb it and wreak havoc with the war effort, but they wanted it as badly as everyone else, and they wanted it intact.

She sent dutiful dispatches to the *Globe* about her insights regarding this theater of war, while at the same time she continued to nag her boss about Russia. She also wired her mother. Cecilia was just as motivated as Cameron, and though it was impossible to picture her mother putting pressure on anyone, she still wasn't entirely helpless.

Cameron was in the hotel lounge late in the afternoon on June 22 trying to keep cool by rolling her glass of iced tea over her forehead when Don Mayfield of the *Journal* came in.

"That Shanahan is a lucky dog. That's all I can say!" He plopped down on a chair at Cameron's table.

They were the only journalists in the place, the only people for that matter, besides a waiter.

"So what's he done now?" asked Cameron.

Mayfield directed his first comment to the waiter. "Gimme a scotch and soda—or maybe I should have a vodka instead, in honor of Johnny."

"What're you talking about, Mayfield? What's going on?"

"Word just got here, Cameron. Germany has invaded the Soviet Union—"

"What!"

"You ain't surprised, are you? I'm sure the only one surprised is Stalin."

"It's still a shock. And Johnny is there." And she wasn't. To keep her mind off her disappointment, she instead tried to focus on Stalin's error. "Well, Stalin should have known. Goodness, Churchill tried to warn him about the German troop movements in the east."

"But he thought the British were just trying to provoke trouble."

"Just as he misinterpreted Rudolph Hess's little jaunt to Scotland last month." That little comedy of errors brought a smile to Cameron's lips. It was still clouded in mystery and confusion. After Hess had "crash" landed in Scotland and was captured by the British, Hitler had declared Hess, the number three man in the Nazi hierarchy, insane. The British locked him up without saying much. Stalin suspected Hess had gone to make a deal with the British, a separate peace that would then leave Germany free to attack Russia and crush the hated Bolshevism. "This is going to make for an interesting war," Cameron mused, again trying not to think of all she was missing. "Churchill and Stalin distrust each other almost as much as they distrust Hitler. It's going to gall them both to have to be allies."

"A week ago Stalin was still trying to cozy up to the Germans," said Mayfield. "Stalin's TASS communiqué just days ago showed incredible naïveté, a trait I would never otherwise attribute to the man. He acknowledged German troop movements on Soviet borders and continued to insist they were not of a threatening nature."

"My father taught me that the first thing a correspondent in Russia must learn is to read between the lines. It's obvious Stalin was still trying to buy time. He knew Russia would not be ready for war until next year at least. He figured if he could hold the Germans off until August of this year, he'd be free until spring of '42. I'll bet he thought even yesterday he was safe because of the absurdity of attacking at this time of the year. Winter is going to set in by October in Russia." She paused, turning in her seat until she saw the waiter cleaning tables nearby. "Salih, is your radio working yet? I'd like to hear some news, if possible."

"I fix it, Miss Hayes, but reception still not very good." The man left his task and scurried behind the counter to where the radio sat on a shelf on the back wall. He turned a dial, and a buzz of static came from the box of the ancient radio, probably one of the first ever manufactured. Salih twisted and turned the tuner dial, hurrying past some scratchy strains of Glenn Miller, until a fuzzy voice with a British accent could be heard.

"Your BBC . . . broadcast . . . we confirm that at 4:00 A.M. Soviet time, the German army, without provocation, attacked its former ally, the Soviet Union. . . ."

More static followed and Salih could coax no more from the box. He switched off the set. In the meantime more guests had wandered into the lounge, having heard the radio and apparently being thirstier for news than for drink.

"Don't turn it off," a new arrival said.

"No work," Salih said.

"Let me give it a go," offered a British captain as he moved behind the bar and began to fiddle with the radio.

Within a half hour business was brisk, and the lounge buzzed with war talk. Cameron joined in, though her mind was also focused on her plight. She considered again Shanahan's suggestion about going on her own to Russia. Yet she might not have to resort to such desperate measures. Arnett knew her desires and qualifications. He would want to send a reporter to Russia now, and she was in the best position to get there, more cheaply than if he had to send someone from the States. She just had to be patient.

"But, oh, how I hate patience!" she lamented, not even realizing she had murmured the words out loud.

"I'd worry about you talking into your beer, if you had one," Mayfield said.

She was about to respond when the blast of a clear voice from the radio stopped her. It was speaking Russian while a British voice interpreted the speech.

" . . . without any claims being made on the Soviet Union, German troops attacked our country. . . ."

"That's Molotov," said Cameron. His voice hadn't changed since she had heard him during her childhood.

Static consumed the voice for a few moments, and the people in the bar began yelling at the poor captain, who then frantically tried to regain the station.

Finally the voice of the Soviet Commissar of Foreign Affairs came again. "This unheard-of attack on our country is an unparalleled act of perfidy in the history of civilized nations. . . ."

He went on about the Nonaggression Pact and how scrupulously the Soviet Union had adhered to all its terms, thus making the attack the total responsibility of Germany. He also emphasized that the war was not the fault of the German proletariat but rather was entirely due to the "bloodthirsty rulers" of Germany.

His final words, not dulled by the interpreter's monotone voice, made a little chill tingle through Cameron's spine.

"The government calls upon you, men and women citizens of the Soviet Union, to rally even more closely round the glorious Bolshevik Party, around the Soviet government and our great leader, Comrade Stalin. Our cause is good. The enemy will be smashed. Victory will be ours."

"Can they possibly win?" Mayfield asked when the speech had ended and the radio air was filled with the sound of Guy Lombardo. "Stalin's purges in the thirties decimated the army of its officers. I've heard tens of *thousands* of officers were executed or imprisoned."

"They have to win," said Cameron, ignoring the grim realities that were Russia. "I refuse to accept the possibility of a Europe ruled by Adolf Hitler. And make no mistake, if Russia falls, Britain will be next."

"And what of you Yanks now?" asked the captain, turning his attention from the radio. "I imagine there will be an even stronger outcry against U.S. intervention from your isolationists when it will mean becoming allies with Communists."

"Let's see how Churchill responds," said Mayfield. "There isn't anyone more outspoken against Communism than he."

"I'm sure Hitler is counting on the U.S. and Britain leaving Russia to hang out to dry alone. He would never have done such an audacious thing if he believed the democratic nations of the world would ally themselves to Communism," Cameron said.

Churchill did not respond to the attack for a full twenty-four hours, but when he finally spoke out, it was in his usually stirring and eloquent fashion. He promised British support to the Soviet Union. He made it clear that if "Hitler invaded hell," he, Churchill, would go to the House of Commons and say a kind word about Satan. Roosevelt also came out in support of Russia, though with more subtlety because of strong anti-Soviet feeling in America.

It was not until a week later that Stalin finally made a public statement regarding the invasion. No doubt it had taken him that long to clean the egg off his face, Cameron thought wryly. She was in the hotel lounge, again listening to the BBC radio announcer read the text of the speech. Stalin made the expected excuses for Russian unpreparedness; then he defended the Nonaggression Pact, saying it had given the Soviet military time to prepare for war. He called upon the Russian people to give their all to victory, to keep the enemy from taking one fraction of Soviet possessions. He exhorted them to destroy and burn their own land to keep it from the hands of the enemy, leaving the Fascist dogs nothing but scorched earth if necessary. He reiterated much of Molotov's rhetoric, but perhaps the most astounding part of the relatively short speech were his accolades to his new Western allies.

"The historic statement of Mr. Churchill on Britain's help to the Soviet Union and the statement by the United States government on its willingness to help our country can only be met with a feeling of gratitude in the hearts of our people."

Cameron had to remind herself that this was the man who had so ruthlessly forced collectivization upon his people and who had unleashed an unparalleled reign of terror upon his unyielding countrymen with devastating purges. Yet he was an ally now, at least in theory where the U.S. was concerned. Stalin was a good guy against the bad guy Hitler.

Yes, this was going to be interesting indeed. But beyond that Cameron feared it would be brutal. Blood would flow over Europe as it never had before. How could it be otherwise with two such lethal opponents?

At that moment an Arab boy came into the lounge and in a thickly accented voice called, "Meez Camroon Hayes! Meez Camroon Hayes!"

"Yes, here," she answered.

He came up to her and handed her a cable flimsy. She gave him a coin for a tip. As the boy sauntered away Cameron stared at the paper. She was actually afraid to open it. It could be anything. News from home perhaps. She had not had a reply to her cable to her mother and thought it possible her father had forbid her mother from answering. But that possibility was not what had her hands suddenly trembling.

Slowly she opened the sheet.

> CAMERON PROCEED AT ONCE TO USSR STOP TRAVEL PAPERS ARE EN ROUTE AND SHOULD BE IN ORDER UPON ARRIVAL STOP DRAW NECESSARY CASH FROM BANK OF ENGLAND CAIRO STOP REMEMBER OUR BUDGET STOP I APOLOGIZE FOR DELAY STOP MAX

Cameron's immediate response was to whoop, but in the interest of professionalism, she restrained herself. Then all at once, shrugging, she tossed the cable into the air and let out a loud, "Whoopee!"

Salih, the waiter, stared at this brazen female behavior. She only grinned at him, then jumped up from her chair. There were a million things to do.

Beverly Hills, California
June 1941

BLAIR CREPT into the house through the kitchen door. It was three in the morning, and she dared not risk waking her family. With quiet stealth she shut the door, then tiptoed across the kitchen floor. She made it to the front stairs—unfortunately, there were no backstairs to her room. She laid a hand on the banister and set a foot on the first step.

"There you are!" came a deep, harsh voice from behind her.

She cringed to a stop but did not turn. Every night for the last couple of weeks since she had started working at Claude's club, she had been expecting to be assailed by that voice. More than ever before she had dreaded hearing her father's ominous baritone.

"It's late, Dad. I want to go to bed," she replied.

"You turn around and look at me when I speak to you."

Suddenly a light flashed on, glaring at her like a prison searchlight. How she wanted to ignore both the light and her father and keep walking, but she knew that would only make things worse. Oozing rebellion, in her stance, in the set of her features, in the tautness of her voice, she turned and said, "Must you be so belligerent?"

"Don't turn this upon me! I am not the one coming home at three o'clock in the morning."

"It's not the first time I have come home late," she challenged. "I am an adult, you know."

Snorting derisively at her bravado, he retorted, "You have pushed me too far, young lady. I have turned a blind eye to your activities for too long, but this is it. I know what you have been doing, and I will not have it."

"What do you care what I do? You have never shown an interest in my life before—"

"Maybe if you had done anything of value."

She didn't know what to say to that. She was in no mood to confront her father just now, especially over this issue. She had just spent the better part of the evening being ogled and fingered by dozens of leering, drunken men. She was now half drunk herself. She knew better than her father that what she did was of little value. And it galled her now to have to defend her life to him, but she braced herself to do just that. Never would she admit to him, or anyone, that she had sunk so low.

When she did not respond, Keagan added, "No daughter of mine is going to flaunt herself in front of a bunch of men, do you hear? I thought you had debased yourself with your so-called acting career, but *this*"—he spit out the final word as if speaking of true evil—"is far beneath even that. Working in a nightclub, for heaven's sake! And not even a respectable one but some seedy dive on the docks."

"It's not on the docks," she shot back. But, indeed, it was very close to them. And it was seedy, and it was a dive.

Poor Claude Fleischer was a sweet, charming fellow but a consummate liar. Oh, he probably hadn't believed he was really lying. He loved his little nightclub. What he had failed to tell Blair was that he had lost his theatrical agency through some bad investments and had been fortunate to have enough money left to buy into the club with another man Blair had not met. She had been foolish enough to take him at his word and sign a contract without seeing the place or meeting the partner. The irony was, she still liked Claude. She supposed she felt as if she deserved him and his disreputable club.

None of this, however, would she ever mention to her father.

"I don't care where it is," Keagan yelled. "You are quitting immediately."

"I am doing no such thing." How she wanted to quit! But where would she go? Movie offers certainly were not pouring in. Apparently Banister had spread it around that she was not a cooperative player. She had nothing now except dependence upon her father. But if she was clear about nothing else, she was certain she did not want that any longer. She'd always hated being under his thumb, feeling that every morsel she ate, every thread she wore had a price beyond what she had actually paid for it. Cameron had finally won her freedom;

perhaps there was a chance for Blair to do the same.

"What!" He was actually shocked by her defiance. She had been defying him for years. Why now should it affect him?

"I like my job," she lied. "I am very good at it, and I won't quit. I have a promising career ahead of me."

"I heard you were singing, but I doubt that is all you are doing," he sneered.

"Why, you—!"

"You'd better watch what you say. I am still your father!"

Suddenly she knew why he had been so shocked at her defiance. This was it—the so-called moment of truth that had been building up for years. This truly was Keagan's last straw—and it was hers, as well. But as this realization struck her with varying degrees of dread and exhilaration, a new voice caught her attention.

"Keagan. . . ? Blair. . . ? What's all this yelling about?"

It was Blair's mother. She was standing at the top of the stairs in her dressing gown. How long had she been listening to the heated exchange? Her voice was thin and trembly. She, too, must sense what was coming.

"Go back to bed, Cecilia," Keagan ordered. "I will take care of this."

"Of what?" Cecilia gripped the banister as if she might be blown over by the slightest breeze. Perhaps her frail appearance came only from the lateness of the hour and the fact that her usually neatly pinned up hair was trailing in graying wisps about her pale face.

"Daddy doesn't approve of my new job," Blair answered, still defiant, despite the fact that her heart clenched at the sight of Cecilia. A break with Keagan would also mean a break with Blair's mother, and perhaps with Jackie, too. They never seemed as important to her as they did now when faced with their loss.

"Surely there must be something else for you to do, Blair!" entreated Cecilia.

"Perhaps something that would make you both happier?" Blair retorted.

But Cecilia missed the sarcasm in Blair's tone, and she replied with pathetic hopefulness, "Yes!"

"And what about my happiness?"

"Are you happy?" And somehow Cecilia made the question seem both guileless and incisive.

Keagan answered, "Quit this sentimental drivel. I don't give a rat's sorry behind who is *happy*." He slurred the final word with disdain. "My daughter is not going to flaunt herself before drunken men in a bar—and that is final!"

"It is not final to me," Blair retorted.

"If you live under my roof, you will do what I say. You quit that job, or you get out!"

There, it was said, the inevitable ultimatum. Blair had always known it would come sometime. She wasn't surprised, yet the words made her stomach twist. She hated living under her father's roof, yet being on her own scared her to death. The first thing she thought of was her wardrobe. Yes, she was *that* shallow. But her clothes meant something to her, the ones she already owned and the latest designs she desired. Would she be able to keep her things if she left? After all, it was mostly bought with Keagan's money. She saw how many of her struggling actress friends lived. Hand to mouth, barely a roof over their heads. How could she live like that?

But the ultimatum before her was unyielding, and Keagan well knew it. He wanted her out, she was certain, and he had finally found the means. She was a thorn in his flesh, an embarrassment to him. He would be well rid of her.

"Keagan, don't!" Cecilia begged.

"Stay out of this," Keagan ordered.

Blair sensed her mother's emotional retreat immediately after Keagan's order. Though she remained standing there at the top of the stairs, she said no more.

"That's okay," said Blair. "I should have left long ago. You found a way of getting rid of Cameron, and now it's my turn." Her tone was steady, belying the wrenching of her insides. And her step was steady as she spun around, brushed past her father, and headed toward the door.

Vaguely she thought she heard a groan from her mother. Keagan was as silent as a rock.

Yet even as she opened the front door, she wondered how she would be able to sneak back in and get her clothes and things. She was going to have no other regrets. This was the inevitable. It should have happened long ago.

———

Jackie found her mother the next morning in the dayroom seated on a window seat, staring out the glass at the gloomy morning with its steady spring drizzle.

"What happened last night, Mom?" she asked as she sat in the Chippendale chair adjacent to the window seat.

Jackie had awakened in the wee hours of the morning to the sounds of discord. She lay listening for some time, thinking it was just her parents arguing, but then she realized the female voice wasn't her mother's—she should have known that in the first place, for most of Keagan and Cecilia's arguments were one-sided, with Keagan ranting and raving while Cecilia squeaked like a mouse or wept silently.

By the time Jackie figured out that the female voice was Blair's, the yelling had ceased. Such confrontations between Blair and Keagan were not unusual, and Jackie had learned to maintain her distance. Too often when she would try to intervene, she only ended up being the one under attack, as had happened during the row with Cameron.

This morning when Cecilia turned dark-ringed, reddened eyes toward her, Jackie was sure what had happened during the night was more than the usual row.

"Blair has left," Cecilia said, her voice thin and strained.

"What do you mean?"

"Well, actually, I'm not sure if she left or if your father kicked her out. But either way, she is gone."

The only surprise in this news was that it had taken Blair so long to leave, and that it had, conversely, taken Keagan so long to kick her out. Nevertheless, it did take Jackie aback that it had finally happened.

"Where did she go?" was all Jackie could think to ask.

"I don't know. It was three in the morning. Where would she go at such an hour? I have been worried sick."

"Blair can take care of herself."

Cecilia shook her head with more clarity in her bearing than usual. "She pretends she can, just as she pretends life is a moving picture. But she is a helpless child, really." Cecilia blinked, and Jackie saw fresh tears form in her mother's eyes. "Poor thing, she is too much like me. . . . Well, at least she stood up to her father, which is more than I did. I still can't believe he let her go like that in the middle of the night. I can't believe I let it happen. I should have said something—"

"Oh, Mom, you know they are both stubborn mules." Jackie moved onto the window seat close to her mother and took hold of her hands. "Sometimes people just have to be allowed to live out their own destinies."

"How did you get to be so wise?" Cecilia managed a small smile.

"I'm taking Psychology 101 this semester." She smiled in response and gave her mother's hands a gentle squeeze.

"It is pretty obvious Cameron takes after your father and Blair takes after me. But I have never quite figured how you fit in, Jacqueline. Maybe you have managed to inherit the best traits from us both."

"I won't argue with that." Jackie shrugged off her discomfort with the praise. "Maybe I have just gotten a good dose of common sense."

"Perhaps it is because you have let God into your life and have allowed yourself to learn His wisdom." Cecilia sighed. "I'm a Christian, too, but for some reason it hasn't taken as well with me."

"Maybe," Jackie said, "it's because you have been praying more for me than you have for yourself." She smiled wryly. "Who knows why God works the way He does?"

Cecilia glanced back out the rain-spattered window. "I'll always wonder why Blair and Cameron have rebelled against God. I know He could help them, especially Blair. I fear so much for her because of her wild ways. I am afraid she will come to physical harm, but I also worry about her heart and her soul. I pray for her, but there is so little else I can do."

"Yes," Jackie agreed. "She practically jumps down your throat if you even hint at something as simple as inviting her to church."

"I suppose you are right. She must find her own way, and we must keep on praying it will lead to God."

"Mom, I've always believed that because you taught us all about God at a young age, faith will come back to Blair and Cameron."

"They have had other influences, though."

Cecilia did not need to say any more. They both knew she referred to Keagan. She may have tried to teach her children about God, but Keagan sneered at her faith, though to the public he put on a fine front of being an upstanding, churchgoing man. But he often hinted that religion was a crutch for the weak, and he had little respect for the overzealous. A little faith, he would say, was certainly not a bad thing, but beware of fanatics.

"Well, I'm going to keep praying," Jackie said with the hope bred of youth.

"It's all we can do," Cecilia sighed, with the resignation spawned by age.

"Maybe I should try to find Blair," Jackie said.

"Before your father left for the office this morning, he told me I should not go after her—as if I knew how to! He said she was not to be let into the house unless she was repentant and had quit that job."

"Did he say *I* shouldn't look for her?"

Cecilia's lips twisted suddenly in a conspiratorial smile. "No, your name never was mentioned."

"Did he say I shouldn't pack her a bag?"

"He said nothing about her belongings." Cecilia's features and the tone of her voice brightened. "Do you have any idea where to find her?"

"I'll check a couple of hotels I know she likes."

Cecilia jumped up. "Wait here a minute." She then hurried from the room, returning a few minutes later. She pressed something into Jackie's hand—a small wad of bills, at least one twenty visible. "It's all the cash I have on hand. It should help her a bit."

Jackie pocketed the money and started to rise, but her mother laid a restraining hand gently on her shoulder.

"Wait, dear." She slid back onto the window seat. "You and I haven't prayed together for a long time. Would you like to now?"

"Oh yes, I would, Mother!" Tears suddenly sprang to Jackie's eyes as she flung her arms around her mother. After the embrace, they took hands and prayed for Blair.

BLAIR'S FINGERS ran lightly over the piano keys as she ended "If I Didn't Care" with a flourish. Scattered applause from the audience indicated at least a few had been listening. She lifted her eyes from the keyboard and through swirls of cigarette smoke saw the Saturday night crowd at the Treasure Cove was lively if not attentive.

She was sliding from the piano bench, ready to take a break, when Claude Fleischer waddled toward her.

"Very nice number," he said in that ingratiating way of his, which Blair had come to identify as his precursor to asking for a favor.

"Daddy's money on piano lessons was well spent," Blair said dryly. And if she derived any pleasure at all from her present circumstances, it was from ironies such as that.

"Come, I want you to meet someone."

"Can't I get a drink first? I am absolutely parched."

"I'll have a waiter bring your usual over. But you must meet Stan. He just arrived."

"Stan?"

"My partner, Stan Welton."

Claude nudged Blair toward one of the best tables in the house. There were several men seated around it and a couple of women. The males looked like businessmen. They were all wearing suits and appeared a better caliber than the Cove's regular working-class clientele, but the suits were obviously cheap. And the women looked little better.

Claude made introductions, and Blair promptly forgot all the names except for Stan Welton. He was a memorable sort with his brawny build and edgy swagger. He was in his midthirties, with light brown hair, a moustache, and an old scar over his right eyebrow. A cigarette dangled between his teeth when he grinned at Blair—the kind of grin she received from most men that clearly said they knew what to do with a beautiful doll like her. There was an odd mixture of sleaze and charm mingled in his look, but Blair had seen it so often she barely noticed as she sat in a vacant chair next to Stan. He immediately put his arm around her.

"Well, Claude, old boy," Stan said, "you didn't exaggerate for once. This is one gorgeous dame!" He turned to Blair. "What're you doing in a dump like this?"

"Isn't it half your dump, Mr. Welton?" she replied wryly.

"Call me Stan, doll. And, yes, it is mine, but even I know the difference between the Treasure Cove and the Coconut Grove."

"We all have to start someplace, don't we?"

He laughed loudly and was so close that Blair could smell the cheap tobacco and cheaper whiskey on his breath. He cozied up even closer, and Blair was relieved when her martini arrived. After a few of those she didn't mind and even began to consider him a handsome, desirable man.

She was quite woozy when she rose to perform her final set for the night. She missed a couple of notes on the piano, and her voice went flat a time or two, but since everyone in the club was as drunk as she, no one noticed.

Apparently Stan had been away on business in New York for a couple of months. Blair never found out just what other business he had, but unlike her older sister, she was not the curious type. Especially where men were concerned, she felt the less she knew the better. Anyway, Stan was now in L.A. to stay awhile and was ready to get involved in the club. Blair saw a lot of Stan over the next couple of weeks. She sat at his table at the club during her breaks. When the Cove closed for the evening, they found private parties to attend, often lasting all night.

Stan was okay, fun, good-looking. He didn't always treat her like a lady, but then again, according to her father, she was no lady, so she reasoned she deserved Stan's demeaning looks. She even thought she probably deserved the slap he gave her because she had made him late for a business appointment and hadn't displayed proper regret for her actions. It helped that she felt no romantic inclinations toward him and was almost certain he felt none toward her. The night he spent with her in her hotel room was hardly romantic, either. She had been so drunk, she hardly knew what she was doing. She had put him off in this area once too often, and he had become quite insistent. She thought he might hit her again. That particular night she was too befuddled to offer her usual resistance. What did it matter anyway? Who was she saving herself for? Prince Charming? That was a laugh. Her virginity was just as worthless as she, so why bother?

Maybe in the past some part of her had felt she owed it to her family to wait till marriage, but any duty there had been shattered the night her father kicked her out of the house and her mother stood by and let it happen. Sure, Jackie had found her the next day and given her a couple of suitcases of her belongings and some money from their mother, along with a pep talk about how things looked bad now, but they could only get better. Poor naïve Jackie!

Nevertheless, Blair realized she did not owe anyone anything. And there was indeed a small part that relished doing something she knew would outrage her parents. What she did with Stan that night was pure rebellion. Someone like Jackie, with her semester of psychology, might call it self-destructive, but Blair really did not care anymore. She just didn't care.

But when she woke in the morning and could, even with a hangover splitting her head, remember what she had done, her insides twisted with shame. What made it worse was that Stan was gone and had left a note by the bed: "It was great, doll. See you around. Stan."

With the note was a hundred-dollar bill. Staring at that demeaning gesture, all she could think was that her father had been right again.

When she got to the club that night, Claude told her Stan had gone out of town again.

"Said he'd be gone indefinitely," Claude told her.

The swine! Blair inwardly seethed. She should have known he had only been building up to a conquest all along. Sure, she hadn't felt anything romantic toward him, either, but still, to take her and then dump her so unceremoniously like that. And then to further degrade her by leaving the money as if she was some common trollop!

She was furious, but a barely discernable part of her knew she deserved to be treated no better.

Her act that night was filled with "torch" songs. Her breaks were filled with martinis. When the club closed, she left with a stranger, a man dressed in an expensive suit, which was, she thought, recommendation enough for him. She never got around to learning his name, or if she did, it quickly fled her fuzzy mind. He took her to a party at a friend's home in the Hollywood Hills. A Hollywood party. She hadn't been to one since the problem with Banister. Not by choice but because no invitations had come her way. She guessed the incident with Banister had put her on some kind of blacklist.

At any rate, she knew a few people at the party. They were friendly enough. Maybe she could get back in with her old crowd. Maybe she could make another picture. Did she want to? Anything would be better than Claude's dive. And now she wouldn't think twice about jumping on the casting couch. Maybe she'd make it this time.

But that was her last coherent thought that night. Vaguely she remembered stumbling down the steps of the outside porch. The music inside the elegant mansion was loud, as was the laughter and noise of the other guests. She and the man in the nice suit were leaving to go to his hotel. She leaned heavily against him, her arms around him for more than mere affection. Her legs were suddenly rubbery. Must be the chill night air.

"Are you feeling okay?" The man's voice came as if out of a fog.

"Wif my hands," she slurred, then giggled.

"Steady, then. The boy is bringing my car now."

"All righty . . ." she chirruped.

As they waited, four people approached, obviously latecomers to the party. One of the men was in uniform. He was tall with dark hair. His face was blurry to Blair, but she knew he was handsome, as well.

"Gary . . . what're you doin' here?" she asked. "Lieutenant Gary . . . church bazaars and Hollywood parties . . . humm. . . ."

The group paused. The soldier said, "I am a lieutenant, but my name isn't Gary."

"Oh . . . course you're not Gary . . . he only goes to church. . . ." Giggling, she waved the group on.

A black blur pulled up just then. Between the man—her date?—and the valet, they managed to get her into the car. The man—what was his name?—came around to the driver's side, got in, shifted into gear, and drove away. Blair fell against his shoulder and knew no more.

Her date could not rouse her when he reached his hotel. He

couldn't help panicking a bit. He was, after all, a married man and it would cause quite a scandal should he be exposed with an unconscious woman in his car—especially this woman whom he had learned at the party was the daughter of the *Journal*'s publisher. The minute he heard that, he should have walked away, but she was so beautiful, and he'd had too much to drink and wasn't exactly thinking straight. He had hoped merely to entertain her discreetly for an hour or two in a hotel room, then help her to leave just as discreetly.

A passed-out woman was hardly discreet!

He tried to wake her several times, but she only responded with incoherent grunts. He grabbed her handbag. If he could learn where she lived, perhaps he could take her there. Her purse contained lipstick, a compact, a few dollars, keys—yes, the keys had a tag that said they were from the Carlisle. A nice hotel, reinforcing the truth of who she was.

He drove to the Carlisle. On the way, after sobering up a bit, he thought about what he should do. He could not call her parents, but he knew she had a couple of sisters. He'd read about them in the paper a few months ago when there had been a birthday party for the old man. What were their names? Unusual names . . . boys' names, he thought. He parked his sedan just around the corner from the Carlisle in case someone there might recognize him. For that same reason, he could not walk her up to her room.

Fleetingly he considered just pushing her out of his car and letting her be found by a passerby—preferably after he was long gone! Might teach the little piece of baggage a lesson for behaving so wantonly. But he was too much of a gentleman to do such a thing. Besides, if anything happened to her and it got out that he had been with her last . . . well, he couldn't let that happen.

He climbed from his vehicle, walked to a nearby phone booth, found the number in the directory, then paused. What would he do if the sister didn't answer and wasn't home? It was, after all, six in the morning. He'd hang up and think of something else. He lifted the receiver from the hook. Could the sister be trusted? He must take that chance. He dialed the number.

"Hello, Hayes residence. How may I help you?" The voice of a servant, no doubt.

"May I speak with Miss Jacqueline Hayes, please?"

"I am sorry, sir, Miss Hayes has not awakened yet this morning."

"It is quite important that I speak with her."

"If it is an emergency, I can get her father—"

"No!" he exclaimed, panic growing again. "I mean, it isn't an emergency. I'm an old friend from out of town, and I am sure she would want you to wake her to let her know I'm here." He knew he was lying miserably. He waited for the servant to hang up.

"One moment," he was shocked to hear the servant reply.

Then he half expected to hear the male voice of Mr. Hayes over the wire and was shocked again to hear a female voice.

"Hello. This is Jackie. Who is this?"

"I am a friend of your sister Blair—"

"Oh, I thought you wanted me."

"I do! This is complicated. Your sister is in a bit of a predicament. Nothing serious, mind you, but . . . she could use a hand is all. Could you come to the Carlisle? And meet us around the corner on Twenty-seventh Street. We'll be in a black Oldsmobile. But Blair would appreciate it if you told no one what you are doing. She is slightly embarrassed, you see."

"I don't know . . . this is all very strange."

"You have every reason to think me a crackpot, but I assure you, I mean well. And your sister does need you."

There was a long pause; then the girl said, "It should take me fifteen or twenty minutes to get there."

JACKIE STARED at her coffee. She had hoped that coming to the school cafeteria when it was nearly empty before the lunch rush would give her a chance to think. But now she wasn't sure she wanted to think after all. Her thoughts were full of her sister Blair—agonizingly full.

How she had hated to leave her that morning, and had it not been that today was Jackie's last final exam and she could not miss it, she would have stayed with her sister in her hotel room. However, Blair had still been asleep when Jackie left, so maybe she wouldn't be missed. Jackie had finished her exam a few minutes ago and decided to have a cup of coffee and think about how she would respond to Blair when she saw her. She supposed she was also stalling, just a little afraid of dealing with her sister's obvious problems.

Blair had been so drunk last night when Jackie had come to get her from her very panicked date that talk had been out of the question. In fact, Blair had passed out the moment Jackie had gotten her to her bed in the hotel. Jackie knew her sister drank to excess, though she had never seen her that inebriated before. There was no telling the cause, but it was clear Blair's life was going steadily downhill. Something had to be done. But what? Jackie knew exactly what her sister needed— faith in Christ. But Blair was completely closed to that.

And there lay Jackie's dilemma. How could she face Blair now when what she had to offer her was something that would likely cause a rift between them?

"Excuse me." A voice came as if out of a dream. "Can you pass the salt, please?"

She glanced up and remembered she was in the cafeteria, though for a few moments she had felt as if she were on an island all alone. It hadn't been a good feeling, and she was rather relieved for the interruption.

"Yes . . . here you go." She handed the salt and pepper shakers to the only other person at her table. In fact he was nearly the only other person in the entire place.

"Thank you." He took the salt and began sprinkling quite a bit on his dish of food.

Jackie stared because the plate was piled full of mashed potatoes, roast beef, macaroni and cheese, rice dripping with gravy, and as the only vegetable in sight, a large mound of creamed corn in a side dish. He began to dig into the food, then seeming to notice her scrutiny, he stopped and looked up with a quizzical smile.

"Oh, my goodness!" she said flustered and embarrassed at her rudeness. "I am so sorry. I didn't mean to stare."

"Is it the amount of food or the balanced selection?"

She laughed, for he had spoken with an amused wryness. "I haven't seen so much starch since the last time my mother did the laundry."

He chuckled. "So it's both. Well, I have just finished my finals, and after studying day and night with little time to eat, I'm starved. That explains the amount. The other . . . well, I hate vegetables. If it's green, forget it, can't stand it."

"How'd you get to be so big and strong, then?" She was enjoying the diversion of the banter and wanted to keep it going.

"My parents still can't figure that out. Certainly can't be in the genes, can it?"

Her cheeks tinged a little pink at that and was perturbed at herself for the reaction. The young man with the plateful of food was Oriental, but defying the stereotypes, he was tall—even though seated, she could tell he must be nearly six feet. He also appeared well built under his tweed trousers and wool V-neck sweater. But she blushed again just thinking of that.

"I've embarrassed you," he said, all his previous wry humor now replaced with earnestness. "I am sorry."

"No need for you to be sorry. Don't know what is wrong with me."

"It's me who should be embarrassed," he said.

"There's no reason—"

"Yes, there is. You see, I didn't really need the salt. Well, I did need salt, but I could have sat at another table." Pausing, he took a breath, then glanced around at all the vacant tables. "We're in the same English lit class, but you probably don't remember me."

"Of course I do! You are the only—" She had been about to note that he was the only Oriental boy in the class, but she hated for him to think she noticed such things.

"The only Japanese boy." He smiled as he finished for her. "You don't have to tell me that! Anyway, I've wanted to meet you all semester, but I'm not great at meeting new people, and you always were with someone or the other."

She held out her hand. "I'm Jackie Hayes."

"I know." He took her hand and gave it a firm shake. "I'm Sam Okuda."

"Nice to meet you."

"And so much easier now. When I saw you sitting here all alone, I decided to quit being foolish. I have really appreciated the things you've said in class, and I've wanted to tell you that all semester. You've never settled for the pat answers and always tried to look into the heart of authors and their characters. You had a godly perspective that even the professor lacked."

"He really did, didn't he?" Jackie replied. "Even in *A Tale of Two Cities* when Lucie's character is so clearly driven by faith, Professor Hawkins tried to interpret it differently."

"And failing that, he just denigrated her faith."

"It was so frustrating. I love Dickens, but Hawkins nearly ruined it for me."

"*A Tale of Two Cities* is now my favorite book. I had never read it before, but thanks to the class and my desire to see for myself just what Dickens was trying to say, I read it several times this semester." He smiled a bit sheepishly. "Forgive me for going on so. I know it was rude of me to break in on your solitude."

"If I'd really wanted solitude I would have gone to the woods or something." She glanced at his untouched food. "I would love to talk, but your food will get cold."

"Okay, but while I eat, tell me how you think you did on the final. What about those essay questions? I'm sure Hawkins will hate my answers."

Jackie spent the next few minutes sharing what she remembered of her answers as the pile on Sam's plate grew smaller. Between mouthfuls he interjected his own insights on the test and on English literature in general. When he finished eating, they continued to talk.

"Is English your major?" Jackie asked.

"Yes, it is. I want to be a writer—very much against my parents' wishes."

"What do they want you to be?"

"Something practical. They definitely don't wish me to follow in my father's profession of farming, so they have encouraged college. But they hoped I would make lots of money. Becoming a doctor would make them absolutely ecstatic. They don't know any rich writers."

"What do you want to write?"

"Fiction. The Great American Novel, you know." His lips twitched into a shy smile. "In my free time this semester, I wrote a Japanese-American version of *A Tale of Two Cities*. It is awful, but it was fun to write."

"Were you born in Japan, Sam?"

"No, I am in fact the first bona fide Okuda American citizen. That's why they gave me an American Christian name—well, it isn't technically Christian to my parents, who are Buddhists. But I'm a Christian, if you hadn't already guessed, though I don't know why you should have." He seemed to become flustered again and had a long drink of his lemonade.

"I thought so from your comments. How'd you become a Christian? I mean, with Buddhist parents?"

"My poor parents . . . I have bucked their traditions in so many ways. But it is they who wanted me Americanized, though I'm not sure they really understood what that meant until it was too late. For instance, they let me attend the Protestant church with one of my father's white friends. Who could have known it would change my life?" Pausing briefly, he added, "Can I get you a fresh cup of coffee? I'd like some of that chocolate cake I saw over there."

"Sure."

Sam took her cup and went to the food counter. Jackie thought of her sister and felt a twinge of guilt for not hurrying back to the hotel. But she was enjoying her conversation with Sam. She had liked him immediately. He had a frankness about him, oddly mingled with shyness, that made a nice mix. He, of course, wasn't the only Oriental student on campus, though there were few enough, but Jackie had not ever really spoken to any. She suddenly realized she had no friends of other races. She decided that didn't say much for her.

Returning to the table, he said, "I forgot to ask how you take your coffee."

"Black is fine."

He sat back in his seat. "Black, really? That seems such . . . I don't know such . . . a mature habit."

"I am mature, don't you know?" she said lightly. "I've been drinking black coffee for years. My father taught me. He couldn't abide his daughters putting in sugar or cream like sissy girls. My middle sister dumps in cream and sugar now just to spite him. But I've grown to like it black."

"But you are a girl," he said, reasonably enough.

"Much to my father's dismay."

"Are you sure he isn't Oriental? You know, we also exalt sons. Women are little better than slaves. I hope I am not like that with my children. I'll love boys and girls equally."

"Sometimes I wonder if it's possible to ever please one's parents." Jackie's thoughts drifted once more to her sister, and a sadness crept over her.

"I can see this is a depressing conversation. Want to talk about something else?"

Jackie sighed. "Well, I really should be going—"

At that moment her name was called out from the door of the cafeteria.

"Jackie! There you are."

It was Jeffrey Meade, and suddenly she remembered they had made plans for after their last final.

"I thought we were supposed to meet at the psych building," he said, striding up to the table. He made no attempt to hide his ire at being stood up.

"Oh, Jeffrey, I completely forgot."

"We are still going to the country club, aren't we?" His gaze flickered briefly toward Sam, but making no acknowledgment of him, he added, "Well, are we?"

"Jeffrey, I can't." Jackie rose from her chair, gathering up her purse and books. "My sister's ill, and I have to see about her."

"Your sister, eh?"

"Yes. Blair. I had to leave her to take my final, but she really needs me now." Funny how she hadn't been in such a hurry to get back to

Blair when she had been talking to Sam. But Jeffrey was another matter. He was getting too possessive, too overbearing. Goodness! He was starting to behave an awful lot like her father!

"I don't like it when we make plans and you break them at the last minute like this."

"It couldn't be helped. I'll walk out with you." She turned to Sam. "It was nice meeting you, Sam. Maybe we can—"

"Come on, Jackie!" urged Jeffrey impatiently. "I at least would like to make my tee time at the club."

"I'll see you later, Jackie," Sam said, but he didn't seem convinced of that.

With a wan smile Jackie hurried away. As she and Jeffrey exited he said, "Who was that Jap you were talking to?"

"Jeffrey, really!"

"Well, it doesn't look good, a white girl and a Jap boy—"

"That's ridiculous!" Jackie said firmly and dismissively. "I'm going to my car. Have fun at the club." Her final statement was made in a tone indicating she hoped for just the opposite.

By the time she reached her car, she had decided to break it off once and for all with Jeffrey. Why had she ever encouraged his attentions in the first place? Oh, she knew very well why. He was from the right family, and her parents heartily approved. In fact, her father had introduced them while they had dined at the country club. It rather irked her that she would go to such lengths to please that man. Of course, she believed a good girl should be obedient to her parents—that's what the Bible taught. But she was certain God would not expect any girl to give herself to an ogre like Jeffrey just to please her father.

Sam Okuda had nothing to do with her decision. Well, in a way he did because she had been furious over the way Jeffrey had spoken of Sam. But that was all. However, she made another decision. She wanted to be friends with Sam. It would be good for her to become more diverse in her acquaintances.

23

BLAIR'S HEAD throbbed as it had never throbbed before. The light coming in through the bedroom window nearly blinded her. Groaning, she rolled over and buried her face back in the pillow. But her urge to visit the bathroom overcame her desire to stay huddled in her bed.

Finally she inched from the bed and made her way to the bathroom. That task done, she had a bit more energy, at least enough to hobble to the telephone and call room service.

"Pot of coffee," she mumbled into the receiver. "No food!"

As she waited for room service, she tried to think about how she'd gotten this terrible hangover. That's when she realized she could not remember a thing about the previous night. Not a single thing!

The waiter arrived with an elegant cart full of coffee service, china, and an assortment of sweet rolls. Blair rolled her eyes, her stomach nearly turning just at the sight of the food.

Fumbling in her pocketbook, she found a tip, paid the boy, and quickly dismissed him. She then poured a cup of the rich brew—strong and black. That would clear her mind.

But it didn't. Neither did a second cup. She thought of the old remedy "the hair of the dog that bit you." She went to the small wet bar and was searching for some gin when the door of the room opened.

"Hi, Blair. You're awake!" Jackie said.

"What're you doing here? Where'd you get a key?"

"Nice to see you, too. I'm fine, thank you!" Jackie returned sarcastically. "But after putting you to bed last night, or rather this morning, I got a spare key from the desk clerk in case you were still asleep when I came back."

"You put me to bed?" She turned from the liquor cabinet but not before Jackie had a good look at what she had been about to do. She cringed inwardly at the hint of disapproval on her sister's face.

"Didn't you get enough last night, Blair?" Jackie asked, her tone full of disappointment.

"Don't start—"

"I'm sorry," Jackie said rather contritely for someone who had really done nothing wrong.

That realization brought Blair up short. She was the one who had gotten so inebriated last night that apparently she had to be rescued by her sister, put to bed, and on top of that was now seeking more of the same. What was wrong with her? What kind of woman was she? A drunk? Is that what she had become?

She turned away from the cabinet and sank down onto the sofa, dropping her head in her hands dejectedly. "I don't remember anything that happened last night," she mumbled through her fingers. "I don't remember who I was with. I don't remember you." Tears stung her eyes.

Jackie sat on the sofa beside her and put an arm around her trembling shoulders. "There, there . . ."

Sobbing, Blair went on, "You were right all along. I-I'm a terrible person—"

"I never thought that, Blair."

"But it's true! I'm a wanton woman . . . I didn't want to be. I wanted . . . oh, I don't know what I wanted! But there is no going back now. I'm ruined." She started to hiccough and could not continue.

Jackie gently rubbed her shoulder, cooing softly. Blair expected no vindication from her. She didn't deserve any. Where she was at this moment was entirely her own fault. Well, maybe not all her fault. Surely part of the blame belonged to Fred Banister and Darla Brooks and some to Claude Fleischer, too, and that cad Stan Welton. Her father, as well. They had all dealt her some tough blows. All she had wanted was to be an actress or a singer, something she could be proud of. But they had ripped the carpet of her dreams out from under her.

But even if it was all their fault, it didn't change the fact that she was indeed ruined. She couldn't remember last night, but it was a sure bet she hadn't been alone. No doubt all her friends had seen her last night so blinding drunk she did not remember passing out and being taken home by her sister. How had Jackie found out about it anyway?

No matter, even Jackie didn't know about her night with Stan. But others no doubt knew. Her parents would disown her now for certain.

Blair lifted plaintive eyes to her sister, hoping that somehow wise-beyond-her-years Jackie would make it all better.

"What do I do now, Jackie?"

"Do you really want to hear my solution?"

"Yes." Blair knew what Jackie was about to say, and . . . well, why not? She had completely loused up everything on her own. Maybe it was time she listened to Jackie.

"Come to church with me, Blair."

With a final sniff, Blair said simply, "Okay."

Church was boring. Blair really and truly was trying to give it a chance, but goodness! She disliked the sermons most, of course. In fact, if they would just get rid of the sermons, it might not be half bad. She did kind of like the singing. But they usually only sang two or three hymns, and they were often slow and dry. Next to the sermons, she hated the visiting after the service. She felt so horribly out of place. Everyone was nice, but she knew they'd be scandalized if they knew about the things she had done.

After three Sundays she was ready to give up her remote hope that church was the answer to her problems. That third Sunday she and Jackie went to lunch after the service, and she broached the subject.

Jackie seemed to understand and even admitted that the sermons weren't always her favorite part. She suggested Blair come to Sunday school, which, she said would allow for more participation. Up until then, since Jackie taught a Sunday school class of five-year-olds, Blair had come to the church service on her own. The idea of yet another hour of "school" did not sound appealing.

"Sunday school is for kids." Blair thought that was a great excuse.

"There are a couple of adult classes."

"I always hated school."

They fell silent for a few moments, then Jackie added with her un-daunted enthusiasm, "I've got the perfect thing! This Friday we are having our July Fourth Sunday school picnic. No sermons, just fun. Come with me. You can help me with my class. How about it?"

A Sunday school picnic. Now, that ought to make me feel right at home, Blair thought with an inward groan. Her mother had made her go to her share of such picnics when she was too young to rebel. Even then, Blair had felt out of place with all the silly games—potato-sack races, pie-eating contests—and food covered with bits of grass and flies. Oh, what fun! But if Blair said no now to her sister, Jackie would know she was making excuses to get out of this church thing altogether. Maybe she was.

But Jackie was looking at her so hopefully. And she had helped Blair out so much already—and never said a word to their parents. Blair supposed she owed it to Jackie to try this. But if it didn't work, she would feel free to forget further involvement in the church. She would have tried at least. And after her three-week hiatus from parties and alcohol, she felt certain she was cured of that foolishness.

When Friday came, Blair chose a cool beach outfit, for the picnic would be at the beach. A red cotton-knit short-sleeved shirt, a full skirt of a lightweight cotton with a red-and-blue floral pattern. She wore a wide-brimmed hat of the same fabric as the skirt and canvas sandals on her feet. She looked quite chic. She opted not to wear or bring a bathing costume because it was a church gathering and she was going to feel out of place as it was, even though Jackie was going to wear a bathing suit, since she would be swimming with the children.

The day was sunny and hot, and Blair was glad for her hat to protect her pale skin from the sun's rays. There were about a hundred people in attendance. The Presbyterian church where Jackie attended had a roll on Sundays of about three hundred. It was not the same Beverly Hills church where her mother went, but it was rather an unpretentious little church in Pasadena. Truth be told, Blair probably would have felt more comfortable in the huge Beverly Hills Presbyterian Church, where many members arrived in limousines and wore designer clothes.

But here she was, so she determined to make the best of it. She refused, though, to have anything to do with potato sacks and pies.

She was having a conversation with a couple of matronly ladies who had offered Blair a corner of their blanket to sit on. They were bragging about their grandchildren, who were just then participating in a relay race on the sandy beach. The children were rather adorable, but hardly the sublime creatures their grandmothers made them out to be. Growing bored, Blair looked around to see if there was another more interesting group she could join.

She couldn't believe her eyes at first and even rubbed them to assure it wasn't an apparition crossing the sand. She hadn't seen him since February and then only that one day. But the sight of him still stirred her. He was no less stunningly handsome than he had been at her father's birthday party, though he was out of uniform now, wearing a blue cotton shirt and tan slacks, with sneakers on his feet.

What in the world was Gary Hobart doing here?

Then Jackie saw him, too, and jumped up. She had been with another group a short distance from Blair. For a moment Blair didn't know what was going on. But she felt a stab of anger as she began to think that somehow Jackie had looked up Gary Hobart and made a date with him. How could she!

The two now headed toward Blair. She wanted to get up and head in the opposite direction, but seated as she was on a blanket in the sand, there was no graceful way to rise and make an unobtrusive escape. Instead, she pasted her most winning smile on her face.

"Well, isn't this the smallest world!" she said cheerily.

"Isn't it?" said Jackie.

"Hello, Blair," Gary said in his deep, earnest voice.

"Forgive me for not getting up," said Blair, "but I am rather stuck in the sand."

"Do you mind if we join you?" Gary asked.

"It's not my blanket."

But the ladies were absorbed in the race and didn't seem to mind two more on their blanket. Gary and Jackie sat down.

"I didn't know you two knew each other," Blair said, unable to restrain her curiosity.

"I ran into Gary the other day downtown," Jackie explained, "and we recognized each other from the party."

"When I asked about you," Gary added, "Jackie invited me today."

"You asked about me?" Blair's stomach fluttered as she wondered what Jackie had told him. But her sister would not have told a complete stranger the truth, would she? She glanced at Jackie, who looked as innocent as could be.

At that moment Jackie was called to join her class in a race. Excusing herself, she hurried off and was soon in the center of a bevy of five-year-olds.

"I shouldn't have come," Gary said suddenly, jerking Blair's attention back to what was becoming a very awkward situation.

"If you want to see my sister, it is perfectly okay—"

"I came to see you."

"Why?" she asked, harshly, she knew, but he had just made a stunning comment.

"I thought we'd hit it off well at the party. And then when we spoke on the phone . . ." He shrugged as if she should understand. "But then you wouldn't return my calls—"

"You only called twice," she said defensively.

"A man can take only so much rejection. Still, if a girl wants to get under a man's skin, that's how to do it. It was puzzling, at best."

"So your male ego was singed? I guess a man like you doesn't get turned down often," she said snidely.

"No . . ." He drew the word out slowly, thoughtfully. "It wasn't that. I don't see a lot of girls. Haven't had the time. But . . ." He paused, then shrugged again. "I guess you were just out of my league. Still, I didn't forget about you."

And I didn't forget about you, Gary Hobart. But she certainly wasn't going to admit how scared he made her. How she desired him and the kind of man he was. Then she remembered she was only good for men like Stan Welton now. What had Jackie been thinking to invite Gary today? As Blair considered that, she realized Jackie had been intending some kind of setup, not for herself but for Blair.

"I'm flattered" was all she could think to say.

"I don't mean to flatter. I don't know what I mean to say or do. I only know that when I saw your sister and we spoke of you, I realized I wanted to see you again. That maybe I'd given up too quickly."

"I just don't think this can work," she replied as honestly as she could. "And not because of me being better than you, or such nonsense. We're different, that's all."

"Hey, we're both Presbyterians! That's a start."

"What?" She blinked, for his statement had come out of nowhere in her mind.

"We have our faith in common. That's the most important thing, isn't it?"

"Our, uh, faith?" She stared at him blankly. Then it hit her. Jackie had told him nothing about her. Gary thought this was her church, her Sunday school picnic. He had no idea that she was a fallen woman trying, rather unsuccessfully at that, to straighten out her life. She was about to clear up his misconception when he spoke again.

"I thought you were having a rather bad time at your father's

party—that is, until we met." He grinned wryly at that final observation, then went on, "Now I know why. You no more enjoy a scene like
that than I do. When I saw you with all those young men, laughing,
drinking champagne, you were just acting, trying to appear to be having a good time to please your father. I kind of thought that at the
time, but now I'm sure."

She stared at him, aghast. This man was a soldier, a West Point
graduate. Was he really as guileless as that? Or was it easier for him
to understand his take on the situation that day than to perceive the
reality? Again she was about to set him straight, but the words that
came out of her mouth surprised her.

"You are a pretty perceptive man, Lieutenant Hobart. I hope my
father didn't notice." Part lie, part truth . . . that was the most effective
lie of all.

"I'm sure he didn't. You were a good actress. Now that I think of
it, you did say you wanted to be an actress."

"Not anymore. I've discovered that to be such a phony, heartless
business." Complete truth there. But not the *whole* truth.

"Say, the sun will be setting in a while. Would you like to take a
walk on the beach and watch it?" he suggested.

They walked toward the pier, which was about a quarter of a mile
away. They both took off their shoes and walked barefoot in the wet
sand with the foamy waves lapping about their feet. Soon the sounds
of the picnic faded and it was just the two of them. At her prompting,
he told her more about himself. It was just as it had been that day at
the party. Blair was amazed that the magical time could be recaptured
so quickly.

What was it about him? About them together? To Blair there was
a sense of unreality about it all, yet, in such a contradictory way, it all
seemed so very *real*. She didn't understand it at all.

Only for one frightening moment did the magic falter—when he
asked her to tell him about herself. Her life flashed before her eyes as
it does for one on the brink of death. But she told him none of it.

Instead, she built the kind of life for herself that she thought he
would understand and be drawn to.

"Oh yes, my church activities are so important to me, but, you
know, I don't attend Jackie's church. I'm ashamed to admit, I haven't
even gone to my church in some time. The schedule with filming that
picture was so grueling that when Sunday came, I often slept in. I

wasn't all that happy with my church anyway. I was going to give Jackie's a try. It is so good to be back! I've missed the fellowship so, and hearing the Word of God, and the singing! How I love the hymns. One nice thing about my old church was that they had a marvelous choir. I'd like to get back into a choir. . . ."

Years of being around Jackie and her mother helped Blair to know all the right things to say. And the words came so easily. She felt it was her best performance yet. Of course she felt a twinge of guilt with the deception. But she wished it were all real. Didn't that count for something?

And the way Gary looked at her felt so good, she could hardly even explain it. She, who had been ogled and leered at by more men than she could count, was for once being looked upon with something very much like respect. Gary Hobart was not looking at her body. Oh, she had no illusion her beauty might have drawn him in the first place, but now he seemed to see something way beyond that. Her spirit. Goodness, her *spirit*!

The whole experience was just too awesome. No one would ever blame her for milking it for all it was worth. When he invited her to come to his church on Sunday, she accepted with ease.

She did make sure she got Jackie alone for a moment when they returned to the picnic. Though Jackie balked at first, she finally agreed to support Blair's story. Neither one of them would ever guess just how far it was destined to go.

PART III

*"Any general who fights against the Russians
can be
perfectly sure of one thing: he will be
outnumbered."*

<small>Paul von Hindenburg</small>

24

Moscow
July 1941

CAMERON TRIED to work the kinks out of her stiff body. She hadn't expected her mode of transport to be glamorous, but wedged in between crates on a freight transport . . . well, what did it matter? She was in Russia at last! Stiff, yes, and she reeked of axle grease and fumes, but otherwise she was sound and even safe.

It had taken nearly a month for her to get out of Egypt, what with delays in getting her travel documents and the frustrations of finding transportation to a country at war. Even without a war, it was no lark getting into the Soviet Union. But she pushed all that from her mind, concentrating only on her final hurdles.

Looking about, she saw the Moscow airport was a hive of activity. Pavel, the pilot of her plane, had to rush off immediately to tend to business, leaving her stretching her body and trying to get the feeling back into her hands and feet. In ten minutes, he returned with apologies.

"Miss Gayes"—the Russians never could get the *H* in Hayes—"I am afraid I cannot see you into town," he said. "Only a civilian driver can be spared for you."

"That is more than I expected, Pavel. You've a war on. I understand."

While Pavel was explaining his need to remain with his shipment for a time, a man sidled up to them. He was a wiry, unkempt fellow in his fifties. Greasy black hair, dark eyes, stubbly, thin face, he was hardly the picture of a hopeful welcoming committee. But Cameron hadn't expected a diplomatic reception. She did have some contacts at the American embassy, but she'd not had time to notify any of them of her arrival. At any rate, she reminded herself, she was only a journalist. She was not going to ride on her father's coattails, even if he would let her, which, of course he wouldn't.

"Ah, Gruk," said Pavel to the new arrival. There followed an exchange in Russian between the two; then Pavel turned back to Cameron. "This is Gruk. He will be your driver. I told him to take you to the Hotel Metropole." Cameron had mentioned to Pavel that her editor was arranging reservations there for her. This was where most foreign correspondents stayed in Moscow. She appreciated that he remembered. "It is good hotel. You will like," he added with a reassuring smile.

"I'm sure I will." She held out a hand to the driver. "Nice to meet you, Mr. Gruk."

Gruk grinned, revealing two rows of rotten teeth. "How-do-you-do!" he said in a rather rote fashion, reaching up an incredibly grimy hand and clasping it around Cameron's. His voice sounded as if he were chewing a mouthful of gravel.

"That is the extent of Gruk's English," Pavel explained with a slanted apologetic smile. "But it should be no problem, since he knows where to take you."

"We'll get along just fine." But Cameron felt less certain than she sounded. She had personally experienced many of the glitches of travel in foreign countries, and the phrase "no problem" was a euphemism that seldom happened. Thus, until she reached the Metropole, where presumably the clerk might speak English, and until she was assigned an interpreter, she was going to be pretty much at the mercy of this seedy-looking man.

"The air raids usually occur at night," Pavel was saying, "so you have a couple of hours to get settled. But be careful and make sure the hotel clerk shows you the location of the nearest shelter."

She bid the pilot good-bye, and though they had known each other just a short time, she felt a bit lonely losing her only friend in this foreign land. She reminded herself that Johnny was here, so she wouldn't be completely friendless. At least they had parted on friendly terms, but one could never tell at any moment exactly where their odd relationship stood.

It took her a half hour to pass customs, which she later learned was an incredibly short time. Then, wishing to appear at her new assignment as fresh as possible, she changed her clothes, ducking into a rest room Pavel had directed her to. She slipped out of the wrinkled and smelly trousers and sweater she'd worn on the plane and put on a simple A-line wool skirt of a subtle tan plaid and a pale blue cotton blouse. Then she met her driver outside the hangar.

The evening was clear and pleasantly cool as they drove off. It was late July and winter seemed a long way off, a lot farther than three months away. Cameron was glad, however, for the cardigan sweater she wore over her skirt and blouse.

She and Gruk rode in a rattletrap pickup truck. It was just as well her companion could not speak English, because he could never have been heard over the coughing and sputtering of the engine.

Remembering the letter that had been given to her just before she left Tehran with Pavel, she pulled it from her handbag. She'd been so tired that she'd dozed during most of the flight, deciding to save the letter from her mother for a more comfortable situation. Since that might not come for a while, she opened it now. The letter was nearly two months old and had obviously taken quite a circuitous route to reach her.

Dear Cameron,

I was so relieved to receive your cable. I knew you had been right in the middle of all that terrible fighting in Yugoslavia and Greece and admit I had many a sleepless night until I heard from you. I have read your articles with great interest and pride. And I will let you in on a little secret. I saw your father reading the Globe *the other day. He made reference to something you had written, so I know he is keeping apprised of your work, as well. The stubborn old coot won't talk about you, but he is proud of you.*

Now on to more pleasant topics. My rose garden received a blue ribbon from the garden club. I am thrilled. You know how dear my roses are to me, and had I more to say in the matter, my girls would have had flower names instead of boy names. Wouldn't you have fancied Violet over Cameron? And speaking of my girls, your sisters are well. Jackie is excelling in college and made the dean's list again. She wants to be a teacher, but I think she is so smart she could be a nurse or even a doctor. She has a beau, a fine young man from a good family. His name is Jeffrey, and he is going into law. Perhaps we'll be hearing wedding bells next summer after she graduates. I wish I had better to say of Blair. I thought she might hit it off with a nice young man she met at your father's

171

birthday party—my, that seems so long ago! His family is not from our social circle, but at least he isn't an actor. Anyway, I don't think she is seeing him, though I had so hoped she would. No doubt he, too, had problems with her current path. Oh, Cameron, your sister is singing in a nightclub! I am mortified, and it is not even a decent Beverly Hills club but rather some awful place on the docks. She moved out of our house because your father told her she had to quit that job or leave.

Oh my, and I wasn't going to saddle you with bad news. But there it is, our life here in Los Angeles. Little changes here, I suppose. It must seem terribly dull after all your adventures. And now I hear you will be heading to the Soviet Union. Yes, I keep in contact with Max Arnett, though your father would explode if he knew. But then, what he doesn't know won't hurt him, will it? Please keep safe, dear! I worry every day about you and miss you, as well. Your sisters also miss you and send their love. I pray for you always and know God's hand is on you, even if you don't see it. I would urge you to attend church, but I don't think there are churches in Russia anymore, are there? Well, if my prayers are any good, you are not alone, even if you will be surrounded by atheists. God bless you!

All my love,
Your Mother

Cameron dashed away a tear as it spilled from her eye. How so like her mother the letter sounded. Cameron could almost hear her voice. She realized now how starved she'd been for news from home. She smiled as she thought of her sisters. They certainly hadn't changed. Jackie was still perfect, but it was hard to resent her for it because she was such a good-natured girl. And Blair . . . what would become of her? A nightclub singer. Yes, their father must have had a total fit about that. She could almost see Keagan's jowls redden and his green eyes spark as he attempted to crush her under his will. Well, good for Blair for having the fortitude to stand up to him. Yet, as Cameron well knew, he had his ways of winning battles.

Cecilia had mentioned nothing about her and Cameron's conversation regarding what had happened in Russia. Well, nothing beyond that "What he doesn't know won't hurt him" remark. But that did not surprise Cameron. It was best for security and for their own emotional well-being not to dwell on these matters, at least until there was something further of import to discuss.

Cameron thought about what she had told Johnny in Egypt about how great Keagan had been in Russia when they had been together there. Well, "great" might be going too far. He had fairly ignored his wife, spending nearly every waking hour working. The only way Cameron had had a relationship with the man was to push her way into his world.

And now she was going into that world again, but this time alone. She didn't want to wonder what her father thought about that. She was certain he must know of her new assignment. She found herself wishing her mother had said something about his reaction. Her mother had said he was proud of her work, but then Cecilia would say something like that because she would desperately want to believe it.

Cameron shrugged as she tucked the letter back into her purse and pulled her attention to the present moment. The airport was about a half hour from the city, and as they finally drew near central Moscow, she didn't want to miss a thing.

Seeing Moscow through adult eyes was like seeing it for the first time. Before coming, Cameron had talked a lot about her experience with the country, mostly, of course, to convince others of her qualifications for the job of Moscow correspondent. Now she knew her words had been like blowing out empty air. She suddenly felt new and green and totally unprepared. She recognized little beyond the vague familiarity of the broadness of the streets and the incongruent narrowness of the sidewalks. There was little traffic on the streets except for military vehicles, especially trucks full of soldiers no doubt heading to the Front. Many people were afoot due, she assumed, to war gasoline rationing. Gruk drove across a bridge, and Cameron caught her first glimpse of the Kremlin. The stout walls that she had remembered as brick were now painted to look like walls of apartment buildings. The elegant cupola domes of St. Basil's Cathedral, once golden and sparkling, were now painted a battleship gray. Despite the effects of the attempts at camouflage, she longed to walk across Red Square. She would truly know she was in Russia then.

A few minutes later the truck began to make some serious new noises. Gruk pumped the clutch as the vehicle began to sputter to a stop. He steered it to the side of the street and, after stopping, continued to fiddle with various items—the ignition and the choke were among the things Cameron could readily identify. The engine groaned to his ministrations but would not turn over.

Gruk shrugged and explained to her what he was doing—in Russian, of course. Then he opened his door and got out. He spent several minutes under the hood, then returned to the cab and tried the engine again with no luck. He stepped out, directing another explanation at her; then he left, not heading back to the hood but rather walking away from the truck completely.

"Where are you going?" Cameron yelled through the open window.

Seldom helpless, she felt very much so now. The man could not even communicate his intentions. She cursed her carelessness in not trying harder to learn the language years ago. She hoped what little she had learned would come back to her soon. In the meantime she fumbled in her purse for her Russian dictionary, she drew it out, but by the time she found the word for "where," Gruk was well out of earshot. She assumed he was going for help.

She waited five minutes, all the while it seeming more like an hour. She did not want to be stranded at this juncture of her assignment. She wanted to get to her hotel, check in with the Soviet Press Department, meet her colleagues, and start to work. After that she would love to wander about the city, but preferably with an interpreter at her elbow.

Pushing open the passenger door, she got out of the truck and walked about, staying within sight of the stranded vehicle. There was no sign of Gruk. It was getting late. The summer gloaming left the sky dusky, but it seemed much darker because of the blackout. It was nine-thirty according to her wristwatch. Cameron paced up and down the street awhile, glancing into shop windows, listening to snatches of conversations of passersby and shop patrons, hoping to hear some English. She didn't, but the sound of the Russian language was oddly comforting, almost but not quite soothing her growing impatience.

After pacing to the end of the street and back several times, she returned to the truck, removed her luggage from the open bed in back, and stowed it all into the cab to make it less accessible to any malicious observers. She was up to two suitcases again, having made some purchases in Cairo. She took the keys from the ignition, locked the doors, then headed off in the direction Gruk had gone. If she had any luck, she would find him. There might be a mechanic nearby that he had found. If she didn't find him . . . well, he wasn't going anywhere because she had the keys. She'd just explore for a short while and then return to the truck. Perhaps she would even stumble upon the Hotel Metropole.

As she walked she realized it was a small wonder she had few memories of Moscow. The city was surely different now, at least slightly, even surrealistically, off-kilter from its norm as it had prepared for war. Piles of sandbags were placed all over in strategic places. These, made from an odd assortment of fabrics—florals, colorful stripes, pastels—appeared very odd until Cameron discerned that the bags had likely been constructed of recycled fabric from cast-off women's clothes. The wall of sandbags had the peculiar look of a patchwork quilt.

Cameron noted that over a waterway, an artificial roof had been constructed to mislead the enemy pilots. On some of the streets, imitation windows had been painted. On the walls of buildings, as with the Kremlin, trees had been painted as camouflage, and some even sported theatrical backdrops to further confuse bombers. Cameron felt as if she had stumbled down a rabbit hole and that at any minute a huge white hare would hurry by scolding her, "You're late! You're late!"

She had a million questions and was frustrated by her inability to communicate. How far away was the Front? How fared the Red Army? Were things as bad as she'd heard? Most outside of Russia predicted the country would be defeated in three weeks to three months. It had already stood for a month. But the sight of bombed-out debris reminded her it hadn't been an easy month. Exactly how much devastation had been wrought by the Germans? How safe was the city? That final mental question was definitely a moot one. Had she desired safety she would have stayed in Los Angeles.

In a few minutes she realized her present course was not going to be fruitful. The street she was on consisted entirely of shops and apartment buildings and offices, not a garage in sight. She turned down a side street, surmising that a mechanic would keep his more unsightly business on a back street. She kept careful track of her path so she would not get lost. Most street signs and directional information had been removed, not that it would have helped her anyway—in fact she wondered how much that or any of the attempts at camouflage would have deterred or confused the enemy.

Cameron came into a residential area, a working-class neighborhood from the look of the simple utilitarian structures, mostly apartment buildings, and all a bit on the shabby side. A few smudge-faced children were playing on the sidewalk while a woman yelled from a second-floor window at them. A couple of vehicles were parked on the curb, but there was no moving traffic except for a bicyclist peddling down the road.

Seeing a woman step from a building, Cameron dug out her dictionary once again. She knew this wasn't going to be the first time she wished she'd retained some of the Russian she had learned as a child. She flipped through the pages looking for the word for "garage" but found "service station" instead—*binzakalonka*. Armed with what she was certain would be her magic word, she quickened her step until she was near the woman. She smiled pleasantly, and the woman smiled also but with more reserve. Cameron was a stranger, a big enough strike against her, but in wartime a stranger could also be a spy or worse.

"*Graspazha*," Cameron addressed the woman, remembering something Pavel had told her on the plane about forms of address. Instead of "Mr." or "Mrs." the Soviet way was, *graspadin* for a man and *graspazha* for a woman, both loosely meaning "citizen."

"*Da?*" said the woman. She was middle-aged, dressed in typical Russian fashion with a long wool coat, even in summer, and a scarf tied around her head. She carried a basket on her arm.

"I'm an American," Cameron explained in English, speaking slowly, as if that would help.

The woman replied in a stream of Russian, and the only word discernable to Cameron was *Amerikanka*. At least the woman appeared to have grasped that fact.

"Da," said Cameron, thankful at least for one word she could not botch too badly, but just in case she nodded her head vigorously. "I am looking for a service station . . . binzakalonka." She added the final word—her magic word—hoping she was a little close in her pronunciation.

"Binzakalonka?" the woman repeated with an arched brow, then in the universal "tongue" shrugged her shoulders and shook her head.

Cameron shrugged back. She tried the word a few more times with different accents on various syllables but to no effect. Finally defeated, she thanked the woman with one of her few remembered Russian words. "*Spasiba*."

"*Pazhalusta*," the woman replied, and Cameron recalled that meant something to the effect of "Don't mention it."

The woman hurried away, and Cameron continued on what was looking more and more like a wild-goose chase. She came to an alley, just the sort of place where one might find a garage tucked away. Then she heard some male voices, one sounding very like Gruk's gravelly bass. She turned into the alley and discovered two men in a recessed area, but there was no garage, and neither man was her driver. They were working on some piping. She tried her magic word again but with no more success. She decided to proceed down the alley a bit farther to where it looked as if a side street bisected it. If she turned right there, she thought she would eventually reach the street at which she had begun. Thus, having made a circle of the immediate neighborhood, she would give up her search and return to the truck, hoping Gruk had been more successful than she.

The turn she had expected to take proved to be a dead end. She continued down the alley because some distance ahead was another turn, and she was certain one must eventually lead to the main street.

Then a loud whine filled the air. An air-raid siren. It sent a shock coursing through Cameron's body. She was no stranger to this sound after Yugoslavia and Greece, but it would never cease to be a tad unnerving. There must be a shelter in the vicinity, but where? Cameron retraced her steps back to where the men had been working, but they were gone. The rest of the area was deserted, and the evening shadows were lengthening in the alley. Her only recourse seemed to be to head to where she thought the alley connected to the street. Once on the main thoroughfare she would be able to see where people were heading, presumably to a shelter, and she could follow them. On the way she tried several back doors hoping to gain entrance to a building and thus to a cellar shelter. The doors were all locked.

25

THE SCREECH of the siren echoed in Cameron's ears, rising and falling in a moaning cadence, making her want to press her hands against them to shut out the sound. She came to a courtyard and heard a different sound, small by comparison to the overwhelming drone of the siren but distinctive and definitely distressful. Her gaze swept the courtyard, and at first she saw nothing but a patch of dirt, a scraggly bush, and a couple of trash barrels. Surmising it was nothing but a frightened animal, she began to turn when the sound came again— almost a wail but different from the siren—and most certainly human.

"Ma . . . Ma!"

Cameron stepped into the courtyard, and a closer search revealed the source of the sound. Crouched by a barrel was a child, knees hugged to chest, face buried as it was pressed against his knees. The child was crying for all he was worth, but she couldn't tell if it was a boy or a girl.

"What is it?" Cameron asked, hoping her tone of concern made up for her foreign words.

The face lifted, displaying huge chocolate brown eyes shining with tears. She saw now he was definitely a boy, though with longish brown hair that curled in waves around his grubby collar. His smudged face was streaked with the tracks of his tears. He was about five years old.

Cameron glanced around frantically, hoping, however futilely, that the boy's mother would appear. She knew there was no use trying to communicate verbally with the boy. Instead, she tried the two doors that opened into the courtyard. Both were locked. Perhaps the locked doors were also the cause of the boy's distress. It must indeed be frightening to be locked out of one's home during an air raid.

"Come on, little fellow, we must find a shelter. S-h-e-l-t-e-r? Understand?" But no matter how slowly she intoned the words, he wasn't going to understand. She tried her dictionary, then realized her hands were shaking and she could not find the word, much less the page.

She reached her hand down to the boy. "We have to get out of here."

His crying had subsided to hiccoughing sobs, no doubt too enthralled with this odd stranger to concentrate on anything else. But he shrank away from her extended hand. His mother had obviously thoroughly ingrained into him the admonition, "Don't go with strangers."

She tried saying "shelter" a few more times but to no avail. In the meantime the siren was screeching, robbing her of concentration, urging her to flee. She then thought of the only other Russian word she knew for a building or house.

"*Dacha,*" she said.

Now the boy just gaped at her as if she were a raving lunatic.

Finally she tried, "Mama? Find Mama?"

The boy responded to that by bursting into tears again and wailing, "Mama! Mama!"

Cameron had long known she did not have a "way" with children. This only proved it. But even a five-year-old in Moscow must understand the meaning and consequences of an air raid. He'd probably been through more than she had. It occurred to Cameron that she'd heard most of the children had been evacuated from the city. Why was he still here?

Concentrating so intently on the child, Cameron had not noticed another new sound mingling with the siren—the sound of an engine overhead, and it was close. She realized she must not be too far from the Kremlin, since she had seen it from the bridge shortly before the truck had broken down. The Kremlin, of course, was one of the prime targets of German bombers.

The first explosion made her nearly jump from her skin. It had a similar effect on the child, only he jumped right into Cameron's arms.

"Too late now, fellow," she said in a gently comforting tone that contrasted with the wryness of her words. She knew well enough he would understand her tone, not her words.

Clutching the now sobbing figure close to her breast, she headed toward the street. The tall brick walls in the alley were way too close for comfort. At least in the street there was much less chance of being crushed by a falling building.

What was she thinking? Outside a shelter there was no safe place if the bombs chose to fall anywhere near. But there was still a chance of finding a shelter, possibly, even a metro station, which would provide the best shelter from the bombing.

At the end of the alley Cameron stopped dead still, her jaw falling slack. In the air overhead the night sky was filled with bursts of light—green, red, and yellow streaks—like Fourth of July fireworks. It would have almost been beautiful if it had not been accompanied by the ear-splitting din of explosions. The ground shook as a bomb made contact with a target. She could see the light of an explosion some distance away. Then came the answering bursts of anti-aircraft guns, which she saw now were the source of the fanciful colors. Cameron could see the streaks of light from a nearby rooftop. It was a stunning display.

Pulling herself back into focus on the task at hand, she looked up and down the street for some sign of a shelter. About two blocks away she thought she saw something that could be an entrance to the subway; at least there was a doorway with an arrow pointing down. She started toward it when a shout behind her made her stop. Turning, she saw a man yelling, presumably at her. He spoke in a frantic jumble of Russian, and Cameron silently began to curse that language she had not long before found comforting. Her frustration level had been reached and far surpassed.

At that same moment the noise of an engine reached her, and less than an instant later the boom of an explosion. It drowned out Cameron's screams as she was shaken to her knees. She threw her body over the child, but just then the man reached them and threw himself over both her and the child. Before she shut her eyes, she noted a plume of smoke on the next street. They were far enough away so that only a spray of gravel and dust peppered them, but it was no less unsettling.

Still, the ground shook and the air belched danger, but the next hits seemed farther away. The man lifted himself away from her, but it was obvious they were still in great peril. Without so much as a word, he grabbed Cameron's arm and yanked her to her feet while she still clutched the child to her.

He paused only to speak to the child in Russian. The boy seemed to recognize him and spoke to the man through sobs and tearful sniffs. The man spoke to Cameron in Russian as he tugged her along after him. This was neither the time nor place to explain her inability to understand him. She knew he meant to be helpful, and that was enough. At any rate, she was in no position to argue.

He paused before an apartment building, and Cameron followed as he ascended the steps leading to the front door. Inside it was dark, but Cameron's rescuer seemed to know the way. She followed him down a corridor, where he paused at a door and threw it open, revealing stairs going down to a cellar. Hurriedly he took the child, then indicated for Cameron to go first. He quickly shut the door, then prodded her down the steps.

The cellar appeared to be full with well over a hundred people. Many were seated on chairs and benches. Some reclined on the few beds pushed up against a wall, while others lay on mattresses or on blankets right on the floor. It was a quiet, orderly group, mostly women in a varying range of ages, some elderly men, fewer young men, and a handful of children. There were no windows in the cellar, but Cameron had the benefit of some dim light from a single bare bulb hanging from a ceiling fixture.

Cameron turned as the man reached the bottom step and nearly stumbled into her. Feeling it was time she thanked her rescuer, she said, "Thank you so much—I mean, *spasiba*—"

At that moment a young woman rushed up to them chattering excitedly and reaching out to the child. "Sasha! Sasha!"

"Mama!" The boy wiggled from the man's arms into the woman's.

The man grinned at the reunion, then turned to Cameron. "So you are American."

"And you speak English!" She wanted to hug him just for that alone.

"I do. I spent a number of years in Chicago."

"You are not Russian, then?"

His English was accented but far less so than she'd noted in other English-speaking Russians she'd met. She eyed him more carefully. A man of about thirty years, give or take a couple. A little more than six feet in height, well muscled—very well muscled, Cameron thought wryly, then nearly blushed at her silly reaction to his appealing physique. Still, even from an objective viewpoint, it was obvious he was a nice-looking man. Square jaw, substantial but not overpowering nose, well-defined, clean-shaven cheekbones, and dark blue eyes. His hair was a sandy color, glittering a bit at the moment as he stood directly beneath the light bulb, which, in fact, nearly brushed the top of his head.

He started to respond to her, but the boy's mother got his attention instead. They spoke for a few moments.

Finally he said to Cameron, "She was trying to thank me for finding the boy, but I told her it was you she should thank."

"I only stumbled upon him in the alley. I was taking a shortcut." Cameron gave a self-deprecating shrug. She had thoroughly botched her would-be rescue and felt no thanks were in order. "I don't know what I would have done had you not come along. That was quite fortuitous."

"Not as much as it appeared. Mira thought the boy was spending the night with neighbors. It was only when the air raid sounded that the neighbors discovered Sasha, apparently homesick, had slipped away and wasn't in his bed. Well, you can imagine there was a bit of a panic here, and I went out to look for him."

"Still, your wife has only you to thank. I was hopelessly foiled by my inability to speak the language."

He shrugged. "Come, let's find a place to settle. We could be here awhile."

Mira made an attempt to thank Cameron, then retreated with her son to a far corner of the cellar. Cameron noted Mira sat next to an older woman who was holding an infant that immediately reached out to Mira. But much to Cameron's surprise, the man did not follow the woman. Instead, he spied a vacant place on the floor against a wall. He glanced at Cameron, then gestured to the place.

Just then another woman approached them. She was middle-aged or older, stout and big boned with a scarf tied over iron gray hair. She exchanged several words with the man, during which she cast suspicious glances in Cameron's direction. She made Cameron dig out her travel documents from her purse, after which she carefully scrutinized them. Then, shrugging with resignation and giving Cameron a final look, she left them.

"That was the shelter warden," said the man. "She had some reservations about accepting a stranger into the shelter. I assured her you were not a spy." His eyes twinkled with amusement at this as he gave her a quick appraisal. "You're not, are you?"

"No, I'm a journalist."

"Well, in Russia that is nearly the same." Smiling to indicate he was only joking, he held out his hand to the wall. "Not all the comforts of home, but we are fortunate to have a wall to lean against."

Perplexed, Cameron took the place while her rescuer settled next to her.

Perhaps noting the confusion on her face, the man said, "Mira isn't my wife. I was just making calls in the building."

"Calls?"

"I'm a doctor. Mira's youngest child is one of my patients." He held out his hand. "Alex Rostov—or if you prefer it in Russian, Aleksei Rostovscikov. Fortunately, the agents at Ellis Island butchered the surname down to Rostov, and I further Americanized my Christian name."

"I'm glad you did. My Russian pronunciation is pathetic. I'm Cameron Hayes."

"Nice to meet you. So you are here to write about the war?"

"Just arrived today. My first story shall be about life in an air-raid shelter." She gave him a relaxed smile. Her heart was actually beating at its normal rate now, and her hands no longer trembled. "Have you come to Russia as part of the various advisory teams sent from the States, Dr. Rostov?" She immediately regretted that her tone had taken on its professional aspect.

"No," he answered rather brusquely.

She thought he might have taken offense at her approach, as well he might. He was trying to be friendly, while she seemed to be turning it into a news opportunity.

Then he added in his earlier, more congenial tone, "I've been here since '38. Before that I was in Chicago . . . for most of my life."

"This is your home now?" She made a pointed attempt to sound casual, friendly.

"Yes." He didn't seem inclined to pursue that topic and proved it by changing the subject. "What part of the States are you from?"

"California. Los Angeles."

"Never been there myself. Must be nice. Eternal sunshine, Hollywood stars."

"It has its merits."

The conversation lagged then, and in the silence Cameron was aware again of the pounding explosions outside.

"Will this go on for long?" she asked. "It must be awful, over and over again, night after night." She shuddered at the thought.

In her previous experience with air raids in Yugoslavia and Greece, she'd been merely someone passing through. She'd sit in a shelter for a few hours, then move on to a new place. Now it began to occur to her that she'd be in Moscow for a prolonged time and the daily trek to bomb shelters would become her routine as it was for these folks, who seemed to be taking it in stride. But at the thought of hours, perhaps every day, spent underground, rooted to one place, hearing the pounding overhead, helpless to do anything but sit . . . endlessly sit . . . and all at once the walls of the cellar began to inch in upon her. She hated sitting still. She hated being helpless.

Swallowing, she ran a finger inside the collar of her blouse. It was suddenly very warm.

Dr. Alex Rostov's responding smile contained a hint of understanding but also just a touch of amusement. "You get used to it. I've seen people sleep right through the worst of them."

Cameron glanced around. Two men were engaged in a game of chess, intent on the game, seemingly oblivious to what was going on outside. Others were sitting placidly, hands folded in laps, eyes closed, dozing or praying—Cameron couldn't tell. Others were involved in quiet conversations, while still others were cuddled close to companions, heads resting on shoulders of friends or relatives. Most wore looks ranging from resignation to sheer boredom.

"Yes, it does seem rather peaceful in here," she observed.

"There are strict rules for conduct in shelters," Alex replied. "Because most raids occur at night, the people who have to work in the morning must have time to sleep. I rather enjoy getting caught in a shelter once in a while. Usually I'm working at my hospital, air raid or not. Generally the red cross of the hospital is respected by the bombers, but this is still a nice respite."

"And here I am bothering you with questions. That is one of my many faults, I'm afraid. I am sorry."

He chuckled softly. "You are not a bother at all. I seldom get to hear an American voice. I . . . miss it more than I thought."

Cameron caught the odd hesitation in his voice. She couldn't read it but detected a hint of sadness or regret. They continued to chat for a few more minutes, then the warden, whom Cameron decided she would not want to cross on rules of shelter discipline, passed out tea.

Cameron took hers gratefully. It was now eleven o'clock—Cameron was glad she'd remembered to change her wristwatch to Moscow time. She gradually became aware of a lull in the bombing outside. At the same time she realized she hadn't eaten since a meager meal of bread and cheese on the plane. She hadn't slept since that last night in Tehran except for catnaps on the plane. She closed her eyes and might have nodded off, but just then the cellar door burst open.

A young boy, fourteen or fifteen years old, came in and chatted excitedly with the warden as another boy of about the same age came up to them. The first boy took off the thick elbow-length gloves he was wearing and gave them to the second boy, who then left the cellar.

"What's going on?" Cameron asked Alex.

"The boys are roof spotters. The boy that just came in said he just pitched two incendiary bombs from the roof. The gloves he had are asbestos, but it's still a pretty heroic act. He probably saved the building from burning."

Cameron started to stand.

"What're you doing?"

"I want to see what's going on, talk to the boy, and see what they're doing on the roof. I'll need an interpreter," she added with an inquiring arch to her brow.

"When I first met you, you were pretty anxious to get to a shelter. Now you want to leave?" He shook his head as she continued to gain her feet. "I can assure you this lull is only temporary."

"I was only anxious to get the boy to safety," she replied defensively, then pausing, she added more sheepishly, "Well . . . I was a bit nervous on my own account, as well. The thing shook me for a couple of minutes. But now—"

"Now you are taking leave of your senses!"

"It's my job."

"Being crazy?"

With a long-suffering sigh, she nodded. "Sort of. At least I will never maintain an edge in my business if I don't take risks. Nature of the beast and all that. However, it was wrong of me to even think of involving you. I appreciate what you have done, but now . . ." She didn't know how to finish her sentence, so she just gave a shrug and started to walk away.

Alex jumped up and was at her side in a moment. "Come on, then," he said simply.

"You don't have to—"

"I know. I have only known you for a short time, but I can already see you will need a doctor for a friend. Let's just hope my medical services won't be called upon today." He grabbed her arm and led the way to the door.

The warden questioned them, and apparently Alex made an acceptable explanation for their departure, because she did not stop them. Cameron did not question Alex's failure to stop for her to interview the first boy. She'd be able to talk to him later, and as much as she was resigned to taking risks, she did understand the advisability of going outside while there was still a lull in the bombing.

26

CAMERON WAS out of breath after running up the stairs from the basement to the roof of the four-story building. But when she gasped, it was not from lack of oxygen. Rather, not far away a blaze of light could be seen, and when she and Alex drew close to the edge of the roof, she saw the building next to theirs in flames. Apparently the spotter on that roof had not been so fortunate in his efforts to remove the incendiaries. Firemen were frantically working to put out the blaze. Cameron knew such fires were like beacons to German bombers, and when they made their return run, they would use them as targets for dropping more bombs.

There were glows of orange light in other locations, as well, most more distant from the apartment building. Cameron shivered.

"It's not a pretty sight, is it?" Alex said.

"Moscow has always seemed to me to be so solid," Cameron replied. "In seven hundred years it has withstood so much. Until now I could not have believed it might truly fall. Yet it is possible, isn't it? What's to stop Hitler? Nothing has yet."

"Do you know that when Napoleon invaded Russia in 1812 and made his advance on Moscow, the Muscovites themselves set the city on fire? By the time the French army arrived, two-thirds of the city had burned down, leaving the French without shelter or provisions. With winter closing in, the French were eventually forced to retreat."

Of course, Cameron knew well much of the history of Russia. She also knew she did not need to say as much. Alex wasn't giving a history lesson; he was merely offering enlightenment to the present and perhaps to the future.

"I suppose," she replied, "that when Stalin delivered his speech last month encouraging the Russian people to leave only 'scorched earth' for the enemy, it was more than mere words."

"I believe the Russian people have the will to stop Hitler," Alex said firmly. As he spoke his face was grim. The handsome, almost youthful cast Cameron had noted previously was now hardened a bit, and the lines had deepened. Perhaps it was only a trick of the eerie lighting from the fire at his shoulder.

"It makes me sick to think what lies ahead if you are right." She glanced out again upon the cityscape. For an instant, like a moment of bitter prescience, she seemed to see an expanse of charred spires thrusting up toward an ochre-colored sky, with wisps of smoke rising from heaps of ashes, the grim remainder of Moscow.

"It'll be long and hard," he said, as if he had seen her vision, as well.

"When is it any other way for Russia?" She let a thin smile ease across her lips. She knew now why this country had always captured her imagination and crept like a burr under her skin. They were a lot alike, she and this tenacious, ornery nation. Never seeking the easy way, always fighting, never satisfied.

She turned her attention from the view and back to her companion. Alex was staring at her thoughtfully, almost solemnly. She immediately thought of Johnny's looks that ranged from patronization to amusement to outright lust. This was quite different. Dr. Alex Rostov was looking at her as if . . . she could think of no other description than that it was as if she were a *person*, not merely a woman, and one of worth, at that. Too often because of her intrusion into a man's world, she was viewed by others, even other women, as only a woman, her gender glaring just when she most wanted to be accepted for something besides her sex. Now Rostov seemed to be doing just that.

Or perhaps she was just imagining it. How could she know what was in his mind?

But he didn't fumble with embarrassment when he was caught in his frank appraisal of her. He smiled. And what a devastating smile! Devastating in its sheer simplicity. No guile, no innuendo, no wry mirth. But it wasn't warm and mushy, either. She suddenly had the strangest urge to kiss this man, this complete stranger, to touch those lips that were firm but pleasant, sincere, but oddly enigmatic.

She swallowed hard and fought back the heat rising around her collar. She was actually relieved to hear the drone of engines in the sky.

"We'd better get back inside," Alex said.

"Uh . . . yes . . . of course. I did want to talk to that boy—" She inclined her head to the young spotter at his post on the opposite side of the roof.

"You'll see him later."

She didn't argue. Even though the object of her sudden discomfiture was going to follow her, she still felt it advisable, for more reasons than a mere bombing, to get off that roof with its ethereal visions and where simple smiles were inexplicably mysterious.

At the cellar door Alex paused. "Go on in. I'll be back in a few minutes."

"Where are you going?" She probably had no right to make inquiries of a stranger, but then he *had* said something about friendship.

"I'm going next door to see if there were any injuries in that fire."

"I'll go with you. I can't bear the thought of being cooped up in that cellar any longer than necessary."

She braced herself for his protests, but none came. Stunned at this, she followed him out the front door. Alex spoke to the firemen, who apparently assured him there were no injuries. They were heading back to the apartment building when a woman hobbled toward them. She was old and wrinkled. Her snowy hair was all askew; the scarf that once held it in place had fallen partially off her head and was tangled in the ends of what had once been a neat bun. Her face was scratched and bleeding, her clothes torn and powdered with dust.

Upon seeing them, she hurried her pace, though her hobble seemed about as fast as she could manage. She called to them in frantic tones.

Alex spoke to her, then turned to Cameron. "Come. I might need your help." His words were practically an order, though more the natural instructions of a doctor in a crisis. Cameron did not think to question them. She followed them both.

Two blocks away a building had been bombed pretty badly. The front was bashed in completely, so that an inside corridor could be seen. In the midst of fresh rubble, the remains of household items were scattered rather incongruously. The front steps were still intact, though the left handrail had fallen over. The woman led them up the steps and into the building. Cameron had no faith at all that the walls and ceiling would not come crashing down on her head with the least movement, much less with another attack. They had to clear away fallen debris as they proceeded down a hall toward the worst of the damage. The building was dark inside, except where gaping holes allowed moonlight to penetrate. The old woman knew her way in the darkness, but there was still much stumbling before they reached their apparent destination.

They halted in a room that showed heavy damage but nothing in the way of a direct hit; however, anyone in this room when the front of the building had been hit would have been knocked about pretty ruthlessly. Picking their way through dislodged chairs, tables, and bits of plaster shaken from the walls and ceiling, the woman finally paused. Cameron's eyes had adjusted to the darkness, but she still almost missed seeing the body sprawled amidst the rubble. A man, as old as the woman, lay unconscious on the floor, a large bleeding gash on his head.

Alex dropped to his knees at the man's side and performed a brief examination. He said something in Russian, to no one in particular, it seemed, but his tone was obviously relieved. Then apparently remembering his companion, he said in English to Cameron, "He's alive. I don't know why he didn't get to a shelter."

"Maybe there are others trapped," Cameron said.

Alex questioned the old woman, then said to Cameron, "No, they are the only ones left." He shook his head. "She—her name is Alla, by the way—says her husband became ill just before the raid, and they were too slow in leaving the apartment. There is no shelter in the building, but a metro station is nearby where they all go."

"Why did no one help them?" Cameron asked, trying, for the sake of the woman, to hide the outrage she felt. It wasn't easy because the woman was weeping and clutching fearfully at Cameron's arm.

Alex shrugged. "Lost in the shuffle, I suppose." He paused as the sounds of a renewed raid wafted in from outside. "We've got to get him out of here, but I have to make sure he can be safely moved. Cameron, would you run back to the cellar and get my medical bag and also see if you can enlist some strong bodies to help carry him?"

"Of course." Cameron tried to gently disengage the woman's grip from her sleeve. "I'm going to get help," she said with as reassuring a smile as she could muster. Eventually Alla let go, and Cameron raced back to the cellar shelter. In ten minutes she returned with the medical bag and two helpers in tow, one a tall, gangly teenaged boy and the other a woman with muscles that nearly matched Alex's.

Cameron saw that Alex had bundled up his own coat for a pillow under the man's head and had found a blanket to lay over his patient. He grabbed his bag while the others stood by waiting for instructions. His eyes were shining in the darkness, full of passion for what he was doing. In the meantime explosions continued to rumble through the air. The walls of the building shook precariously. Dear Lord, Cameron thought miserably, won't they ever stop?

"Cameron," Alex called. "Take this blanket and hold it like a tent over me—that's it," he encouraged as she took the shabby wool cover that had been draped over the patient and held it over both the injured man's head and Alex's. Alex then took a penlight from his bag and, lifting each of the patient's eyelids, flashed the light into his eyes. He murmured something in Russian.

"What is it?" Cameron asked. She was beginning to see that the doctor had been in Russia so long that Russian had become his first language—if it ever had been otherwise—and he spoke it without thinking.

"His pupils are reactive to light," he answered. "That's good." He flicked off his light. "You can remove the blanket. I just didn't want to break the blackout," he added in explanation. "I can work in the dark now." As Cameron tucked the blanket back around the patient, Alex placed his stethoscope against the man's chest. "Heart sounds are weak but regular. He's got a broken leg, though, apparently from falling during the raid. That's when he struck his head and got knocked out."

Cameron appreciated Alex's efforts to keep her informed, especially in that he had to say most of the same things in Russian to the old woman, who had calmed a bit and was now clinging to the big woman from the cellar.

"How are we going to move him?" Cameron asked.

"I'd like something to splint the leg with," he said as he dabbed an antiseptic-smelling concoction on the old man's head wound. He issued some instructions to the boy, then spoke again to Cameron. "Would you and Ivana—that's the woman you brought from the shelter—see if you can find a mattress that we can use as a stretcher?"

Cameron went about her task marveling at the doctor's presence of mind and calm efficiency. She had heard horror stories about Russian medicine, but if this man was any example, then the stories could not all be true. But she was forgetting—he was not Russian—was he? He had no doubt immigrated to America. She wondered how old he had been at the time. Where had he received his medical training? And why had he come back?

Searching through the darkened apartment was no easy task. Cameron bashed her shin a couple of times and walked into a wall. The moonlight streaming through the windows helped, but Cameron did not forget it was also an aid to German bombers. Balancing a thin mattress between them, which Cameron had found in another room of the building, she and Ivana finally returned to Alex. The boy had found a broomstick, and Alex had put it to use as a crude splint for the old man's broken leg. Between the four of them, they eased the patient onto the mattress. The old wife looked on, obviously too frail herself to offer any assistance.

The journey from the bombed-out building to the one where the cellar shelter was located proved a bit harrowing. The Germans were concentrating on another part of the city now, but the sounds of attack were no less disconcerting. Besides this, the patient had regained consciousness and was highly agitated, crying out for his wife and trying to vault from the mattress to search for her. Poor old Alla was hobbling behind them as fast as she could, trying to catch up so she could ease her husband's fears. The stretcher-bearers slowed and finally had to stop altogether or lose their patient. After the man was calmed by the sight of his wife, the trip went more smoothly, but they had to move at a snail's pace so that Alla could keep up with them because her husband refused to let go of her hand. It was excruciating to move so slowly when at any moment a bomb could fall on top of them.

Cameron tasted fear in the back of her throat but did her best to ignore it.

Back in the cellar the light was out and soft snores could be heard from various corners. The warden warned them to be quiet, an impossibility considering their burden. But they managed to get the new arrivals settled without causing too much of a stir. Alex spent a few more minutes tending Alla's cuts and scratches and seeing that the old man was comfortable. Then he went to where Cameron had found her old place against the wall and collapsed beside her.

"He should be all right," Alex sighed. "We'll get him to a hospital as soon as the raid is over." He leaned his head against the wall and took another deep cleansing breath. "I could sleep for a month."

"When was the last time you slept?"

He cocked a brow wryly. "What day is it?"

"Good grief, Alex!" She marveled at the ease with which they had fallen into the use of first names.

"I was on my way home just before the raid. I was kicked out of the hospital after working a thirty-two-hour shift and had planned to get a very good night's sleep, but I wanted to stop here and see a couple of patients first . . ." He smiled tiredly, eyes half-lidded. "Only for a few minutes . . ."

"Hopefully, there will be no more excitement for a while then," she said.

"Somehow I take you to be the type who thrives on excitement."

"Normally, yes, but I haven't had much in the way of sleep in the last two days either. A bit of boredom would be rather appreciated."

By mutual but unspoken agreement, they fell silent, and for a rare time in her life, Cameron actually enjoyed the quiet—if quiet it could be called with bombs still reverberating uncomfortably close at hand. Cameron leaned her head against the wall listening to the peculiar mix of sounds, bursts of bombs mingled with the purr of sleepers. She thought about the Muscovites of 1812 burning down their city to save it, and she thought also about those of 1941 sleeping placidly through the air raid. The same blood coursed through both generations. If Adolf Hitler somehow walked into Moscow, he would find only the charred remnants of a mighty civilization.

Such lofty thoughts eventually lulled Cameron to sleep. She did not feel herself slump over but was pleasantly aware of the nice firm cushion her head found to rest upon. With a sigh that bordered on a soft snore, she snuggled closer to the cushion. All else faded to oblivion—the stranded truck with her belongings, including her precious typewriter, at the mercy of thieves; her work that should be calling loudly to her but was only a whisper that faded in and out of her dreams; and a city in flames while its stouthearted citizens slept.

She was having a dream of Johnny Shanahan standing on a stage dressed like an opera singer. He opened his mouth and the most horrific, piercing wail poured forth.

"It's over," a soft voice came to her, closer than the wail.

"Huh?" Cameron croaked, then sat up with a jerk. She had fallen asleep, soundly asleep. And the cushion for her head was the shoulder of Alex Rostov! "Oh, my goodness! I was asleep!"

He was smiling benevolently. "Yes, you were." She hadn't noticed it before, but his voice, with its husky timbre was oddly comforting, soothing. But he was a doctor; that was part of his trade. "That's the all-clear signal."

"The siren, of course. I thought I was dreaming it. How long—and oh, your shoulder! I am so sorry."

"Don't give it a thought. I hardly noticed. It was . . . nice. That is, I didn't mind, and to be honest I fell asleep a bit myself and found your head a nice pillow, as well." He offered her a slanted smile, half apology, half entreaty.

"Oh." She didn't know what else to say. Then, still flustered, she blurted the first stupid thing that came to mind. "Guess we slept together on our first meeting." And immediately she reddened. She could not remember when was the last time such a full and complete blush had overcome her. She might have fought it off if she wasn't still so sluggish from sleep. Ah well, it was done now.

Alex laughed, not condescendingly, but more of a shared amusement. Shrugging, she joined him. It *was* funny. He then rose and held out his hand to her. Oddly, the gesture didn't strike her as a man doing the "gentlemanly thing" by giving a hand to a helpless female. She had no inclination to fight it, at least. She grasped his hand and let him gently tug her to her feet.

"Come on," he said, "let's see what remains of the city."

27

THE METROPOLE, built during Tsarist times and renovated in the thirties, was, as Pavel had assured, a good hotel by Russian standards. It was but a short walk from Red Square, other major hotels, and the American embassy. Gruk unloaded Cameron's baggage in the lobby, then bid her a *dasvidaniya*.

After the air raid Alex had walked her back to the truck, where she found the driver making repairs on the engine. Apparently, while he had holed up in a shelter during the air raid, a mechanic had suggested to Gruk a likely problem with the vehicle. It did the trick, at any rate, because the truck's engine roared—or at least coughed—into motion. She thanked Alex and they parted, but not before she told him she owed him at the very least a dinner sometime. He accepted the offer but warned her he often had a difficult time getting away from his work at decent hours.

She reflected on this as the hotel porter took her up to her room. Were the doctor's words a polite brush-off? Somehow she'd had the impression of him as being more direct than that, but still, he was little more than a stranger, even though they had spent the night together and shared some rather harrowing moments.

The porter, carrying her bags, led her to the elevator and up to the fourth floor. As he took her luggage to the room, the floor manager, or "key lady," as Cameron learned everyone referred to the woman, greeted her. She was a fat middle-aged woman with an affable enough smile beneath small cold eyes. Cameron remembered that doormen, porters, and no doubt key ladies in Russia, and especially in hotels catering to foreigners, were almost certainly agents of the secret police, or NKVD as it was now called. A fact of life here she must accept.

The woman led Cameron to her room, which was small but adequately appointed. Perhaps in New York or London or even Los Angeles, for that matter, it would have passed as no more than third-rate, but here in Moscow it was considered first-class. There was a balcony overlooking a busy side street, a bed set off in a small semi-alcove, and adequate but slightly threadbare furnishings—a desk, a table with two mismatched chairs, a sofa, and a couple of upholstered chairs. But best of all, it had its own bath! Cameron had not bathed in as long as she had not slept, and she knew that need must take precedence over all others.

The key lady let her tiny eyes settle on Cameron. "You like?"

"Yes, it is fine. Thank you very much."

"You want breakfast?" The woman's voice seemed to rumble up directly from her ample chest like a muffled foghorn. Her English was thickly accented, and Cameron had to listen closely to decipher it.

"I would very much, but first I'd like a bath." Cameron glanced at her watch. It was eight in the morning. "Could you bring breakfast at nine?"

"Good. Here are towels." The key lady opened a dresser drawer, removed the two towels it held, and set them on top of the dresser.

Cameron thanked the woman effusively and breathed a sigh when she exited. The first thing she did was haul her luggage up onto the bed. She took out her makeup bag and her silk dressing gown and carried them with the towels to the bathroom. Turning on the light, she tried not to be disappointed. The tiny room did not exactly sparkle and was, in fact, quite dingy. She was certain she saw a cockroach scurry away to some dark corner the moment the light flashed on. She cringed when she used the stained toilet and groaned when she saw there was no toilet paper. The flushing mechanism needed a great deal of prodding to work. She now also remembered that very few things in Russia ever work as, or when, they should.

The tub was the gravest disappointment. Its small size didn't bother her as much as the chipped and stained porcelain. She wondered when it last had been cleaned. Then she shrugged at that minor inconvenience when she turned on the water and it came out pale brown no matter how long she let it run. The hot water was tepid at best.

"Thank goodness you are no neat freak," she murmured to herself as she stepped into the water.

She had her own soap that smelled like roses—Blair had given her two bars as a going-away present. Cameron had thought the gift frivolous at the time, but now she wished her sister were here to receive a grateful hug. The rose scent made her forget what she was bathing in. She scrubbed it vigorously into her skin, inhaling the fragrance hungrily.

However, a tepid bath did not invite lounging, and in five minutes she was ready to get out as soon as she washed her hair. But as she started to dip her head into the tub to do so, she heard a noise in the other room.

"Who's there?" she called. Perhaps the porter with her breakfast.

Then the knob of the bathroom door jiggled as obviously someone grasped it.

"Hey!" she yelled as the door opened a crack. Only her quick reflexes saved her modesty. She grabbed the towel lying by the tub and flung it over her body as she sank back into the water. Luckily the towel was large enough to cover her as she drew up her knees in the water.

"Don't come in," she yelled.

"Is that any way to greet your favorite fellow?" Johnny's voice came from behind the door.

"If I'd had a gun, I would have shot you as a burglar." She clutched the ends of the towel, now quite wet, more tightly around her, for it would be just like Johnny to come in.

"Don't take another step nearer, Johnny Shanahan!" she warned. "What are you doing here, anyway, and how did you get in my room?"

"Heard you were in town, and I just couldn't wait to see you."

"Well, close the door and wait for me in the front room. I'll be there in a minute."

"Whatever you like, doll," he said, closing the door. His voice had that devilish, part-charming, part-evil sound that made gooseflesh rise on her skin. Or was her reaction merely because the water had steadily gone from tepid to ice-cold? She shook her head, bemused and most definitely befuddled. He never failed to catch her off guard.

Cameron gave her hair a quick wash and rinse, then stepped from the tub, rang out the soaked towel, and wrapped it around her head, thankful there was still a dry towel for her body. Once she finished drying, she slipped into her dressing gown, oddly conscious that the burgundy silk was a nice compliment to her particular skin tones and auburn hair. Actually the dressing gown was probably the most luxurious thing she had at the moment, even more so than the simple black evening dress, both of which she had purchased in Cairo. But she belted the robe with a secure knot.

Toweling her damp hair, she came into the front room to find Shanahan lounging on the sofa, legs sprawled out before him, puffing languidly on a cigarette. He looked as if he owned the place.

"You didn't answer my second question," Cameron said. "How did you get in my room?"

Johnny smiled benignly. "A packet of sugar persuaded the key lady to let me in."

"A packet of sugar? Oh, it doesn't matter." Her tone was now more patronizing than angry as she sighed and rolled her eyes. She *was* glad to see the idiot. Before she could say anything more, a knock came to the door. It was her breakfast. The waiter placed the tray on the table, then paused.

Cameron started to reach for her purse but realized she had no money to tip the man. She hadn't had time to change her money yet, and her smallest bill was a twenty—no doubt a month's wages for a Russian waiter! She'd also failed to tip the porter, and she hadn't been able to communicate that she would do so later. Shanahan must have perceived her quandary, for he jumped up, reached into his pocket, and handed the waiter three cigarettes. This seemed to more than mollify the man, and he left with effusive *spasiba*s.

"Thanks, Shanahan, that was generous of you." Her tone carried a hint of sarcasm, which he caught.

"You'll soon learn, my dear, that goods around here are more valuable than money, because even if most Russians had any money, there are few goods to purchase. That waiter would have to work quite a long time to have enough for a pack of smokes, and he might have to forgo milk and bread to do it." He resumed his seat, puffing on his own cigarette with renewed vigor. "So how long have you been here? What do you think of the place?"

"Not long enough to make many impressions. I spent the night in a bomb shelter. The room's all right. But no toilet paper, Johnny! A minor inconvenience, I suppose, but . . ."

"That's Russia," he said with a sigh. "They think that's why newspapers were invented."

Cameron chuckled and turned her attention to the breakfast tray. She was suddenly starved, and with great expectation she lifted the lids of the various dishes on the table. An omelet in one dish, toast in another, and a small bowl of caviar. None of it seemed hot, or even warm.

"Caviar for breakfast," she murmured, "now, that's a first."

But she went first for the pot of coffee, frowning a bit when she noted that it did not steam when she poured it into a cup. She glanced at Shanahan. He was wearing a smug grin.

"Your first breakfast in Russia," he said dryly.

"I'm too hungry to care." She sat down. "Would you like to join me?"

"No thanks. I've already had the pleasure."

Though everything was cold, she ate every morsel. She no doubt had caught the kitchen off guard by requesting the meal later than usual. Tomorrow would be different.

"So, Johnny, how has it been here?" she asked around her food. "How is the war going? No one says much."

"That's because no one knows much."

"Of course you—"

"Journalists know the least of all," he said with a frustrated edge to his voice. "I expect Stalin knows something, but he ain't talking. Any news we get usually comes a week after the fact. Sometimes, if the news is good—which is seldom—we only have to wait a couple of days for it. I can tell you that the Germans have pretty much swept through Lithuania, Latvia, and the western Ukraine. They are starting to put the squeeze on Leningrad. And the most recent Soviet communiqué has admitted that Hitler has reached Smolensk—"

"Johnny, that's only three hundred miles from Moscow!" Cameron gasped, nearly choking on her toast.

"The good news is that Papa Stalin seems to have stopped Adolf there—for now."

"You don't think the Russians can hold them?"

"Russia wasn't ready for this," he replied as he leaned toward the table and casually picked up a wedge of toast. "They don't have near enough war matériel." He spread a dollop of caviar on the toast and took a bite. "They don't have guns, but at least they have the best caviar on earth."

"The situation can't be that bad!"

"The factories are churning out weapons now with dizzying speed. The Reds are gonna catch up, no doubt, but until then . . ." He shook his head. "The best they can hope for is to hold the Germans long enough for winter to set in and do its work."

Cameron sipped her cold coffee and smiled.

"You actually like that stuff?" Johnny asked, rather incredulous.

"Every summer my dad makes iced coffee—he thinks he invented it. I grew to like it, and it reminds me of home." As she thought of her father, she suddenly realized much of her ire toward him had dulled. Foremost in her mind now was that if it hadn't been for him, she might not be here in the very midst of what must be one of the most exciting times in history.

"I'm not surprised," Johnny replied dryly. "That old tyrant probably believes he invented movable type. But even he would not appreciate cold coffee during a Russian winter."

"You haven't been here during a winter yet, Johnny. As I recall, many Russians believe winter is the best time here."

"Not during a war. There are already shortages. The last snows came this year in June. Even the oldest peasants said they hadn't seen a worse winter. The first snows will come in October. I'm no farmer, but even in Russia four months can't be an adequate growing season. And with nearly all manpower—and womanpower, too—focused on either fighting or churning out hardware for the war, the prospects don't look bright."

Cameron thought of her discussion with Alex on the roof of the apartment building. "Johnny, if history has taught the world nothing else, it is to never, ever underestimate the Russian people. That was Hitler's greatest mistake, and he will pay for it."

A laconic smile eased across Johnny's face. "I love it when you get passionate."

"This place does something to me, Johnny. I spent the night in a bomb shelter with people who were so strong, yet so very lackadaisical about their own strength. You can't easily crush something like that. And it makes me feel good to see it. Maybe a little of that has rubbed off on me."

"Nah, you were always strong, Hayes." He took a long draw from his cigarette, then crushed it out in the ashtray on the table. "I only hope this place doesn't rob you of that spirit."

"How can it when a lot of it is simply derived from being here?"

"The Russian people and the Soviet government are two different animals. You were very lucky if you spent a whole night with the people, because it is a rare occurrence for foreigners. The Russian people are discouraged from mingling with us—it may even be illegal."

Now that she thought about it, Cameron had wondered why the people in the shelter made so little attempt to relate to her. She'd decided it had been due to the language differences, yet she had been in other foreign countries where people's natural curiosity about foreigners had been enough to scale the difficulty of communication. It hadn't been so in the shelter. They had watched her but with a reserve that now Cameron realized might well have been a reticence born of fear. Yet that seemed so inconsistent with her impressions of such a strong people in the face of war.

"I suppose it has always been that way," she admitted. "When I was here as a kid, I didn't realize it. I thought it was because I was a kid."

"Well, prepare yourself," he said gloomily. "It's the government, not the people, you'll be dealing with—and that will be an experience akin to smashing your head against a brick wall."

"I've got a hard head," she said confidently.

"Don't I know it. I just hope it's hard enough."

After Shanahan left, Cameron fell asleep and did not wake until late that afternoon. She dined in the hotel dining room, as the hotel only provided breakfast in the rooms. But she did not mind because this was an opportunity to meet with many of the other correspondents. The foreigners had their own dining room and sat at one large table with another table to the side for their Russian secretaries and interpreters. Cameron was the only woman at the correspondents' table, but they greeted her with enthusiasm.

"What news have you from home?" asked Jed Donovan from the *New York Tribune*. "I heard Joe DiMaggio is on one beaut of a hitting streak."

"Sorry, Jed, I left home before baseball season started," she answered.

"Boy, I miss baseball," sighed Donovan, "almost as much as I miss sweet-smelling, smart-dressing American dames."

"Forget baseball and dames," said Ed Reed of the *Chicago Daily News*. "I'd give anything for some decent food. My mama's fried chicken smothered in gravy and creamy mashed potatoes . . ."

Most of these men hadn't been in the country much longer than Cameron, but they were already missing the comforts of life. Nevertheless, she enjoyed their company and decided they were basically a great group of men to suffer through a war with.

However, she begged off an invitation to attend the theater with several of her colleagues. She wanted to work on an article instead.

"Ah, the eager beaver new kid on the block," sneered Henry Cassidy, the *Associated Press* correspondent.

"You fellows have a head start already," she said. "I just want to catch up a bit."

"Leave her be, Hank," said Shanahan. "We'll have plenty of time to corrupt her."

She spent a couple of hours on an article about her first Moscow air raid in which she highly praised the intrepid fortitude of the people she encountered. Realizing that the milieu of war meant there must be certain restrictions upon imparting details of what she encountered, she made a pointed effort to keep her words within the guidelines that had been acceptable in other war zones she had been to. When she finished, she felt she had crafted a fine piece. And, amazingly, at only ten o'clock, she fell asleep again and did not wake until well after sunrise.

After breakfast, again a cold but hearty affair, she gathered up her article, stuffed it into her leather satchel, and headed out to report in officially for her duties. It was then that she learned the dismal truth.

At the Commissariat for Foreign Affairs, or the Narkomindel, located at the former Greek Legation Building, Cameron was directed to the office of Nikolai Palgunov, the Chief of the Soviet Press Department. Palgunov impressed Cameron immediately as a consummate bureaucrat. He was a small man imbued with enormous power over foreign correspondents, and it showed in his tedious, indeed, nitpicking approach to his job. He peered with cold eyes over thick wire-rimmed lenses at Cameron and seemed to relish the prospect of yet another green foreigner to rake over the coals of his tedium.

"The Soviet government has, for the benefit of foreign correspondents, formed the Soviet Information Bureau," he said in a monotone.

He spoke French, so he and Cameron were able to converse without an interpreter. Since Cameron had been forced as a kid to attend elite boarding schools, this was one language she could understand fairly well and speak, if only brokenly.

"You will find our system perhaps a bit complex, but naturally in a state of war certain precautions must be instituted."

"Of course," Cameron agreed. She might be green, but she quickly interpreted this to mean that the Soviet government would do everything in its power to control the flow of information from their country. "I do hope I will be able to follow a combat unit—"

"That, of course, will be impossible, Miss Hayes. Perhaps when it is deemed safe to do so, a tour of the Front will be permitted."

Cameron took that to mean that correspondents would be allowed to see the Front when the war turned in the Soviets' favor. She now remembered once again what her father always said: *"The only way to survive as a journalist in Russia is to learn to read between the lines. Seldom does a Russian ever say exactly what he means."*

"There will, however, be regular press conferences," Palgunov said almost proudly, as if he were offering a great boon. "They will be delivered by Comrade Lozovsky, Deputy Commissar for Foreign Affairs. It is a rare privilege for such a high official to communicate in this way to correspondents."

"Then I do appreciate it," she replied, and he did not appear to perceive her droll tone.

"I also deliver a daily communiqué at around three in the morning. This timing will allow time for the dispatches of most of the correspondents to make their morning editions. Most of the journalists make use of the pressroom for the writing of their dispatches. The censor's office is conveniently located nearby."

"Very good," said Cameron, careful to hide any sarcasm, of which she was feeling much, from her voice. "I understand I will be assigned an interpreter and a secretary."

"We are rather short at the moment of office help, but you will have an interpreter as soon as one becomes available. You will also be issued a ration book, and if you inquire at the American embassy, you will be shown the embassy commissary, where you can make most of your purchases."

He went on for several minutes about shopping, but Cameron was still groaning inwardly about his bombshell of no available interpreters and heard little else. What was she going to do without an interpreter? Palgunov had already mentioned that most—which she interpreted as *all*—news was to be gleaned from the major Russian newspapers, all, of course, written in Russian. The interpreters translated the papers for the correspondents, who then wrote their dispatches from that. The government restrictions made the reporters work with one arm tied behind their backs, but she was to work blind as well, and there was no telling when the inefficient wheels of the Soviet bureaucracy would come up with an interpreter for her.

Finally her meeting with the chief came to an end. He rose from his chair, and Cameron did, as well.

"Oh, one final thing," he said offhandedly, and she braced herself for another bombshell, "all dispatches must be stamped with an official stamp from your newspaper."

"But the *Globe* has never had a bureau here, and we have no stamp," she argued logically enough.

He wrote something on a scrap of paper and handed it to her. "This is a shop that will make a stamp for you." As she took the paper he added, "At the moment, however, they are not operating due to having been bombed." He wasn't smiling. His lips remained thin and taut, but Cameron could swear she saw a slight twitch to them, accompanied by an evil glint in his eye.

"Then surely I can be given some leeway regarding this—"

"That is not possible, Miss Hayes. The rules must be followed, or there would be chaos in my department. We can't have that, now, can we?"

"What am I supposed to do, then?"

"I am certain you will work it out, humm?"

She left his office feeling that not only had her arms been tied and she had been blinded, but that her legs had been cut out from under her, as well. She wondered why Shanahan and the other correspondents she had dined with last night had not enlightened her about all this. Competition was stiff, yet she had noted a level of camaraderie among the men, also. Had they deliberately neglected to fill her in because she was a woman? Of course, this wouldn't be the first time she had been forced to pay for her membership in this predominately male club. But the men last night had been friendly enough and even glad to see her. They had seemingly welcomed her as an equal.

She shrugged, turned a corner, and ran into Shanahan.

"Hi'ya, sweetheart!" he said in a chipper tone.

She responded only with a sour look.

"Uh-oh, I bet you've just had your little introductory talk with our best friend, Nikky Palgunov."

"You could say that."

"You're feeling a little cut off at the knees, eh?"

She gaped at his incredibly correct summary of the situation. "Why didn't you say anything, Shanahan? Why didn't anyone say anything?"

"Listen, honey, would you have believed us?"

"Why shouldn't I? It would have been nice to have some warning." She paused, suddenly realizing just what she was expecting—the very thing she spent much of her time disdaining, that is, help from others regarding her work. She had made great noise about her independence, and now she was expecting her colleagues—or competitors—to coddle her as if she were helpless. "Never mind, Johnny, it is not your place to hold my hand."

"You wouldn't let me if I tried."

"You're right." Then remembering her satchel and the article it held, she added, "There is one bit of help I'll happily accept. Where is the censor's office?"

"You already got something to send?"

"I just wrote up a little something about my air raid experience—"

"Cameron, let me tell you now, if it didn't come from Palgunov's communiqué or from *Pravda*, it probably ain't gonna make it through."

"Oh, it's just an innocuous piece about—nothing seditious, that's for sure. I was very careful not to mention anything sensitive."

"But—"

"Thanks, Johnny, but I am sure it will be okay."

Shrugging, he gave her directions to the office. Cameron found it easily enough. Fifteen minutes later, she exited the censor's office holding in her hand what was left of her thousand-word article. "Last night I experienced my first Russian air raid."

Feeling completely wrung over, she found her way to the pressroom. She was greeted by the familiar and surprisingly friendly *clackety-clack* of typewriter keys. Then followed the verbal greetings of her colleagues. Yes, she felt definitely that she had entered a club, but despite everything, she felt very much a part of it. She realized that all these men had experienced the same disheartening blows she had that day. And she knew that had they sat her down and spent hours warning her about the woes of the Soviet Press Department, she would never have believed them, or at least she would have believed she would somehow rise above it all.

But there was another hopeful note to be gleaned from this moment. These men were busy writing. They had somehow found a way to surmount all the Soviet restrictions. They were working. They were reporting the war. Somehow she could, too.

Someone jumped up and cleared a space for her at a table. She didn't have her typewriter, but there was a spare she could use. One of the men advised that she keep her portable at the hotel so she could use it there should she be cut off from the press department for any reason. Others stopped work and listened with great sympathy to her miserable tale. The correspondent from the *London Times* offered his official stamp to use, saying his paper would forward her dispatches on to the *Globe*. Another man loaned her his interpreter, and as the men resumed work—for deadlines would not wait—the woman interpreter began reading *Pravda* to Cameron.

———

Cameron returned to the hotel just before two o'clock for lunch. She was in her room freshening up before the meal when her telephone rang. It was the desk clerk announcing that a Dr. Rostov would like to see her. She said she was coming down anyway and that she would receive her visitor in the lobby. She took extra care with her makeup and hair, and instead of her usual skirt and blouse, she slipped into one of her nicer day dresses, a beige wool that had a dark brown suede yoke with decorative tabs and matching long sleeves and belt. It was very chic, and she wished now she had packed the matching Breton-style hat. Blair had always said it looked charming on her. It was a bit warm out for wool, but not nearly as warm as July in Los Angeles would have been. She hadn't worn this dress yet in her travels because it was one of her few designer outfits and she was saving it for something special.

So why wear it now? she asked herself as she took one last glance in the mirror before exiting her room. Then again, why not?

As she entered the lobby, she saw Alex Rostov standing beneath the regal chandelier, looking even more stunning than he had in a dim bomb shelter. He certainly looked taller, and his hair was definitely lighter. With his ruddy skin, broad shoulders, and vivid blue eyes, he looked very Russian, the strain that had come down from the Norse invaders of old. He was dressed in a tan suit of a subtle plaid with a darker brown sweater vest, white shirt, and brown necktie under the jacket. His clothes had a worn look, but he seemed to have taken care with his dressing.

"Hello, Alex! What a pleasant surprise." Her voice sounded strange, and the smile on her face did not feel right. What was she doing—? Then it hit her with the force of a blow. She was flirting!

"I hope you don't mind my just showing up like this. I had some time off and knew if I gave it too much thought, an emergency would come and rob me of it." He took her outstretched hand. His hand was warm, his grip firm. She was amazed at how large his hand was. She somehow thought a physician's hand would be slim and dexterous.

"I'm glad you came. I desperately need a break." She forced her voice back to some semblance of her normal timbre. "I was just about to have lunch. Would you care to join me?"

"I doubt the hotel would appreciate an unexpected mouth to feed. Russian hotels are funny about that. But perhaps I can entice you into having lunch with me somewhere in the city?"

"Oh, I'd love it! I haven't had much chance to explore yet."

They were about to leave when Shanahan ambled toward them from the elevator. He was with a couple of their colleagues, who continued on to the dining room while he paused. She wished she could have pretended not to see him and didn't know why. But she didn't get her wish.

She made hasty introductions and felt the awkwardness of being caught between two beaus. It was silly, of course, for Alex was definitely not a beau. Shanahan was hardly one, either. Maybe it was more like a girl being caught with a boy by her big brother. She knew Shanahan would taunt her unmercifully about Alex Rostov later, despite the fact that there was absolutely no reason for him to do so. She already saw it in his expression as he eyed Rostov with the shrewdness of an art dealer authenticating a masterpiece. Shanahan missed nothing. He probably also had noted the unnatural quality to Cameron's voice. He'd give her absolutely no peace about that, either.

"So, Cameron," Johnny said, "you mean to tell me you spent all night with the good doctor in a bomb shelter and you never said a word about it? And I thought you told me everything."

"Not everything, Shanahan. You're the enemy, remember?"

"I almost forgot during your bath yesterday—"

"Johnny!" she actually screeched. Then to Alex she said, forcing her tone to calm, "This man is a consummate liar and rogue. The only time he speaks the truth is on paper."

Alex smiled, though obviously he was feeling the discomfort of being an outsider while they talked inside jokes. He then said with incredible aplomb, "You must be starved, Cameron. Perhaps we ought to get you some lunch."

"Yes, I'm positively famished. You will excuse us, won't you, Johnny?"

"You're not eating in the hotel?"

"Alex is going to show me some of the city."

"Well, have fun then, kiddies. And, Alex, bring her home at a decent hour." Shanahan smirked as he turned toward the dining room.

Alex and Cameron left the hotel. The afternoon air was warm but not stifling so. The sky was blue and a cool breeze eased down the street.

"Nice fellow," Alex said conversationally as they walked. Casual as his tone was, she could tell he was curious about Johnny.

"Nice? Shanahan? The last word I'd use to describe Johnny is nice."

"You're old friends?"

"Dr. Rostov, are you trying to find out if Johnny and I are . . . well, if we are involved?"

He grinned, revealing two rows of white teeth, mostly straight except for a slightly crooked incisor on the bottom row. "I'm not very subtle, am I? I'm not implying I have any expectations of you and me, that is, well—" Laughing, he shook his head. "I guess there is no way to express my curiosity without immense awkwardness. But it was just idle curiosity, really, nothing more."

"Johnny and I used to work on the same paper in Los Angeles. Then I . . . well, I quit and went to work for the rival paper. We used to . . . well, date. It's over now." She could hear the lack of confidence in her voice. It was over. Wasn't it? "My father didn't approve of Johnny—not that his approval mattered. Believe me, I would have married the man just to defy my father. But Johnny let himself be bought off—oh, you don't need to hear all that. Sounds like one of those radio soap operas." She paused, desperate to change the subject; then she glanced up and saw where they were. "Red Square!" she breathed.

She had been so intent on getting to the Narkomindel earlier that morning she had not taken the time to notice it as she passed by. Now she let it sink into her senses. About a quarter of a mile in length, it was more vast, more impressive than she remembered from her childhood. At the far end was St. Basil's, and even its camouflage could not hide the fact that this had to be one of the most beautiful structures in the world. It was said that Ivan the Terrible had gouged out the architect's eyes so that the marvel could not be copied.

Set almost right in the middle of the square was a flower kiosk, bursting with color—yellow, white, blue, pink, snapdragons, stock, marigolds, daisies.

"I wish I were an artist," Cameron murmured. "Though I am a writer, there are some things words just cannot capture."

"You still should write about it," he said. "Your readers would love it if only you could give them a glimpse of the wonder there is now in your eyes."

The glow momentarily dimmed. "Even if I could, the censors would cut it all out."

"I see you have already run into Soviet bureaucracy."

"Like bashing my head against the Kremlin Wall! And to make matters worse, I can't even write what they will allow, because they haven't got an interpreter for me yet."

"I know how to take your mind off it temporarily." He nodded toward a woman who had a large box suspended over her shoulders. He took Cameron's hand and strode toward the vendor. He spoke in Russian to the woman who lifted the lid of her box, withdrew two packages, and exchanged them for a couple of kopecks. Alex gave one to Cameron, and they continued their stroll. "Eskimo Pie," he said.

She opened up her bundle and saw it was exactly that. "What do you know, just like in America!"

"We even call them by the same name."

"And who said our countries were that different?" She bit into her ice cream. "Very good."

"It will tide you over I hope until we find someplace to eat. I'm afraid restaurants are far and few now that so many have evacuated from the city." Pausing, he chuckled dryly. "Even in the best of times we cannot boast fine dining."

"Now, there it is again," Cameron said. "You used 'we' again. I didn't have the impression that this was your home."

Before answering, he took a bite from his ice cream. Cameron wasn't certain if it was just coincidence or if he was avoiding her comment. But he finally did answer. "I suppose it is my home now. Five years of my life have been spent here."

"Oh, I thought you said you'd only been here since '38."

"Yes, but then there were the two years from my birth until my family emigrated."

"To America. Chicago, right?"

"Yes." He drew out the word, then pointedly turned his attention back to his ice cream.

"I suppose I am prying, but it was just idle curiosity, nothing more . . ." she said matter-of-factly.

He smiled at her obvious reference to his earlier comment. Then he seemed to relax. "We both probably have fascinating life stories. I'll tell you mine, but you must reciprocate. Agreed?" When she nodded, he continued, "I was born in St. Pete—I mean Leningrad—in 1910. However, it was St. Petersburg when I entered it rather ingloriously during a miserable blizzard in the month of April. My parents were Socialists, both of them. Avid followers of Lenin, for which they paid by being forced into exile in 1912. They went to America in hopes of raising support for their cause. My father had a friend in Chicago, so that is where we ended up and where I lived and grew . . . until three years ago."

"And what brought you back to Russia?"

He hesitated, then suddenly pointed toward the GUM department store at the south end of the Square. "*Piroshki!*" he exclaimed.

"What?"

"Lunch. Come on."

She followed him the rest of the way across the Square to a vendor who was indeed selling meat pies. Cameron had a distinct feeling Alex did not wish to tell her everything about himself. Of course that was his prerogative, but it made her no less curious. It took all her discipline not to throw her hard-driving journalistic powers against him to ferret out the untold story. It wasn't any of her business. Dr. Alex Rostov was not a "breaking story."

They bought piroshki and a syrupy drink that was supposed to be the Russian version of Coca-Cola. Then they found a place to sit on a low wall just outside of Red Square. Cameron slaked her hunger a bit on the pie, then simply could not resist the temptation to ask her guide one question.

"So your parents were really revolutionaries?"

"That surprises you?"

"Well, your noble bearing cries Russian aristocracy," she responded with a touch of playful sarcasm. "But if they were Socialists and exiles, why didn't they return after the Revolution?"

"It was their greatest disappointment that they could not return to reap the rewards of all they had worked so hard to promote. My mother became ill with a heart condition, and returning to Russia would have killed her."

"How sad. Are they still in Chicago, then?" Cameron simply could not help the questions. His story was fascinating even if he probably didn't really believe it to be so.

"They are both dead now. Oddly enough, my father went first, killed in an automobile accident about ten years ago. My mother died . . . three years ago."

Something in his tone, something sad, almost broken, made her know it was time to cease her queries. His eyes seemed to sink almost visibly inward. The blue became very pale, empty of color.

Feeling bad that she had been the cause of this downward slide of the previously pleasant mood of the afternoon, Cameron jumped in with a determined but light tone.

"My father was an immigrant, too," she said hurriedly. "From Ireland, though. No big deal there, however. Just forced away because of poverty. And before you could say Horace Greeley, he went west to California and made his fortune. He's the publisher of the *Los Angeles Journal*. I'm only telling you this because you told me about your parents. I try never to speak of my connection to the paper, especially since I happen to also be in journalism."

"You wish to make it on your own volition?" His tone now matched hers in lightness. His eyes had become vivid once again.

"Yes," she answered emphatically. "I *have* made it on my own—" She stopped abruptly as she heard herself, then smiled sheepishly. "I sound like I really don't know for sure, don't I? Well, I do have my doubts sometimes. That's partly why I quit my father's paper and went to work for his rival, but even that is filled with . . . I don't know, pitfalls. You don't know how many times I wished my name was Smith, or anything but Hayes."

"I was right. We both do have interesting stories." There was a sardonic quality to his tone.

"What we're telling."

"Yes . . . what we're telling. Perhaps everything is not interesting—or pleasant."

"I have to confess, Alex, I have this annoyingly curious nature. I've been told I resemble a puppy dog always sniffing around for something and when I find it, I sink my teeth in and refuse to let go. I will try to curb it, I promise."

He laughed softly, almost tenderly. "Puppy dogs may be annoying at times, but they do have a way of worming into one's heart." His eyes, a startling blue now, focused on her, and they held both a mirth and a gentleness that caught her breath.

"So do mysterious doctors," she heard herself say, and she didn't know why.

"I don't mean to be mysterious, Cameron. It is only that—" He shook his head as if shaking off a spell. "Please do not take it personally, but there are simply things I don't wish to talk about."

"I understand, Alex." She, too, made an almost visible attempt to shake off whatever unwelcome spell had seemed to hover over them. She brushed her hands together, ostensibly divesting them of the crumbs from her lunch, though the underlying meaning of the gesture was more than obvious. She jumped up. "Come on, there is so much more of the city I'd like to see. Do you have time?"

"I most certainly do."

29

CAMERON WAS EATING breakfast in her room the next morning when there was a knock at her door. Answering it, she encountered a young woman.

"Miss Gayes?" said the woman in English, thickly accented. Like most Russians Cameron had encountered, this woman had trouble with the *H* in Hayes because there was no equivalent of *H* in the Russian alphabet.

"Yes, may I help you?"

"I am Sophia Gorbenko. I was sent from the Narkomindel . . . to be your interpreter."

"Oh, wonderful!" Cameron dropped all her previous reserve and flung open her door. "Do come in."

The young woman looked like a child, petite and fine featured with hair the pale tan color of a fawn. Her skin was also pale—but then all Russians seemed to be pale—and her eyes were a greenish gray and fringed with the thickest brown lashes Cameron had ever seen. Sophia Gorbenko looked like a porcelain doll. Next to her Cameron felt like a tall, gangly giraffe.

Cameron gestured toward the table and, as she drew up a second chair, said, "Please sit down. Have you had breakfast?"

"I have, thank you." Sophia sat down opposite Cameron.

"Some tea, then? It's not hot, but it never is. There's a spare cup."

"Thank you very much."

Cameron filled the cup. "Well, I never dreamed they would come through with an interpreter this quickly. I am just thrilled. And you speak very good English."

"I was taught by my father and my grandmother. My accent is very bad, but I keep working on it. I am very happy to have this job and to have a real American to talk to. I also speak French and German if you have need." Her tone was soft and self-deprecating. Cameron had the feeling a single hard look would knock the poor child over. So she modified her usual overbearing nature as best she could.

"How old are you, Sophia?"

"Nineteen."

Cameron thought she looked twelve but kept that impression to herself.

Sophia added, "I have brought the morning papers. I am told the correspondents like to get started as soon as possible." Sophia took the newspapers from her bag. There were copies of *Pravda*, *Izvestia*, and *Red Star*, the military paper.

"Excellent! Let's get started, then." Cameron pushed aside the breakfast tray.

"Please to finish your meal," Sophia said, and it was part entreaty and part the gentlest command Cameron had ever received.

"I'd rather work."

Sophia glanced quickly at the food, then just as quickly looked away. In that brief moment Cameron noted disapproval in the girl's eyes, though little Sophia no doubt would have been mortified had she realized she had been found out. This girl had probably suffered through famine and privations of which Cameron could not even imagine. It must seem to the girl the height of arrogance to waste even a spoonful of caviar and a slice of toast.

Somewhat apologetically, Cameron added, "Perhaps we can save this for a snack later."

Sophia's lips, which were rather full and large in proportion to the rest of her, twitched into a smile. "That would be nice, Miss Gayes."

"But before we begin work, you must call me Cameron. Not only because you seem to be having trouble with the *H*, but also because I have no female friends in Russia, and I would count it an honor to have you as my first."

Now Sophia's lips spread into a large smile. "I would like that. Dr. Rostov said you were very nice person."

"You know Dr. Rostov?"

"He is a good friend of my family. It was he who put in a word about your need of an interpreter to the Narkomindel and suggested me for the position."

Cameron had mentioned the problem to him, but only in passing. She had never imagined he had such pull with the foreign office as to solve her problem. "I shall have to thank him, then."

"It is I who am grateful," said the girl. "I am not a regular employee of the Narkomindel, so I am very blessed to have this job."

Cameron was happy to hear these words, especially because it was usually a given among foreigners in Russia that, in addition to hotel staff, all secretaries, guides, and interpreters were to some degree agents of the NKVD. For Sophia to be that much removed from the regular bureaucracy seemed a very good thing.

They spent the next several hours until lunch at work. It was a slow, tedious process. There were problems in actual translation because as good as Sophia's English was, she had not had enough exposure to actual English-speaking people to be familiar with idiom and such. But this was fairly minor compared to the difficulties of wading through the newspapers themselves and gleaning out gems that would interest Cameron's readers in California. Sophia had to read through many a boring, dry article before Cameron realized it held nothing for her to use.

The hours of work did produce two good articles that Cameron typed up and which Sophia then hurried over to the censor. When Sophia returned an hour later with the censored material for Cameron to proof, the whole effort seemed wasted. She was left with barely enough to fill a couple of inches in the paper. Her lead had been completely decimated, leaving only a few sentences taken verbatim from the Russian papers.

In the meantime Cameron received a phone call, which Sophia took and translated. There was to be a press conference at the Narkomindel at nine that evening. She asked Sophia to drop off the article at the cable office and then to take the rest of the day off until nine, when she would be needed again.

Cameron went to the dining room and quickly realized that her colleagues had all scooped her on the day's news. She was curious, however, about what news the others had lifted from the newspapers and if she had chosen wisely for her own dispatches. Much to her surprise, she discovered that even the old hands had this same curiosity. And just as she would never have asked outright what they had sent, the others also approached it subtly.

Barton of *Reuters* asked casually, "What did you think of that story in *Red Star* today about the capture of Pskov?"

"Yeah," Shanahan replied, "it's the first admission that the Germans are even that close to Leningrad, and rumor has it Pskov fell a couple of weeks ago."

"What article is that?" asked Donovan from the *New York Tribune*.

Everyone knew then that Donovan had missed it. They were certain of this fact when he jumped up and headed out the door with the lame excuse that he had forgotten to lock his room. He was going to file a dispatch, because it was, of course, better late than never. Cameron felt rather smug because she hadn't missed the article and had filed the story. She hadn't scooped Shanahan this time, but at least the *Globe* would print this important news of the Russian war effort.

At nine the correspondents made their way to the Narkomindel for the press conference to be held in a back parlor on the lower floor. The correspondents took seats around a green felt-covered table, which made the gathering look every bit like a Saturday night poker game back home. Cameron slipped in beside Shanahan while interpreters found seats at their respective correspondents' elbows. Someone provided a sugary sweet fruit drink reputed to have come from the Caucasus.

"Good evening," said Solomon Lozovsky, the Deputy Commissar

of Foreign Affairs. "I am so glad to see such a good attendance." He spoke Russian through his own interpreter, but Cameron knew he was fluent in French and English. Cameron was glad to hear Sophia's pen busily scratching notes on her pad.

Lozovsky delivered a rather innocuous statement. Cameron immediately saw that he lived up to his reputation of being the master of propaganda dispensing. He had perfected the art of saying much without saying anything at all. But he did not look like a devious sort. His slightly unkempt goatee and moustache gave him a benevolent air. He looked more like a scholar than a politician. He was in fact more cosmopolitan than many of his comrades, having spent time abroad.

When he paused and invited questions, Cameron decided as the new member of the "club" that she should strike first. "Comrade Lozovsky, can you tell us where the Front is at this time?"

"The Front, you ask? What can I say? The Front is unstabilized."

Donovan then asked the same question the correspondents had been asking for weeks. "When will we get to visit the Front?"

"Perhaps when the Front is more . . . stabilized." The tiniest hint of a smile twitched the commissar's lips.

"What can you say about reports out of Berlin that the Germans have surrounded Smolensk?" Shanahan asked.

"Just another fried duck out of the rumor kitchen," the commissar smirked. "There is an old Russian proverb, 'The maggot gnaws on the cabbage, but it dies before it is done.' The Fascist barbarians have gotten their fill of the cabbage. They will soon crawl away and die."

"So Moscow will not be threatened?" Donovan asked.

"The only way Hitler will see Moscow is from a postcard."

Lozovsky proved himself full of such witticisms, far more so than he was of actual information. But he did have a small treat that night. Lifting his large briefcase up onto the table, he unfastened it and withdrew a stack of documents.

"These," he said with great relish, "are documents captured from the Fascist bandits."

He passed them around, and though all were written in German, they looked authentic. Sophia looked them over and said they seemed to be regarding gas attacks. Lozovsky verified this.

"These documents prove that the Fascist dogs intend to use poison gas against our troops." Then he leaned forward, his lowered voice only adding emphasis to his words. "And in fact there have already been reports from the front lines of substances being released in Soviet trenches that have caused our troops varying degrees of lung and stomach discomfort."

The room erupted into a squabble of questions, but Lozovsky would give no more details. He then switched gears by commenting on the success of the press conferences themselves. He hoped all were happy with the progress. It seemed a perfect opening for widespread complaint from the correspondents, but no one said anything except the Japanese correspondent.

"Comrade Lozovsky, I would humbly request that since my language is so difficult that you would allow the Japanese correspondents to receive their daily communiqué two hours earlier than the others. We also feel that because of the language, censorship is an especially lengthy process, and it should be suspended altogether for the Japanese."

The commissar listened with great interest to the request, nodding as if he truly understood the problem. Then he said, "I have never heard the problem stated in such a succinct fashion. Thank you so much, Comrade Hatenaka."

And with that, the question was addressed and neatly dispensed of without the commissar making any commitment at all. The meeting was adjourned, and the correspondents trailed up to the pressroom to try to eke an article out of the nothing they had received. But even that attempt was thwarted by the drone of the air-raid siren.

Everyone filed down to the shelter in the cellar of the building. Cameron had her pad and pencil with her, and she used the time to write. There were three censors in the shelter, but they shook their heads when she tried to give them her finished article.

"We have no dictionaries with us," they said. "We will look later, eh?"

Of course. Using the hours holed up in a shelter for work was far too efficient for Russians!

Cooped up again in a shelter, Cameron wanted to scream. She was far too restless to join the men in their games of cards or chess. Nor was she interested in Palgunov's little game of quizzing his staff on his favorite subject, Western literature.

"Who wrote *Call of the Wild*?"

"How many books did Dickens write?"

"What is Mark Twain's real name?"

She visited a bit with Sophia, but soon the conversation lagged between her and the obviously shy girl. Cameron let her head fall back against the brick wall. She had used that very analogy to describe her dealings with the Soviets and had been in the country only three days. Yet she had already been thwarted on many levels. She'd tried to get in to see officials with no luck. She'd requested tours but had been put off with lame excuses. How was she going to survive an entire war? She almost wished Hitler would make speedy work of the country.

30

ALEX STRIPPED OFF his rubber gloves and his bloodstained surgical gown, tossing them into the laundry basket. He had just finished a particularly thorny bowel reconstruction on a strapping young boy, a soldier—his patients were nearly all soldiers these days. This boy with his broad peasant face and burly shoulders, who had been made for tilling the soil, not for killing, would never be the same again. With only half his intestines intact and a colostomy to help the other half to function, he would probably waste away to a shadow of his former self. If he survived at all. He still must face the threat of infection and the myriad of other complications that still could set in. The only good news in the matter was that the boy would probably never have to go back to the Front—unless the war dragged on for several years.

But the peasant boy had been only one of Alex's surgical patients that night. It was now five o'clock in the morning, and he had been at it since the previous morning with only a short break for supper. His surgical team hadn't even paused to take note of the air raid. Thus far the Germans had respected the red cross on the roof of the building—

and well they should, because many of Alex's patients were German prisoners.

At any rate, he was going to get off his feet for five minutes.

He went to the doctors' lounge, drew a cup of strong tea from the samovar, and sat in one of the chairs at a large round table. There was a sofa in the room, but he didn't dare recline on something so comfortable. He'd heard ambulances arrive as he left surgery, and no doubt he'd be paged over the loudspeaker very soon.

Alex sipped his tea and gave his familiar surroundings a casual perusal—the drab, dingy walls, the worn, rickety furnishings, the tattered curtains on the dusty, now blacked-out windows. He'd been a stark idealist when he had entered medicine a dozen years ago. Money had never been his motivation. But to have sunk to this . . .

"It's my own fault, and I know it," he murmured, not even realizing he had spoken aloud.

Still, despite his idealism, maybe even because of it, he'd had grand visions of medical glory, of making a real mark, doing something impressive for mankind. There was no hope of that anymore.

"That's my own fault, too."

"Talking to yourself, my boy?" A voice came at Alex's shoulder. He hadn't heard the door open.

Alex chuckled in response. "I'm so tired I don't know what I am doing."

"Yes. I heard you had a difficult case."

"Do come and join me, Yuri, so I have someone more interesting than myself to converse with."

The newcomer, a tall, lean man in his early fifties with dark hair that had grayed in a most distinguished manner, strode into the room, drew himself a cup of tea, then sat at the table. He was wearing a white lab coat over neatly pressed black trousers, a white shirt, and a carefully knotted necktie. Care had obviously been taken with his appearance, despite the fact that his garments were neither fashionable nor new. He wore a stethoscope around his neck and a badge on his coat identifying him as Dr. Yuri Fedorcenko, Chief of Staff.

"So what are the boy's chances? The bowel resection?" Fedorcenko asked.

"Fifty-fifty at best. His intestine was like a sieve. I stitched up what I could, but I had to remove a good portion. We are, of course, low on blood, so I could not transfuse him with as many units as he needed.

If he survives all this, there is still the hurdle of sepsis to surmount."

"Well, at least the boy has one of our best doctors."

"That's kind of you to say."

"I mean it!" Fedorcenko said emphatically. "America's loss was our gain."

"They weren't exactly crying about my leaving."

"Alex, none of us should have to spend our lives paying for past mistakes." Fedorcenko rubbed his clean-shaven chin as he peered at his colleague over steel-rimmed spectacles.

Alex knew the man was not speaking empty platitudes. He knew his boss and mentor had struggled through his own share of personal mistakes. Alex only hoped that if, or when, he rose above the ashes of his own failures, he might come out as fine a man as Dr. Fedorcenko. The problem was, Yuri made it clear that his victories had not been won by his own strength. His hope rested entirely on a higher power, on a faith in God to whom he gave all glory. Alex was not ready to follow that path. He'd been there before, and it had failed him—or perhaps he had failed it—but either way, the whole matter of faith was now beyond him.

"Dr. Fedorcenko," blared the loudspeaker, "you are wanted in Ward C."

Yuri rose, rinsed out his cup at the sink, then headed toward the door. Pausing momentarily, he said, "Alex, let's talk again later. I had a fascinating case yesterday I'd like to tell you about. Why don't you come to dinner soon? Katya asked only the other day why we had not seen you in such a long while."

"Thank you, Yuri. The first chance I can get away—"

"I'm your boss, you know. I will schedule you an evening off to-morrow."

"And we can pray there are no emergencies."

"That may be asking too much, even of God, but we shall see, eh?" Fedorcenko grinned before exiting.

Alex thought fondly of the family that had taken him under their wing since he had come to Moscow three years ago. They had practically adopted him as a son, with no more recommendation than that Alex's parents had been good friends of Fedorcenko's brother in America. Without Dr. Fedorcenko, Alex would never have been able to re-build his life to the extent he had. He would be . . . He shuddered visibly as he thought about just where he might be now. He shook the dismal image from his mind.

He was about to finish his break, having taken well over five minutes, when the door opened again. This time it was no doctor.

"Ah, Aleksei, my friend! They told me I might find you here."

"Hello, Anatoly," Alex replied. "You are rather far out of your element, aren't you?" But somehow Alex was not at all surprised at the confident manner with which the new arrival dominated the lounge.

If there had been football in the Soviet Union, Anatoly Bogorodsk would have been recruited as a linebacker. He was only five-eleven, but his two-hundred-twenty-pound frame was solid muscle. Lacking the game of football to put all that brawn to its best use, Anatoly had found instead a nice position with the NKVD, the current appellation for Russia's secret police.

Anatoly strode into the lounge, grabbed a chair, and straddled it, facing Alex. The old piece of furniture groaned and wobbled under the man's weight. "As you well know, I have a deep aversion to the odor of antiseptics, but I did wish to see you. Do you have a few minutes, my friend?" The fact that he had already made himself comfortable indicated Alex's response to the question was moot at best.

"I never have a minute, but for one of the NKVD's finest, I can make the time."

Anatoly laughed. "How I love your Americanisms! 'NKVD's finest'—very funny. But I won't argue with the truth of it. It's been a long time, Aleksei, since we have seen each other. My wife and son both have asked why Dr. Aleksei has not come to see them."

"I practically live at the hospital since the war started."

"Your loyalty and dedication are to be commended."

Alex merely gave a deprecating shrug in response. Anatoly was indeed a friend, though an odd one for a man in Alex's position, but Alex had the feeling Anatoly hadn't come by the hospital to slather him with praise. "So, what brings you here today?"

"I wish I could say a friendly visit."

"But?"

"I owe you a great deal, Aleksei."

"You need not mention it."

"I will mention it!" Anatoly's small, dark eyes lit with passion. "Because of you, my son lives today. You alone spared me the greatest grief a man can know."

Uncomfortable, Alex tried to steer the man from his mode of praise. "How is Stephan?"

"Excellent! Perfect! My pride and joy!"

"I can see that. And I would love to talk more with you, my friend, about your family—I truly would. But I was just finishing my break and must get back to work."

"And so I can no longer avoid unpleasantness, eh? Believe me, I do not like what brings me here. I do not like when my job forces me to censure my dearest friends." Anatoly shifted and the chair creaked. "I am concerned, Aleksei, about recent reports regarding your—how shall I say?—associations."

"My associations?"

"With the American journalist. Apparently you spent the entire night with her during an air raid—"

"Purely a coincidence, I assure you."

"No doubt. And what of the afternoon you spent together two days ago? Please realize, I hate asking such questions. It is merely routine, and if it were entirely up to me, I would ask no questions at all. To me your loyalty is unimpeachable."

"I am still a foreigner."

"You are in an unfortunate gray area. Though you have been away from the country for nearly thirty years, you are still a citizen and a member of the Party, and that counts for much and allows you much latitude. You have conducted yourself impeccably these last three years. The Union of Soviet Socialist Republics holds you in high regard. For this reason I understand the Narkomindel took your recommendation for an interpreter for the foreign woman. Nevertheless, I would not want to see your freedom—and I use that word only for want of better—jeopardized by . . . well, questionable associations."

Alex steepled his fingers and tapped them thoughtfully against his lips. He knew better than anyone his peculiar position in Russia. The Soviet government did not quite know what to do with him, thus he was wildly free by the standards of the average Russian citizen, and he was dizzyingly free compared to nearly all foreigners. The government might hold him in high regard, yet he was still watched, as Anatoly's observations revealed. Membership in the Communist Party and his elite status in the desperately needy medical field could cover him only so far. He was never certain if his place was to be lauded or pitied. He could be arrested in the blink of an eye, and the American embassy would not lift a finger for its wayward doctor, who had not in thirty years bothered to become an American citizen.

With a sigh, he finally responded, "Anatoly, I am committing no crime and doing nothing seditious, I assure you. The journalist is very attractive, and I did not see the harm in trying to get to know her better."

"There are many Russian girls who would enjoy getting to know you, Aleksei. My own niece—"

Alex held up a hand. "I know! I know! And she is a lovely girl. They are all lovely girls."

"But?"

Alex shrugged. "There is just something about this one. She is—"

"American, humm?"

"That's the last thing that would appeal to me," Alex answered quickly, his vehemence surprising him. "But I am attracted to her."

"She is feisty, independent. You like that type, yes?"

"I suppose so, but there is more to her than that."

Anatoly leaned forward, his eyes dancing. "You know this in only two meetings?"

"In a way, yes. But I hope I could have more time with her to see if I am right." Alex arched a brow suggestively.

"You would like me and my men to look the other way, yes?"

"Yes."

"You ask a lot, my friend." Anatoly pushed his torso away from the chair back and folded his arms in front of him. "But then, I owe you a lot." Anatoly swung his leg over the chair and stood. "I'll tell you a secret, Aleksei. I think this country needs a little more romance. Just because we had a revolution of the workers doesn't mean we must work, work, work all the time. We need more of the spice of love."

"I wouldn't call my association with the American love. Far from it," clarified Alex.

"Good, because falling in love with a foreigner would place you in a very difficult position. Avoid love, but indulge all you want in romance!"

"Thanks, Anatoly. And believe me, I would not be foolish enough to fall in love with a foreigner, especially an American."

Later, as Alex stood before the basin in surgery scrubbing his hands for the next case, he considered his conversation with Anatoly. He didn't know why he had pressed for the latitude in being allowed to see more of Cameron. He'd thought when he told Anatoly that he was attracted to the American, he had just been conjuring an excuse. But to be completely honest with himself, he'd have to admit that he was indeed attracted to Cameron. He'd felt it almost immediately in the bomb shelter. Yet he was toying with danger by continuing to see her—danger on many levels. The wise thing to do would be to drop the pursuit entirely and continue his life along the path he had followed in the last three years. A quiet, fairly isolated existence, devoted almost entirely to his work, some visiting with his very small contingent of Russian friends, having a few dates with Russian women, but mostly keeping to himself. That was the safe route, the path, perhaps the only path, that would allow him to do what he truly loved, that is, to practice medicine.

The intrusion of Cameron Hayes was a complication he could and should live without. There was no reason to see her again. And he shouldn't. But he knew he would.

Cameron was entering the Metropole when two men approached and moved to either side of her.

"Miss Cameron Gayes?" one asked in barely recognizable English.

"Yes."

"You will to come with us, please."

"Why? Who are you, if I may ask?" Choking back alarm, she forced her tone to sound casual. The two men, though dressed in plain clothes, glared NKVD.

"You will come."

"But—"

They each took one of her arms, not violently but firmly. She knew it was no use to argue. Not only was it clear their English vocabulary had already been exhausted, but if they were NKVD, then they had nothing against her, and she had her rights as an American citizen. Furthermore, Cameron was growing so bored and frustrated with her current assignment that a stint in a Soviet prison might be a nice change. Even a stroll with muggers would be an improvement.

"Okay, okay!" she muttered. "But I can walk on my own." She shrugged away their grasps.

She proceeded with them to a black automobile parked across the street from the hotel and slid into the front seat, wedged in between the two goon-sized agents. Fifteen minutes later, after driving nearly across town, they stopped before a nondescript office building. She was taken upstairs, and her escorts deposited her in a reception area of one of the offices, then they departed. The drab office certainly did not look like a gulag, or even the first step to a gulag. Cameron relaxed. Maybe she had somehow won a coveted interview with some high Soviet official. Maybe Stalin himself. She had already sent a letter to Stalin, and like all the other journalists, she would continue to make weekly appeals for an interview—which the Big Man never granted. Still, the journalists tried.

However, Cameron realized this was not going to be that moment. They weren't even close to the Kremlin. One could hope, though.

The secretary, who had thus far ignored Cameron's presence, looked up just as Cameron was about to make herself known. The woman spoke Russian, but her meaning was clear. "Please sit."

Cameron did so as the secretary spoke into an intercom. In a moment an inner office door opened, and a gentleman about sixty years old stepped forward. He was dressed in an ill-fitting suit, like so many Russian bureaucrats, and if it ever had been fashionable, it had been years ago.

"Miss Cameron Gayes?" he said. He was a big man, nearly filling the doorway. He had thin gray hair and very thick, bushy gray eyebrows over cool gray eyes. He held out his hand, saying in English, "You do not maybe remember me."

"I'm sorry—" Something clicked in Cameron's brain. The bushy eyebrows hadn't been so gray, but she clearly remembered fingering the long strands in amazement. Even now she felt a sudden urge to stroke the strands that, had they not been so curly, would have stretched to a full two inches in length. "You do look familiar. . . ." The veil of the past finally lifted. "Oh, Colonel Tiulenev!"

"Yes, but you used to call me Uncle Boris!" He grinned.

Completely assured this was not to be an arrest, Cameron took the man's hand. He laid his other hand over hers warmly.

"It is a very long time!" he exclaimed. "You were no higher than my knee."

"I might have been a little taller than that," Cameron laughed.

"Come into my office."

He sat behind his desk, and she sat in a chair opposite. He apologized for the formal setting, but they were the only seats in the shabby, utilitarian office.

He said, once they were settled, "I hope you forgive the manner in which I . . . uh . . . sent for you."

"I don't mind, but was it really necessary? Could you not have telephoned me?"

He snorted a laugh. "You have not been here long enough to understand the unreliability of the Russian telephone system. Not always are calls private." He shrugged. For him this was merely a way of life. "And I thought for both our sakes it would be best to maintain the appearance of business. This is Russia, as you will soon learn."

"I am learning. So, Colonel, I see you are no longer in uniform. Are you retired from the army?"

"Alas, when I most want to be in the military, I cannot. Several years ago I hurt my back and was given a desk position. I am a deputy commissar of the State Planning Commission in the division of Defense Industries. I still hold the rank of colonel, so it is not amiss for you to call me thus, but you may call me Uncle Boris if you like."

Smiling, Cameron remembered that Uncle Boris had been an awfully nice man. Besides tolerating her fascination with his eyebrows, he had also been quite generous in giving her sweet treats. "I will always think of you as Uncle Boris," she said warmly, "but perhaps if we need to maintain an aura of business, I should stick with a more formal form of address."

"Ah yes." He fingered his brow, a nervous habit she now also recalled he had, and gave her a regretful look. "Tell me, Cameron, how is your father? It has been many a long year since I heard from him."

"He is well." She was trying to think of more to say about her father when the colonel spared her the effort of dredging up chitchat about a man she hardly knew.

"He is still a big newspaperman?" asked Tiulenev. "You work for him, yes?"

"He still publishes the *Journal*, but I . . . work for another newspaper. The *Globe*."

They spent a few more minutes discussing Cameron's family and the "good old days" in Russia, but quickly exhausted the topic. When the conversation lagged, Cameron could think of only one other thing to discuss.

"What are your impressions of the war, Colonel?"

He waved his hands nonchalantly. "I have no time for impressions. Every minute of my day is spent prodding factories into more production or finding more and more raw materials with which to make weapons. I have no time to wonder what becomes of the supplies I produce for the war."

"Will production meet the demands?"

An easy smile bent his lips. "I forget you are a reporter."

Cameron offered him an apologetic smile. "I am so sorry. I really didn't mean to take advantage—"

"*Nyet, nyet!*" He was still smiling. "I do not mind the questions. I am only sorry I cannot answer them. It is natural you might hope for me to be a source. I was for your father sometimes, but it was different then. This is wartime, and it is far less advisable to bend the rules. Please to understand."

"I do, Colonel. Let's just keep this on an entirely friendly basis— however, appearing like it is business." Cameron grinned ruefully.

"A funny world we live in, yes?" He scratched a bald spot above his temple—a place that could have benefited from a few strands of his eyebrows. "Still, there is no reason why I cannot have some part in broadening your experience in Russia. The Intourist offices are closed for the war, so you will need a helping hand."

"What do you mean?" In spite of herself, she leaned forward expectantly. Suddenly she remembered her mother and what she had promised her. This man might well be able to help Cameron find a missing person.

"You would like to go—how is it you Americans say?—off the beaten track? I remember your father always wanted to see anything he could that was out of the ordinary and behind the scenes."

"I would like that, Colonel, very much." This was no small offer, and she appreciated it.

His smile broadened and his brows flapped. "I will see what I can do, little Cameron ... *Camrushka!*" He paused then, drawing his brows together, and added, "But there is something else?"

"I didn't think I was so transparent."

"I have merely learned to be a perceptive old goat." He grinned. "Tell me what is on your mind."

"I fear it may be asking a great deal, perhaps even the impossible. But it is important." His nod urged her to continue. "How difficult would it be to find someone here in Russia?"

"Of course it depends on the circumstances."

"He is an old acquaintance of my parents. Yakov Luban, or his son, Semyon Luban." Cameron wondered how much to reveal. Boris was, after all, a friend of Keagan's, not Cecilia's. But the chance of the colonel going to the trouble of contacting Keagan seemed slim. Still, at this stage, keeping things simple would probably be prudent.

"I never heard the name, and I thought I was close to your father. He was in government?"

"No. Yakov owned an English bookstore in Leningrad. He was kind to my parents, and they were always worried about him when they lost contact after the Revolution."

"I see . . ."

Cameron was certain Uncle Boris *saw* a great deal. One did not rise in the hierarchy of the Stalinist regime without being perceptive and also very cagey.

"I realize it is a long shot. I just promised my parents I would inquire."

"I will look into it, Camrushka. But I must warn you that in these times it is difficult to find anything of value, much less someone who has been missing for twenty years."

Cameron wanted to hug him. And when he stood to see her to the door, she did just that. She even pecked him on his florid cheek. But she still did not dare touch his eyebrows.

"OH, MISS GAYES, I was so worried when I heard they came to take you away!" exclaimed Sophia when she saw Cameron later. She actually shuddered when she uttered the words "take you away." Cameron wondered if this sweet girl had had some personal experiences along those lines. She hated to think so.

"It was all completely innocent," Cameron assured. "An old friend sent them, and he only wanted to visit with me." Cameron held up an envelope. "And it has all turned out very well. Look at this."

What she had was an invitation for her to tour some Moscow factories, two munitions plants, and a bakery. Later, when Cameron crowed about her good fortune to her colleagues at dinner that evening their estimation of her rose considerably. After dinner Shanahan offered to buy her a drink at the hotel bar. He reeked of ulterior motives.

"Sweetheart, you aren't gonna go on that tour all alone, are you?" His eyes large with concern, he gazed at her over the rim of his glass of vodka, his drink of preference since coming to Russia.

"Why shouldn't I?"

"Maybe you haven't noticed the peculiar place of women in this country. Many do a man's work, especially now. Economically they are afforded much equality with men. But socially . . ." He shook his head and drained his glass as if in sympathy to the poor downtrodden female. "Do you know Soviet government officials—male officials, of course—seldom bring their wives and daughters to state gatherings for fear of them being corrupted by foreign hounds?"

"And you, of all men, should know there are no hounds or wolves among the foreign community," Cameron said drolly.

"There are hounds and wolves wherever there are men, but most civilized countries don't see the need to protect their women to that extent."

"And so your point would be. . . ?"

"I fear you won't be taken seriously on your little tour."

"I live with that all the time, Shanahan."

"I only thought it would be helpful for you to have a male along—"

"Goodness, Shanahan! If you want to come, why don't you ask outright?" She gave her head a shake, but she rather enjoyed the feeling that for a rare instance she was in a superior position to Shanahan.

"Because, doll, you'd have no reason to invite me. I am the competition."

"That wouldn't prevent me nearly as much as having to keep listening to you call me doll, or sweetheart, or baby!" She gave a disgusted growl and screwed up her face as if she'd just sucked a lemon.

"Hey, it's just me. Nothing personal. You know that. Part of my charm, ya know." His grin, wide, mocking while at the same time unassuming, was also part of his charm.

She rolled her eyes. There simply was no other way around that look of his.

"Listen, d—I mean Miss Cameron Hayes!" He kept grinning. "Let's cut a deal here. Take me along on your tour, and I will never call you by anything but your proper name again."

"Oh, Shanahan!"

"Please, Cameron! I'm dying of boredom. My liver is getting pickled with the endless drinking, and I'm broke from playing poker with the boys."

"Well, in the interest of your liver—and my identity, mind you!—I suppose you can come. But I will have first shot in sending out any dispatches regarding the tour."

"That's jake with me, d—Cameron!"

She loved the sense of power this situation gave her. She wondered if she could have extracted more from him.

———

A car came for them in the morning. No interpreters would accompany them, because each plant would provide one for the tour. That was just as well. Cameron had given Sophia a long list of tasks to do, since she had also offered to act as Cameron's secretary.

Their first stop was an automobile factory. Cameron was a little disappointed because she had expected to see war production. But as it turned out, this plant that normally produced a Russian passenger car called a "Zee" was now largely involved in producing trucks, half-tracks, and even some munitions. She and Shanahan were received enthusiastically by the plant manager. He obviously was thrilled to brag about his factory.

He freely divulged statistics about output and the wages of his workers. The employees, the majority of which were women, often worked sixty-hour weeks. Though they received overtime pay, they still earned only seven hundred to a thousand rubles a month, roughly between twenty and forty American dollars in terms of buying power. Cameron busily jotted down all these numbers. This was just the kind of thing American readers wanted to know.

The plant itself was in a sorry state, and Cameron felt just as sorry for the manager, who seemed so proud nonetheless. The infrastructure itself was old, with cracked floors, poor lighting, and obviously faulty wiring. Besides this, there was a general unkempt atmosphere—the floors badly in need of sweeping and disorganization apparent everywhere.

Cameron whispered to Shanahan, "And this is the factory they chose for us to see!" Obviously it must be considered a model.

"So much for the Five-Year Plans," Johnny replied in an undertone.

Midway through the tour they were taken to a small but nicely appointed lounge-type room and served a lavish meal. And it was only ten o'clock in the morning! But there was pork and beef and caviar, pastries, and several different kinds of wine and champagne and vodka. Cameron had the feeling they were trying to dull her senses so she would miss the lower aspects of Russian factories.

The next stop was the plant where the Stormovik plane was produced for the Red Air Force. Cameron found, much to her dismay, that here especially she was happy she had taken Shanahan along. Cameron was not well versed in mechanics, but for some reason Johnny seemed to know a great deal not only about auto mechanics but also about airplanes. He knew the right questions to ask, and he knew how to make comparisons between Russian design and American design. He brought an element to the visit that would have been missing without him, because the factory men were reticent to speak too technically to a woman, and Cameron didn't know enough about the subject to ask leading questions.

"Is this a dive bomber or a level bomber?" Johnny asked.

"Both," beamed the manager. "We kill two birds with one rock, as you Americans say."

"I've noticed you are not using large quantities of aluminum."

"Some parts are of aluminum, yes. But Soviet production is low since Fascists have taken control of some of our plants."

This visit also was broken up by a lavish late-afternoon meal. No matter what the Americans had to say of Soviet industry, they could not fault their catering talents. There were many toasts to American friendship, the success of Lend-Lease, and the hope of a Second Front. The manager and his staff assigned to entertaining the two journalists joined heartily in the consumption of vast quantities of food and alcohol. Cameron hoped this would work to her advantage. She wanted to get away and mingle with the workers, from whom they had thus far been kept carefully isolated. She hoped her guides would be too numbed by alcohol to notice her absence or to care if they did notice.

Shanahan was definitely smashed after the luncheon. He had no more intelligent questions about the airplane industry—he barely could form an intelligible word, much less a full sentence. But he nevertheless kept the group of Russians thoroughly entertained with bizarre, ribald, and probably fictitious stories of life in American aircraft factories. Much to Cameron's surprise, she learned he had worked at Douglas Aircraft once between newspaper jobs.

While the men had paused to listen to one of Johnny's long and amply drawn-out tales, Cameron wandered away from the group. Of course, now she wished she had been allowed to have Sophia along. But she had picked up a little of the language since her arrival in Russia, so with that and her dictionary, she determined to get along.

Two women were standing idly by a conveyor belt, which proved to be little more than a strip of canvas stretched between a couple of gears. Even this makeshift arrangement seemed to have broken down. The women were waiting while it was being fixed. Cameron had noticed many such delays at the factories.

"Zdrastvuytye," she said, wrapping her tongue around the word for "hello" as best she could.

One of the women smiled, obviously amused by her sad attempt at the language. The other woman, who was older and apparently wiser, scolded the younger woman's rudeness.

"Hello," the older woman said in English and held out her hand.

"You speak English!"

"Nyet, only small."

"Well, it is wonderful. I wish I spoke better Russian. What is your job here?" Cameron had to speak loudly, because despite the fact that this station was idle, there were other machines groaning and rumbling noisily.

"I take . . ." The woman thought hard, then added, "And put. Like this." She demonstrated by taking some metal object, presumably a part to an airplane, from the stalled conveyor belt and placing it on a nearby cart. "Take . . . put!" she said with a grin.

"Do you like your work?"

"Like work?" Cameron could not tell if the woman's quirked brow was due to problems of interpretation or the fact that she just never considered *liking* her work. "Good. Work good. Work for our blessed Comrade Stalin! Defeat Fascist pigs, eh?"

"I see . . ." Cameron was thumbing through her dictionary to get some help for another comment when she heard her name.

"Miss Gayes!" It was the manager. They must have just noticed her absence. He was calling from the door of the large room into which she had wandered. He started moving toward her.

She thanked the women and bid them *dasvidaniya*, then headed back toward the tour group. What happened next occurred too quickly for her to assimilate in any rational way. The blast knocked her to the floor. She thought the damage to the conveyor belt must have been more serious than it looked. Then she heard the screams. She wrenched around.

Where were the two women she had just been talking to? But Cameron's vision was blurry from the dust and debris. She rubbed her eyes as she scrambled to her feet and hurried to where she had just been standing with the women. But the little workstation was gone, or rather crushed beyond recognition by a large beam. The younger woman was on her knees screaming, blood oozing from a wound in her head. Cameron started toward her, but the woman was pointing at something else.

Cameron paused and gasped. The friendly older woman was sprawled out on the ground, pinned beneath an end of the beam. Cameron did not stop to think that had the explosion occurred a moment earlier, she would have been under that beam, as well. She was too stunned to think much at all as she dropped down beside the older woman and slid her fingers under the beam. But there was no budging the thing, which was a huge iron beam that had been a ceiling support. It didn't matter, though. The woman was not moving. With shaking fingers, Cameron tried to feel for a pulse and found none. Shakily she rose to her feet to see if she could help the other woman.

Though these moments seemed to Cameron to have stretched over an eternity, in reality only a few seconds had passed since the explosion. People were yelling, screaming, and running about—some in sheer panic, others attempting to help their co-workers who had been injured.

Vaguely, Cameron heard her name shouted again. She was certain it was Shanahan, but she did not get a chance to respond.

Another blast ripped through the factory, and again Cameron was wrenched from her feet. Only this time, the instant after she hit the floor, something struck her in the head. Pain seared through not only her head but her entire body. She was certain another beam had fallen on her. She tried to move but couldn't. She was struck again and again, as if the ceiling was raining on her.

"Cameron!" Shanahan was bent over her.

Cameron opened one eye, but her vision was so blurry that the attempt to use it only made her insides quake.

"Johnny . . . she's dead . . ."

He was frantically pitching away fallen debris, which she vaguely realized had been covering her. But she remembered no more as the world around her went black. No more, that is, except a voice infused with heartrending agony:

"Cameron, you can't be dead!"

32

HER VISION WAS blurry when she opened her eyes again. She was surrounded by dull light. It could have been the factory, but there was no hard cement floor beneath her. She was in a soft bed. She moved her head to look around, but pain throbbed as she did so.

She closed her eyes but not before noting the figure seated beside her bed. Johnny. His head was resting against the back of his chair. His eyes were closed. And despite her blurred vision, she saw he looked a wreck. His face was smudged with soot and dirt, along with a definite five-o'clock shadow on his chin, and his hair was disheveled and dusty, as were his clothes—the same clothes, if she remembered correctly, that he'd had on for the factory tour. Then she realized something else. He was holding her hand.

"How come you never told me you used to work in an aircraft factory?" she asked, her voice hoarse with disuse.

His eyes popped open. "Cameron! Holy cow, woman, it's about time you woke up."

She smiled and squeezed his hand. Suddenly he jerked his hand from her grasp, looking as if he'd been compromised in some horrible way. She chuckled, but the effort hurt her head.

"How long. . . ?"

"You've been in and out for hours."

"And you've been here the whole time?" She couldn't help grinning. The motion hurt, but she'd never known Shanahan to be so sweet before.

"Someone had to stick around to make sure these Russian quacks didn't kill you," he replied roughly.

235

"What happened, Johnny?" That initial sense of well-being left her as she was reminded of the terrible events at the factory. "The woman I was talking to—she's dead, isn't she?"

"Yeah. Five people were killed in the blast. You came within"—he shook his head and swallowed hard—"a hairsbreadth of being one of them."

"Was there some kind of malfunction?"

"Sabotage."

"Johnny, no!"

His usual rakish glint gleamed once more in his eyes. "Biggest story since the invasion, and we were there, baby—I mean, Cameron."

"Well, it's a sure bet Palgunov won't let us print it."

"The Soviets won't even admit to its being sabotage," he replied. "The only way I found out was because they came close to arresting you—"

"Me!"

"Sure. You had wandered away from the group just before the explosion. You were saved from arrest only because they caught the culprits who did it."

She shut her eyes once again trying to assimilate all that had happened. People were dead. Sabotage. She'd been a suspect. And it was a news story that would never see print. She shifted her position, then was seized by a sudden new panic. Was she critically injured? Would she be sent home? For all her complaints of boredom and frustration with the Soviet system, she desperately did not want that to happen.

She wanted to ask, "Am I going to live?" But the words sounded so pathetic in her mind that she could not voice them, especially to Shanahan. She'd find out soon enough. Besides, she didn't *feel* near death, despite the pain in her body. To get her mind off these things, she asked, "Who did it, Johnny? Traitors or German infiltrators?"

"That I can't find out." The frustrated crease of his brow indicated he had tried hard to do so. "But I got enough."

"Enough for what?"

"A dispatch, of course."

"They'll never let you send it—" Abruptly she stopped and shook her head, ignoring the ache the movement caused. "Johnny, you didn't! How? The diplomatic pouch?"

"Nah. The embassy guys couldn't agree if this would help or hurt the Russian cause back in Washington. I had a friend who was leaving the country. It wasn't hard to arrange."

She couldn't believe how casual he sounded. He'd been here longer than she and must know the consequences. "Johnny, if the Narko-mindel finds out, you'll be deported. You know they monitor international newspapers. If they see the article in the *Journal*—"

"No one monitors papers in a nothing berg like Los Angeles." There was a touch of defensiveness in his tone. "London, New York, maybe even Istanbul, but not Los Angeles."

"It's an important story. What if it's picked up by the wire services?"

"Quit worrying, Hayes. You just lay back and worry only about getting on your feet."

Something else penetrated her foggy mind. "Hey, wait a minute! We made a deal that I'd get first crack at any dispatches."

"You really want this one, Hayes?" he said snidely. "I could—"

"Aw, shut up, Shanahan! I liked you better when you were holding my hand and crying over me."

"Crying! Ha ha!" He barked a fake laugh. "I have never in my life cried over a woman."

She opened her mouth to reply but stopped because just on the edge of her vision she saw a tall figure in a white lab coat approach. It hadn't even occurred to her that she might be in Alex's hospital or that he might be her doctor. She smiled as she thought her injuries might work out for good after all.

"Well, I am happy to see you are in good spirits," Alex said in reference to her welcoming smile. He held a metal clipboard in hand and now flipped a couple pages. "Your vital signs are stable except for a slightly elevated temperature. But on the whole very good, considering what you went through." He smiled, and Cameron was glad no one was taking her pulse just then.

All of a sudden a thought struck her, and it hit with a force nearly as staggering as the earlier explosions. Here she was with two desirable, devastatingly handsome men doting upon her and at her beck and call. She suddenly had a better understanding of her sister Blair, and she glimpsed just how pleasant such a circumstance could be. Yet her pragmatic side jumped in immediately and sharply pointed out the downside to the situation. Two men interested in her? She didn't even want one man. She was happily single and independent, and that's how she wanted to stay.

But she looked back and forth between the two men, ignoring the way the movement made her stomach quake. Either one of them might be worth sacrificing just a tiny bit of her independent life.

"Are you my doctor, Alex?" she asked, trying to push all those other unsettling thoughts from her mind.

"For the most part I am a surgeon, and thank goodness you didn't need surgery." He strode to the side of the bed opposite from where Johnny sat and took Cameron's hand in his.

At first she thought he was being friendly; then she realized he was taking her pulse. She rolled her eyes and groaned inwardly at her foolishness. That blow to her head must have scrambled her brains.

"Good," he said, laying her hand back on the bed. "I have been overseeing your care, if that is agreeable to you."

"Of course." She paused uncomfortably as he bent over her. Her heart was actually fluttering!

"I want to check your eyes," he said in a very clinical, very doctor-like tone. He lifted each of her eyelids and flashed a penlight into them just as she remembered his doing to the old man that first day they had met.

She started to worry again. That man had been seriously injured. "Is . . . is it okay, Alex?"

"Yes. Reaction to light is a bit slow. You have a mild concussion. No broken bones, though I imagine you hurt like the dickens. You were banged up pretty badly."

"I feel like everything is broken." She detested admitting fear and hated even more the slightly fearful tremor in her tone, but she had been through an explosion. Didn't she have a right to a little fear?

He laid a hand on her shoulder, a familiar gesture and unaccountably comforting. She gazed up at him, smiled, and was rewarded by a similar response from him that made warmth tingle right down to her toes.

"I want to keep you in here for observation for a couple of days," Alex said.

"Are you kidding, Doc?" Shanahan said. "You'll have to hogtie her—"

But just as he spoke, Cameron said languidly, "If you say so, Alex." Out of the corner of her eye, she caught the surprised quirking of Johnny's brow.

"I say so. And you ought to get some rest now." Alex turned his gaze upon Johnny. "And Mr. Shanahan, if I can tear you away from her side, you look as if you could use some rest, too."

"Maybe I can use a cup of joe." Shanahan rose. "You get some sleep, doll."

Cameron did not even think to upbraid him for the use of "doll." She felt too good wrapped in the care of these two men, these two friends. That's all. And she was happy with that.

———

Shanahan and Alex left the ward.

"You got any coffee in this joint?" Johnny asked.

"I believe the doctors' lounge has the wherewithal to make a pot. Come with me."

Johnny strode beside the handsome, broad-shouldered physician, giving him a covert perusal as they walked. He was just the sort of man women usually went gaga over. Of course, Johnny couldn't complain about his own prowess with women. He could have any woman anytime he wanted—well, here in Russia it was a bit more difficult because the local girls tended to keep their distance from foreigners. But in general Johnny was fully aware of his own effect on women, though his came from pure charm, not from stunning looks. And it wasn't always easy. Pouring on the charm took a good deal of effort. But a man like Dr. Rostov didn't have to do anything. He walked into a room, and women responded. And few women could resist a *doctor*. Double threat.

Still, Johnny had thought Cameron was different from most women. Yes, she had fallen for his own charms, but there was no denying they had a mutual chemistry and a lot in common. He would never have believed she could fall for a man just because he looked like Apollo. She was a woman, though. And Johnny had seen the way she practically drooled over the good doctor.

That bothered Johnny more than he wanted to admit, but what bothered him even more was the responding look he'd detected in the doctor's eyes. Dr. Rostov may have been taking Cameron's pulse, but that wasn't all he was checking out.

Rostov opened a door and gestured Johnny into a room with a table and chairs and kitchen area. It was pretty shabby looking, and Johnny thought about rich doctors in the States. This room might have served the janitorial staff in an American hospital. Whatever had reduced Rostov to this? Pure idealism or something else?

Johnny found a seat on the sofa, which was worn and lumpy but looked more substantial than the ancient chairs around the table. Rostov opened up cupboards, found a coffeepot and a can of ground coffee, and began scooping the coffee into the basket of the pot.

"So, Doc, is Cameron really gonna be okay?" Johnny asked, anxious to smooth the way to what really interested him.

"Yes, she'll be fine with some rest."

"She tells me you were born here but raised in the States," Johnny said casually.

Alex brought the pot to the sink and filled it with water. "That's right."

"So you received your medical training in the States?"

"Yes, I did."

Alex's forced tone made Johnny realize his questions were starting to sound like an interrogation. "I just want to know she's getting the best care . . . you know how it is?"

"I think so." He put the pot on the hot plate. "This might take some time. You sure you wouldn't like some tea? It's already brewed."

"I don't know how you people can stomach all that tea. You and the Limeys—with all that tea in common, your two countries should get along a lot better than you do."

"We are allies now." Alex drew himself a cup of tea from the big stainless steel samovar, then sat at the table. "Is that all you had on your mind, Johnny—it is okay if I call you Johnny, isn't it?"

"Sure, Alex. I never did go in for all that formality." Johnny leaned back more comfortably on the sofa, wondering if the doctor's question was truly inviting a frank conversation. Why not? he thought, then proceeded. "What exactly are your intentions with Cameron, Alex?"

"My intentions?" Whatever the doctor had been expecting, this certainly wasn't it.

"Yeah. I feel sort of responsible for her, you know, kind of like her old man wanted me to look out for her. Anyway, a lot of grief could come from her getting involved with a Russian."

"Well, I . . ." He was still obviously at a loss for words. He sipped his tea before continuing. "I'll be honest with you, Johnny, I do like Cameron, but we are definitely not involved. However, she did lead me to believe it was over between the two of you."

"She did?" Now it was Johnny's turn for surprise, not from the fact that Cameron had told the doctor they were over, but that he had come up at all in a conversation between them.

"But if you two are still . . . or even if you—"

"Naw, we called it quits back in the States. It's just that . . ." What was it? There was no future for him and Cameron, yet even Johnny knew she was different from all his other women. She had gotten under his skin like no other had. He wasn't in love—he was incapable of that—but something was going on in him, and he didn't like it much.

"Did her getting injured make you reevaluate your feelings for her?" asked Alex.

Johnny gaped at the forthrightness of the man—his rival? Was that it? Was Johnny just feeling sentimental because Cameron had been injured?

"I don't want to see her hurt emotionally. That's all," Johnny said somewhat defensively.

"Neither do I. But I think that our competing for her could hurt her worst of all."

"We ain't competing," Johnny said firmly. He squirmed uncomfortably; then noting that the coffeepot was steaming, he jumped up and strode to the counter. "Where do you keep the cups?"

"Top shelf to your left."

Johnny found a cup, turned off the hot plate, and poured some coffee, taking the cup back to the sofa. It was too hot to drink and he blew on it. "Are you an American citizen?" Johnny asked abruptly.

"No, Russian. My parents always dreamed of returning to Russia, so they kept their citizenship. I felt as if I'd be betraying them if I became an American citizen, so I didn't."

"They Reds?"

"At first, yes, they were." Alex spoke shortly, as if reluctant to answer that question. "Later, they were not as . . . zealous."

"You a Red?" Johnny persisted, though he clearly saw the subject made Alex ill at ease.

"Are you still sizing me up as a romantic interest for Cameron? If so, I can tell you it makes me mighty uncomfortable. I still can't tell if you are a rival or a big brother with a shotgun." He leaned forward for emphasis. "I can tell you one thing, though. I haven't known Cameron long, but I am pretty certain she would be furious if she knew she was being discussed in this manner."

Johnny let it pass that Rostov had so adroitly sidestepped his question about his ideology. An easy smile bent Johnny's lips. "You know her pretty well, Doc."

"Why don't we talk about something else, then?"

"Okay, what?"

"You want to know about my politics?" Alex deadpanned, then smiled wryly.

"Only because of my concern about Cameron. To tell the truth, I don't give a hang about politics except if it makes news. I don't care if you are a Commie, a Republican, or a teetotaler." He paused, took a drink of coffee, then added sheepishly, "Okay, I'm curious. Are you a Red?"

"I'm a member of the Party."

Johnny nearly choked on his coffee. He really hadn't expected that. "The *Communist* Party?"

"So now how are my chances with Cameron?"

"Zilch! Her father would kill you before you even had a chance. But we weren't going to talk about Cameron." He jumped up, refilled his cup, then leaned against the counter. "I'm surprised being a member of the Party didn't harm your admission to medical school in the States."

"I didn't join until after."

"Do you believe all that stuff? Marx, *The Communist Manifesto* . . . the whole nine yards?"

"I believe in medicine. I did what I felt I had to do in order to continue to practice."

"What do ya mean?"

Alex shifted in his seat. "It's involved." He shoved his chair away from the table and rose. "I have to get back to work."

"And I thought you were an idealist. Guess I had you wrong, Doc." Johnny was rather glad about that. He didn't like idealists, and he was starting to like the doctor.

"I was," Alex answered. "Once . . . before life intruded."

"It's obvious what Cameron sees in you. Mystery, angst—women go for that stuff."

"How do you know she sees anything in me?"

"Aw, Doc! Haven't you noticed how she makes goggle eyes at you? She never even got mushy like that around me."

And from the look of stark disbelief on the doctor's face, Johnny

242

realized this was actually news to the man. Johnny could have thought of a way to work this to his advantage, to twist and fashion the truth to suit him. But he had never yet had to win a woman through deceit . . . well, except for the usual kind of deceit like telling a woman he only had eyes for her or that he'd do anything to please her. He figured he could beat the doctor fair and square if he decided he wanted to.

33

CAMERON WOKE TO find a new visitor seated beside her bed. It was Sophia. Her head was bowed and her lips were moving slightly, though no sound came from them.

"Hi, Sophia."

The girl lifted her head and smiled. "Oh, Miss Hayes!" Cameron had not yet been able to get Sophia to call her by her first name, but she had learned to pronounce the *H*. "Did I wake you?"

"No, I've been dozing off and on all day. It was awfully nice of you to come." Cameron tried to ease herself into a sitting position.

"I was so worried I had to come see that you were all right," Sophia replied as she jumped up to assist Cameron.

"It was still nice of you. Sophia, were you just praying for me?"

Sophia's cheeks pinked a bit, but Cameron had found that the young girl grew embarrassed quite easily.

She nodded, almost apologetically. "You do not mind, I hope?"

"Of course not." Cameron shifted once more in her bed to get a better look at her visitor. The movement was hurting less and less, which was a good thing because the bed was growing more and more uncomfortable. "I have to admit, I'm not a religious person myself, but it is touching to know you spent the time for me."

"You do not believe in God?"

The guilelessness of the question rather surprised Cameron, given the time and the place—this was, after all, the atheistic state of Soviet Russia. "Goodness, that's a complex question," Cameron replied, then adroitly turned it around. "I'm surprised you do. I thought most Russian young people had turned away from religion, and I would have especially thought that one with a position in the foreign office such as yours would certainly adhere to atheism."

"This is, as you say, also complex." Sophia resumed her seat, and as she did so, she glanced quickly around. There were three other patients in the ward besides Cameron. Lowering her voice, Sophia continued. "The war has brought about many changes in this area. You have not been here long enough perhaps to notice that many churches have reopened. Not only the Orthodox Church, but other sects, as well, are enjoying new freedoms."

"That shouldn't come as a surprise," Cameron said. "Stalin is looking to Christian nations for help, which they might have been less willing to give under the old practices."

"Yes, I am sure that is true, but there is more to it," Sophia replied, her tone becoming more animated than usual. "Even Comrade Stalin acknowledges that in time of war, when the people must make terrible sacrifices, there is a deep human need to reach out beyond oneself for strength. Have you visited any churches since you have come here? You would find them very crowded these days."

"I am ashamed to say I haven't been to a church." Cameron smiled ironically. "My mother would be very disappointed in me, though I didn't attend regularly at home, either. I think Mother hoped that the dangers of war would drive me to God, as it has with you Russians."

"So when you are afraid, you do not talk to God nor seek Him?"

"No, I don't." Cameron paused, then thought about her experiences in Yugoslavia and Greece. "Well . . . maybe once or twice I have. I don't mean to denigrate your faith, but I want to be stronger than that."

Much to Cameron's relief, Sophia did not appear offended, but she did seem perplexed. "You believe seeking God is a weakness?" When Cameron nodded, Sophia added, "You agree, then, with Lenin that religion is the opiate of the people?"

"That seems kind of a harsh viewpoint." But Cameron did agree with Lenin in that one area at least, yet it was difficult to come right out and say so, especially to this fragile young woman. She'd never been able to admit such a thing to her mother, either, but it was true, wasn't it? Religion was for the weak. It certainly had appeared so where her somewhat weak-willed mother had been concerned. It did not mean there was no God, but rather that God was relegated to the needy. Sighing, Cameron stalled by reaching for her pitcher of water.

"Let me," Sophia said, taking the pitcher from Cameron.

"Really, Sophia, you needn't wait on me like that." Cameron wrestled the pitcher from her, then twisted around to get the glass. But she was at the wrong angle and knocked the glass off the table, sending it shattering to the floor.

Sophia scooted out of the way of the crash, then, smiling wanly, rose. "I will get a broom."

"I am so sorry."

Sophia gave Cameron a reassuring pat on the shoulder before leaving the ward. Cameron cursed silently. Yes, she prided herself on her strength, and now to be reduced to a hospital bed and to be so weak that she couldn't have cleaned up the mess if she wanted to was a horrible state of affairs. But she was not about to turn to religion just because of that. If there was a God—and because of her mother, she had to allow for the possibility—He could not respect a person who turned to Him only in times of need. But if God was in the business of helping people, it didn't stand to reason that He'd appreciate someone who didn't need Him at all. Now, there was quite a quandary!

When Sophia returned a few minutes later with a broom, Cameron debated posing this quandary to her but decided against it because the last thing her throbbing head needed was a theological debate.

Sophia swept up the broken glass, and when she had disposed of it, she returned once more, this time with another glass. Pointedly, she filled it with water and handed it to Cameron.

Cameron smiled sheepishly. "I am a real hard case, Sophia, I hope you can get used to it. It always drove my mother mad. She used to shake her head and say, 'The bigger they are, the harder they fall.'"

Sophia set the water pitcher back on the table. "But, Miss Hayes, you are not big. This is metaphor, yes?" She screwed up her face trying to decipher it, then shook her head. "But I don't understand."

"My mother believed that everyone was bound to fall sooner or later," Cameron explained. "You see, the only question was just how hard the fall was going to be."

"And a big person, a strong person, would fall harder because they expected it the least?"

"Something like that, yes. According to my mother."

Sitting back in her chair, Sophia said, "Even if I knew I would fall, I still wish I were strong like you, Miss Hayes."

"You are probably stronger than you think, Sophia. You are Russian, after all." Cameron took a thoughtful sip of the water. "You are only nineteen, but I'll bet you have been through more hardship than I will see in a lifetime. You were born in 1922 during that terrible famine. My father was one of the foreign correspondents Stalin finally let into the country so that he could get wheat from America. Dad was permitted to see only some of the effects of the famine, but I remember how appalled he was, and he is a tough old bird. You were old enough later during the purges of the '30s to remember them. They must have affected you in some way. Yet you survived. That is strength, Sophia."

"I survived because others protected me," Sophia replied, a deep pain darkening her eyes. "They are the strong ones. In '32 my father was targeted by the GPU, which is now the NKVD. Fearing for us children, he and my mother planned to get us out of the country, to send us to our relatives in America. My two sisters and brother, all teenagers at the time and older than me, refused to go. They did not want to desert my parents and their country in time of need. I might have still gone, but I wanted to stay also, yet it was not because I was brave like them. I wanted to stay because I was more afraid of going away all alone to a strange land."

"You were but a child."

"I am not a child now, and I am afraid all the time. My brother and oldest sister are in the army. My husband is in the air force. He is in the most danger of all."

"I didn't know you were married," Cameron said, genuinely astonished. "You never said anything."

"I do not wish to burden you with my personal life."

"It is not a burden," Cameron said in a scolding tone. "I don't wish to pry into your life, but on the other hand, I want you to feel free to talk to me. Sometimes sharing a burden like that with a friend makes it easier."

"My mother says that also. She, too, gets upset at me for not telling her things." She paused, thought for a moment, then added, "My husband's name is Oleg." Her expression softened, obviously pleased to be able to speak of him. "We were married in April before the war."

"You were married only three months before he left? How terrible!"

"My papa thought we were too young to be married. Oleg turned twenty only a week ago. I do not know where he celebrated his birthday—on some awful battlefield, I fear." She touched a corner of her eye, and Cameron saw moisture glistening in the large brown pools. "Papa consented to the marriage, for though he wished we were older, he loves Oleg like a son. He was in prison with Oleg's parents and cared for them both before they died."

"They died in prison?" When Sophia nodded sadly, Cameron asked, "Your father was a political prisoner, I assume, arrested during the Great Purge?"

"No, earlier. In 1932 he spent two years in the Gulag."

"Why was he arrested?"

Sophia glanced around the ward again. The other patients appeared to be sleeping. She lowered her voice anyway. "It was never clear. Papa has always held a rather unusual place here. He was of the aristocracy before the Revolution. His own grandfather was an advisor to Tsar Alexander II. Yet, his father, my grandfather, was firmly tied to the proletariat."

"He was a revolutionary?"

"In a way, but it is more complicated than that. My grandpapa, whom I never had the honor of knowing, was greatly esteemed by the common people. He was killed on Bloody Sunday in 1905. He believed in political freedom, but he believed even more deeply in spiritual freedom."

"You mean religious freedom?" Cameron knew she'd regret the question, but her natural curiosity forced her to ask it regardless.

"That, too, but more." Sophia ran a hand through her hair. She appeared conflicted. "It is difficult to explain, but this is the heritage passed on to my father. He came to believe in these things, as well, and he, too, suffered."

"Are you saying he was arrested because of religion?"

"My family had a church in our home—"

"An underground church?"

"Yes, that is what you call them."

"And that is why he was arrested in '32?"

A rather mysterious smile bent Sophia's lips. "The church was never discovered, but the GPU knew it existed. They could not catch us holding illegal meetings, so they claimed my father's aristocratic background made him a subversive. He was never tried, merely sent to the Gulag."

"But he is out of prison, isn't he? I seem to recall Alex saying your father is Chief of Staff at this hospital."

Sophia nodded.

"How did he get out, then?" Cameron leaned forward. This was fascinating stuff. She might never be able to tell the story of Sophia's family, but she was still intensely curious.

"My father is one of the foremost cardiac specialists in the country," Sophia replied, obviously proud of the fact. "When a high government official developed heart disease and it was discovered that the best heart doctor was in the Gulag . . . well, he was quickly released."

"And he treated this official?"

"Yes, he did," came a new voice to the conversation.

Cameron had not noticed the arrival of the two lab-coated men. Alex was with an older man. Cameron quickly noted the man's name badge, but it was written in Cyrillic letters and thus no help in identifying the stranger. Yet she would have wagered her whole paycheck that this man was Sophia's father, a fact especially evident around the man's eyes, which were not as large as his daughter's, but just as expressive. They were now glinting with a twinkle Cameron guessed was for Sophia. She was the apple of Daddy's eye, no doubt about that.

He spoke to his daughter in a teasing tone. "Little Sophia, are you boring your employer with family stories?" His English was very good, with just enough accent to give him an exotic air.

"I am far from bored," Cameron interjected before Sophia had a chance to answer. "I gather that you are Sophia's father?"

Sophia had risen and now moved next to the man, placing her arm around him and gazing up at him in an adoring fashion. "This is my father."

"Dr. Fedorcenko," he added.

"I am Cameron Hayes." She held out her hand.

He took it, not in a typical handshake, but more in the old-fashioned manner in which a gentleman would click his heels and kiss a lady's hand. He didn't kiss Cameron's hand, but he did bow ever so slightly over the proffered hand.

"I have heard about you, Miss Hayes. I am sorry we must meet under these circumstances, but I am most happy to meet you at last."

Cameron wondered if he had heard about her through Alex or Sophia, not that it mattered. "Well, as I was saying, I am not bored at all," said Cameron. "This is very interesting. Who was the government official that you treated, and did he survive?"

Fedorcenko laughed, glancing at Alex. "I see you did not exaggerate, Alex," he said. Then to Cameron, "Alex told me he had never met anyone who asked so many questions."

"Occupational hazard, I suppose." Raising an eyebrow, she continued, "So did he?"

"Yes, he did. But physician's confidentiality and other considerations constrain me from revealing the man's name."

"Someone high on the totem pole, I'll bet."

"Totem pole? Now that is an English idiom I have never heard, and I thought I'd heard them all from my brother-in-law, who is also an American journalist."

"Who is that?"

"Daniel Trent."

"Oh yes, I've heard of him. He's with the *New York Register*."

"Recently retired. So what is this totem pole?"

"To tell the truth, I'm not really sure. A Native American religious symbol—a tall carved pole in which, I suppose, the best gods are on top."

"Not unlike the Soviet hierarchy," observed Fedorcenko.

"It isn't that I wouldn't love a rousing political discussion," Alex said, stepping closer to Cameron's bed, "but this isn't entirely a social visit." He checked her pulse as he continued. "How are you?"

"Fine."

He laid a hand on her forehead. "You feel warm."

"What do you expect with the attentions of two such charming men?" she teased.

Alex chuckled but tried to maintain his medical decorum. "Has your vision cleared?"

"Oh yes. I count only four men in white jackets now," she replied lightheartedly.

"It is good to see you retain a sense of humor. Very important curative aid, especially in a Russian hospital," said Fedorcenko.

"Oh, Papa," Sophia said, "this is the best hospital in Europe."

"I might not go that far," he said, shrugging, "but we do the best we can with what we have. Now, Sophia, Dr. Alex wants to examine Miss Hayes, so we should be on our way, eh?"

"Yes, Papa."

"Thank you, Sophia, for coming, and you also, Dr. Fedorcenko," Cameron said.

Fedorcenko responded with another bow.

"I will come again tomorrow," Sophia said.

"I hope not to be here." Cameron glanced at Alex, who only gave her a noncommittal quirk of his shoulder. "Well, if I am still here, Sophia, could you bring my typewriter and my satchel? Oh, and I left a notebook—"

"Hold on!" interrupted Alex. "You're supposed to be resting. It would be counterproductive to turn this ward into a tiny pressroom."

"Actually, this ward is bigger than the pressroom at the Narkomindel." Cameron smiled sweetly. "But I guess I must follow my doctor's orders," she added contritely. However, as Sophia turned to leave, Cameron caught her eye and silently made sure she understood that she still was to bring the items mentioned.

When they were alone, Alex pulled the curtain around Cameron's bed. He did a brief neurological exam, then checked her heart and breathing with his stethoscope. He noted that she still seemed uncomfortable when she moved and said she had probably bruised her ribs. She merely shrugged as if it were nothing. She wasn't going to let on how much it did hurt and be doomed here another day. Not that she didn't enjoy Alex's company, but his visits were very few and far between, due, he had once apologetically explained, to his heavy workload.

In the middle of the night Cameron woke burning up with fever. Alex was called, apparently to confirm what she thought was obvious. She had a fever of a hundred and four degrees. Alex apologized profusely.

"It's not your fault," she murmured.

"It may be from something you picked up here. We have had some problems lately, but I thought we had it under control."

She tried to smile but could not feel her numb lips to know if she succeeded. "Not many doctors would admit that."

"No, I suppose not," he said in that vague, mysterious way of his that she was coming to know quite well and liked very little.

She thought he was with her most of the night, but she wasn't certain if it was really him, or if he was just part of the dreams that assailed her. Once, she dreamed people had circled her bed and were praying. They wore glowing white robes and had bodies like Sophia, but when they lifted their heads, they all wore Johnny Shanahan's mocking grin. Another time she dreamed of Alex sitting on top of a totem pole. He wore that inscrutable look of his until he rose, stretched out his arms, and took flight. Then there was such an open, joyous expression on him that Cameron, as she observed from far below the pole on the ground, wanted to weep. In fact she did weep, and the tears flowed all over her body, soaking her to the skin.

When she was once again lucid, she realized her fever had broken during the night, and she was drenched with perspiration.

CAMERON MISSED seeing Roosevelt's special envoy, Harry Hopkins, during his visit to Moscow. Her fever had forced her to accept a longer stay in the hospital.

Shanahan, Levinson, and Donovan came to visit the afternoon after the fever had broken. Cameron still had a low-grade fever and was weak. Johnny was carrying a big bouquet of flowers that cheered her immensely.

"It's from the guys in the pressroom," he said. "I told them you weren't one of those sappy women who drool over flowers and that you'd prefer a breaking news item—"

"I love them!" Cameron reached out for them. No, she wasn't a flower person, but she was moved by the gesture.

"I told you she'd like 'em!" said Levinson.

"Well, I chipped in on them, too," Shanahan said defensively.

"It was sweet of you all. Be sure to tell the rest of the guys. Donovan, would you see if a nurse has a vase?"

For a few minutes the men stood around rather awkwardly, fingering the brims of the hats they held in their hands, shifting from foot to foot, then someone mentioned the Hopkins visit, and all relaxed as they forgot themselves in the familiar milieu of their work.

"Came as a complete surprise to us," said Donovan. who had returned with the vase and was rather ineptly stuffing the bouquet into it. "Hopkins was here several hours before any correspondents even knew."

"At least he was willing to talk to us after he met with Stalin," Levinson said.

"For what it was worth," groused Shanahan. "He confirmed the president's commitment to Lend-Lease, both now and for the long term. No surprise there."

"What did you expect?" asked Cameron. "A U.S. declaration of war?"

"Well, if this war is to go into the *long term*, Stalin is gonna want more of a commitment from Roosevelt."

"He should be happy to get supplies," argued Levinson. "And FDR will have to do some smooth talking to get the American people to commit that much to a bunch of Commies. Anyway, we're not even their allies. What about England?"

Donovan chuckled. "Here's a joke my secretary told me the other day. It appears God was up in heaven wondering about all the battles on Earth, and he wanted to talk with those responsible, so he sent Saint Peter to fetch them. First, he got Stalin. 'I was the one who got attacked!' said Stalin. 'It's not my fault. It's that fellow Hitler.' But when Hitler came, he said, 'Who me? I didn't start it. It was the British who declared war on me. It's that fellow Churchill.' Then Churchill came before God and said innocently, 'You can't possibly blame me. Just look down there. You won't find a single Englishman fighting anywhere!' "

After everyone expressed their amusement at Donovan's humor, Cameron said, "I suppose the Russians have a legitimate reason for feeling hung out to dry. But even Churchill, one of the most outspoken opponents of Bolshevism, has proven this war isn't about ideology. It's about stopping a madman who wants to conquer the world."

"You want a flag to wave, Hayes?" sneered Shanahan.

"Which flag?" queried Levinson.

Cameron didn't know whether to be angered at the response or embarrassed by her speech. She'd always thought herself a cynic, and her passion surprised even her. But she certainly wasn't going to grovel apologetically before her colleagues.

"I'll wave a 'hammer and sickle' if I have to," she rejoined. "The Soviets are the only ones at the moment shedding any blood in this war."

"The Brits weren't sitting on their haunches at Dunkirk or the Battle of Britain," argued Levinson. "They have bled a good deal."

"Hayes, you shed a little blood the other day," Shanahan said softly.

Cameron knew his words were his idea of a peace offering. She shrugged. "I guess these Russians are just getting to me. I don't want to see them fall."

"No one does," said Shanahan. "If Russia falls, Europe will be lost."

"If only the American people can be made to see that."

"All they see is Red."

"And it may never change," lamented Cameron, "as long as the Narkomindel slashes our dispatches the way they do."

"It ain't our responsibility," said Shanahan. "It's not our job to change the world—just to write about it."

"Which I believe Hayes is saying we are having a cursed time doing," said Donovan. "And the Soviets are merely cutting their own throats with that policy. If we could write more freely, we could have a positive effect on public sentiment."

"They don't trust us," said Levinson. "And they never will. They will make nice with FDR and Churchill and put on a show of cordiality toward correspondents, but only as long as it serves their purpose."

"Well, something better happen soon," Shanahan growled, "or I'm gonna shake the dust of this berg off my shoes."

"Are you thinking of a new assignment?" Cameron asked. It didn't surprise her. Shanahan was too much of a rebel to put up with Soviet repression for long.

"Only problem is," said Levinson, "this is still the best assignment around at the moment."

"If only we could get to the Front," sighed Cameron. However, she silently hoped such a trip did not occur while she was still in the hospital.

"Ain't gonna happen while the Krauts are kicking Soviet—"

"Shanahan!" scolded Donovan, "watch your tongue. There is a lady present."

"Where?" rejoined Shanahan, looking around in utter surprise, his eyes quickly passing over Cameron.

Cameron laughed. "Thanks, Johnny. That's the best compliment you could pay me."

Just then a nurse came into the ward. She barked something in Russian to Cameron and her visitors. When they indicated their lack of understanding, she pointed to her wristwatch, then gave a shooing gesture with her hands. The message was clear then.

"Say, fellas, I sure appreciate your coming," Cameron said.

"Everyone wanted to come," said Donovan, "but they didn't want to overwhelm you."

"Tell them thanks."

She was surprisingly relieved when they were gone. She would never have said anything, but the visit had tired her. After the nurse took her temperature and pulse, Cameron closed her eyes and went to sleep. She woke two hours later well rested, and she was almost certain her fever was gone. Another bouquet of flowers sat on her bedside table. The card said they were from the State Planning Commission. But there was a personal note signed "Uncle Boris." He said that since she had been sleeping so soundly, he did not wish to wake her, but he apologized for what had happened and said if ever he could do anything for her, she should ask. It hadn't occurred to her that Colonel Tiulenev might feel responsible for what happened. She wished she had been able to see him and set his mind at ease. Also, now that she was awake and feeling better, she was sorry to have missed the distraction his visit would have afforded.

It would be a few hours until dinner offered another distraction, and Cameron quickly grew restless. She slipped from her bed, found her dressing gown, which Sophia had brought along with a few other personal items, and slipped it on over the drab hospital nightgown. Her knees were a bit shaky and her head was woozy, but after the room quit spinning, she was certain the sensations were nothing a bit of exercise wouldn't help. She had read somewhere that a new theory of medicine encouraged patients to be more ambulatory than in the past, that it aided in blood circulation and general well-being. The idea probably hadn't reached Russia yet, but it was time it did.

Her feet snugly shod in bedroom slippers, she shuffled from the ward. She had to use furniture for support to get to the door, and once in the hall she walked close to the wall. She'd never been sick before, and this sense of helplessness was new to her, and totally unwelcome. She was determined to fight it all the way.

No one seemed to pay attention to the escaped patient. She'd already discovered this was a busy hospital. Though not strictly a military hospital, this was one of the major medical facilities for war casualties. Cameron passed many uniformed men in the corridor, no doubt visiting wounded soldiers or attending to other military business. She suddenly realized this was the perfect chance to gather some human-interest material on wounded soldiers. Palgunov could not possibly reject an angle that would surely raise sympathy in the States for the Russian cause.

The only problem was the language barrier. How she wished Sophia were here now. She supposed she could wait until her interpreter came later. But waiting was definitely not Cameron's style. Coming to the end of the corridor, she paused before a door. Only then did she hesitate. Should she knock? She was a woman, and this could be a ward of men. But her own experience indicated that staff and visitors entered the wards freely. If there were delicate procedures going on with a particular patient, the curtain was usually pulled around the bed.

She grasped the door latch.

"There you are!"

Cameron gasped and a shock shot through her as she jumped guiltily. She was only a little relieved when she turned and saw Alex.

"Goodness!" she chuckled nervously. "Alex, you nearly gave me heart failure."

"I had a similar response when I saw you weren't in your bed." Then he nodded toward the door she had been about to open. "You are heading into the wrong ward," he offered guilelessly.

"I know that."

"You do?"

"Yes, I was just . . . well, I thought I might explore a bit. Perhaps meet some patients." She smiled lamely.

He nodded, and she thought she detected a touch of amusement in his eyes. "You were thinking of taking a tour of the hospital?"

"Yes, something like that. I was hoping to visit with some soldiers."

"For your personal edification?"

"Well, yes, I suppose so—oh, I can't lie to you, Alex. I think an article featuring the viewpoints of wounded soldiers would make for great copy in the States."

He folded his arms in front of him and was silent for a long moment. Finally the small glint of amusement was given full rein. A grin spread across his face. "You had only to ask, Cameron. You need not go about like a thief in the night . . . or afternoon."

"It's okay, then?"

"Of course. Would you care for a guide?"

"It's more than I deserve for sneaking about."

"I happen to have a few spare minutes. All I ask is that you don't let yourself tire out." Pausing, he cocked his head toward the door. "That, however, is not a military ward."

He took her upstairs to a large ward of about twenty beds. He explained that these were enlisted men, that officers were in a separate ward. The noise level was quite high, unlike other parts of the hospital Cameron had observed. Cameron was reminded that these were young men who had been healthy and active before their injuries.

When Alex introduced her around, they all appeared quite pleased that a woman, a foreigner at that, would come visit them. One young man had an animated exchange with Alex.

"He wants to take you to the cinema," Alex translated.

"You mean on a date? Tell him he hardly knows me," Cameron replied glibly.

The soldier laughed and replied that it didn't matter. He was already in love. Cameron laughed with him; then with a casual glance, she noted that he was missing an arm. She looked away quickly, pretending not to see. But it didn't work.

Through Alex the young soldier said, "I would give two arms to stop the Fascist bandits!" He grinned as if to comfort her. "I'll get a medal, too."

"I'm sure you deserve it. Where are you from?"

"My village is near Pskov. I am told it is now occupied by the German scum. We will get it back soon."

Another man called out, and Alex translated, "I am from the Ukraine. Will you tell about me in the American newspaper?"

"As much as I am allowed. Where were you wounded?"

"Near Smolensk—"

"She means where on your body, stupid," interjected another man in a good-natured manner.

"Is that what you mean?" he asked, appearing embarrassed at having made a fool of himself before a foreigner.

She gave him an encouraging smile. "Both, I suppose."

"I got shrapnel in my foot." He poked his left foot out from beneath the covers, showing a cast nearly covered with autographs. "Will you sign it, yes?" Alex gave her a pen, and she did so as the soldier added, "The doc here fixed my foot up good. I will go back to the Front soon, right, Doc?"

Alex nodded and his voice was strained as he replied, "It looks that way."

"I will shoot more Fascist pigs! I only wish I had bullets as big as this cast to shoot at them!"

The other men laughed at this bit of humor. Cameron chuckled politely. Their enthusiasm was oddly disturbing. She supposed they had a right to it, considering what they had suffered, but there was something about it that gave her a chill nonetheless. They were too young to be so eager about killing. One man she spoke to however was more reserved.

Alex explained that he had been badly shot in the abdomen and had a large portion of his intestines removed. He'd lost thirty pounds in less than a week. His taut features hinted he was still in a great deal of pain.

"Before the war I worked on *kolkhoz*, or collective farm," he said quietly, speech coming with difficulty. "I do not know what has become of my family. The Germans overtook my village, too."

"I'm sure they are all right," said Cameron lamely.

"All I want is to go back to them and work our farm. I am a good farmer."

A lump formed in Cameron's throat, and she felt a tingling in her eyes. And why shouldn't she feel like crying at the boy's simple but profoundly poignant words? She blinked a few times until the unwelcome feeling passed. Still, Cameron didn't know what to say to the boy. The only words that came to mind were just as inane as her silly encouragement about his family who had probably been killed. So she just reached out and took the boy's hand and squeezed it gently. His own grip was weak and his skin was hot to the touch, like hers had been last night.

"Comrade Stalin says we can pray again if we like," he added. "If I could get to a church, I would light a candle and pray for my family and that I could get to them soon. Do Americans pray?"

"Yes . . . some do."

"If you go to a church, would you light a candle for me?"

"I . . . yes . . . of course I will."

"And pray that the war will be over soon."

Several men who heard chimed in their support of this. But one voice added, "Soon or not, we will fight to the end."

And there was a chorus of agreement to this, as well.

Cameron visited several more bedsides, and each soldier was eager to tell his story, where he was from, what family he had, and how he'd been wounded. Often all this was interspersed with Party rhetoric and slurs against the Germans. When it was time for her to leave, they told her to come back, and she promised she would.

Once in the corridor, the stoic front she'd tried to present to the soldiers began to falter. She leaned against the wall a moment to catch her breath or at least shore up her slipping emotions. She felt as if all the strength had been sapped from her, and the faces continued as vivid pictures in her mind's eye. The broad, homely, wonderful faces. They had made her forget all her journalistic instincts. Instead, they had seemed to bring out something quite foreign to her. She had wanted to gather each of them under her wing like a mother hen and protect them from further pain.

There was something more. A sudden thought came to her, as painful as it was disquieting. Her own brother might well be among those men in the ward, or more likely, he might be one of the many soldiers she'd seen marching in the streets or riding in trucks on the way to the Front. He'd be twenty-six now, the prime age for a soldier. She had not thought of him in a long time. It had seemed so clear when she had talked to her mother about it in California. She would come to Russia and find her brother. The fact was, since then she had probably tried hard *not* to think of him. She should have already been making inquiries into his whereabouts. But, except for that brief and rather lame mention of him to Uncle Boris, she had avoided it since coming to Russia.

She supposed reality had intruded. And the reality was that nothing was clear anymore. Though hard to admit, she was probably afraid of how this young man Semyon Luban might shake up her world. If he were even still alive. And if he was dead? How could she ever tell that news to her mother? It seemed best to just leave it all alone. Yet that resolution did not prevent a thought of him to prick her at unwelcome times. Her brother could be so close.

She now knew why she suddenly felt so exhausted, and it had nothing to do with her own injuries. It was solely because she was so completely helpless to shield those boys, even her own brother, from the harm of this detestable war.

Cameron laid a hand on Alex's arm. "I appreciate your taking me to see them. They are all sweet young boys, aren't they?"

"Some a bit more bloodthirsty than others," he said lightly.

"I expect they were just spouting off, trying to look tough. Alex, the boy from the *kolkhoz* . . . will he make it home?"

"I think you should light that candle quickly if you are of a mind to do so." His grim tone belied the glibness of his words. "He worsens every day. He is battling infection now, but nothing we have done has helped."

"I wish I could pray and light a candle for him." Cameron shook her head and sighed. "I wish I thought something like that could work for him."

"You don't?"

"Since I have come to this hospital, I have been asked about religion more than I have been in years." She tried to give a dry chuckle to match her words but could not manage it.

"That's not surprising. Hospitals seem to encourage spiritual thoughts."

"That sort of thing isn't for me." Sighing, she added, "But I almost would try a bit of prayer if I thought it would help that boy."

"But it's not for you—religion, that is?"

"I don't need it. How about you?"

That look flickered across his face, the one that was part shadow and part abyss. If he had intended for it to beguile her and lure her toward unearthing the secrets behind it, he was being very successful.

She was drawn to him in a way she knew she should fight, but for once in her life, she longed to submit rather than fight. She could leap into that abyss and not mind it at all.

She tried to lightly brush away the rising emotional tension between them. "Oops, I've stumbled upon the mystery man again. Sorry."

"I'm afraid you are making more of it than there is." He wasn't being entirely honest, she realized, yet there seemed no point in debating the issue. He had a right to his secrets. Then he went on, "Faith in God used to be very important to me, but when I needed it most, it failed me."

"That's why it is best not to need anything," she said flippantly.

"You are an arrogant woman," he breathed, almost tenderly. His face was very close to hers, and her breath caught as a desire to be kissed by him overtook her. Then the corners of his lips curved into a gentle smile, and the electric moment passed. "Everyone needs something, Cameron," he said. "Even strong, independent female journalists."

"You don't strike me as a needy sort, Alex."

He rolled his eyes derisively. "I am, believe me. I suppose I put on a bit of a front because doctors are supposed to be something close to gods, but I have fallen far enough to know I am rife with weakness."

"Do you want to talk about it?"

"The middle of a hospital corridor isn't the place for that discussion." He must have read her mind, though it probably was not much of a stretch to realize she was thinking him mysterious again, but he added, "Sometime we'll talk." He then linked his arm around hers and said briskly, "Come on, there's another ward I want to show you."

"The officers?"

"All you'll hear from them is even stronger Party rhetoric. No, what I want to show you will be better . . . and worse, too."

She arched her brow with curiosity and let him lead the way.

35

THEY SOON CAME to a section of the hospital, toward the back it seemed, or at least it was set apart from the rest. A guard let them through a locked door, and they came to another door off a corridor where there was another guard standing outside. He let them in.

Closing the door behind them, Alex finally explained. "This is where the wounded German POWs are."

This ward also had about twenty beds, but it was quieter, more subdued than the one they had just visited. These men had a reason to be quiet, because they were the vanquished, stranded in enemy territory. Yet despite that, Cameron did not sense hostility in the atmosphere. Nor was there despair. These were merely men who had come face-to-face with their weaknesses, not only physical, but emotional, as well. They had thought they would sweep through Russia in a matter of weeks, as they had in so many other countries, but they had failed.

"This is Helmut Othman," Alex said, pausing by a bed. He conversed in German with the soldier for a moment, and the man brightened considerably at the attention, or perhaps merely at hearing his native tongue spoken by his supposed enemy. Alex examined the man's thickly bandaged right arm. He felt the fingers and seemed pleased. To Cameron, he said, "I operated on him two days ago. His arm was shattered pretty badly. But I think we saved it."

"Where are you from, Helmut?" Cameron asked with Alex translating.

"I am from Hamburg. I haven't been home in a very long time."

He was young—they were all young—but he seemed especially so, the fresh-faced, wide-eyed kind of youth. His blue eyes and close-cropped blond hair hinted at that so-called Aryan purity much touted by Hitler. Yet his eyes were sad and his voice soft, almost self-effacing.

"What did you do before the war?"

"I worked in my father's bakery. He is the best baker in Hamburg. I was soon to be in charge of cake decorating. My father said I was good enough. Thanks to the doctor here, I will still be able do it, because you need two arms for that job. I liked working in the bakery, but they did not have me work in the kitchen in the army. I am in infantry."

"Do you know why you've gone to war, Helmut?"

"My country has gone to war, and I was called." He shrugged. To him it was that simple. "I have no personal bad feelings against the Russian people. They killed some of my friends, but I killed some Russians. All I want to do is go back to Hamburg and decorate cakes."

A knot once again swelled in Cameron's throat. She didn't like looking into the eye of the enemy, especially when what she saw were honest common boys. All their stories were similar to Helmut's. They had parents and girlfriends and wives and children, and all they wanted was to go home to them. They were grocery clerks and factory workers and farmers. They were not the automatons, the tin soldiers Americans had been led to believe of the Wehrmacht. And they were not consumed with dark hatred.

One boy said his best friend had been killed at his side during the fighting around Kiev.

"I wanted only to kill Russians then," he said. He had freckles on his nose and red hair that was mostly covered by a thick bandage around his head. "But they have been kind to me here in the hospital. I don't know what to think now."

Neither did Cameron.

When she and Alex left, he took her to a small physician's lounge on that floor. He drew them each a cup of tea from the samovar, and they sat on hard wooden chairs that wobbled and creaked when they moved.

"Why did you take me there?" Cameron asked, speaking for the first time since leaving the prisoners' ward. Her voice rasped with barely concealed emotion.

"You seemed to me the kind of journalist who would want to see both sides of a matter," he said simply.

"I am, but . . ." She stared into her cup of dark, strong liquid. "I thought you were a patriot, and yet you must know, it isn't good for the cause to stir sympathy for the enemy."

"To me they are not the enemy," he answered rather forcefully, as if he had defended himself in this area before. "They are my patients. I have fought no less to keep them alive than I have the Russian boys. As for patriotism . . . I don't know. I have adopted Russia as my country, but I remain an outsider here. I am definitely an outsider in America. As for Germany, I hate the politics of Hitler. I see every day the horrors he has wrought, and if I could, I would personally put a bullet in the man's head." He jumped up suddenly and strode to the samovar. "Do you want more?" he asked as he refilled his cup.

"No. I still don't know why you showed me that ward."

He turned toward her. She had never known a man with such an expressive face. In rather peculiar contrast to his enigma, he wore his emotions quite close to the surface. The problem was in discerning the cause of those emotions. And Cameron wanted to know. She had never known a man whose soul she so desired to touch, or for that matter, a man who had a soul at all. She was sure her father had no soul, and as for Shanahan—oh, he had his tender moments, but she was almost certain it went no deeper than that. And she began to glimpse what probably had been missing from their relationship all along.

Alex's eyes were a dark blue now as they studied her. His tone was soft as he resumed his chair. "I guess I wanted to share with you my conflicted world. Maybe I thought you would become as confused as I, and I would find comfort in company. Pretty cruel of me, eh?"

"Yes, it was," she replied with only a hint of humor. "If I'd had a choice, I wouldn't have wanted to see what I just saw. But I suppose I'll have a much better understanding of this war. Still, those stories of German atrocities we hear about, are they all lies, then?"

"It's the SS who are the real beasts of the German army and who are, I'm fairly certain, responsible for the atrocities. The common soldiers take the towns and villages; then the SS moves in and takes the hearts and souls of the people. I've never had to treat any of them. They are probably too mean to get captured alive."

She saw more conflict in his eyes and knew, even if he didn't, that if he had an SS officer on his operating table, he would fight as hard for that life as for any other.

"Cameron, did you think war was a simple black-and-white matter?"

"I'm not sure what I thought—no, that's not true. I thought it was pure glory, filled with exciting stories to write. I've been strafed and bombed and seriously scared, but it's always been rather a lark. I've seen one dead person, at least one who has died right before my eyes. I never knew her and spoke only a few words to her. It was shocking, but it would make wonderful copy." Now Cameron felt the tension of inner revelations she wasn't comfortable with. She jumped up, and for want of something better to do, she brought her cup to the samovar. "I suppose I should thank you for this eye-opening experience," she added, her back to Alex as she refilled her cup.

"I'm sorry, I shouldn't have—"

"No! I wanted to talk to soldiers. I want also to go to the Front, to see battlefields, to see the battles! But I thought I could do that without being affected by it all." Suddenly she thought once more of the factory, of the woman who had so cheerfully conversed with her and then had died moments later in the explosion. She had tried not to think of the woman in the factory. The broad-faced, friendly worker who had reached out to Cameron—and then died so quickly. Cameron had tried to avoid the pain caused by seeing the light in a human being's eyes one moment, only to watch it darken with death the next. She, too, might have been killed. But she didn't want to think about all that. She didn't want to be touched.

She hadn't heard him move and didn't know he'd done so until she felt the warmth of his nearness. He put his large, warm hand on her shoulder.

"It was bound to happen, Cameron." His voice was as gentle as his physician's touch. "Your soul is too tender not to be moved by such experiences."

No one, including herself, had ever thought of her as tender before. She felt as if something were cracking around her, the shell of armor she wore. She knew it was no coincidence it was this man who was gently chipping it away.

She turned suddenly and found herself a mere two inches from him. His face was filled with an expression she could not read—and one she could not resist. She drew even closer to him and touched her lips to his. She had meant only a friendly brush, but the contact over-whelmed her. Her arms went around him and she pressed closer. When he responded, tightening his own arms around her, lengthening the kiss, nearly taking the breath from her, she only then realized how desperately she had wanted to be held like that. Perhaps she had wanted it but been denied it her whole life.

His lips were soft and firm all at once, gentle and passionate. Like him, the kiss was conflicted in its own way, not knowing whether it was merely a comforting gesture or one of desire. But after a full min-ute locked in his embrace, Cameron was certain the latter had won out. When the door burst open, she didn't know if she ought to be relieved or angry.

Two laughing nurses bumbled onto the scene, and their laughter stopped abruptly as Cameron and Alex just as abruptly fell apart. There were several awkward moments as apologies were stammered on both sides, and she and Alex made a hasty exit from the lounge. They were silent as they walked side by side down the corridor. Cam-eron's heart was still racing, her lips still tingling with the reminder of his touch.

All she could think about was that she wanted to kiss him again. She didn't care if she had been the aggressor and still wasn't certain if he had responded only to spare her dignity.

Suddenly he stopped walking and nudged her against the drab white wall. He was very close to her again, and she could have so easily kissed him, but he wore a dark, almost forbidding, look that checked her raging emotions.

"Cameron," he said, his voice low and rough, "I am not the kind of man you should get involved with."

"What?"

"There are too many complications. You should—"

"Wait a minute!" she burst. "No one tells me what I should or should not do."

"Really?"

She smiled in spite of herself at his earnest expression. How stupid she must sound! "Did you want to kiss me, Alex, or were you just being kind?"

"Kind?" A flicker of amusement momentarily lightened him. "Do you think that is how a man kisses a woman when he is trying only to be kind?"

"Well . . ."

"I have wanted to kiss you almost from that first night I met you when we were on the rooftop and the fires of the bombing were reflected in your eyes. I was certain it was no mere reflection but that it had come up from your very soul. I knew then I wanted to crack the walls that I perceived were just a façade around you." Pausing, he sucked in a breath, and it was obvious he'd said more than he wanted. He then added with just a touch of defiance, "But there are things in my past . . . that would repel you." He glanced around, aware that they were in a corridor once more.

An orderly hurried by pushing a gurney. Nurses and doctors and others passed back and forth. The life of the hospital churned on around them. Noises came from the wards, hushed conversations, cries of pain, even a distant rumble of laughter. But it all blurred in the immediacy of the moment between Cameron and Alex.

"Listen, Alex," Cameron said with determination, "corridor or not, I think it's time you revealed all these horrible mysteries about yourself. Are you an ax murderer?"

He sighed and the look on his face clearly said he knew it was time, and there might never be a better place. "I came to Russia three years ago because I was running away—not from the police. I was trying to escape my private shame. I lost my license to practice medicine in the States because I killed a patient on the operating table."

"Oh, Alex! You couldn't have—"

"Yes, I did!" he said emphatically, as if refusing any misplaced sympathy. "It was pure incompetence. I was a very ambitious surgical resident. I wanted to be the youngest Chief of Surgery to ever hold the post at my hospital. I had pushed myself to the limit, and then I tried to reach beyond that by taking drugs. I pumped myself full of stimulants so I could do without sleep. And when I absolutely had to get some sleep, I took depressants. Then more stimulants to counter the depressants. I was heavily addicted for a full year, and the irony was that I continued to function amazingly well, effectively hiding my problem. I suppose that was the real irony—I was a very good surgeon. I no doubt would have attained my ambitions on talent alone." He paused and gave a self-deprecating laugh. "And I said *you* were arrogant! Still, the truth is I didn't need the drugs at the beginning. Even now I am not sure how it all began. Slowly and innocently, I am sure, until I found myself caught in a vortex I couldn't escape. And then a woman died. It was a delicate procedure, and my hand slipped and incised an artery. My friends said it could have happened to anyone. Maybe so . . ."

"Such things do happen—"

"Don't, Cameron! I am not telling you this for sympathy. That is the last thing I want or need. And I am glad I had colleagues back then who weren't willing to give me sympathy, either, who refused to protect me. I got what I deserved. I do regret that my mother suffered from the scandal. I'm sure that is what killed her. She was so proud of my accomplishments, and then to lose it all so ignominiously. . . ." He had been standing stiffly before her, but now he turned to the side and leaned against the wall as if just talking about the loss sapped him of strength.

She didn't care how it sounded, she still felt a need to say something, to offer understanding if not sympathy. "Still, you did not give up. You came to Russia, and you continued to practice medicine."

"Medicine was all I had, all I ever wanted to do. And that need forced me to clean up my life. A family friend, another Russian immigrant, put me in touch with his brother here in Russia, who turned out to be Dr. Fedorcenko." Pausing, he turned his head toward her. "Now you know my secrets, most of them at least. Now you know what causes my reticence. Every day I am haunted by my past, by fear that it could happen again. Once you have an addiction like that, it is indeed like a ghost forever haunting you. I do not even take aspirin because of the fear in me. I don't touch alcohol. But there are times, God help me, when I have worked an especially long day and am so tired I can barely think straight and then an emergency comes in . . . I think about it then. I think that perhaps one pill—"

"But you fight it." Her words were part question, part hopeful statement.

"Yes, I fight it. But I can never know for certain when or if I will lose the fight."

"Thank you for telling me these things, Alex." She wondered if he'd thought his tale would really change what she was feeling. "But do you think I am so shallow that knowing this would change anything?"

"You are far from shallow. And I think I know a lot more about you that you try to keep hidden." A hint of a smile played upon his lips.

"You do?"

He nodded. "You are not as tough as you pretend to be. And I am very drawn to you, Cameron." His eyes seemed to envelope her with their intensity. "But I can't inflict my personal demons upon a woman. There are just too many complications for there to be a future for us."

"Future?" she rolled her eyes. Men! They thought all women were dying to get married. She was only partly aware she was hiding behind her suddenly glib attitude. "Alex, rest easy. I am not looking for a future with any man."

"What do you want, then?"

"I don't know," she replied just a bit testily. "All I know is when you held me—or when I held you, whatever it was—it seemed to ease a need I had, maybe just a need to be close to someone."

"Anyone? And I just happened to be around?"

She did not understand the undertone of ire in his voice. A minute ago he was trying to reject her! "Oh, please!" She started to walk away, but he reached out and laid a hand on her shoulder, gently restraining her.

"This is all sounding pretty ridiculous, isn't it?" he said apologetically. "I don't understand any of it. We both have obvious needs, yet we both also have this drive to protect ourselves from them. It's confusing."

She smiled. "I'll tell you what I believe appeals to me about you. You are a deep and complex man. There is so much to you that I find intriguing. Half the time I have no idea what you are going to say or do, but I rather enjoy the uncertainty. On the other hand, Alex, it is also the most frustrating thing about you. Can't you just once accept something without trying to analyze all its aspects?"

"And what would I be accepting?"

"Simply that we are attracted to each other and we should enjoy it."

"I fear I am too Russian for simplicity or enjoyment, much less both at the same time."

"Well, I am Irish. We are all simplicity and enjoyment. I'll show you the way."

His eyes, dancing and sparkling, roved over her face. They held a hungry aspect. "I want to kiss you again."

"Now you are getting the hang of it!"

She leaned toward him, and their lips brushed. Then the loudspeaker blared.

"Dr. Rostovscikov . . ." The rest was in Russian, but the name was clear to Cameron, even though the voice used the Russian equivalent of his name.

"An emergency," he said reluctantly. "I have to go. You'll be all right to get back on your own?"

"Yes . . ."

"I'll come to see you later."

She watched him hurry down the corridor; then she leaned back against the wall and sighed. As if the complexities of war were not enough in her life right now, was she also—? No, she was not falling in love. But she was falling into *something*, and she feared it was far more dangerous than war.

PART IV

"A censored press only serves to demoralize."

KARL MARX

36

BLAIR KNEW GARY was falling in love with her. And it was more than a feeling. He'd told her as much.

They had gone to a potluck at his church. She'd brought a hot dish—scalloped potatoes and ham. He had raved about how good it was. One of the other men at the dinner had winked at Gary and said wryly, "And she can cook, too! She's a keeper, Gary."

Gary had agreed.

Blair did not admit that she'd sneaked back home while her father was at work and bribed her parents' cook to make the dish. What was another lie, after all?

After the dinner they had fallen into the task of washing up. They were at the big sink in the church kitchen, hands steeped in soapy water. Somehow they found themselves all alone. Gary looked at her in that way he had so often in the weeks since that Fourth of July picnic when they had started dating. It was a look she could easily lose herself in. His eyes dark, intense, warm, and inviting, all at the same time. It was the look she could spend the rest of her life immersed in. There was caring in that look but more, as well. He looked at her as if she had value, not because of her beauty, but because of her inner self. Sometimes she wondered if he even saw her beauty.

"He's right, you know," Gary said, handing her a dish to rinse.

"Who's right?"

"Mr. Thomas, when he said you are a keeper."

"Oh, Gary, really!" She chuckled lightly, a bit embarrassed.

"You should know by now how I feel about you, Blair."

"You hardly know me."

"I know enough, and I love what I know . . . and I want to spend the rest of my life learning about and loving all the rest."

"I didn't think you were such a doe-eyed romantic, Gary." With a giggle, she flicked some soapsuds at him. "Now, get serious. We have work to do."

He retaliated good-naturedly by splashing her. They laughed, and for the moment the intensity dispersed.

But the awful knot in Blair's stomach did not. He loved her. But whom did he love? The lie, or *her*? Was there truly a difference between the two? She tried to convince herself there wasn't, that only the form was a lie—the churchgoing, domestic girl might not be her, but she'd never lied to him about what was in her heart. If he truly loved her, then it must be the heart of her he loved, not the *form*.

Or was she merely justifying what she had done, what she was doing even now as a woman came into the kitchen and complimented her hot dish.

"You must give me the recipe. The particular combination of spices was wonderful!"

"Thank you so much," Blair replied with just the right balance of pride and humility. "I'll bring the recipe Sunday."

How easily the lies came. Fred Banister didn't know what he had lost. She was a better actress than Lillian Gish, Helen Hayes, and Jean Harlow all rolled into one!

Gary suggested that after the potluck she come back to his parents' house—he stayed there when he was on leave from where he was stationed at Fort MacArthur—to play some bridge with them. Yes, she had met his parents and they seemed to like her, and she liked them. They, unlike her own rather deviant family, were down-to-earth folks. Ed Hobart was an ebullient man with a story or joke about everything, while his wife, Marjorie, was quiet and sweet. Blair liked to be around them. But she declined Gary's suggestion, saying she had to get up early for a job interview.

Sometimes all the deceptions, piling one on top of the other, wore her out. Her life was becoming a house of cards. There was always another lie that had to be told to cover a previous one. One of the most difficult deceptions was her job. She had been ashamed to tell Gary where she really worked, so she said she volunteered at a hospital, the night shift, and that was why she couldn't spend many evenings, except for her days off, with him. It was an easier ruse to pull off in the first couple of weeks when they saw each other only two or three times and his work schedule conflicted with hers. But two weeks ago, he had taken night duty, so they were seeing each other nearly every day now.

Then there was her family. She'd put off for quite a while his meeting them, but finally she had to succumb to his requests or find herself having to build yet another tower of lies. The biggest problem had been Keagan, but that was solved quite easily because he still refused to speak to her. She honestly told Gary there was some bad blood between her and her father and he wasn't speaking to her, but her mother would love to meet him. They met at a restaurant and Jackie came, too. They had a lovely time—almost like normal people.

Yes, Blair was loving every moment with Gary. She loved the way he treated her like a princess—not in the sense that he spoiled her, but rather that he simply responded to her as if she were something very special. She had never had a man treat her that way before. He listened to her when she talked about herself and her life. Really listened, as if her words had merit. She even revealed about some of her rebellion and let him assume she had now become a Christian and changed. She told him the truth about her father, about his disappointment with her. And he didn't press for details when it was obviously a difficult subject for her to talk about. She also told him the truth about her dreams.

She almost smiled at that. Her dreams. She didn't really have to lie about them, because her dreams were changing. The things she had scoffed at when Jackie would tell her about wanting a simple home and family were becoming more desirable to Blair. Maybe it was because Gary came with such things.

Perhaps what had started as a lie had actually evolved into truth.

However, she thought of a recent conversation with Jackie. Her sister had remained true to her word and not revealed Blair's secret, but she still took every opportunity to try to make Blair give it up.

"You can't fool God," Jackie had said just the other day.

"I'm not trying to fool God." Goodness, could Jackie really think Blair was that evil?

"But you are pretending to be a Christian, aren't you?"

"Well . . ." Blair had tried not to think of these issues. "I do believe in God, you know. I wouldn't lie about a thing like that."

Jackie had given a noncommittal response and let it go, for the time being at least.

Blair knew she was pretending a faith that was not there. She knew to be a real Christian one had to do certain things, the first and foremost being to pray a prayer "accepting Jesus into your heart." So just to have an answer next time Jackie hounded her, Blair had decided to do it. Not in a mocking sense, to be sure. But what would it hurt to pray the prayer? So she did. She had felt no different afterward, but the pastor of Gary's church had preached a sermon—one of the few Blair actually listened to—about faith being based on fact, not feeling. So she didn't have to feel anything; it wasn't one of the requirements. She must be *in*. She must be a Christian. Yet the harder she tried to convince herself of her faith and of her other changes, the more she knew they could not be real. Something was missing. Though she had turned away from Hollywood, everything about her life reeked of a motion picture. Pure illusion. Even the words she spoke seemed to have been written by another.

Again she thought of a house of cards. And like any such structure, it was doomed to come crashing down on her.

————

But it didn't seem so when Gary took her out for a special dinner he'd said was for their two-and-a-half-month anniversary. She had poked fun at him for celebrating a half month, but he said he felt like celebrating every week they were together. They went to a very fancy restaurant—not the kind her Hollywood acquaintances frequented, thank goodness!—but it was a place where the waiters wore white jackets and black ties and which had to cost far more than Gary's army pay could afford.

"This is so nice, Gary," she said as they finished their meal of prime rib, "but we didn't have to come to a place so fancy."

"It's a special day." He smiled, reaching across the table for her hand.

"You are really too good to me. But you must know I don't expect these kinds of things." Her hand rested so comfortably in his. She knew she expected nothing more than the warmth and security of his touch. This was all she had truly ever wanted, and she had finally found it in him.

"Don't worry, okay? I know you don't expect it. I also know I will never be able to keep you in the manner to which you are accustomed." He grinned at his words that had to be straight from a movie. "I know you like nice clothes and such, but they are not important to you. You are a loving woman of God, and He is the center of your life."

"Gary . . ." For one brief instant she considered revealing all. With great clarity, she saw in that instant what a mockery of *him* her entire sham was. He would hate her if he knew. And so she remained silent.

"Shush," he went on. "I've been waiting all evening to say something, so let me get it out. I've got new orders. I'm being assigned to the Philippines—"

"Oh no, Gary!"

He squeezed her hand and gave her a reassuring smile. "I didn't want to rush things with us. But I know what I want, and I think you know what you want, as well. So why wait? Let's get married, Blair. I love you so."

His eyes roved over her like she was some holy thing. Couldn't he see? She was a liar, a deceiver, a mocker. How could she have fooled him so? Was he so gullible? But she knew he was an intelligent, perceptive man. There was simply no reason why he should not have believed her lies. Why would any reasonable person suspect such a deception?

"Gary, this is so sudden."

"You mean to say you didn't see this coming?" He grinned. "That's one thing I can't believe, Blair, my love. I can read you like a book—"

"Gary, really . . ."

"It's true. I have never felt more connected to a girl before. I know you feel the same way. I have prayed about this, and I feel certain that you and I are supposed to be together. The only thing that would make me feel otherwise is if you said you didn't love me."

And that, of course, was the worst part of her rotten sham. *She did love him.*

"I—it's just—we . . ." She couldn't think of any reason against his proposal except the truth.

"Is it the army life that bothers you? You're afraid of it, aren't you? We haven't talked much about it. I guess that's my fault. I suppose I didn't want to scare you away. Maybe it is unfair of me to marry you and then leave for foreign parts—"

"You mean I wouldn't go with you?" She grasped at this as if it were a life belt.

"The families of military personnel in the Philippines are being returned Stateside. The situation over there is just a bit dicey, what with Japan's aggression in China and such. The trouble is centered more in the Far East in general, not so much directly in the Philippines, which is still rather an idyllic spot," he added quickly, as if to reassure her. "As soon as things cool off a bit, I am certain the families will return. It might only be a matter of months, maybe by the first of the year. I know the practical thing would be to wait until then to marry, but I'm not sure when I'd get leave to come back, and we'd want our families at the wedding."

She looked up into his eyes, then down at their hands still clasped on the edge of the table. He loved her and wanted to make her his wife. And she loved him. He was everything she had only just discovered she desired. For the first time in her life true happiness was within her grasp.

Gary need never know of her lies. She could do this. She could pull it off. She had done so for nearly three months. His parents loved her. The folks at church loved her. *He* loved her. She could play this role forever. She knew it. And really, it *was* far more truth than lie.

"Yes," she said. "Yes, Gary, I'll marry you!"

37

JACKIE WALKED with Sam Okuda along the treelined path not far from the campus. The day was warm, even a bit sultry. They had just finished registering for the new term in a crowded, stuffy building and had hurried outside for some fresh air. Jackie had gotten all her classes for this, her last, year of college. She had no classes with Sam this term because she would be concentrating on her teaching requirements, while Sam, who had graduated in June, was now working on his master's in English.

They talked about their schedules for a while, but soon Jackie edged the conversation toward a more serious topic she had been wanting to get his advice about. They had seen a lot of each other over the summer, and she had come to value his wisdom and his friendship.

"Sam, I have this awful dilemma," she said. "I need advice."

"Ah . . ." He stroked his beardless chin as if he wore a venerably long white beard. "Tell me your troubles, my child. The wise Sam shall solve all your problems."

Giggling, she rolled her eyes. "Well, you're not exactly Solomon, but you are the best I've got."

"Ouch! Shot down again!"

"I don't want your head to get too big." She sighed. "Really, Sam, I enjoy talking to you. You know you are becoming my best friend. I have never had a best boy friend—" Flustered, she added quickly, "Not *boyfriend*, of course, but . . . well, you know what I mean."

"What do you mean, Jackie?" His dark eyes twinkled, and she knew he was just teasing her.

"Have you ever had a girl friend?" she asked.

"You don't mean *girlfriend*, of course," he continued to tease, "but girl friend, two words, right?"

"It is kind of different, don't you think?"

"Yeah . . . it is that." The teasing briefly died from his tone, and the twinkling left his eyes. "All right, girl . . . friend, what is your problem?"

She was relieved to move away from the discussion that she sensed was becoming just a tad awkward.

"It's about my sister," Jackie began. "I don't know what to do about her. She has sworn me to secrecy about something, but I want to tell you, if you swear it will stay between just us."

"Okay, shoot."

"I've told you about my sisters—"

"Sure. The competent, savvy reporter and the flaky, confused actress. I can't wait to meet them someday."

Jackie chose not to respond to that comment. Neither one of them had broached the subject of meeting the other's families. Jackie didn't know why. Somehow it seemed it would complicate their friendship.

Instead, she continued with her problem. "Well, this is about Blair, the confused one. Her life was really messed up, Sam. I don't want to get into details, but it was bad. Anyway, she has met this guy—they had met once before and she told me at that time what a great guy he was. Then she wouldn't return his calls, until he finally gave up. I think she was scared because he wasn't like the other men she usually went out with. He is a really decent Christian man. I ran into him one day and sort of arranged for them to meet at a church function—"

"I didn't think your sisters went to church," said Sam.

"They don't. But things had become so bad for Blair that when I invited her to church, she finally came."

"So your sister has started going to church and she has met this terrific Christian guy. What's the problem?"

"Did you wonder why this straight-arrow Christian man is interested in my wild sister?"

"I hate to admit it, but us males can be pretty ridiculous where beautiful women are concerned. Remember, you took me to that movie your sister was in, and she is mighty beautiful."

"It's worse than Gary just being blinded by a beautiful woman. You see, my sister has been playing the part of the kind of girl Gary would be attracted to. She's pretending to be a Christian."

"I guess she could pretend to be worse things."

"Don't be glib, Sam. This is serious."

"I'm sorry. I didn't mean to make fun. But tell me something, is your sister going to church by day and maintaining her wild life by night, so to speak? Does her attitude seem mocking or malicious?"

"Not that I can see. She still has her job singing at a nightclub, but I think that is only because she signed a contract and can't get out of it. I am pretty certain she isn't drinking anymore or going to the wild parties she frequented before. If I didn't know the truth, I would think she really had changed, you know, in her heart."

"Then maybe it isn't as bad as you think."

"But you can't pretend to be a Christian!" Jackie exclaimed. "It's just wrong."

Sam scratched his head thoughtfully. "Of course it is wrong. But something also tells me that God may just have her where He wants her. You have been a Christian all your life, Jackie, so you might not have as good an idea of what it's like to be on the outside looking in. I became a Christian in high school because my father's white friend invited me to church, and every time I went, I saw something very appealing. It was so much more alive and affirming than my parents' Buddhism. The more I was around the people at that church, the more I wanted what they had."

"And you're saying it might grow on Blair?" Jackie was starting to see the situation in a new light.

"Yeah, in a way. Who knows what's going on in her heart? Well, God does, that's for sure! If you really want my advice, I think you should let nature take its course. Let God deal with your sister. He may want to punish her for doing something evil, for mocking the faith, or maybe He is gently nudging her into that faith. Let Him have His way. Anyway, I have gotten the idea that you've been trying for years to get your sisters to turn to God but without success. If Blair hasn't listened so far, do you really think she will listen to you now?"

Jackie stopped walking, and when Sam stopped also, she just looked at him. Then shaking her head with something like awe, she allowed a smile to slip across her face.

"Maybe you are Solomon, after all," she said.

He laughed. "A yellow, slant-eyed Jewish king—now, there's a picture."

"Don't say such things about yourself, Sam," she said, not masking her ire at his self-denigrating tone. "You are not yellow. And your eyes are very nice."

"I haven't known many white people like you, Jackie. My dad's friend, and my namesake, Sam, and his wife, Joan, are like that, and there are some folks at church. But even there I am regarded by many as different and somewhat suspect. Well, I am different, I know," he said earnestly. "But it doesn't bother you at all that I am Japanese. You hardly even seem to notice."

"I truly don't, not anymore."

"But you know other people do. Don't you see them look at us?"

She gave a dismissive grunt. In truth, she and Sam seemed to stay out of the public eye as much as possible. However, it was true that when they did encounter others, Jackie was aware of looks of disapproval.

But she said with conviction, "I don't care about them."

"Well, with the way the Japanese have been burning their way through the Far East, sometimes even I am ashamed of who I am. People look at me suspiciously now more than ever. They don't seem to realize I am an American citizen. I was born here. I've never seen Japan!" He paused and looked down intently at her. "Jackie, I don't know what will happen if we go to war with Japan."

"That will never happen."

"How can you be so certain?"

"It is such a small country. How could they have the audacity to go to war against us?"

He shook his head without hope. "It is just because they are small that it *could* happen. They have a desperate need for space and more natural resources. They are not bullying all those little countries in Asia for their own sake. Many don't give much credit to the Japanese because of their typically small stature and the size of the country itself, but I believe they have the will to be a dangerous adversary." Again he shook his head with a dry laugh. "Listen to me! 'Their' and 'they.' That's how far removed I feel from my Japanese heritage. I am *Nisei*—"

"*Nisei*. That means you were born here?"

"Yes, and *Issei* means someone born in Japan like my parents. But I am an American citizen *by birth*." Sam spoke the words defensively, as if he needed to do so with her. She was a little hurt by this, and he saw it immediately in her face. "I'm sorry, Jackie." He ran a hand through his thick black hair. "Did you ever make a pact when you were a kid?" When she nodded, he continued, "Well, it may sound childish, but let's do it, okay? No matter what happens, you and I will always be friends."

"It could not be otherwise, Sam. Your friendship really means a lot to me. I . . . don't know what I'd do without it."

He grasped her hand between his and raised it. Obviously not knowing what to do with it at first, he suddenly placed her hand against his chest near his heart.

"Then we make a solemn vow. Friends forever," he breathed.

Oddly, she did not feel foolish. It was childish, but he had a way about him that made it very natural and very vital.

"Friends forever," she echoed.

He did not let go of her hand quickly. There was such an intensity to his grasp, a heat that seemed to make her whole arm tingle. Her heart raced as she gazed up into his eyes. For a moment, which seemed to last as long as the eternity of their friendship, their gazes held. She knew he felt what she was feeling—whatever it was. She could not define it, and maybe she didn't want to. Friendship was a good enough definition.

He dropped her hand suddenly, then laughed a nervous laugh. "Boy, do I feel like a dope. I'm twenty-two years old!" he quipped.

"That's why I like you. You are not afraid of being a dope once in a while."

"Hey, I'm starved. I'll buy you lunch."

"It's three o'clock in the afternoon. We already had lunch."

"Then I'll buy you an early dinner."

"Okay, because I sure can't afford to buy you food the way you eat!"

BLAIR BRACED herself for arguments when she told Jackie of her plans to marry Gary. She was surprised at how relatively mild they were.

"Are you sure?" Jackie asked.

"I've never been more certain about anything." That was another lie, but only a small one. She was full of fear and doubts, but she'd had time to effectively swallow them.

"Have you told him about . . . anything?"

"What's to tell, really? I am the person he expects to get. I truly am, Jackie." That was quite convincing. She even believed it herself—mostly.

"What about the nightclub?"

"Yes, I'll tell him about that."

"Promise me you will, Blair? You can't start a marriage with that kind of deception."

"He'll be leaving for the Philippines in a few days."

"What? You are going to the Philippines?"

"No, I can't go right now because the families of military personnel have been evacuated. But while he's away, I can straighten out the mess with the Treasure Cove."

"When do you plan to marry?"

"Tomorrow."

Jackie's head snapped up almost comically. "What!"

"Well, it's either now or wait months."

"What about Mom and Dad and his parents? Blair, do you really know what you are doing?"

"His parents will be there, and I hope Mom and you will come. Dad,"—she blew out a dismissive puff of breath—"I don't care about him. Ed, that's Gary's dad, said he'd walk me down the aisle. He also said he'd talk to Dad, but I begged him not to. That would only make things worse." Blair shuddered inwardly at that near disaster when Ed had put an arm around her and said he'd talk to Keagan, "Man-to-man, you know." Only Blair's tears—very real tears!—had put an end to that well-meaning notion. She didn't want to think what secrets such a talk might reveal.

" 'Down the aisle . . .' " Jackie said. "The wedding will be in church?"

"Gary's church. But no guests except you and our parents. We want nothing fancy."

When the interview—or was it a third degree?—was over with Jackie, Blair had sagged with relief. It was surprisingly easier to tell the news to her mother. Cecilia was actually thrilled. She loved Gary. For once in her life Blair felt she had gained her mother's approval. And Cecilia had even hinted that her father would be pleased, also. This truly solidified Blair's resolve and covered most of her doubts. Would this indeed garner her father's approval? Amazing.

———

Blair was in the back of the church waiting for her cue to enter. She ran a trembling hand over the sleek fabric of her ecru satin dress with its bias cut skirt in the appropriate afternoon length. Within herself, she had refused to wear white. No one had commented on her choice of ecru, which complemented her skin tones better than white anyway. She prayed the subject of color would not come up. At any rate, the gown was quite simple; the draped peplum around her hips, forming a bow at the back, was its most elaborate feature.

She had insisted on keeping everything simple. No cake, no reception afterward, no chance for the families to have time together to talk. Luckily, Gary wanted it simple also. He would have only two days after the ceremony with his new wife before shipping out, and he wanted every minute selfishly spent with her alone.

Silently, Blair praised herself at how smoothly all was proceeding. In a few minutes Ed would come and walk her into the church, and within ten minutes it would be over. But it wasn't Ed who approached her in the church narthex.

"Dad!" she gasped.

"Do you think I'd miss my own daughter's wedding?" he asked tightly.

"Well, I . . . I'm glad you came." She decided it was best to keep her response to her father simple, as well—though her mind was whirling and she felt slightly dizzy. Her father had come to her wedding!

"Looks to me like you have decided to settle down."

"I . . . I think so, Daddy."

"That's all I wanted, you know."

It sounded so simple when he put it that way and when, of course, she was complying with his wishes.

"Thank you, Daddy."

"For what?"

"For being here to walk me down the aisle."

"And who else would do that, I'd like to know?" he replied with mock affront—at least she thought it was mock.

She smiled at him, and she couldn't remember the last time she had smiled at her father. Then the organ began the "Wedding March." Clutching her small bouquet of fragrant gardenias in one hand, she linked her other around her father's arm, and they entered the church.

After that, everything was rather a blur to Blair until the minister said, "By the power vested in me by the state of California and by our Father God, I pronounce you man and wife."

Gary kissed her delicately, almost shyly. Then the families gathered around them for hugs and congratulations. Still, the reality did not settle in.

Not even when Keagan said expansively, "I wish you newlyweds would let me take you out to dinner to celebrate. But I understand the lieutenant here is anxious to begin his wedded . . . ah . . . bliss."

"They only have two days before Gary leaves," offered Jackie.

"Don't let me stand in the way," Keagan said good-naturedly.

Blair really began to wonder if she was dreaming. Maybe her father had merely been properly coached by Cecilia and Jackie. Maybe he, being in the public eye, understood about guarding the family's "dirty laundry." At any rate, he never let on a thing.

"It couldn't have been a more perfect day," Blair said to her new husband as they walked on the beach.

They had rented a honeymoon cottage at a seaside inn in Malibu.

"I knew it would be." Gary's arm was laid firmly across her shoulders, holding her as if he never wanted to let go. "Everything about this union is perfect. But when your father showed up! That was the clincher, wasn't it?"

"Yes. I am still reeling from that surprise."

"We are very lucky, Blair."

"Except for your having to leave—"

"Shush." He held a finger over her lips. "We won't think of that now."

"I just want to think of being Mrs. Hobart. Blair Hobart. I like the sound of it."

"Perfect . . ."

The way he said that word, with such contentment, made the doubts inside Blair surface. "Gary . . . we will have a perfect life, I know it. But . . . what if . . . well, you and I both know people aren't perfect. We make mistakes. You know that, don't you?"

He chuckled. "I don't know about you, honey, but I'm perfect. I will never make any mistakes!"

"Oh, you!" She playfully poked him in the ribs. "I am being serious."

He stopped in his tracks and turned to face her fully. "Here's what I believe, Blair, with all the strength God has given me. Love suffers long and is kind; it doesn't envy and isn't easily provoked; thinks no evil . . ." He paused. "I can't remember all the verses, but it's First Co-rinthians, chapter thirteen. Anyway, here's the part I really wanted to say. Love bears all things, believes all things, endures all things. Love never fails. That's my own rendition of it. But that's what I feel for you, and it goes beyond the superficial. It goes into the heart, and it covers a multitude of sins."

"Oh, Gary . . ." She knew then that she could tell him everything, and it wouldn't matter. So why bother? It would not change a thing.

On the morning of their final day together, they were having break-fast on the deck of their cottage. A warm breeze, tangy and lazy, wafted over them. Both were studiously avoiding talk of what would come in a few hours, actually at midnight, when Gary would have to board the aircraft that would take him thousands of miles away.

"I wish our wedding pictures were ready so I could take one with me," Gary said, coming closer than they yet had come to the taboo subject of his departure.

Blair smiled coyly. "Maybe wishes do come true."

"I know they do—they have for me at least. But I wasn't going to stretch it by thinking a photographer might comply with me."

"I hope to have a special present for you."

"And what would that be?"

"It would spoil the surprise if I told you. But"—she glanced at her wristwatch—"in a bit, I am to call home and that will tell if the present is ready."

"The photographs?"

"Are you are going to be impossible at Christmas, too, trying to guess all the secrets? Do you peek into the packages under the tree?"

"If I can get away with it." He grinned mischievously. "Don't you?"

"I never peek. I don't want to know. I love surprises."

"That doesn't surprise me. You are ever the romantic." He rose from his chaise, came to her, and took her into his arms. "I love you so, Blair! I can hardly believe God has been so generous to me." He gently pressed his lips against hers, then when the kiss melted away, he continued to hold her.

He hadn't shaved yet that morning, and his beard, a dark shadow on his chiseled features, was a bit scratchy. Blair loved the feel of it, the nearness of him, the sweet fragrance of orange juice on his breath, the flutter of his eyelashes against her hair. These were details she sa-vored and would not forget. She sighed with contentment, but her breath also shuddered as she remembered why she must remember such things. The hours were ticking away. A panic began to grip her. Midnight was much too close.

"What are you thinking, my love?" he asked.

"I want to remember what you smell like."

"Not before my morning shower!" His humor was forced. He knew what she was thinking. They both could hear the clock ticking.

"Then I'll smell you afterward, too."

"I will look forward to it."

"But first I should go to the office and make that phone call."

"I wish we had paid extra and gotten a phone in the room. Then you wouldn't have to leave at all."

"Take your shower, and you won't even realize I am gone."

Blair made her phone call and was pleased to learn from the photographer that the wedding photos were ready. The only problem was that he had sent them to her parents' house, the only address he had. She had hoped to have them sent to Malibu and avoid spending precious time at her parents', but now that would not be possible. When she told Gary with a disappointed sigh, he suggested it was for the best.

"I want to say good-bye to my parents anyway, and it is only right I see yours, too, before I go. Let's go by your folks, say good-bye, get the pictures, then stop by my house. It will help my mother to have the photos to console her, you know."

"Yes, that's a good idea," Blair said, with not as much enthusiasm. She wanted him all to herself.

But they lingered in Malibu for a couple of hours, both reluctant to return to the "real world." They didn't get off until after noon. Blair had called ahead so they'd be expected at her parents'.

She was nervous when they greeted her parents. Would her father maintain his good behavior? Her mother had the cook prepare a light luncheon for them. Donna, the housekeeper, also had a message for Blair.

"A gentleman called for you, Miss Blair."

"Oh, it was probably the photographer."

"That must be it. He did not leave a name but was glad to hear you would be here today."

Seeming to take the cue, Cecilia brought out the photographs. For a few precious moments Blair forgot all else as she and Gary relived their beautiful wedding day. The pictures had turned out wonderfully. Keagan had hired the best photographer at the *Journal* to take them, had paid him well, and had given him a bonus for expediting their development. It was the best wedding gift, besides his presence, that her father could have given her.

Blair had asked her mother to specially frame one smaller photo of her and Gary, which she now gave to her husband.

"I made sure it was small enough so it would not take up too much space in your duffel bag," she said, and just those innocuous words made the emotion rise up in her.

After admiring the photo, he kissed her lightly, then tucked it among his things. Then Donna called them to luncheon.

They were seated in the dining room when the doorbell rang. The housekeeper answered it. A few moments later, instead of Donna, a man strode into the dining room. Blair dropped her fork.

"Well, I've found you at last!" the man exclaimed in a rough tone.

"What is the meaning of this?" Keagan demanded.

"I'm here to see your daughter—"

"Stan—" Blair gasped, only barely finding her voice.

"You know this man?" Keagan asked.

Blair glanced at Gary just then, and the same question was in his eyes.

"Oh, she *knows* me, all right—in every form of the word, eh, baby?"

"Stan, please, not here!" Blair fumbled to her feet, knocking over a water glass in the process. She hardly noticed.

Gary jumped up and put an arm protectively around Blair as he glared at the newcomer.

"I don't like the tone of your voice," he challenged.

"Ain't that too bad," sneered Stan Welton. "This little strumpet—"

"I'm warning you!" growled Gary.

Blair had never heard Gary speak so threateningly. He had always been so kind and gentle that she had almost forgotten he was a highly trained military man. He could indeed protect her from Stan. But would he want to now that the awful truth was surely about to be revealed?

"Yeah, well, she has a contract with me that she has broken for the last several days. I got customers expecting to see her—"

"What—?" Gary began.

But Blair cut in desperately. "Please, Stan, let's talk about this outside." She began edging away from Gary.

"Sorry to interrupt your little tea party," Stan mocked. "I don't need to say nothing more except you will fulfill our contract, or I'm gonna slap you with a big lawsuit, ya hear? Don't think just because ya got a rich daddy, you're gonna mess with me. I can eat tarts like you for di—"

But he didn't finish his sentence because Gary's fist slammed into his jaw. Stan stumbled back as blood spurted from his lip. Only the wall behind him kept him from hitting the carpet.

"I told you not to talk to my wife that way," Gary said. He looked as if he was ready to strike again. Blair had the feeling he could have hit Stan much harder and would if given further provocation.

"Wife?" Stan laughed. "When did that happen, doll? Before or after you and I made music together? And I don't mean at the nightclub. However, you will sing at the club tonight, or else!"

The protective fury hardening Gary's expression changed to utter bemusement. "Blair. . . ? What does he mean?"

"Gary, it's not how it looks," Blair said lamely. But would that be her final lie? Her house of cards was finally crashing upon her—upon them.

Stan burst out laughing. "Oh boy, it is just how it looks. Now who you gonna hit, buster? I think you've been cuckolded, soldier boy." He snorted derisively. "Well, my work here is done. You be at the Treasure Cove at nine, doll." Pausing, he shot a look at Keagan. "Unless Daddy here wants to pay." With that, he spun around and stalked away.

The silence that followed Stan's exit seemed to go on eternally; however, it wasn't a complete silence, for it was broken by Blair's sobs. Gary was still standing beside her, quiet and stiff. A million explanations careened through Blair's mind, but she could not find the will or the courage to say any of them. Instead, she turned and ran from the room.

She was out the back door before she realized she should have instead gone out the front, jumped into the car, and driven away—far away, never to return. She was about to run to the front of the house when the kitchen door opened.

"We'd better talk, Blair," Gary said, his tone full of control, a military control.

Again she thought how odd it was that she had so seldom thought of him as a soldier. "Do you really want to hear what I have to say?"

"Of course I do—" There was a slight catch in his reserve. "You are my wife."

She thought about what he'd said yesterday about love bearing all things, believing all things, hoping all things, enduring all things . . . never failing. She knew that could not mean *everything*, not the kind of things she had done. It was time, anyway, to test this love. She had no choice about it.

"I sing in a nightclub," she confessed as if that was the worst of her sins. "I didn't want to after I met you, but I had this contract."

"Why didn't you tell me?"

"I didn't think—I was afraid you'd not be interested in a girl like that."

"You don't think very highly of me, do you?" He quickly added, as if he didn't want her to answer that question, "And what about this Stan fellow? What about you and him?"

"That was before you. I was so ashamed. . . ." She paused as a sob caught in her throat. She choked it back and forced herself to continue. "I didn't think you'd want a woman who wasn't . . . pure."

Weeping, she could say no more. A silence loomed for a very long time before Gary spoke.

"You said these things happened before me." His tone had reclaimed its military reserve. "You mean before you found God, right?"

She couldn't answer his question, his challenge. It was clear he was beginning to see the whole ugly picture. Why say more?

"Blair, was everything a lie?" Still, she could not respond. "Tell me. Was it?" He demanded, harshly now, sounding almost like Stan. She wouldn't have been surprised if he struck her. But he didn't. His eyes flamed, but they were brimmed with moisture, as well. Yet his hands were stiff at his sides, his fingers balled into fists.

She felt as if one of those fists were jammed into her throat, for no speech could be coaxed from her. She just nodded.

He gasped in a breath, sharp as a knife. All fire and fury in him dissolved then. He suddenly looked wasted and worn with despair.

"Dear God, Blair," he mumbled before he went into the house.

A few moments later Blair heard the engine of his Ford start and the screech of tires against the cement drive. He was gone now.

Because Blair had no place else to go, she returned to the house. Maybe it was because she felt she needed more punishment. Her parents were still in the dining room. Cecilia's eyes were red, and she gripped a handkerchief in her hand. Keagan grasped a glass of whiskey in his.

"So you ruined things again, didn't you?" he said, in a tone so matter-of-fact it made Blair's insides quake almost as much as Gary's final look of despair had. Her father had expected her to fail.

Still that fist gripped her throat, and she could not speak. She did manage to call a taxi on the phone in the foyer. She waited for it outside. Cecilia came out to try to console her, but she brushed her away.

"Don't waste your time, Mother. I'm not worth it."

And that's what she truly believed, no matter what her mother said.

GARY HAD ALWAYS had life pretty easy. He'd grown up in a close, loving family who had taught him a strong faith in God, a faith that had carried him over the few rocky places he'd known. He had breezed through school, and though he had needed to be persistent to get his West Point appointment because of his serious lack of social connections, it had worked out quite well in the end. The academy had been all he had hoped and dreamed, and he had graduated high in his class. And now, his first foreign assignment was rather a plum. The Philippines was, after all, the Pearl of the Orient.

To top off all this good fortune, he had met a woman who was beautiful, godly, and a delight to be with. A woman who shared his faith, his dreams, and, he was certain, his love. A week ago he had seen no reason why they should not marry, have a passel of children, and live happily ever after.

What had happened less than an hour ago had hit him completely from out of left field. Well, that wasn't entirely true. He'd always known she was hiding something. He'd assumed it had something to do with her relationship with her parents, her father in particular. She had told him they didn't get along, and he sensed she was ashamed of that. He supposed that as a Christian she felt she had failed somehow with them. She wouldn't talk much about it. And he hadn't pressed because he could see how it hurt her, and the last thing he wanted was to hurt her in any way.

The fact that Keagan Hayes—Gary's father-in-law now!—had showed up at the wedding had somehow lulled Gary into believing everything was all right.

He had never suspected Blair's secrets could have gone so deep or been so twisted. She had tricked him into believing she was basically a decent girl with a bit of a wild past, but who had found God and put it all behind her. It truly would not have bothered him had she told him about the nightclub. He understood contracts and word of honor. Maybe, just maybe, even this Stan fellow in her past wouldn't have bothered him had she told him. Sure, he'd always imagined marrying a pure Christian girl. But that wasn't a requirement as long as her heart was pure toward God. Christ had known prostitutes and forgiven them. Gary was no better than his Lord.

Where it all fell apart, however, was in Blair's lies. Not trusting him with the truth. But, of course, it went deeper than that. She had used him, made a royal fool of him. That's what really sent him into a spin.

Yet they were married now, even if Blair was not the woman he thought he'd married. He had made a commitment, and they had sealed that commitment by becoming one flesh. He had believed with all his heart she was the woman God wanted for him.

"You gullible fool!" he muttered as he gripped the steering wheel of his dad's Ford.

But thoughts of their wedding vows kept coming back to him. He had made a commitment. They had their own contract. He was a man of his word, a man of honor.

He wasn't surprised when he found he had driven to the Long Beach pier. As he had meandered around the county, from Beverly Hills to Long Beach, he'd found a telephone book and looked up the Treasure Cove. But before going there, he had stopped by his folks' place. He had to leave the Ford and take a taxi from there. He'd also said his good-byes and told them what had happened. They had prayed with him and assured him they knew he would do what was right.

Now it was ten o'clock at night. He had to leave in two hours. He shouldn't have put it off so long, but he still wasn't certain what exactly was *right*. Maybe he had waited till now because he wanted to see Blair in her own element. He hoped that would help him to know the true extent of her lies. Of course he was desperate to believe that at least some of the Blair he had come to know and love was real.

"Somewhere over the rainbow . . ."

Blair's fingers ran lightly over the keys of the piano, her eyes closed so she could perhaps imagine she was in some enchanted land called Oz. She didn't want to be reminded of where she truly was—the haze of smoke in the air, the pungent smell of cheap liquor mingled with the body odor of men fresh from their jobs on the docks.

" *. . . bluebirds fly. Birds fly over the rainbow, why then, oh, why can't I?"*

"Hey, baby, give us a dance." A voice in the audience jarred her back to grim reality.

"Yeah, sweetheart, somethin' lively!"

She finished the tune and did not move, keeping her eyes shut. Claude sidled up to the piano.

"C'mon, Blair. I get the feeling you are hiding behind that piano." His voice, though too soft for anyone else to hear, forced her to open her eyes. He did not appear overjoyed at his words, nor had he seemed proud of sending Stan after her today. But he added, "I'm not paying you to just sit and sing sad songs, honey."

Saying nothing, she rose and spoke to the band. They struck up a Latin beat, and taking the microphone in hand, she launched into "South of the Border." In her red satin gown, trimmed in silver sequins, she looked far more the gay señorita than the dour torch singer. Who cared what she was like *inside*?

Incorporating the rhumba into her movements, she worked her way around the tables. She was an actress—a good one, she was learning. Few would dispute that the smile on her face and the alluring twinkle in her eyes was not real. The men whooped and regaled her with wolf whistles. Soon she became immersed in the role. She fingered a customer's shirt collar and bent low as if she would kiss him, pulling away at the last moment with a coy wink. She flicked another man's necktie in his face and ran her hand along another's shoulder. The audience loved it and cheered for more.

She moved to the back of the room, losing herself completely in the snappy beat of the song. It wasn't hard to do because she had been doing it all her life.

She reached out to tease another man, caught a glimpse of khaki, turned fully, and saw Gary!

She missed a whole beat of the tune as she stared, or rather gaped, at him. She wanted to turn and run, but the performer within her was stronger than she ever believed possible. Never let 'em see you cry, she silently reminded herself as she whirled away as if the pause had been part of the act.

The show must go on.

She finished navigating the room and reached the stage as the band played the finale. She had rehearsed some showy moves to finish the song. A swing of her hips, a shimmy of her shoulders, and a couple of high leg kicks. She did them all and with flourish, not just because that's how she had rehearsed them, but something inside her wanted Gary to finally see the real her.

She hurried off stage the moment the last note sounded and fairly fled to her dressing room.

Though she had hoped her display would have scared Gary to run far away, she half expected the knock on her door a few minutes later. Still, she hesitated before finally forcing herself to say, "Come in." She was sitting at her dressing table pretending to touch up her makeup. She didn't turn but saw Gary's reflection in the mirror.

"That was quite a show," he said.

"I guess so," she replied, dabbing a powder puff against her skin. "I didn't think you went in for places like this, Gary."

She saw him step closer. Still, she did not turn.

"Turn around and look at me," he said.

"You ask an awful lot," she replied tartly.

He came up beside her, bent over, and forced his face between her and the mirror. "Look at me, all right? And let's talk." He dropped to one knee and seemed to plant himself firmly as close to her as possible.

"Do you think we really have anything to talk about?"

"How can you say that?"

The utter devastation in his tone cracked the hard shell she tried to portray. Tears sprang to her eyes. "I've lied to you, Gary, about everything," she confessed. "I don't think anything I ever told you was true." Her voice trembled over the words. Tears continued to sting her eyes, but she didn't want to cry. She hated for him to feel sorry for her.

"Nothing. . . ?" he said plaintively.

"Surely my lies mocked any small truth there might have been in anything I said or did."

"At least you are being honest now," he said glibly.

But she knew the words came from desperation, just as her lies had, and now even her honesty. "It isn't worth much when I've been forced into telling the truth," she said.

"No, I suppose not." He let out a frustrated breath. "What now? We are married."

"You can get an annulment. It may be enough grounds just that I deceived you into thinking I was pure."

"I made a commitment to you."

"To a lie."

"I don't believe leaving you would be the honorable thing to do."

She gaped at him, torn between laughing at such pie-eyed decency and crying that he felt she still deserved to be treated so decently. But what truly shocked her was the sudden rise of hope within her at the realization that she could still have him.

Only then did she know what she must do. She had hurt him enough.

"Gary, it is time I tell you everything. You'd better sit more comfortably." She spoke in hard tones as she jerked her head toward the small sofa. Then she licked her lips and prepared herself for her greatest role yet. "I'm gonna give it to you straight, so there will never be any question. I'm not a Christian, not a real Christian, not like Jackie, or the people at church. I never even went to church before that day I saw you at the picnic. Well, I had just started going . . . I'd gone a couple of times—" She realized she was trying to justify herself and added harshly, "And I was bored silly. Do you know why I started going? I came home drunk one night—so blinding drunk I could not remember anything that I'd done. It wasn't the first time such a thing had happened, either, but it was the worst time. Guess it put the 'fear of God' into me. Just the *fear*, mind you. Not real faith."

"But why. . . ? I . . . I don't understand why. . ."

The look on his face now was more what she expected—disappointment, utter bewilderment. "To snag you, of course." Then, because she knew she didn't deserve his sympathy and feared he might end up giving it to her, she added, "Guess I was bored with the men of the fast Hollywood crowd. Slumming a bit, I suppose. Stan was the ultimate act of slumming. What a scoundrel, but more my type, don't you think?"

"Don't do this, Blair."

"You are a nice guy, Gary. I shouldn't have played you the way I did . . ." But her voice betrayed her. A tear escaped her eye. She swiped it away. "I feel bad. That's all," she added to explain the betraying emotion.

He stared at her, his eyes wasted with hurt. Her insides twisted, but she was not going to play upon his pain. She had a feeling she could, that she need only tell him that despite all she had done to him, she did love him. That at least was true. But she did not deserve a reprieve. She deserved no good thing.

"Did you ever really love me?" It was the one question she hoped, yes, even prayed, he would not ask.

But what was another lie? "No, Gary, I never did. You were a lark, that's all." She allowed no more tears to escape her eyes. Instead, she fixed a hard gaze upon him. "I know now it was a raw deal. You didn't deserve it. Sorry."

He let out a dry, brittle laugh. "You are a very good actress. But I'm not sure what is the act. I don't know what to think."

Trying to maintain her harsh demeanor, she wrenched her wedding ring from her finger. "You may as well take this. I certainly have no use for it."

When Gary made no move toward the ring, Blair thrust it at him. Only then did he take it. Their fingers brushed, and she saw the tremor in his hand. She tried, unsuccessfully, to block out the moment two days ago when he had slipped the ring on her finger. He just stood there staring at the circle of gold in his hand, as if he had no idea what to do with it.

"My advice is to not think anything," she said coldly. "Just get out while you can."

Nodding, he sighed. "Yeah, I should. But I loved you, Blair. Maybe it was a lie I loved. I don't know . . . I just don't know. I can't think straight right now." He lurched to his feet. "I gotta leave in less than two hours."

"That's for the best, don't you think?"

"Maybe so. Maybe it'll give me time—give us both time to think about it—"

"Forget about me, Gary," she cut in sharply.

"Do you think I could ever forget about my own wife?"

The word "wife" excised her heart with pain such as she never thought a person could feel except on a physical level.

"We got married, and I cannot throw such a commitment into the garbage so easily."

"Maybe it would be easier if you kept in mind you married garbage."

He shook his head, not so much in disagreement, she thought, but more in frustration and despair.

"Gary, don't you know when you've been licked? It's finished. Over!"

He opened his mouth to reply, but nothing came out. His dark, passionate eyes were slick with moisture. For a brief moment, he struggled with his emotion, then seemed to steel himself against it.

Dropping the ring in his pocket as if he had made a decision, he started to leave. But before he did so, he focused on her that look, the one that used to make her feel so special. It was as if he was desperate to connect with the woman he loved just one more time. If even a shred of her lurked within Blair's body, his look seemed to say he wanted to embrace it, at least visually, one last time. But Blair arched a brow and merely smirked at him in response.

Then he exited the dressing room.

A moment later Blair laid her head on the table and wept.

Moscow
Late September 1941

AFTER CAMERON was released from the hospital, her life in Russia fell into a rather dull routine. Even the almost nightly air raids became tiresome events that raised more grumbling than fear.

The foreigners passed the long days with visits to the theater and the ballet, for the Bolshoi continued to perform. But such pursuits had never been of much interest to Cameron. The men also managed to find diversion in playing poker and drinking copious amounts of vodka. Cameron tended to absent herself from these gatherings, as well, because there were still some of the men who felt uncomfortable with the presence of a woman at these activities, and rather than force the issue and make them and herself even more miserable, she often avoided the social life.

As summer faded away and the air took on a crisp bite that could only be the harbinger of a Russian winter, Cameron wondered how her dream could have faded so quickly. Sometimes she thought wistfully of chasing even society stories in Los Angeles. At least they were her stories and not a regurgitation of *Pravda*. To appease this lack, she spent much time writing a journal, things that would never pass the censor's pen but that perhaps one day when she returned home could be organized into a book of her experiences. Of course all the correspondents talked about writing books of their "Russian exile," as some called it. She thought of the glut of memoirs there would be after the war, and tapping on her typewriter keys, she shook her head.

"What a life!" she murmured.

"Miss Hayes, did you say something?" Sophia asked from her perch on the couch.

Cameron hadn't realized she had spoken aloud. She had also nearly forgotten Sophia's presence, which had become a regular daily fixture in the hotel room. The girl was reading *Red Star*. She had taken to reading the newspapers to herself rather than translating to Cameron, since she had by now gotten a pretty good idea of the kinds of things Cameron was looking for. Any items she thought of interest, she would then read to Cameron. The girl could probably write the dispatches, as well, and eliminate the need for Cameron's presence altogether.

"No, I'm just bored. Find anything yet?"

"There is an article about Leningrad, but you have already written about the completion of the German blockade of Leningrad. There is a story about a factory that makes machine guns and has far surpassed its quota this month. It received a special commendation from Comrade Stalin. It lists some production figures that are interesting."

"Palgunov and his boys don't like too much detail, especially facts and figures. What if the Germans find out how many machine guns Stalin has? Could mean the end of the world as we know it." Cameron flung back the typewriter carriage with special force. The machine nearly bounced off the table. She caught it in time, but what did it matter, for as much use as it was to her?

She glanced at the paper in the typewriter. Another article that would never see print. But she had needed a way to vent her soul-wrenching experience in the hospital. Who knew, though—maybe she could find a way to get it to Arnett.

THE TWO FACES OF WAR

This reporter has spoken to generals and strategists to whom war has been reduced to mere percentages. One general told me that in a certain battle, he expected a thirty-percent reduction of his troops. Weighing that against the importance of a particular military objective, it seemed to him a fair exchange. Perhaps it was. A hill, a town, a bridge . . . these are vital steps toward victory.

But recently I saw another side of the matter that will forever change my perspective. I spent some time in a Russian hospital, a place where one cannot avoid the human element in the global conflict. There is no glory to be found within the walls of a hospital. There is pain and loss and death. But more than that, there are men, human beings. When one looks into the human face of war,

*it is easy to forget strategic objectives. A hill, a town, a bridge—
these lose essential importance in the wake of this human face, a
face, I might add, that has hardly seen the shadow of a beard. Yes,
they are mere boys. In their nightmares, I imagine they still cry out
for their mothers. As Russian boys, I am certain their lives were
never as simplistic as their counterparts in the States, but I do not
think their hopes and dreams differ too greatly from young Joe
Smith in Madison, Wisconsin. They all have girls back home and
family they want only to return to. They tell ribald jokes and listen
to music I am certain their parents find far too loud. Less than a
year ago they worried only about their marks in school or whether
there would be enough rain for the wheat to grow.*

*There is no doubt that lying in a hospital never figured into
those dreams, much less the loss of an arm or a leg. I met a boy
who spoke of his family and the farm he had worked before the
war. He wanted only to get back to that life, but his wounds were
extensive, and it is doubtful he will make it out of the hospital.
Another young man wanted me to sign his cast—he would be
thrilled to show off a foreign signature. Another said he was proud
to have lost an arm for his country.*

*These men were cheerful and talkative. They wanted no pity,
and I was forced to carefully hide any I felt. I repeat, there is no
glory to be found in a hospital military ward, but heroism
abounds.*

Cameron thought about the wounded Germans. But she couldn't
mention them, for even American readers would have a hard time accepting anything written sympathetically about them. And, like Alex,
she was conflicted. As individuals, those boys had touched her heart,
but as a part of the evil that was Nazism, they were abhorrent. She
wondered if she could word it in just that way. Then she shrugged with
frustration. No one would read any of it anyway. Except for Shanahan. She had showed her first draft to him the other day, and he had
been impressed.

"I see you are finally learning from the master!" he had quipped,
not even pretending modesty.

But there were only a few such moments to lift her from a growing
sense of futility. Shanahan was responsible for some, but the rest were
compliments of Alex. He was a true light in the fog of Russian bureaucracy. Too bad he was so busy with his work. His visits were far
too seldom.

As Cameron let out another lilting sigh, the telephone rang. Sophia answered it, as was her habit.

"That was the American embassy," she said when she had hung up the receiver. "They invite you to a cocktail reception tonight at seven."

"Did they say who it was for?" Perhaps some dignitary had come to relieve the daily grind. There were always rumors afloat that Churchill had come to Moscow. None ever materialized.

"I am sorry. I did not ask," said Sophia.

"That's okay. But goodness, I hope it's someone interesting. I can use the diversion before I go bonkers."

"Bonkers, Miss Hayes?"

"You know, nuts, crazy, *insane!*" Cameron said the final word with a dramatic flourish, then flicked her lips several times with her finger, a wild look in her eyes. She laughed in response to Sophia's astonished look. "Sorry." She took a breath. "Why don't you read me the articles about Leningrad? I suppose I can use that again."

That evening at Spaso House, Ambassador Steinhardt's residence, Cameron tried not to be disappointed that the cocktail party appeared to be just a routine gathering. Again she found herself in the minority, because all eight embassy wives had evacuated at the beginning of the war.

Ambassador Lawrence Steinhardt was an urbane, intelligent man, but most of the correspondents had not warmed to him. They did not believe him to be forthcoming to them regarding his dealings with the Soviets. But his greatest affront was his habit at parties of reserving the best imported wines and spirits for ranking guests while serving the substandard Russian spirits to the lesser guests, which usually included lowly correspondents.

He also was not entirely happy with his post. He would not admit it, but anonymous embassy sources had informed several correspondents that he was anxious to get away on vacation, a permanent one if possible.

Naturally it was Shanahan who had the nerve to broach the touchy subject. Balancing a martini in one hand and waving a cigarette in the other, he ambled up to Steinhardt, who was talking to one of his attachés.

"I was surprised when I received your invitation to find that you

him a luminous smile. She was so bored she had actually sunk to flirting with this stuffy Brit.

Out of the corner of her eye, she saw Shanahan roll his. She didn't care. Tramble was a pleasant distraction.

"I say, it just occurred to me," Tramble went on, "I have two tickets for the ballet tomorrow. Would you care to accompany me, Cameron?"

"I'd love to, Bill."

"Now, you don't want to tax yourself, Cameron," Shanahan said.

Cameron gaped at the wholly unexpected words. "What?"

"I think you have been overdoing it since you were in the hospital."

"That was weeks ago, Johnny." She glared at him, realizing he was not in the least concerned with her health. He couldn't be jealous, so he must simply be enjoying the sport of ruining her fun.

"You were in the hospital?" Tramble asked. "I did not know. Whatever for?"

"Oh, it was nothing. I got a bit too close to an explosion, and I came out with a mild concussion. I am perfectly all right now."

Tramble sucked in a lungful of smoke, then blew it out in the most graceful manner Cameron had ever seen the act performed.

"I daresay, I have heard Russian medical facilities are nightmarish."

"I was quite impressed with my care," Cameron responded with enthusiasm.

"It helped that you were pretty chummy with your doctor," put in Shanahan.

"A Russian doctor?" Tramble said as Cameron unobtrusively poked an elbow in Shanahan's side. What was his game now?

"Yes, quite a competent one, too."

Just then Levinson joined them. "Are you talking about your doctor, Cameron? I didn't want to say anything about that business in Chicago while you were laid up, but I have since wondered if I should have, so you could have gotten someone else."

"What're you talking about, Lev?" Shanahan asked.

With a quick movement Cameron tossed back her nearly full glass of wine. "Oh, look," she said quickly, "I'm empty again. Lev, would you be a dear and fetch me another?"

"You've had enough," Shanahan said, snatching the glass from her hand. He was probably right, because Cameron was suddenly feeling a bit giddy. Realizing her diversion wasn't going to work, she could only listen dully as Shanahan pressed on. "What about the doc, Lev?"

"The incident didn't make national news, but I was working on the *Tribune* and followed the story, which made a bit of a splash in Chicago. Seems he killed a patient, a society dame he was operating on while under the influence of drugs. Lost his license to practice in the States."

Cameron moved her lips to attempt a defense of Alex, but her tongue felt thick and unwieldy.

"Was that before or after he became a Communist?" Shanahan asked.

"He'd had ties to the Party all his life. His parents were Reds," Levinson replied.

"What's this?" asked Tramble, obviously fascinated. "This was Cameron's doctor? Dear me, I am so glad you survived the ordeal. Had I been privy to this whole matter, I would have seen to it that you received better care—"

Finally Cameron found her voice, sluggish and numb as it was. "Wait a minute! I re—re—I got the best. Alex is a . . . a great doctor. You don't know what—oh, my goodness!" She stopped abruptly as the lump forming in her throat suddenly seemed more than a mere lump. She remembered she hadn't eaten anything but a couple of canapés since lunch. Her stomach churned, and she was certain she was going to be sick.

"Cameron, are you okay?" That was Shanahan, though his voice was slow and distorted.

Tramble reached a hand toward her. She shrugged him away.

"Never-you-mind-I'm-okay," she insisted, then turned on her heel and shambled away from the circle of men.

She should have found a bathroom, but the balcony was closer and the idea of fresh air was inviting. She had never vomited in her life, and she wasn't going to start in the middle of the U.S. ambassador's residence.

The air outside was crisp and refreshing. Actually it was sharp and quite cold, but she didn't mind. She sucked it in like Tramble had his cigarette, with nearly as much relish. What was wrong with her? She did not have a weak stomach. How much wine *had* she taken? She tried to count from the moment of her arrival an hour ago and quickly realized it was more than was good for anyone.

She heard the scrape of shoes against the stone floor of the balcony.

Please, don't let it be Tramble! But she was no more pleased when Shanahan came up beside her.

"You gonna live?" he asked.

"Of course!"

He glanced over the edge of the balcony. It was only two floors up, and he had a clear view of the garden below even in the darkness. "You feed those plants down there?"

"I did not! And I'd prefer to be alone." The fresh air had cleared her head a bit, and her anger was definitely taking the edge off her numbness.

"What're you mad at me for? It was Levinson who spilled the beans about the doc. That's what's got you upset, isn't it?" There was actually the merest hint of sympathy in his tone.

"It is not. I had too much wine, that's all. But I am furious about the discussion about Alex. You all sounded like a bunch of gossiping hens."

"You think it's true about Rostov?"

"Doesn't matter. It isn't right to be spreading malicious stories about someone." She gripped her hands around the balcony rail and stared into the night sky. Clouds let only a few stars twinkle through.

"Cameron . . ."

His voice was so soft and unlike him that she swung her head around to look at him. That was an unwise move because it made her head spin again.

"You care for this guy, don't you?" he added.

"Of course not," she insisted. "I just don't like seeing anyone maligned so—"

"You do. I saw it in the hospital."

"No, I don't." Her voice was soft now, her denial hardly believable.

"You're asking for trouble with him, Cameron."

"He's a good man."

"I ain't saying he isn't. But he is loaded with red lights, as they say. A Russian citizen, a Communist, and to boot, an ex—I hope ex—drug addict, if what Levinson says is true. You really want to get mixed up with all those complications?"

"I am not getting mixed up with anything." She turned her gaze back to the cloudy sky because she was afraid he'd see she was lying. "Alex is a friend, like you, Shanahan. That's all."

"Okay, if you say so."

She was certain he meant it. Shanahan could understand that kind of relationship. It was all he'd ever known himself, never having experienced anything deeper with a woman.

"You want to go back to the party?"

"I think I'll walk home."

"Want company?"

"No, you'd better stay and see why Steinhardt called this little party. I'll want a full report in the morning." She started to turn from the balcony, then paused. "Johnny, would you see that Tramble and Levinson, especially Lev, don't spread that story about Alex any further? True or not, he is trying to make a new life for himself here and doesn't need that right now."

"I'll take care of it, Cameron."

Cameron walked the several blocks back to the Metropole. She had worn her evening gown with its thin silk fabric and unsubstantial jacket. The cold autumn air penetrated it easily, and she was chilled through by the time she reached her hotel. Her stomach felt better, but she longed to get into a hot bath and prayed a bit of hot water could be coaxed from the tub faucet.

But the idea of a bath was quickly forgotten when she entered her hotel room and found Sophia sitting on her couch. Sophia was seldom there after dark. Something must be wrong.

41

"WHAT IS IT, Sophia?"

"I am sorry to come into your room like this without calling first. But it is not good to use the telephone anyway. I prayed you would not be too late from your party."

"It looks like your prayers have been answered. I left early. What's going on?"

Cameron tossed her evening bag on the table and kicked off her shoes, slim high heels that pinched her feet. She sat on the couch beside Sophia and tucked her sore feet up under her.

"It is my husband—"

"Oh, Sophia, he's not—?"

"No, Miss Hayes, he is alive, thank God, but—" Sophia stared down at her hands folded tightly together in her lap, her expression creased with distress. "He is here in Moscow." That statement certainly contradicted her grim look. Cameron was both concerned and curious. Sophia went on, "He was captured by the Germans weeks ago—I did not learn of this until just now. But he escaped, and . . . and he . . . is here."

"I don't understand what the problem is," Cameron said.

"I would wish for you to hear his story from his own lips." Sophia smiled wistfully, and obviously she was about to ask a lot of her employer and friend. "Would you come with me and meet him and hear him?"

"Of course I want to meet him, but is this something you want me to do as a friend or as a reporter? Not that it would matter much. I'm just curious."

"I do not know which. You will have to decide."

Cameron laid her hand over Sophia's. "Well, I will come at least as a friend. But won't it be dangerous?"

"I know I ask much of you—"

"You take me wrong, Sophia! I don't care for myself. But you and your family could get into much more trouble than I by having a foreigner come into your home."

A little sigh, perhaps of relief, escaped Sophia's lips. "We have decided it is worth it if you do not mind. We will do what we did in the old days to elude the police in order to get to our church meetings."

"You mean play cloak-and-dagger?"

Sophia smiled. She apparently was familiar with that idiom. "Yes, only no daggers, I hope!"

"Did anyone see you come here tonight?"

"No one saw me come into the hotel. When I came to your floor, I waited until the key lady was occupied, and then I took the key to your room from her drawer." Her brow arched with cunning. She was rather pleased with herself. "If you distract her again, I can replace the key and leave unnoticed."

"We'd better be on our way, then, before we are caught in an air raid." Cameron glanced at her watch. It was nine-fifteen. "But do you mind if I change first? A black silk evening gown is likely to draw some attention. Besides, I am freezing."

Ten minutes later Cameron was garbed in her wool A-line skirt, heavy cream sweater, and warm winter coat. While Sophia hid in the closet, Cameron got the key lady to come into the bathroom to see a problem—it was not hard to conjure a problem, since there was always something going wrong with the bathroom.

Cameron occupied the woman for five minutes, giving Sophia ample time to return the key and exit the floor. Cameron then dismissed the key lady and left the room herself, telling the woman she would be upstairs in Shanahan's room if anyone wanted her. She couldn't worry that Shanahan wasn't home. It didn't really matter if anyone realized she had slipped the "coop," just as long as they didn't find out where she had gone. She took the elevator up to Shanahan's floor, then following Sophia's directions, took the backstairs down to the ground floor and to the corridors that led to the lower-class rooms and to the service areas of the hotel, then finally to a back door. She met Sophia in the alley outside the door. They had to go the rest of the way together because of the difficulty Sophia would have had in giving directions to her home across town. And at that, they took a circuitous route so that by the time they reached Sophia's building, they were as sure as they possibly could be that no one had followed. But to be certain, Sophia took Cameron into the building also by a back way.

Cameron had lost track of the exact location of the building, and the darkness had not permitted her to make much of an assessment of the kind of neighborhood in which Sophia lived. One would assume that being the daughter of the Chief of Staff of a large metropolitan hospital, she would live in an elite district—Cameron did recall Sophia mentioning that she lived with her parents. But once inside the building Cameron saw a décor that in the States would be considered lower middle class. The walls were in need of paint, the floors were scuffed, and the elevator was not working. Because of the blackout, the windowless corridors were lit only by one low-wattage bulb—a bare bulb without any fancy shade.

They climbed three flights of stairs to Sophia's flat. Cameron tried not to gasp for air as they reached the floor, because poor Sophia was apologetic enough about the need to walk. Sophia let them into the flat, which was also dimly lit, though Cameron noted heavy blackout shades were over all the windows. She had only a moment to appraise the flat itself—a homey affair but hardly first-class—before she was immediately accosted by greeters.

"You're safe!"

"We were starting to get worried!"

"Come in . . . come in!"

"Welcome!"

Everyone spoke English, which was welcome enough. But the faces, too, were friendly, and the hands that took her coat and nudged her into a parlor were warm. Cameron recognized only one face, that of Dr. Fedorcenko. There were three other women and a young man besides.

"Sophia, why don't you make introductions?" said Fedorcenko. Obviously the patriarch of the family, he was purposely deferring to his daughter.

"Yes, Papa."

Cameron marveled at the girl's tone, not only at the respect in it but at the deep fondness, as well. She thought of her relationship with her own father but quickly pushed the unpleasant memories from her mind.

Sophia turned first to the oldest member of the group. "Miss Hayes, this is my grandmother, my father's mother, Anna Yevnovona."

Cameron towered over the elderly woman who held out her hand. Anna Yevnovona had clearly always been of a petite stature, but a slightly bent back made her even shorter than she must have been in her youth. She was thin and as frail appearing as her granddaughter, with white hair pinned into a bun on top of her head, giving her a bit more height. Cameron guessed the woman's age to be at least eighty, with each year accounted for by the wrinkles lining her face. The hand she proffered was knobby and arthritic, but her grip was surprisingly firm. When she smiled and lifted bright blue eyes, Cameron was only then reminded that Sophia had said something about there being aristocracy in the family. Surely this woman had once graced the corridors of palaces.

"I am happy to meet you," Anna Yevnovona said in accented but incredibly refined English. "Sophia talks all the time about her work with you. She is so happy to have such a good job."

"She is a true gem," Cameron replied. "I would be lost without her, Mrs. . . . uh . . . Fedorcenko?"

"Actually, by American reckoning, I would be Mrs. Grigorov, for my second husband. I am a widow twice now, but I would be pleased if you'd just call me Anna or Anna Yevnovona. It is simpler that way." Her eyes, clear and bright for an elderly woman, glittered as she released Cameron's hand.

Cameron recalled Sophia saying that her grandfather, her father's father, had died in 1905. Anna could not have been older than fifty then, so it was no surprise she had remarried. At any rate, Cameron stifled her curiosity and said, "I would be happy to if you would also just call me Cameron. I can't seem to get Sophia to do so, but I keep trying."

"We Russians tend to be very formal in such situations, but I know you Americans are just the opposite." She paused and smiled at her granddaughter. "Go on, Sophia dear, I know the others are anxious to be introduced."

Next Sophia introduced a woman who was obviously her mother. Her name was Katya, and she was an older version of her daughter, with pale amber hair now gently streaked with gray and a delicately lined face. She was quite beautiful and held her shapely figure straight, emanating nobility, as well.

The third woman was Sophia's sister Valentina, who, Cameron learned later, was two years older than Sophia. She resembled more her father with dark brown hair and eyes. Her English was not as refined as that of the others, and she said little.

Finally, Sophia presented her husband. If she had been presenting according to age, it was obvious Oleg was the youngest, besides his wife. But Cameron had a feeling from the adoring expression on Sophia's face that she had not only saved the youngest for last but also the one whom she obviously considered the best.

Oleg took Cameron's hand and bowed formally. "It was very good of you to come, Miss Gayes." His English was easily the worst of the group, heavily accented, but there was an intensity to his tone that somehow transcended his difficulty with the language.

Oleg Gorbenko was as dark and substantial, in appearance at least, as his wife was pale and ethereal. His hair was black, thick, and curly, and his chin was dark with a day or two's growth of beard.

There were thick black brows over green eyes. Cameron immediately was reminded of a black cat, sleek, lithe, and just a bit mysterious. Physically, he was only an inch or two taller than Cameron, and he was thin, though Cameron attributed that to his time spent as a prisoner of war.

"Oleg," Cameron said with a smile she hoped would ease some of the tension she felt from the young man, "you could not have kept me away."

"Why don't we be seated?" said Katya, taking her place as hostess. "I will fix some tea."

"Mama," Oleg interjected, his voice intense but uncertain, "tea will not sit well with what I must say."

"We know that, Oleg," Dr. Fedorcenko answered. "But we have a guest, and it is proper to offer refreshment. Besides, a little tea sometimes soothes harsh words, eh?"

"Perhaps they should not be soothed. Even when spoken harshly, they have been dismissed—"

"Not by any of us, son," Anna said. "Come now." She placed an arm around his shoulder and nudged him gently but firmly toward a chair. "Katya and Tina have heard your story. They will fix tea while you get started. I know you are anxious."

Oleg nodded with respectful deference toward the old woman. He sat in the chair even as Dr. Fedorcenko directed Cameron to a comfortable upholstered chair adjacent to Oleg's. Sophia drew up a chair close to her husband. They continued to grip each other's hands. The rest of the party found seats, as well.

"So, Oleg, what is it you have to say?" Cameron asked.

He needed no more encouragement than that. With occasional help with his English from Sophia, he launched into an incredible tale.

"A few weeks ago my plane was shot down near Kiev. I am from a village in the Ukraine, and I still have some family there." He paused and glanced at Sophia. "Did you tell her I am Jewish?"

"I am not sure if I did or not. It did not seem important."

"It is very important," he said emphatically. "It may mean the difference between her believing me or not, but I will not lie about my heritage. Others have thought that because I am Jewish, I have exaggerated—" He had trouble with this word and it took a couple of minutes, with assistance from everyone, to find the right word. "Well, I have not! What I am saying is the truth. It would be a sick man indeed who would fabricate these things.

"I am not a practicing Jew any longer. I am a Christian now. Still, I tell the truth!" His gaze fell upon Cameron, and her breath caught at the passion in his eyes. She knew now why Sophia wanted her to hear these things directly from Oleg. The passion exuded from him in a nearly tangible manner. If he hadn't been surrounded by this eminently refined group, she, who practically knew no fear, might have been a little afraid of him. He brought to mind the voice crying in the wilderness that she'd heard about as a child in Sunday school. He needed only an animal-skin tunic and a handful of locusts and honey. Without seeing them together, Cameron might have wondered at the pairing of sweet Sophia and her fiery Oleg. But seeing them side by side, Cameron concluded they were a perfect match. She was day and he was night, perhaps a very stormy night.

Cameron took a breath and said with her own emphasis, "I am prepared to believe you, Oleg. I see no reason why I shouldn't."

"Three of my comrades and I escaped from the Germans," Oleg continued, apparently assuaged. "They were eventually shot or recaptured. I don't know how I was spared, or indeed, if I was spared at all. I headed toward Dniepropetrovsk, the town where I had family. I was afraid to return directly to my unit. You probably do not know this, but Russians taken prisoner by the Germans are often considered traitors by their own people. I could have been shot just for having been a prisoner. My family could have been arrested. I am just a lowly private, a mere gunner on my aircraft, and of little importance. No doubt because of that, thank God, my family was not harassed. I hoped my Ukrainian relations would tell me what to do."

"Are you AWOL?" Cameron asked. Then amplified, "That is, away from your unit without leave?"

"For all they know I am still a prisoner of war. But I cannot remain as I am forever. I will soon have to report to my unit and take whatever they would do to me. This gap of time since my escape and my return to my unit will not be good, and I fear things will not go well for me." Sophia groaned, and he paused, drawing her closer with his arm. "I had to risk it. I am sorry. Now I will tell you what I saw. I escaped from the Germans, and I headed toward Dniepropetrovsk because, as I said, I have people there. I found my relatives in the town, and they took me in and hid me in their home. I was there for so many days I lost track while we awaited a safe time for me to get on my way again.

By now the city and the entire area was occupied by the Germans. We heard of executions, at first of captured partisans and city officials who would not be expected to be loyal to the Germans. This kind of thing is commonplace. I have heard the German SS also summarily execute members of the Communist Party in towns they occupy. I heard many prisoners are shot, too, if they don't starve first. I suppose I was fortunate to have escaped.

"Soon the German SS came into the Jewish sectors of the town. Whole neighborhoods were cleared out—men, women, children! These people were civilians, and there was no reason to arrest them save for the fact that they were Jewish.

"I was hidden in a place under the floor of my uncle's house, but I heard the cries and screams of people being taken prisoner. I heard the SS soldiers come into the very house where I was hiding and drag out my relatives. And—God forgive me!—I stayed in my hiding place and was not discovered. Soon after, deeply shamed, I came out and saw truckloads of people being taken away. I followed on foot, hoping to see where they would be taken. It was dark and the caravan moved slowly, so I was able to keep up, but they only went a few miles out of town. I kept to the woods by the side of the road, wondering what I could do. But I knew, even back at the house, I could not have done anything. I was helpless."

Oleg paused, took a breath, and swallowed. Just then thunder rumbled outside. It seemed most appropriate. As he was about to begin again, Katya and Valentina returned with the tea. Katya served Cameron first. When she got to Oleg, he, who had protested the service before, now grasped the cup eagerly and gulped down half the liquid in one swallow.

"Forgive me," he said, "I talk so much it makes me thirsty." He attempted a wan smile, but it did not fit on his dark and drawn face. He was silent after that, instead studying each face around him as if gauging the effects of the tea and whether his listeners were soothed enough to hear the rest of his story.

He set down his cup and shifted in his chair. Cameron heard the patter of rain outside. She hoped that German bombers would not come tonight because of poor visibility. Everyone in the room remained silent, but tension could be felt from all, and the lone sounds of clinking of china and silver only emphasized the heavy atmosphere.

Oleg finally began again, his voice soft and distant. "When I was a boy, I remember my uncle taking me into those woods—they are only a few miles from town. We fished one summer, and I caught my first fish ever. Miss Gayes"—the intensity, the immediacy returned to his voice—"did I tell you there were hundreds, maybe over a thousand people, taken from the town that day? I could not imagine what was about to happen, but when I saw the trenches dug in the field . . . I should have guessed. The Germans shot them all—every man, woman, and little child. Oh, God!" His eyes suddenly filled with moisture and were like lumps of coal washed in a dark stream. A tear spilled over and tracked down his face through the dark shadow of beard and pain. "I have not been able to blot that picture from my mind. It is as vivid as a photograph." His voice remained steady, belying the tears, one after the other now dampening his face. "Do you know what it is like to see hundreds of people being gunned down? The incredible amount of blood, the screams. It does not take a minute to do such a ghastly deed, or five minutes, but it goes on and on until, if you happen to be the unlucky brute viewing such a thing, you want to scream, as well. For a time I thought I should run out and join them—they were my people." He stopped abruptly and wiped a sleeve across his eyes. His lips had begun to tremble, making speech difficult.

"Oleg, you couldn't have stopped it even with your own death." Cameron's own voice was shaky, and tears had begun to sting her eyes.

"No . . . but I could have stopped the dying inside me every time I think of it." His reserve crumbled completely now.

For all Oleg Gorbenko's dark and foreboding countenance, Cameron had a strong urge to hold this young man. She was glad when Sophia took him into her arms, soothing him with whispered endearments and gently stroking hands. He clung to his wife as a child clings to his mother. His shoulders shook with emotion. It was a strange sight indeed to watch the frail little Sophia hold up this man as if she were a pillar of iron.

Again the room was silent. Even Oleg's grief was mute, his sobs silent as they wracked his body. Glancing around at her companions, Cameron was surprised to note that none were looking at Oleg. But the truly surprising thing was that, to a person, all heads were bowed, eyes closed.

They were praying!

It was just as well that there was absolutely nothing she could say to Oleg or anyone at that moment, because had she wanted to speak she would have felt extremely awkward. She was uncomfortable enough as it was and very glad no one expected her to say a word. She only hoped they would not expect her to pray. She remembered the times she had gone to church with her mother when she was young and feeling, when the congregation prayed, that she had to bow her head and pretend to do so also, though instead she would occupy herself by planning the rest of her day. Oddly, she felt no need to pretend now, but even more oddly, she wished she could pray. At least it was *something* to do.

The creaking of Oleg's chair brought her attention back to him. He had moved away from his wife and turned to face Cameron. His lips no longer trembled. His voice was steady once more, the glint again sparking from his eyes.

"You have heard, Miss Gayes. Now what will you do?" he said. Was it a challenge?

Me? She thought. Who was she? What could she do? Then she remembered. She was a reporter. This was the kind of stuff she lived for. Stuff? This was murder of such magnitude that it was far beyond a trivial scoop. And it was beyond her. She did not want it. Why had he dumped it into her lap?

"Oleg, this is a complicated matter," she hedged. Yes, it was an odd thing for her to be faced with something so momentous, so stupendous, and not regard it in terms of journalist glory. This alone was a frightening place for her to be in.

"Complicated? I don't understand."

Cameron met his gaze and realized, of course, that men crying in the wilderness were apt to see things in black and white. How else could they remain so single-minded and passionate about their causes?

"Certainly you must see this is a sticky matter," she answered. "Why have you told me and not your Soviet superiors?" It was a loaded question, she fully realized.

"My government represses practically everything, and I feared they would do the same with this, especially when a friend of my father-in-law's, a government official, came this morning to hear me. He did not believe me. He said because I am Jewish, I would do anything to raise sympathy for my people. He warned if what I said was true, I should tell no one else. There was no telling what the government would do with such a story. But it would make me no hero, he told me, especially as an ex-POW. I don't understand why they would repress it. If the rest of the world knew, if the world leaders knew—"

"There's no telling what *they* would do." She cut in a bit more harshly than was necessary, but that came mostly from her own reticence.

"America would enter the war!"

She shook her head. All she could think of were the many reasons why this might well *prevent* them from declaring war on Germany. But she was not prepared to dash this young man's hopes—perhaps his only hope of quelling the screams in his head and the flow of the blood of his people. Helplessly she looked around the room. Did any of them understand the awful position she was in?

"Oleg, you must back away a little," came Dr. Fedorcenko's voice. Cameron thanked him with her eyes. "You must give Cameron time. For one thing, she is as much a prisoner of our system as we are."

Grasping the straw offered by the doctor, Cameron added, "There is no way I could get a regular dispatch about this out of the country. And if I tried to use the diplomatic pouch, I would need the support of the ambassador."

"But if they knew, if they heard . . ." Oleg's voice trailed away as if he was suddenly realizing the futility of his hope. "There must be a way. . . ." he murmured.

"If I did write your story," she relented just a bit, "I would need some confirming proof."

He brightened at this and reached into his shirt pocket, where Cameron now noticed a paper had been placed. He took it out and handed it to her. "I have written everything out. I have signed it, and it was witnessed by my father and mother-in-law. See, it is legal."

The last thing in the world she wanted to do was take that paper. Who knew what might happen if she were caught with it? But she wrapped her fingers around it and stuffed it into her pocketbook.

"I will do what I can," she said and thought she'd never heard more feeble words in her life.

"Thank you, Miss Gayes." Either Oleg had not perceived her subtle but definite brush-off, or he had enough sense to know when to cease pushing.

SHORTLY THEREAFTER, Dr. Fedorcenko offered to take Cameron home. She practically raced to the door. He led her through the rain-washed streets, a single umbrella protecting them both, though rather inadequately, from the drizzle. The metro had stopped running at ten o'clock, so they had to walk the entire way.

Pausing under an awning to catch their breath after walking for twenty minutes, Fedorcenko thanked Cameron again for coming. "Oleg is a good, honest boy—"

"I don't doubt that," Cameron put in quickly.

Dr. Fedorcenko smiled. His glasses were slightly fogged, and she could not see his eyes, but she guessed there was some apology in them as well as irony. "He can be a bit overzealous at times—not a bad quality, but in this case, it may work to his detriment."

"You must impress upon him to not tell anyone else what he has just told me—not yet at least. It is important to think it through first. I'd like to talk it over with a colleague I can trust."

" 'In many counselors there is wisdom,' " he said and seemed to be quoting something Cameron did not recognize. But it was a good quote regardless of its origin. "But," he added crisply, "we will all be careful to keep those counselors to a minimum. None of us wishes to bring harm to the war effort, but I know Oleg enough to say that he will soon come to a point where he will place purely moral obligations over more pragmatic ones. Men like Oleg have a difficult time under-standing concepts like 'for the greater good.' Some of us, however, can be too pragmatic for our own good or anyone else's."

"I wouldn't take you for a cynic, Doctor."

"Why do you say that?" He cocked a brow, sincerely curious.

"Well, it doesn't seem to fit with the doctor image, you know, helping mankind and all that."

"Perhaps doctors are the worst, especially old doctors such as myself. We have seen more death than even the vilest criminal. We have seen humankind at its worst. Yet I have seen miracles, also. I have seen hope. I have observed the hand of God intercede when my own hands have failed. I don't think I am a cynic about God, only about people, especially myself. I wonder how God can stand us. Perhaps He is a cynic, as well." Pausing, he chuckled softly. "I have been told I tend to analyze matters far too much, and now I have wandered off the subject. Where were we. . . ? Ah yes, Oleg. He is no cynic. He will expect action from you, Cameron. In addition to his idealism, he has a good dose of impatience."

"Impatience is a disease of youth, is it not?"

"You are what—? Only four or five years older than Oleg?"

She laughed. "Goodness! I am, aren't I? I feel like an old woman compared to him." She grew serious once more. "I will try to decide what to do soon, but I must caution you that I am not entirely my own person in this. My hands may be tied. But I will try."

"I know you will," he said. "I have heard nothing but good about you from those who know you. That is why I encouraged seeking you out."

She didn't quite know what to say to that but was spared as the rain let up a bit and Fedorcenko suggested they take advantage of the reprieve and be on their way.

As a precaution, he bade her good evening about a block from the hotel. He tried to give her his umbrella, but she refused, insisting that her coat would afford her enough protection traversing the short distance to her hotel. She was dripping by the time she sloshed into the hotel lobby, but she was fairly dry under her coat, which she hung on a coat tree before making her way to the hotel common room.

It was late, nearly eleven o'clock, and she didn't expect to find anyone, but she wanted to talk to Shanahan right away, and this seemed as good a place as any to start looking for him. She was shocked when she reached the open doorway and saw Shanahan sitting at the bar with Alex!

At the same moment she saw them, Shanahan saw her. He turned to Alex and said, "Alex, did I ever tell you it was a woman who drove me to drink?" Raising his glass of a clear liquid that certainly wasn't water, he added in his best W. C. Fields impression, "And I never remembered to thank her!" He tossed back his drink and grinned at Cameron.

"I thought I'd find you here, Shanahan," Cameron said dryly, striding up to the two men. "But, Alex, I thought you had better taste in company."

Alex smiled, and there was an element of relief in his aspect. The glass in front of him was larger than Shanahan's and filled with a clear fizzy liquid that Cameron guessed to be club soda, though she wasn't about to judge the man.

"I came by to see you," Alex said. "I found Johnny instead, and he said you should have been home from the party a couple of hours ago. We were . . . uh . . . worried about you."

"Well, neither of you *look* like nursemaids." But as much as she tried to be offended by their protective attitudes, she couldn't help being warmed, as well!

"Alex, Alex," Johnny said in a superior tone, "haven't you learned yet to never, ever show this woman any condescending emotion such as worry?"

"Well, never mind that," she said dismissively. "I'm glad you are here anyway. I need to talk to you both."

"Pull up a stool," Shanahan said. Then to the bartender, "Ivan, a glass of vodka for the lady—"

"No thanks," Cameron said. "I have a serious matter to discuss." She held up her hand and shook her head at Ivan. "Let's go sit at a table—" She glanced once again at the bartender. In all the time she had been there, no one had yet to determine just how much English the man understood. But it was safe to assume he understood more than he let on and was probably an agent of the NKVD. "On second thought, let's go up to my room." With glinting eyes, Shanahan opened his mouth to make some snide remark, but Cameron cut him off. "This is serious, Johnny."

Nevertheless, he grabbed his glass and the vodka bottle from Ivan before exiting the bar with Alex and Cameron. In her room, they all found seats, and Cameron immediately launched into an account of her visit to the Fedorcenko home. When she finished, there followed several moments of stunned silence. Even Johnny seemed nonplussed by the story. He filled his glass with vodka and had a long drink.

"Good heavens!" he breathed. "I've heard of such things but never believed them. I'm still not sure I do."

"I know Oleg," Alex said. "He doesn't tell lies."

"Yes, but the mind does play tricks. This Oleg fellow had been a prisoner of the Germans for weeks. I've heard how they treat their prisoners, and doubtless he was starved the entire time, perhaps tortured, and fearing he would be shot any day. Then the ordeal of escape and eluding the enemy culminated in watching his friends and family gunned down. Twenty victims could easily become hundreds to such a distressed eye."

"I don't want to waste time discussing the truth of Oleg's story," Cameron said. "Let's just assume that's a given."

"You cannot just assume it," Johnny said with rare earnestness. "Your career could well ride on the truth of young Oleg's statements. The kind of story he wants you to write could easily make you appear a crackpot at best, especially if you have no proof to back it up. Solid sources are the backbone of journalism. That's a basic rule of our trade, and that you should know, Hayes!"

"All right!" she replied with frustration that he had hit so closely to her own doubts about the story, which, perhaps for Alex's sake and his relationship to the Fedorcenkos, she had wanted to downplay. "That's a strong consideration. But what are the other implications I have to deal with?"

"The most immediate would be the Soviet response," Alex said. He leaned forward, a grim look on his face. "And that may well take you off the hook if you so choose."

"That is exactly what I want—to be let off the hook," Cameron said emphatically. "But . . . what I want doesn't matter."

"Okay," Shanahan said, his eyes focused on Alex, "you are the Soviet expert here. What's their most likely response?"

"You must know that Stalin is as anti-Semitic as Hitler," Alex answered. "He would feel little sympathy toward slaughtered Jews, and I doubt he could conceive of a world that would feel any more sympathy than he. But he is a smart man, and I'm sure if he thought it would save Russia, he would use it in spite of his personal prejudices—"

"He won't use it, though," cut in Johnny, "because he would realize it could blow up in his face."

"Maybe I am just as naïve as Oleg," Cameron said, sighing with frustration, "but why? No sane, civilized person could hear of such atrocities and not be moved to action."

"I never thought I'd say this, Cameron, but you *are* naïve." Johnny sipped his vodka, a thin smile on his face. "Few Americans are gonna want to fight a war to save Jews. I wouldn't be surprised if many Americans, secretly or otherwise, applaud Hitler's *Mein Kampf* view of Jews. We are a very anti-Semitic nation. What would FDR do if he knew about these things? He's got to know, to some extent at least. We've known for years that Hitler is persecuting Jews. But the president can't just ride roughshod over Congress, not even if he's Roosevelt."

"There are Jews in Congress, Jews in Roosevelt's government," Cameron argued.

"The owners of many top newspapers are Jews," Johnny said. "But have they ever published anything about this persecution of Jews? Everyone's got to protect their own backsides. And that's what you've got to do, Cameron."

"I would hate myself if that were my motive," Cameron said firmly. "I am not an idealist, but I'm no coward, either. I'm going to do what's right—I just can't decide what is right!"

"Cameron," Alex said in that soft but vibrantly compelling way of his, "I think you'll agree that I am an idealist—I *know* Johnny here will agree. I don't want to believe Americans are that heartless, even if they are anti-Semitic. I think if they are presented with irrefutable evidence of these atrocities, they will be appalled and demand action. But you must see, you have no such evidence. And without it, the average citizen simply won't be able to believe such a story. It is *utterly* unbelievable! It is far beyond stories of Jews being forced from their businesses or of mass evacuations of Jews from their homes. And even knowing Oleg's honest character, I don't want to believe it. This is probably why Jewish leaders in the States have not responded in the way you'd expect. No one *wants* to believe such evil is possible."

"Here's another thought I've toyed with," Cameron said. "What if this is an isolated incident?"

Both Alex and Johnny shook their heads in unison. Johnny said, "If it *could* happen, if it *did* happen in one village, you've got to accept that it has happened in others."

"I feel sick." Cameron groaned.

Alex said gently, "You mentioned how helpless Oleg was, and he was there. Even if he'd had a gun, he could not have stopped it. We are that much more helpless. Cameron, you have the power of the written word, but even it is useless in this case. The only way to stop Hitler and his murder is to shorten the war."

"And the best way to do that is for America to enter the war."

"It's gonna happen," said Shanahan, uncharacteristically optimistic. "But Oleg's story isn't gonna be the catalyst to bring it about. In the worst case, it could actually delay it. But it will happen. FDR is chomping at the bit. He'll get us into this war."

"It better be soon," Cameron said.

"Does that mean you will sit on this story?" asked Alex.

"I feel for Oleg's sake I must make some further attempt to get it out."

Alex smiled. She saw something like admiration in his eyes. He had counseled her to stonewall the story, yet it pleased him that she was not ready to give up. Before she realized what she was doing, she glanced quickly toward Johnny. He was smiling, too, but rather than showing admiration, his expression seemed to say, "Oh, you foolish girl! When are you gonna learn?" And she realized with a start that she was once again comparing these two men. Alex, with his genuineness that was neither saccharine nor repulsive. And Johnny, whose smirk even now did not put her off because she understood him as only a like-minded soul could. Yes, she and Johnny were definitely soul mates, if ever there were any.

Alex, on the other hand, constantly baffled her sensibilities. Yet he stirred her in a way no man, not even Johnny, ever had before. She understood that as little as she understood the man himself. But there it was.

Two men, so different, it was silly to even attempt drawing comparisons. How could she be drawn to such divergent characters? Maybe they were more alike than mere surface appearance denoted. Maybe they were like two sides of the same coin, each completely different, yet drawn from the same essential material. Perhaps if she could have both men, she'd have the perfect man.

If she wanted to have any man at all! But she might waver in that attitude if she could have a man with Johnny's incisive wit and cocky style along with Alex's gentle, compelling touch and his completely unaffected honesty.

Sighing, she shook away the momentary lapse. How could she be thinking such blathering, romantic rubbish when there was before her a conundrum of such magnitude she was for the first time in her life nearly paralyzed by it? Well, fantasizing about these two men was certainly a preferable diversion.

"Okay," she said in a crisp, businesslike manner, "I think we have covered all our bases. I appreciate you both for listening and offering opinions."

"My pleasure," Johnny said wryly, and she wanted to kiss that twisted grin he wore.

"You'll do the right thing, Cameron, I know it," Alex said. And only he could make such a statement sound like more than the cliché it was. She wanted to kiss him, as well.

And suddenly she felt like a very evil woman. But she couldn't help it. She loved both men—well, not *loved*. She *liked* them both immensely.

THE NEXT MORNING Cameron was far more clearheaded when she called on William Tramble at the British embassy. She supposed she shouldn't have been surprised when he smiled benevolently down upon her and told her in that proper British way of his that he wouldn't touch such a story. His reasoning was that it could not possibly be true and he'd be a laughingstock were he to repeat it to anyone.

She then went to Bob Wood at the U.S. embassy—he was second on her list only because Tramble had been available to see her first.

Wood didn't come right out and say he didn't believe the story, but his expression became an unreadable mass that she interpreted as his diplomatic way of hiding the fact that he thought she was being led down a proverbial garden path. He did, however, speak to Steinhardt—at least he said he spoke to the ambassador—Cameron could not be certain he was telling the truth. In any case, when they had a second interview a few days later, he said the ambassador could not sanction sending such a story via the diplomatic pouch.

"I guess that's it, then," she said, turning to leave. She wasn't entirely convinced of her words, and even as she turned, her mind was spinning about for other avenues of help.

"Cameron, you've got to understand the position the embassy is in—"

"Bob," she cut in sharply, mostly from frustration, "it is really not necessary to make more excuses. You are hanging me and my source out to dry. Maybe that's for the best."

"What else can we do? You have no concrete proof."

"All I have is an honest young man devastated by the very real things he saw."

"If he is as compelling as you say, he could well be your best proof."

"Oh, and how do I use him?" she asked snidely. "Do I smear some of his blood on my story?"

Wood scratched his head, rose from where he sat behind his desk, and strode to a window. He gazed out on the street below for several moments. Cameron tried to gauge his behavior. Had she somehow misread his earlier reluctance? Was it possible he had believed all along what she told him about Oleg?

"I have a feeling you didn't quite believe me when I said I spoke to the ambassador." His tone was pensive as he kept his gaze toward the window.

"Well, I—"

"I did speak to him. In fact, we had quite a conversation. I actually became very animated. He wondered why it should concern me so." He turned now to face her, his brow was creased, his eyes intent. "I couldn't tell him, of course. God knows what would happen if it got out."

"Bob—"

"Let me finish, Cameron. I'm about to tell you something only a select few know. About fifty years ago, a family named Grunwald came to America from Germany. They settled in New York, but because of his Jewish ancestry, the head of the family had difficulty finding work in his chosen profession. He was a lawyer, a highly educated man. He ended up as a custodian in a factory and only got that job after he changed his name on his application to Wood."

Cameron gasped and Bob nodded.

"We have been Wood ever since," Bob added. "Staunch members of the Presbyterian Church. My father is an elder, for heaven's sake! Jacob Grunwald was my great-grandfather, and because of him my father is now president of our country club—a club, I might add, that does not accept Jews. I attended Harvard, was in the right fraternity, and later joined a law firm which has no Jews among its legal staff. Of course, today there are many known Jews in powerful positions in our country. I applaud them. And I won't say I am not ashamed of this lie my family has perpetrated. I wish I'd had the courage years ago to stand up and claim my heritage."

"Why are you telling me all this, Bob?"

"When I stood before the ambassador yesterday and said we ought not to discount your information, I knew my words would have had far more impact if I'd have told my secret and indicated it meant so much to me that I would take that risk. I wanted to be that kind of man. I have always wanted to be that kind of man. But I have failed. I suppose by telling you, I hope to exonerate myself a little."

"You still can be that kind of man, Bob." But Cameron knew what she was asking and knew it wasn't her place. She shook her head. "I'm sorry. I am not going to ask such a thing of you. But it should not have to be such a professional risk for you. These things should not be happening in a civilized world. Yet that is in reality what this is all about. We do live in a world where a good man can be ruined because of a quirk of birth, because of the god his people believe in. And now we must accept the fact that we live in a world where men are murdered for those same reasons. *Murdered*, Bob!"

Wood sucked in a shuddering breath. His eyes glistened with moisture. "If it's true. . . ?"

"Are you weeping now because it is a lie?" she challenged.

"My people . . . I have never thought of the Jewish race like that before. I learned I was a Jew the summer before I entered Harvard. My father thought I should know so I would realize what a gift I had been given. I pushed it from my mind almost immediately after he told me and have not looked back . . . until now." He dashed a hand across a corner of his eye. "I'll never forgive you for this, Cameron." But an ironic half smile slanted his lips. "But I'll always thank you. My people are being murdered. I believe it."

"Thank you, Bob," Cameron said. "I realize we can do very little about it, but I appreciate your taking me seriously."

"Perhaps we are not completely helpless."

"You just said—and rightly—that we can't do much without hard evidence."

"And you said the only evidence you had was a passionate young man named Oleg."

"Yes. . . ?" Cameron eyed him curiously. What was he driving at?

"He could be your evidence. If we could get him out of the country."

"You're kidding!"

"I may be a blubbering idiot at the moment, Cameron," he said as he pulled a handkerchief from his pocket and blew his nose, "but I am not kidding. Think of Oleg speaking with powerful men in Washington—perhaps even with the president himself! What impact could that have? Perhaps not an immediate declaration of war on Germany, but it could help to move men in that direction."

"You don't think it could backfire?"

"I've had the advantage of being able to observe the American people from both sides of the fence while I sat firmly *on* the fence," he said wryly. "I agree with your friend—the doctor, right? The American people are basically decent. They may hate Jews on one level, but few would ever condone acting out that hatred with murder. The worst that could happen is they would simply not believe such things."

Cameron rubbed her chin and began pacing across Wood's fine Persian carpet. "Could we do it? Could we actually get him out?" Her mind raced.

"He wouldn't be the first Russian defector."

"Have you—?"

"Never. I haven't a clue how to go about sneaking someone out of the country."

"Johnny might know. He's smuggled a few articles out—"

"I'll pretend I never heard that!"

The two paced back and forth together for several moments, then stopped when they realized no earth-shattering ideas were likely to descend upon them immediately.

"We're going to have to give this some thought," Bob said. "If you don't mind, I would also like to speak with Oleg myself."

"We may not have a lot of time. Oleg lives in fear he will be arrested, as an ex-POW if nothing else."

"I will put out some discreet feelers."

"So will I."

"Cameron, you must be careful. I can stand upon diplomatic immunity. You will not be able to claim that."

"I am always careful, Bob." Her confidence surprised her. She knew it was ninety percent feigned.

Still, confidence was all she had to offer at the moment. But she left Wood's office feeling for the first time since speaking with Oleg that she could do more than offer the young man a sympathetic ear. But when she saw Sophia, she debated within herself whether to tell her of Bob Wood's idea and finally decided not to say anything until she had something more concrete than mere confidence to offer. Defecting from Russia was a huge step, and it did not seem fair to force them to consider it until there was even a small possibility that a plan could be implemented.

A secret meeting between Bob and Oleg was arranged, and afterward Bob was more determined than ever to help the young man.

But such things did indeed take time, and as the days passed, Cameron's silence and inactivity regarding Oleg did seem to create a terrible awkwardness between her and Sophia. They had just been developing a nice rapport, if not friendship. Now Cameron could not even look the girl straight in the eye. Of course, Sophia had the grace not to mention Cameron's seeming inaction, but Cameron was still bothered by it.

Then a new distraction came along, and Cameron embraced it eagerly, not that she wouldn't have anyway, because it was the long-awaited visit to the Front.

44

ON A DRIZZLY morning ten British and American correspondents met together in front of the Foreign Affairs Commissariat. Five black M–1's, the Russian version of a Ford sedan, pulled up to the curb. Besides the journalists, there was a full complement of armed guards and a couple of officials from the press department, including a censor and a staff colonel who would act as their military liaison.

Cameron was quite surprised when Alex stepped out of one of the M–1's.

"I obtained permission to join the group in order to observe front-line medical facilities," he explained.

Cameron was more pleased at the prospect of his company than she had a right to be.

Though there would be several stops on the way, the group's final destination was Yelnya, about a hundred fifty miles southwest of Moscow. Heavy fighting had taken place in that area less than a week before, and the Russians had finally eked out a victory—one they now wished to publicize to the world, thus the visit by journalists.

Just outside Moscow, not far enough outside in Cameron's opinion, the little caravan encountered the red-and-white road barrier that indicated the beginning of the military zone. Beyond this point, there was no denying that Russia was in the midst of a desperate war. Columns of military vehicles rumbled down the road in a constant flow, and Cameron was gratified to note that there were among the Russian-made vehicles some Fords. Lend-lease matériel was already flowing into the beleaguered country. There were also Russian soldiers posted along the road, standing guard, wrapped in rain cloaks, ever vigilant.

The roads, never much to begin with, steadily disintegrated into deep ruts caused by the stream of heavy vehicles and now also by the constant autumn rains. Vehicles, even big trucks, stuck in the mud became a common sight along the roadside, and their own M–1's were not spared, either, becoming mired in the mud at frequent intervals. But they reached the little town of Vyazma, their first stop, by late afternoon.

Cameron scrambled from her car, anxious to stretch her cramped legs. Because she was one of the smaller members of the party, she had been given a seat over boxes of supplies, some of which were marked "Vodka." Alex joined her as she took a brief walk. The guards warned them not to wander too far.

"It doesn't look too bad," Cameron said with a sweeping gaze up and down the street.

"Yes, and it's heartening. I imagined far more destruction."

There were, of course, bombed-out buildings, but on the whole the town was intact and seemed to be operating "business as usual." Flowers bloomed in gardens, women gossiped over their fences, shopkeepers sold their wares. There was a heavy military presence, but that was to be expected.

"How far do you think we are from the actual Front?" Cameron asked.

"Yelnya is about seventy-five miles southwest of here, and we know the Russians have retaken that. All looks secure around here."

"Yes, but almost too secure for a Russian operation. Maybe we shouldn't grow too comfortable."

Alex grinned. "I think that is just wishful thinking on your part."

"And what do you mean by that?" she asked with mock offense.

"Well, Miss *Gayes*," he replied, thickening his Russian accent for effect, "I think you vant nothing more than to be in the thick of a good battle. Your Russian protectors vill be hard pressed to keep you in tow."

Laughing, but a little embarrassed by the truth of his statement, she said, "I do. I really do."

"As they say, be careful what you wish for."

The group was put up for the night at the Vyazma International Hotel—a euphemism by any standard. They slept three to a room—except for Cameron, whose gender afforded her a private room that was little more than a converted broom closet. The beds were old, rickety, and the mattresses were filthy. There was an indoor toilet, but for washing up, the guests had to use a communal faucet at the end of the corridor on their floor. But they were well fed that night and the champagne and vodka flowed—well, better than the rusty, undrinkable water.

They interviewed a general who assured them that the "Fascist swine" would never get close to Moscow. He also piled on the propaganda thicker than the mud on the road. It was far more interesting later to speak with some airmen who had just returned from bombing a German airfield in Smolensk. These young men were quite cocky with their successful run. The commander of the aircraft said they made as many as seven raids a day over German-occupied territory. Each run was about an hour round trip.

But early the next morning, while the correspondents still slept, the Germans retaliated for that raid by bombing Vyazma. Cameron was awakened by the blare of the air-raid siren and only had time to roll under her bed before the first bombs fell. It wasn't long, however, before she heard the drone of Russian fighters rising to combat the bombers, chasing them away.

Venturing into the hall after the all-clear siren blasted, she saw several men clustered in front of one of the rooms, apparently laughing. She hurried to join the group, which parted to give her a view of the room. Inside, their censor was lying on his bed, a fallen window frame neatly framing his body. Though Cameron on several occasions had wished to kill a few Russian censors, she was thankful he was unhurt beyond a few scratches and bruises. The town, as well, had not suffered badly in the bombing.

The picture of destruction grew grimmer as they got back on the road after breakfast. As they penetrated territory only recently reclaimed by the Russian army, the entourage of correspondents passed the remains of villages, many bombed out of existence. One had been a town of over ten thousand inhabitants. Only a hundred now remained. No one knew how many had been killed or how many had been carried off to labor camps by the occupying Germans. Fields of rye and other grains lay all around unharvested, for there was little manpower to take care of the crops.

The caravan stopped for the day at a divisional headquarters some forty miles northeast of Smolensk and only three miles from German lines. They were surrounded by thick forests, and Cameron had the comforting sense that they would provide good cover for partisans. There were also the less comforting sounds of bursting artillery not far in the distance.

But in this coarse milieu, the Russians seemed determined to be good hosts to their foreign guests. The journalists were taken to a large mess tent and treated to an incredibly lavish feast of caviar, succulent roasted pork, and even chocolate. Of course, there was also all the champagne and vodka they could drink—and drink it they must, not only so as not to offend their hosts but also because the water was not to be trusted.

After the usual drone of speeches, the toasting began.

"*Pobeda budet za nami!* Victory will be ours!" cried the divisional commander Colonel Kirilov.

"To victory!" came the response, and down went the vodka.

Cameron would have been out cold in ten minutes if she had not followed Alex's example of pretending to sip but covertly spilling as much as she could get away with, down her own chin if necessary. But there was always a vigilant host nearby whose duty it seemed was to ensure that the foreigners were made insensible by the alcohol.

Then the music began. Someone beat out tunes on a piano—yes, there was actually a piano three miles from German lines in a mess tent! Some of the tunes were Russian, but there was a recognizable selection of good old American songs, too. "And the Angels Sing" and the "Beer Barrel Polka" were especially well received. But the crowd roared with delight when the pianist turned out "Jeepers Creepers," with one of the men singing the tune in a hilarious mixture of Russian and broken English. And all this within the sound of gunfire.

Soon dancing accompanied the music. The Russian soldiers had no compunction about dancing with each other, since there were not enough village girls, who had come to serve the guests, to go around. Only after imbibing much vodka were the foreign men as uninhibited. As one of the few females, Cameron could have danced nonstop the entire night, but after a while she became giddy and light-headed from the exertion. At one point between partners, she managed to slip from the tent to get some fresh air outside.

Strolling to the edge of the camp, she sucked in the crisp night air. There were definitely signs of frost in that air. Some predicted snow soon. It was actually quite a peaceful night. The guns had quieted down, and the occasional bursts lent a rather mournful tone to the evening. She turned toward the west and imagined the Front only three miles away. A brisk walk would take her there in a matter of minutes. Of course, there was a labyrinth of forests in between and, no doubt, land mines and who knew what other booby traps.

"No more shooting," came a voice at Cameron's back, startling her.

"Goodness, Shanahan! You shouldn't sneak up on someone this close to a battlefield."

"Sorry, sweetheart." He came up beside her. "It is close, isn't it? Can't you almost feel it?"

She knew he meant the proximity of the Front. It was as if he'd known exactly what she had been thinking.

"Do you think they will take us much closer?" she asked, not caring that she sounded like a starry-eyed schoolgirl.

"It won't matter. We'll all be too sloshed to care. That's their game, you know—numbing our heads with booze and our stomachs with rich food so we will be too dull witted to see any of the fine details of this little excursion."

"You've got to admit this is still exciting. Why, we are the first foreigners to lay eyes on these battlegrounds! We are finally going to get to report some *news*. I can't wait to write my first 'With the Russian Army' dispatch!"

Johnny was looking down at her, an easy smile bending his lips. He reached up a hand and brushed back a strand of her hair blown by the wind. "You are so beautiful all flushed with journalistic zeal!" Pausing, he continued to gaze at her, his eyes seeming to glint with . . . was it hunger? She tingled inside, but it was Shanahan who added, "You do get to me, Hayes. Yes, you do!" He leaned close, his face inches from hers, his breath warm and strong with the scent of alcohol.

"Johnny . . ." She didn't know if she wanted him to stop or keep going, but she didn't move away from him.

"I love you, Cameron!"

The words may as well have been a blow for the way they made her flinch away. "What?"

"I love everything about you," he went on. "I love that sharp tongue of yours. I love the way your nose turns up, and the way your nostrils flare when you are angry." He grabbed her hand. "I love the tinge of typewriter ribbon ink around your nails." He kissed her hand.

What was happening? This could not be the real Johnny Shanahan. This had to be an imposter.

"Johnny, you are drunk," she said sharply, mostly to counter the unwelcome tingly response she was having to his words. She told herself once more that she did not want Johnny. She did not love him, but he still had a crazy effect on her.

"Very, very, very drunk!" he agreed. "But you know that never stopped me from speaking the truth."

"In all the time I've known you, you have never said you loved me."

"Would you have wanted me to?"

"Heavens no!" But she thought, yes, there might have been a time . . . before . . . what? Alex?

"I just wanted to see what it would feel like," he was saying. "Just for your information, I have never told any woman I loved her."

"It doesn't surprise me."

"Maybe I love you like a sister, huh? I never had a sister. I got a brother, but he hasn't spoken to me for twenty years."

"Why?" she asked, eagerly grasping at the diversion.

"He thinks I'm responsible for our father's death. Good ole Dad killed himself shortly after I left home when I was fifteen." He shook his head ironically. "Now, you tell me, the man beat my brains out nearly every day and lost no opportunity to tell me how worthless I was when I was home. Does that sound like a man who'd despair so at my departure that he'd shoot himself when I was gone?"

"Johnny, you never told me this. I'm so sorry."

"Must mean I love you if I'm telling you my deepest, darkest secrets." He leaned toward her again, his lips almost brushing hers, then pulled away. "Probably like a sister . . . so better not kiss ya." He took a deep breath. Was it of regret or relief? Cameron couldn't tell, but she was certain she had felt a bit of relief herself. Then he said quite casually, as if she were his sister, "I gotta see a man about a horse."

"Huh?"

But then he headed into the woods and she understood.

She stared after him, torn between tenderness and anger. And for the next ten minutes her mind was in a complete turmoil. Why had he chosen now to speak words of love? And what could such words possibly mean to him anyway? Brotherly love? She wasn't certain that he understood that emotion, either. After all, there apparently was no love between him and his own brother.

Oh, she could kill him for muddying the water like that. It was far too muddy as it was.

Then as if on cue, Alex strode up to her.

"I needed a reprieve," he said.

"Same here. Too much of a good thing."

He cocked his head toward the tent. "That's a good thing?"

"Guess it's the perspective. I mean, here are these Russians, practically cut off at the knees by the Germans, surrounded on all sides by death and destruction, and yet they can still dance and sing louder and drink longer than anyone I have ever seen."

"Yes," he mused, "there is seldom any middle ground for Russians. All or nothing."

"I am beginning to see that."

They chatted for several minutes, mostly about their experiences thus far on the tour, then Cameron became distracted, until she finally said, "You know, I am getting kind of worried about Johnny."

"Why is that?"

"He went into the woods a good twenty minutes ago to . . . uh . . . take care of business. He should be back by now."

Alex's brow creased. "That's not good at all. We are close enough to German lines that there could be enemy strays roaming the woods."

"We'd better go look for him."

What they really should have done, Cameron well knew, as did Alex, was to go for help. But until absolutely necessary, neither wanted to deal with suspicious Russian military men, much less the NKVD agents who had accompanied them from Moscow. They went into the woods, thinking to go only a short distance and staying together the whole time so as not to lose each other in the darkness.

"Johnny!" They took turns calling, but not too loudly so as not to elicit a response from the wrong side.

Ten minutes later they were about to return to the camp for help when they were startled by a stirring in the bushes. Alex grasped Cameron's arm and pulled her protectively close. Neither of them was armed, of course.

In a moment Johnny himself stumbled into the small clearing in which they stood. He stumbled because he was being roughly pushed by another. Soon Cameron saw that a khaki-clad soldier was gripping

Johnny around the neck with one arm while holding a pistol to his head with the other. As the light from the sliver of moon, which had a moment before been hidden behind clouds, shone into the clearing, Cameron got a good look at Johnny's captor. It was a woman.

Weakly, but with a definite hint of his usual mockery, Johnny said, "I don't know if she wants to shoot me or make love to me."

Alex conversed with the woman, who, Cameron decided, was quite attractive in a statuesque way. She towered over Johnny by several inches and she was definitely of the "big-boned" type, but her layers of warm clothes probably hid a well-formed figure. Her face, however, had well-defined features that were a sculptor's dream—high Nordic cheeks, almond-shaped eyes, and a nose that divided all like a shapely icicle. Her blond hair was covered partially by a visored cap.

Alex finished his discussion with her and said, "She is a partisan and thought you might be a German spy, in which case she most definitely planned to shoot you."

"Well, would you kindly inform her otherwise?" Johnny said with a pathetic half smile.

"I have, but she wants to see our papers."

They quickly obliged her, Johnny taking great care to remove his so she wouldn't panic and pull the trigger. Finally satisfied that these were foreigners but not Germans, she lowered her weapon. Johnny stepped away from her, then turned to get a better look at his captor. He grinned that smile of his that was usually death to a woman's sensibilities. But this woman continued to gaze stonily upon him.

"So you are a partisan," Johnny said, looking her up and down now with frank admiration. "You would never have gotten the better of me except . . . well, you had me in a rather precarious position."

Alex translated, then repeated her response. "She—her name is Tatiana—wants to know why you went so far from the camp to do your business."

Shanahan shrugged. "I'm a city boy. I had no idea what protocol demanded in such situations." Then he added as soon as Alex had finished translating, "Ask her if she knows the way to the Front."

Alex cocked a brow. "Of course she knows the way to the Front."

"Then ask her if she'll take us there."

"Now?"

"Yes, and I mean the real Front, not this insipid rear echelon stuff the press department is trying to foist on us. I want to smell sauerkraut, ya hear?"

"You're crazy. She'll never—"

"Ask her!"

Cameron remained silent during the exchange. Shanahan's idea was crazy, of course, but if Johnny could make it happen, she was not going to argue.

Alex asked, and it was obvious the woman was not about to take such an enormous risk. She shook her head obdurately, causing the ammo belts across her chest to rattle like cheap jewelry. Alex did not have to translate her words.

"Listen here," Johnny said, his white teeth sparkling as his lips parted in a smile that could at the very least melt stone, "I'll be very grateful if you do this little thing for me." His words did not have to be translated, either. She shook her head again. Then, like a magician, Johnny reached into his coat pocket and pulled out a pair of silk stockings!

"What in the world—?" Cameron exclaimed, shocked. "You actually carry stockings?"

"Hey, they are better currency than rubles," Johnny defended himself.

But what was even more shocking was the immediate transformation that came over the partisan statue. She actually grinned and reached a hand toward the treasure.

"Yeah, baby, I knew we spoke the same language," Johnny said, still grinning. He draped the stockings over her dirty, calloused, outstretched hand.

She rubbed them once against her cheek, then tucked them away somewhere deep and safe within the layers of her clothing. And the deal was sealed.

A TREE BRANCH slapped Cameron in the face, sending a spray of moisture over her like a rain shower. Ahead, Tatiana was plowing through the thick growth of forest, seemingly oblivious to her followers. Shanahan hiked at the partisan's side. They were carrying on a muted but animated conversation, he in English, she in Russian. In no way could they fully understand each other except in that elemental language, perhaps, of the soul.

Cameron glanced at Alex striding at her side, then nodded toward the couple ahead.

He shrugged. "Amazing, isn't it? I asked if he wanted me to translate, and he waved me away."

"Well, Johnny does have his own private way of communicating, especially with women."

Alex looked at her, and she could see, even in the deep night, the questioning in his gaze. Was he wondering just how much personal experience she'd had with Johnny's communicative skills? Surely he knew she and Johnny had been close.

Just then Tatiana signaled for them to be still. They halted the moment they saw the sharp wave of her hand. Then Cameron listened. They had to be close to German lines now, but she had yet to see any Russian soldiers, gun emplacements, trenches, or other evidence of the proximity of the Front line.

All was silent. Not even a stray rifleshot pierced the stillness of the night. In the next moment their guide motioned them to continue moving, but a finger over her lips clearly indicated there was to be no more conversation. She made a sharp turn to the right, then continued to move through the woods with the stealth of a cat. Cameron tried to mimic her example. But, like Johnny, she was definitely not a forest kind of person. Her clumsy foot snapped a twig. Tatiana turned and scowled at her.

Ten minutes later, Tatiana stopped again, then spoke in a rough, low voice.

"*Kakaya sivodnya pagoda?*" she murmured.

"That's odd—" Alex started to whisper in Cameron's ear, then was cut off by a muffled voice coming from the thicket.

"*Sivodnya tiplo.*"

"*Duyit vyetir,*" Tatiana replied.

Then the owner of the voice stepped into view. And he was not alone. In the next instant Cameron, Alex, and Johnny were surrounded by heavily armed men and women, at least six of them. Cameron swallowed. Had they been led into a trap? But none were in uniform, at least not German uniforms. Some wore flak jackets with civilian trousers, or military caps with Red Army insignia, or khaki pants, but there was not a complete uniform among them, and certainly they wore nothing with German insignia.

Tatiana spoke to Alex, and he explained that these people were her partisan comrades and that her rather confusing words before about the weather had been an exchange of passwords.

"We're behind German lines," he said almost too matter-of-factly for the import of his words.

"What!" Cameron and Shanahan exclaimed together.

Tatiana "shushed" them soundly, then had a long whispered interchange with Alex.

Finally Alex explained, "Before—when we first met—I told her I was a doctor and you were journalists. Well, it seems she acceded so easily to Johnny's request not because of her insane love for silk stockings—" He tossed Johnny a knowing look. "They've got an injured comrade. She promises that as soon as I look at the man, she will take us back to a Russian frontline unit."

"Aw, sweetheart," Johnny said to Tatiana, "and here I thought we could trust each other." He shook his head, then grinned. "Well, I forgive you. Let's just take care of business and get the blazes out of here. I never wanted to be so close to the Front that I was on the other side!"

They were taken deeper into the forest about a hundred feet, and there in a small clearing lay the patient. Another man was kneeling beside him, blotting his forehead with a cloth. Alex hurried up to the prostrate man and knelt down. Cameron was at his elbow. She nearly gasped when she saw the patient was a mere boy, no more than fourteen years old. The man ministering to the boy was at least forty, with a gray-streaked beard. Was he the boy's father? When he lifted pain-filled, beseeching eyes to them, there could be no doubt of his close relationship to the boy.

Alex spoke in English to Cameron as he quickly examined the patient. "Tatiana said they were afraid to move him to the field hospital, which is more than five miles away. When we encountered her, she'd been heading to the hospital to attempt to get a doctor to come to their camp." He lifted a blood-soaked shirt, exposing the boy's wound. "It's a good thing they didn't move him. Probably would have killed him."

Even the darkness could not hide the glint of passion in Alex's eyes. She'd detected the same look when he had treated the old man during the air raid the day they had first met. It was the look of a man involved in a task that touched the very core of his being. She could easily understand why he had sacrificed much to come to Russia in order to continue doing what so obviously gave him life.

"Of course I never have my bag when I need it," he grumbled. But he spoke to the older man, who quickly rose and went to rummage through a pile of supplies. In a moment he returned with a first-aid kit. "Sutures! Dear God, let there be sutures in there!" Alex said as he opened it and assayed the contents. "Hallelujah," he exclaimed, pulling out a packet of what Cameron surmised were sutures. "I have to get this bullet out. Cameron, come here and help me."

Cameron glanced around, thinking Tatiana was certainly a better candidate to assist the doctor. But she was nowhere near—Johnny was not in sight, either. In fact, only one other partisan remained in view. She hoped that meant the rest were diligently guarding the perimeter. Nevertheless, there was no one else around, and so she was forced to drop on her knees next to Alex, who had put the older man to work distracting the boy and soothing him however he could.

Alex murmured, half to himself, "I need light."

He spoke to the man, who responded with a vigorous shake of his head and a firm "*Nyet!*"

Cameron understood and said, "Alex, there's a flashlight in that pile of supplies. Why don't you do like you did during the air raid with that old man?"

"Of course!" He grinned. "You know, you are turning into a first-rate nurse!"

"Thank you, Doctor," she replied with a crisp efficiency she did not feel.

Alex issued orders to the man and to Cameron until they had made a snug little operating tent with a couple of blankets. He then put the man to work holding the flashlight.

"Have you ever operated like this before?" Cameron asked.

"You mean outside the sterile environment of an operating room?" He shook his head. "When the war started, I wanted to be assigned to a field hospital, but I guess I hadn't been here long enough for them to trust me so far from Moscow and the protective eyes of the NKVD. So, no, I haven't, not like this." He lifted his eyes to meet hers. "I could be a little afraid if I let myself think about it."

"Then don't think about it."

"It will be some story to tell our grandchildren, though, operating on a wounded partisan behind German lines. Not many will be able to top that—" Stopping suddenly, he added sheepishly, "I meant our respective grandchildren. That is—"

"I know what you meant, Alex." She smiled to assure him she was in no way alarmed by his words. But . . . well, she was glad when he started to work.

After giving the boy a dose of morphine from the kit, Alex lifted a scalpel from the first-aid box and poured alcohol over the instrument. He also sloshed a good bit of the stuff over the wound. Then he incised it. His hands were incredibly steady. Cameron's were shaking.

"There's going to be a lot of blood," he said. "There's not enough disinfectant for our hands, but use the sponges in the kit carefully, and it should be all right."

"Sponges?" She rifled through the box. "I don't see any sponges—"

"Gauze—there." He pointed out packages of sterile gauze pads.

Cameron became so engrossed with the drama of the operation that she forgot to be sickened by the blood or the probing or the groans of the boy, who even in his agony had the sense not to scream out and risk alerting any Germans who might be near. In an hour it was done. The bullet was removed, and Alex was stitching up the wound.

"He still can't be moved right away," Alex murmured. "But they can't stay here indefinitely without risk of exposure."

When he finished, the light was switched off and the tent removed. The older man offered effusive thanks to both Alex and Cameron. His eyes filled with tears as he took Alex's hands and shook them, then gathered him into a suffocating bear hug. At least it looked suffocating, and Cameron was glad the big, bearded partisan only kissed her cheek.

Cameron put away the first-aid kit as Alex hovered anxiously over his patient, muttering things like, "If infection doesn't set in . . . if the stitches hold when they move him . . . he's young . . . but he needs a decent diet . . ."

Cameron had always thought she and Alex were as complete opposites as there were, yet this sight of him as a doctor at his work suddenly made her see an elemental likeness between them. She behaved the same way when she was tracking down a story or writing one. She understood that gleam in Alex's eye, because she was certain the same one often glinted from her own. She smiled at the idea, not knowing why that should please her so.

A few minutes later there was some stirring in the woods, followed immediately by the appearance of Johnny and Tatiana. Johnny's hair was messed and imbedded with grass and twigs. Tatiana was not in much better condition. Except for the besotted looks on both their faces, Cameron might have thought they had just tangled with a German division. She knew better. Johnny had just been up to his old tricks.

Yelnya looked more like a graveyard than the site of the first major Russian victory. But perhaps it was that, as well.

In the two days since the encounter with Tatiana, the entourage of journalists had passed through enough shattered villages, woods chewed up with gunfire, fields rutted with tank tracks, and what was left of those fields covered with grain, ripe and uncut, so they should have known what to expect when they reached their final destination. But there was no possible preparation for the ghastly sight that greeted them. Yelnya had once been home to fifteen thousand inhabitants. They were gone now, only God knew where. All that remained of the town was charred beams and stone chimney stacks. So fresh was some of the destruction that small tendrils of smoke still rose from the ruins.

Cameron had seen some of the ravages of war in Yugoslavia and Greece, but never anything like this. It was as if this village had been victim to some special rage. She thought of the German POWs she had talked to in the Moscow hospital. They had seemed incapable of this kind of thing. Yet here it was before her eyes, and she now realized that this war between these two ancient adversaries went deep to the core of some bestial drive Cameron could only imagine.

Later, Shanahan found an old man digging among the ruins of a house. A few of the other reporters gathered around, and with Alex translating, the man told them what he had experienced.

"The German devils took away all able-bodied men and women when they conquered my town," he said. "My son was among them. I think he is safe in a work camp. They let us older ones stay. But the night that the Russian army began to close in, the Fascist pigs locked us all in the church." He jerked his ancient gray head, and following the direction of his gesture, Cameron noted a stone church, the only building still standing. "We heard the battle sounds, we saw the fire and smoke rise as the enemy razed our homes. But the windows of the church are high, and we could see little else. Until our boys broke into the church, we had no idea who the victor would be."

When he finished, returning to his futile attempts to find what was left of his life, Cameron wandered away, finally pausing before the church. She thought of the terror those people must have experienced that night. She tried to imagine what it would be like to listen help-lessly to a battle raging, quite literally, in your own backyard. She thought of her own home, her parents' home, safe and sound in Bev-erly Hills. Would the war touch them? Like this? She shuddered at the thought and quickly hurried back to her friends.

But even the most hardened of reporters in the group were stunned by what they were seeing. Colonel Pitinov, their military liaison, didn't help by choosing that moment to badger the foreigners about the Sec-ond Front.

"You must write in your newspapers how desperate this need is," he harped. "Russian soldier is best in the world but can only do so much."

The reporters didn't even have the heart to counter that if Soviet censors wouldn't tie their hands so, maybe their writing could have an effect on public opinion. They just sighed, shook their heads, and were glad when the guides told them to get into the cars for their next stop.

They spent that night in a field hospital, which was actually little more than several dugouts in a hillside. Alex was pleased to see it was fairly well equipped, with even an X-ray machine and decent, clean operating rooms. The staff consisted of seven surgeons, six doctors, and forty-eight nurses. There were only a handful of patients here now, the most seriously wounded who could not yet be moved, but in the heat of the battle a few days before, these medical personnel had been treating more than three hundred patients a day.

That night there was no dancing, no vodka, save quiet drinking by some to numb the horrors of the day. Few even had much appetite for the spread of food laid before them.

Cameron didn't know how it happened, but after the barely touched dinner, she found herself strolling around the compound flanked by Alex and Shanahan.

"I've seen it, but I still can't believe all the loss and devastation we've witnessed," Cameron murmured, thinking aloud more than making a statement to her friends.

"The other night after we ran into those partisans, I prayed for the first time in years," Alex said.

"Really, Alex? I thought you had given up your faith," Cameron said.

"So had I, but it seemed the only way to find a release for all the emotions churning inside me. Probably didn't do any good."

"There is something about war, I guess," Cameron replied, "that makes a person think of spiritual realms. I've been wondering a bit about God myself."

"Come on, you two!" cut in Shanahan in that snide way of his. "I would have thought the both of you had more backbone than that."

"I don't think it has anything to do with backbone or weakness," rejoined Alex. "There was a time when I believed faith in God was as much a part of my life as my heart or lungs."

"You used to be a religious fanatic, Doc?" Johnny barely hid his incredulity. "What happened? That mess in the States set you straight?"

Cameron gasped at Johnny's crassness.

Casting Cameron a look, Alex replied, "You told him?" She could tell he was disappointed in her, even though he hadn't said it was a big secret.

"No, I didn't," she answered quickly. "One of the other journalists was in Chicago at the time. He brought it up. I wouldn't—"

"I'm sorry," Alex said with earnest apology. "It's not a secret anyway. And yes, Johnny, that is what killed my faith. I learned I wasn't equal to it."

" 'Not equal to it,' " Johnny mimicked snidely. "You're a doctor, a good doctor, a smart man. You don't need it. You ought to just say good riddance."

"It's funny," mused Alex, "but despite all that has happened to me, I can't do that. I can't deny the existence of God or His innate power."

"Okay, if there is a god, then how can He let war happen, let the kind of destruction we've seen happen?"

A smile slanted Alex's lips. "That's an argument nearly all non-believers raise at one time or another. I've no answer, and I'm not sure it matters. But I am the last person right now to debate theology. I wonder what the meaning of it all is, too. I question God, as well."

"Oh, I'll tell you what the meaning of war is." Shanahan's smug look made Cameron roll her eyes. He had all the answers, or so he thought. "Warmongers, madmen, and tyrants perpetrate war in order to give reporters like me and Cameron grist for the mill. Wars are journalistic opportunities, and I say bless them! Praise them on high! Glory hallelujah!"

"Johnny," Cameron said, "if I believed you really felt that way, I'd have nothing to do with you."

"She's right, Johnny. I read your Pulitzer Prize–winning article—"

"Really?"

"Yes. It was nationally syndicated, wasn't it? It hit the Chicago papers, and I remember it. It was about a police standoff with a man holding his wife and two children hostage. He'd been beaten down by the Depression and had decided to end both his and his family's suffering. What you wrote moved me, and I don't think you could have done that without having been deeply moved yourself."

"I always say the most important thing in journalism is sincerity. If you can fake that, you got it made!" Johnny grinned.

If he had a soul, Cameron thought, he was going to guard it with his life.

"You weren't faking," Alex said firmly.

"Let's talk about something else," Johnny said. "All this talk about religion gives me the heebie-jeebies."

It seemed Alex was growing uncomfortable with the topic, as well, and he quickly changed the subject. "So what're you two going to write about this excursion?" Alex asked when they paused beneath a big oak that had lost all its leaves.

The evening was cold, but it wasn't raining for a change. An icy wind sliced through the compound, and Cameron shivered. Winter had not even begun, but she felt as icy as that wind, right to her bones.

"Do you mean now, or when we get home and can say what we really think?" Shanahan rejoined.

"What do you really think?" Cameron asked.

"War just ain't as much fun as I thought it would be," he said dryly.

Cameron thought of his previous seemingly contradicting words about the glories of war. Perhaps then he was just blowing hot air. She thought, too, of him frolicking in the woods with a pretty partisan and wondered at his statement. Yet, he had been awfully quiet since that night. What really had gone on between him and Tatiana?

"Do you ever feel that no matter how you represent what you've seen, you are going to cause problems?" Alex asked. Was he thinking as well of the affair with Oleg Gorbenko?

"Yeah," Johnny said. "What if I write about the devastation of this country, about the stinking little battle of Yelnya that the Russians won at the cost of—how many thousands of lives?—and of how they are retreating everywhere else in the country? Why, the folks back home might just say, 'What's the use? Let the Germans have Russia. They're just a bunch of Reds anyway.' No offense, Doc."

"What if we told about these Russian soldiers we have seen?" Cameron mused. "Sometimes they seem almost invincible—"

"Oh, that's easy," Shanahan cut in, his lips twisted smugly. "Then they'll say, 'Hey, them Ruskies don't need us. It ain't our war, anyway!'"

"And if you told the truth?" asked Alex.

"Come on, Doc. The first casualty of war is the truth," Johnny replied. "Nope, we are just left with the degree of untruth we wish to embrace."

"I disagree," Alex said. "You remember, I spent many years in the States. I believe the American people are not that dumb. They want the truth. They can deal with it. And no matter what comes of it, at least that outcome has been born of truth not of . . . well, propaganda."

The smirk that flitted across Shanahan's face seemed to say, "You are the idealistic fool I thought you were." But he had the good grace to keep quiet.

Instead, he said, "Well, let's just see what the press department lets us get away with—"

He stopped suddenly as an ambulance raced into the compound, its horn blaring. Several doctors and nurses ran out to meet it. Alex, whose instincts were honed to respond to that stimulus, instantly turned and hurried toward the ambulance, as well. It took Cameron and Shanahan a couple moments to follow.

The back doors of the vehicle had been flung open, and a stretcher was being lifted out. Cameron saw the strands of yellow hair hanging over the edge of the stretcher first. But that was all she could see because medical personnel were hovering over the patient. Someone was shouting orders. Then Alex, who was also bent over the patient, turned and focused a quick glance on Johnny. It was so brief that it could have meant nothing, but Cameron knew differently. Johnny did, too. He let out a sharp groan.

Cameron laid a hand on his arm. "Johnny, it might not—"

But he wrenched away from her grasp and propelled himself closer to the stretcher, which was already being pushed into the surgical dugout. Johnny raced to the door and would have gone in, but Alex was there blocking him.

"They've got to do surgery," Alex said grimly.

"It's her, then?" Johnny's voice was strangely hollow.

"Looks like she took a hit by a grenade."

"No . . ." Johnny groaned.

Cameron put an arm around him. "Let's find a place to wait. She'll be okay. These doctors see that sort of thing all the time, don't they, Alex?"

Alex licked his lips and shook his head. "It doesn't look good."

In less than fifteen minutes, the surgical team came out, their grim faces indicating their lack of success. The beautiful young partisan was gone. Tatiana had been as good as dead when they brought her in. Under normal circumstances—that is, in the heat of battle—the doctors would not have even tried to operate but would have taken someone with a better chance of survival.

Johnny walked away, and Cameron did not see him again until much later. He was sitting on a bench in the mess tent, his hands wrapped around a cup of coffee. She slipped onto the bench beside him.

"Don't say anything, Cameron. I know you mean well, but don't, okay?"

"Okay." She rose, poured herself a cup of coffee, and returned to her seat beside him.

They were silent for a good ten minutes. It was late and there were only a couple others in the tent, and they were quietly sipping coffee or tea, taking a break from the evening labors.

Finally Johnny said, "She knew she was going to die."

"You mean like a premonition or something?"

"No. They, the partisans, that is, all know they are going to die. She expected to die. If the Germans didn't get her, she would die of starvation because as the Russians retreat, the partisans are cut off from supplies. They are pretty much fighting a lost cause, and they know it." He paused, lifted his cup to his lips, and drank. "Bah! Its cold." He flung the rest of the contents onto the dirt floor.

"You want me to get you more?"

"I can get my own coffee!" he burst, then recanted. "Never mind me." He took a pack of cigarettes from his pocket and lit one, drawing in a deep lungful of smoke. "Every day she lived was like a gift to her."

Cameron remained silent. There was absolutely nothing to say.

"I'm not mourning for her, you know." And his tone sounded defensive. "I barely knew her. We shared . . . something nice, that's all."

"I know," Cameron murmured with sincere sympathy.

"She said—she did speak a little English, you know—she told me she didn't mind dying. She truly didn't. Everything she had and nearly everyone she loved had been destroyed by the war. Killing Germans was all she had left." He turned wasted eyes toward Cameron. "Why do I feel so rotten then, Hayes? She was already dead when I was with her."

"She couldn't have been, not really, for her to have touched you so."

"That's it, I guess. She was alive, so cursed alive!" He lurched suddenly to his feet. "I hate this war, Cameron." Then he strode away.

Cameron drank the rest of her now cold coffee. It did nothing for the chill consuming her body. Hugging her arms tightly around herself, she wanted to weep. For a woman she didn't know?

It was a crazy, ugly war, and she tried to remember why so many eons ago she had been eager to be part of it. She couldn't remember. She couldn't even cry.

PART V

"History knows no greater display of courage than that shown by the people of the Soviet Union."

Henry L. Stimson
U.S. Secretary of War under FDR

46

Los Angeles
October 1941

BLAIR HAD TWO DAYS to vacate the hotel. Seems she was compromising the sterling reputation of the place. Fact was, she had staggered into the lobby one too many times, and apparently the other night she had caused a bit of a scene at the elevator. She remembered none of it but took the manager's word for it.

Her impending eviction was just as well, since her money was running out and she could no longer afford a posh Hollywood hotel. Her mother had cut off the small dole she was slipping to Blair via Jackie. Apparently her father had found out about the money and had blown up. Her father was not about to be made a fool of again by his daughter.

Blair looked in the bathroom mirror, grimacing at the image that looked back at her. Dank platinum hair with serious darker blond roots showing—why bother to touch them up? Her audience at the Treasure Cove hardly seemed to care. Her once luminous blue eyes were dull, bloodshot, and the skin surrounding them was ringed in dark circles. She suddenly thought of Cynthia Bell, the gal she'd worked with in the chorus line of *Three on a Match*. How pathetic Cynthia had seemed, clinging to her fading youth. Now, Blair realized, she looked far worse than Cynthia ever had.

Who cared, anyway?

Blair certainly didn't. She seriously wondered why she continued on at all. Every day when the effects of the previous night's binge began to dissipate, she'd think about ending her life. She would lie on her bed and devise any number of creative ways to end her miserable existence. The simplest would be to use up the bottle of sleeping pills on the top shelf of her medicine cabinet. She opened the cabinet now. Yes, there it was waiting. . . .

There were twenty pills in the bottle. She had counted them only yesterday. They would be enough. If only . . .

If only she had the courage. But she was a coward. Why else did she try to numb her sensibilities every night with alcohol? She simply could not face the reality that the only time she had been truly happy was when she had been acting a lie—when she hadn't been her true self. That was pathetic enough, but there was more to it than that. She stayed drunk because she hadn't even been successful at perpetrating her lie. She was a worthless failure, just as she always knew she was—just as she had been told countless times by her father.

When the phone rang, Blair tried to ignore it. No one called her these days but Jackie. And she was the last person Blair wanted to see. Jackie would only preach at her, confront her with the stupidity of her deceptions.

The incessant ringing did not cease. Blair had not answered her phone in several days. The only way she knew it was Jackie calling was that her sister had sent her a couple of notes begging her to answer her phone. Blair knew she was torturing her sister, but she received no pleasure from the knowledge. The true irony was that down deep in her heart, Blair knew Jackie was her only true friend. How pathetic was that? Her only friend was someone she had nothing in common with.

Blair glanced once more at the bottle of sleeping pills sitting enticingly on the shelf.

"Not yet . . ." she murmured.

She shuffled into the sitting room. The phone continued to ring. Jackie was being more persistent than usual. The shrill sound seemed to pierce through Blair like sharp jabs of loneliness.

Yes, it made her feel lonely because she knew comfort and caring lay on the end of that telephone line. There would be someone to talk to, someone to listen to her. And deep in her heart, Blair knew Jackie would not really preach at her, nor would she say "I told you so." That's probably why she really wanted to avoid her sister. Blair had no idea at all what she would say to a listener such as Jackie, but oh, how splendid it would be to have another pair of eyes to look at that weren't leering and filled with lust. But Blair still hesitated in picking up the receiver. She longed for her sister, but she feared her, as well. Jackie had cajoled Blair to church the last time she was so down in the dumps. Blair did not want to risk that now. Though she had clearly used the church and religion and even God for her own ends before, she could not deny there had been a twinge of something real in the mess of her lies. Maybe it hadn't been in her own heart, but she had seen attributes in some of the people she'd encountered that had caused a deep longing within her. Though she had not seen perfection in a single person she had met at church, she had seen a peace in some that she knew came from knowing a God who accepted them no matter who they were. Of course, she reminded herself that none of them had likely done the kinds of things she had done. There was only so much God could accept, wasn't there?

Still the temptation to pick up that phone was strong in Blair. She even reached out her hand.

The ringing ceased as abruptly as a slap, but the sound continued to echo in Blair's ears. She had been so close to answering this time. But where could it lead? She did not deserve friends, nor a loving, accepting God.

———

Jackie hung up the phone and sighed. "Are you certain she hasn't moved out yet?"

The desk clerk shrugged. "All I know is she came in last night . . . like she usually does. And, well, I doubt she will be awake this early, much less in any shape to pack and such."

Jackie had just learned the news of Blair's imminent eviction. She had tried to talk the manager out of it but to no avail.

"Would you let me into her room?"

The man hesitated.

Jackie added, "She could be sick or something."

A doubtful smirk twisted the man's lips. "Sick, eh?" He then reached under the desk, fumbled a moment until he brought up a ring of keys. "It's nothing to me, anyway. Maybe you can help her pack."

Yes, Jackie supposed she could help Blair pack. But where would she go? Too bad Cameron had written a couple of months ago asking Jackie to see to the subletting of her apartment. Apparently she was confident enough in the success of her job that she did not feel the need to keep the apartment as a fallback. Jackie had found new tenants quickly—a couple of her girlfriends at UCLA who wanted to live off campus. They were now well entrenched in the tiny place, and there was no room for a third roommate.

Perhaps another hotel. But even before the blowup with Gary, Blair had confided to Jackie that she could no longer afford a hotel. Maybe things were desperate enough so that Blair would consider quitting her job—there must be a way for her to get out of that contract, if that was all that was keeping her there. If she quit her job, maybe she could come back home. But even Jackie hated to see Blair do that and, in essence, come crawling back to their father. Blair's shaky self-esteem might not withstand that kind of blow.

Jackie went through a list of acquaintances in her mind. There were some who might take her on a temporary basis but none who would put up with Blair's present excesses. Perhaps one of Blair's Hollywood friends, but Jackie decided that would be worse than sending a drunk to a liquor store for a loaf of bread.

There must be some way to help Blair. Jackie remembered her talk with Sam and her decision not to interfere, but she *had* interfered, and now it seemed she must keep doing so to make things right. It wasn't Jackie's fault Blair had perpetuated her deception, but she had orchestrated getting Blair and Gary together. Yet despite the fact that Blair had been living a lie with Gary, Jackie was still certain the lie had started becoming truth within Blair. Had she only been allowed a little more time, her heart would surely have changed for real. The changes Jackie had seen in Blair had been real, she was certain, only for some reason Blair had been unable to admit it. Jackie had even felt hopeful when the two had married. She'd been so confident it all would come out okay.

Well, it hadn't. And Jackie felt she had to do something about it. If only she could get Blair and Gary back together. He was the best thing that had ever happened to Blair. But Gary was thousands of miles away.

The desk clerk cleared his throat to get Jackie's attention. She'd nearly forgotten he was there. He jangled the keys in her face.

"Look, I'm busy. You want to go up to her room, or not?" he asked sharply.

At Blair's door, Jackie knocked several times.

———

The sound of that knock was like a reprieve to Blair. When the phone had stopped ringing, she had accepted her loneliness, only this time, for some reason it was harder. Everything was harder. She knew now, if she hadn't before her deception, that there was something better out there. A life of peace and happiness beckoned her. If only she had been able to tell Gary that she really did love him. Why had her pride reared up then of all times? She certainly hadn't had enough pride to keep from lying about herself then or to stay sober now. But for some crazy reason she was too proud to open her heart and soul to the man she loved. Her husband.

Goodness! She was a mixed-up girl. Probably crazy, as well.

Now someone was knocking on her door. Jackie? Had she been calling from the lobby? Most likely it was just the hotel manager come to expedite her eviction.

She walked to within three feet of the door and stared at it.

"Blair, are you in there? I really want to see you," Jackie's voice came, the voice of reprieve.

Blair just stood there.

"Come on, sis! I've cut my classes today to come here," Jackie pressed.

Blair reached out her hand, her need *not* to be alone overcoming her desire for punishment.

Blair opened the door a crack. Much to her chagrin the desk clerk was with Jackie.

"Look, Miss Hayes, you had best start packing," said the desk clerk.

Blair nodded, let Jackie squeeze in through the smallest crack possible in the door, then closed it. Turning, she noted her sister's doe eyes just gaping at her.

"You look a fright, Blair!"

"I'm so glad I let you in," Blair said with affront that was only partly feigned. "I really needed to hear that."

"I'm sorry, but it's kind of a shock, that's all." Jackie moved into the room, then sank down on the sofa. Patting the place beside her, she added, "Come on, sit down. Let's talk."

Blair found herself obeying. She wanted to be hard, sarcastic, closed, but seeing the warmth and love Jackie was offering made that attitude impossible for Blair. She sat beside her sister, curled her feet up under her, and waited. She didn't know what to say or what her sister wanted to hear, so she decided to let Jackie take the lead.

"I'm sorry I interfered," Jackie launched ahead. "I'll probably be sorry for interfering now. Sam said I shouldn't, but I just can't stand by and see you do this to yourself—"

"Who's Sam?" Blair cut in. "I don't much like the thought of you talking to total strangers about me."

Jackie got a wounded look on her face. She obviously realized she'd made yet another mistake, but Blair felt sorry for her. Jackie was just trying to do the right thing. She was barely twenty years old and was having to carry a heavy load because of Blair.

"I just needed to talk to someone," Jackie replied. "He's not a stranger to me. I value his opinion, and you have had me awfully confused these last couple of months."

All Blair's lingering ire dissipated completely. "I'm sorry for doing that to you. I put you in a bad position. I put everyone in a bad position. What a mess I've made of things!"

"Anyway, you can trust Sam to keep my confidence."

"Well, who is he? A new boyfriend? What happened to Jeffrey?"

"Jeffrey never meant anything to me. Mom liked him far more than I ever did. But Sam is only a friend, a very wise and dear friend."

"A *friend*, huh?" It felt rather good to Blair to focus on someone besides herself for a moment.

But Jackie wasn't going to let that happen. "We're here to talk about you, Blair."

"That is a far too depressing topic."

"I want to know one thing." Jackie's doe eyes lost some of their warmth, replaced by an incisiveness that made her look much like Cameron for a moment.

"What?"

"Do you love Gary?"

"Who cares?"

"I care. Gary cares."

Blair wanted to deny her true feelings yet again. What would it help to dwell on something that made no difference now? Even though Gary had made no moves toward annulling the marriage, Blair had to accept the fact that it was over. She hadn't heard a single word from him, so that must be proof enough. But looking into her sister's honest, guileless gaze, Blair was suddenly very sick of lies. She wanted someone to know what was in her heart, even if that someone couldn't be

Gary. She needed someone to believe that she wasn't a completely evil person, that there had been some small particle of truth in all her deceptions.

"Yes, Jackie, I love . . . him . . ." The words caught as unexpected emotion clogged her throat. Sudden tears spilled from her eyes.

Jackie grasped Blair's hand. "Did you tell him?"

Blair shook her head. "W-what g-good would it have done? How could he b-believe me with all my other lies?"

Jackie fished a handkerchief from her purse and gave it to Blair, who took it, blew her nose, and tried to staunch the flow of tears.

"I want you to think about something," Jackie said, with a look of acumen that belonged so much more to Cameron than to sweet Jackie. "What's the real lie, sis?"

"What do you mean?"

"Is the lie the person you tried to be with Gary? Or is it the person—the empty, rebellious, bad girl—that you have tried to be all your life?"

Blair barked a mirthless laugh. "That is even crazier than all the other craziness I have caused lately! And I am surprised that you of all people are trying to justify what I have done. I mocked the things you hold dear, didn't I? I mocked God, the church, Mom, apple pie, probably even the flag!"

"I'm not trying to justify anything. I know what you did was wrong. Yet I also know you didn't do it maliciously."

Blair jumped up. Unthinkingly, she strode to the wet bar in the corner of the room. The bottles of liquor glittered before her, but oddly they offered no enticement. She was more clearheaded now than she had been in days, and that sensation held an appeal. Talking to her sister had taken some of the edge off her depression. Jackie's words wedged a hope within her that she found herself desperately clinging to.

"I didn't do anything with maliciousness in my heart, Jackie, though I don't know why I did do it," she said, still staring at the bottles. "It just felt so good to be treated tenderly and with respect by a man. I would have become a real Christian in order to deserve it. But it was all so confused. I knew any confession of faith would have been just too weird. Even God wouldn't have been able to separate the real from the fake."

"Yes, He would, Blair."

"I tried, you know . . ." Blair turned and forced her gaze to meet her sister's. "Once I said the prayer, like you told me, accepting Jesus into my heart. But I did it just so I could say I did it, so you wouldn't harp on me anymore. Nothing happened. It wasn't real."

"Did you want it to be real?"

Blair let out a ragged sigh, then strode to a chair opposite the sofa and flopped down dejectedly. "I don't know what I want! Do I want to pray the prayer in order to get Gary? Do I want it to help erase all the lies? Do I want it so I can escape the miserable pit my life has become? Or . . . do I want it because I love God?"

"I never knew you were so complex, Blair," Jackie said with a little chuckle.

"Neither did I. I am finding out things about myself lately that—" She stopped abruptly and shook her head. "It's all rather scary."

"Okay . . ." Jackie hesitated, seeming to find her direction even as she was speaking. "What is at the very core, Blair? What do you really and truly want?"

"I want what I had with Gary these last two months. I want it to be real," Blair answered without hesitation.

"But you can't have that until God becomes a reality to you."

"You see why I can't pray the salvation prayer, don't you? I just can't sort out my motives. Maybe in time . . ." But what Blair feared most was that in time she would destroy herself before she could work out her motives. If only she'd had more time with Gary. She wasn't sure how that would have helped, but she knew something inside her needed him. Perhaps if she needed God that much all her problems would be solved. Yet, in a way, she knew that need was deep within her as well. Each was wrapped up in the other. On one hand she knew it wasn't right to find God in order to get Gary, but conversely, she sensed she might not be able to truly work out her confusion about God without Gary.

But Gary was thousands of miles away.

Then the idea came to Blair. It was as insane as everything else. Nevertheless, she leaned forward in her chair, a sense of expectancy growing inside her. Hope, for the first time in a long time welled up in her heart.

"Jackie, do you think I could finagle one last loan from Mom?"

"Dad is keeping a pretty close eye on things."

"I would probably need several hundred dollars."

"What are you thinking?"

"I'm thinking about doing some traveling."

Jackie's eyes narrowed. "Are you considering going to the Philippines?"

"I've got to see Gary again," Blair said emphatically. "I believe that's the only way I can work all this out."

"I don't know, Blair . . . what if—?" But she stopped abruptly.

Blair somehow knew what she was thinking. "What if Gary rejects me outright, tells me that he doesn't want some lying, mixed-up woman in his life?" She smiled ironically. "Then I'll need God more than ever, and I can turn to him without fear of my motives."

Jackie blinked, then allowed herself a reluctant smile.

"I know now I have to do something." Blair rose. "Come with me a minute."

Jackie followed her to the bathroom. Blair opened the medicine cabinet, took out the bottle of sleeping pills, and handed them to her sister. Jackie stared at the bottle, aghast. She understood clearly the significance they held.

"Maybe I'll find myself in the Philippines, Jackie, maybe I won't. But I am pretty certain what's going happen to me if I stay here."

Jackie wrapped her hand around the bottle, then dropped it into her pocket. Tears brimming her eyes, she put her arms around Blair. They held each other for a long time, both crying. For the first time, perhaps in her entire life, Blair felt good. She had been honest at last, with her sister and with herself.

47

Moscow
October 1941

"GOT YA AGAIN, Hayes!" Shanahan gloated as he passed Cameron on his way out of the cable office.

"You may have speed, but I have quality," she rejoined gamely.

There had been quite a race among the reporters to get to the cable office upon their return to Moscow from the Russian Front. But Cameron wasn't too upset that Johnny had beat her on the West Coast scoop. He appeared pretty much back to his old self since the death of Tatiana. Only Cameron could see the haze of hollowness about him. The snide remarks, the wisecracks, held a kind of desperation, as if he was just going through the motions. But she also knew him well enough to know he wasn't going to become maudlin about recent events, and he definitely did not want others to become so toward him. His attitude of "business as usual" suited Cameron. It simply didn't help to dwell on the negative.

When she returned to the Metropole after filing her "With the Russian Army" dispatch, she found Bob Wood waiting for her in the lobby.

"Perfect timing!" he said. "I was about to leave you a message but a person-to-person talk is preferable. Shall we take a stroll around Red Square?"

"Of course." She did not question his urge to stroll outside where the autumn breeze was chilly and ominous clouds portended rain. She knew there must be only one reason why Wood, who had seldom socialized with her in the past, would seek her out now. And if this visit had to do with Oleg Gorbenko, it best be held out of doors, away from prying ears and possible listening devices.

"Sorry," Bob said as a chill breeze caught them in the face almost immediately upon stepping outside.

"I'm getting used to the cold. You should have seen what I had to put up with at the Front."

"I'd like to hear about your experiences sometime," he said. "I hope to join some of the diplomatic staff on a tour soon."

"It better be soon. It didn't appear any too secure out there, though the Russians made a great deal of their 'victory.' " A gust of wind skittered toward them, and Cameron paused in order to hold her woolen beret to her head. "Well, another time for all that, Bob," she added, "perhaps over hot tea *indoors*. I have a feeling you have other matters to discuss. I hope so, at least, and I hope it is good news."

He smiled. Cameron hadn't noticed before, but he appeared so young. He must be thirty, but he looked twenty and fresh out of college. And he didn't fit the Jewish stereotypes, either. He was rather pale with sandy hair, and adding to his youthfulness, his chin seemed covered only with peach fuzz. His wire-rimmed eyeglasses added to his collegiate air.

"I think I do have some good news," he said. "I have come up with a way to get your friend out"—he paused and glanced around before continuing—"of the country." He was looking very nervous.

"You have? How? My goodness, I wondered if there was any way of doing it. I couldn't believe all the checkpoints and such we had to go through on my jaunt in the country, and we looked quite official. A lone man traveling . . . well, it just isn't happening, especially not without papers."

Though Cameron's focus had, much to her embarrassment, been on other things during the tour of the Front, she had given some attention to such matters. But it had seemed too negative to waste much thought on. She really couldn't get very enthusiastic about Bob's announcement.

"Going north, west, or south is out of the question, of course," agreed Wood. "The only possibility is east."

"The only way he could do that is on the railroad. Any other way of crossing Siberia this time of year would be impossible. I hate to sound so negative, Bob." She turned to face him. "I have to confess, I haven't even broached the idea with him. Seeing the state of the country this past week hasn't exactly filled me with hope for anything."

"Anything we attempt will be fraught with danger," Bob admitted. "He must weigh this against his desire to get his story heard. Didn't you mention he lives in fear of arrest anyway? So it may be six of one, half a dozen of the other to him. In any case, I have solved the key problem with escape. I have found a way for him to obtain forged papers."

Cameron chuckled dryly. "I didn't even think of that." She tried not to think of all the other details they might forget. Perhaps Bob was more competent in these matters than she thought.

His next words did not make that hopeful. "I hadn't considered it, either. But I spoke to a colleague—"

"You told someone else about Oleg?"

"I had to, but I did so only in general terms. But I needed to talk with someone, and it was a good thing because it was he who mentioned the need for travel documents. I was rather thinking we could simply stow him away aboard one of the diplomatic airplanes that arrive from time to time."

"That sounds like a good plan."

"Too many people would have to be involved and give their approval. And we will not receive embassy sanction of this or any plan for getting your young man out of the country. You understand, we must act completely on our own in this?"

With a sigh, Cameron nodded. "So then . . . forged papers and a trip east on the railroad. Sounds simple, too simple."

"You are beginning to sound quite Russian in your pessimistic outlook." He gave her a sympathetic grin. "Just keep thinking that the simpler, the better—less to go wrong."

They had been walking briskly and by mutual agreement paused by the GUM department store for breath. Though it was midafternoon, there wasn't much activity here. Stalin had requisitioned many of the shops in the building for use as office space. The remainder simply had little goods to entice shoppers these days. Cameron was tempted to suggest they duck inside out of the wind to continue their conversation, but she suddenly felt too vulnerable in this all but deserted space.

"Bob," she said as they continued once again on their way, "do you think the risks are worth it?"

"I wouldn't be taking them if I didn't." There was a confidence in his tone she had not noted in the past. "I know from personal experience that one cannot look Oleg in the eye without being deeply moved by what he has to say. It is imperative that others also hear him."

"Okay, that's enough for me. I'll run this by Oleg as soon as possible. I'm almost certain he'll agree to the plan. He will have his family's safety to consider, but I have a feeling they are accustomed to these kinds of risks." Her own confidence was returning. "Tell me about this forger you know."

———

Cameron told Sophia that evening when they met to attend the nightly press conference. The idea of defecting was not an entirely new one to her; in fact, Oleg had been talking about trying to escape the country. The family had talked him out of it.

"Does that mean your family won't support him in this?" Cameron asked.

"They will not like the idea, but they will support him—us."

"Him," Cameron corrected pointedly.

"No, Miss Hayes. If my Oleg goes, I will also go."

Cameron blinked with surprise at the girl's hard stand on this issue. She didn't even try to argue with her. Of course "day" and "night" must remain together. They needed each other too much to be parted.

"Then the first step is to get the travel papers," Cameron said. "You must have photos of you and Oleg taken by the forger. The man who does the documents is at—"

"Miss Hayes, I know I am expected to go to this man, and normally I would not hesitate, but I am being closely watched. We are fairly certain the NKVD has learned Oleg escaped from the Germans and has not reported to his unit. They are watching me and the rest of the family. I don't believe they realize he is in Moscow, but they do expect him to show up here sooner or later. It is more difficult than ever to lose my watchers. I can come here to the hotel, to the Narkomindel, and to my home, but anyplace else raises great suspicion."

"I'm in a similar position." Cameron glanced at her wristwatch. Soon they would have to leave the hotel for the press conference. "Perhaps if you could take your own photos with appropriate disguises—"

"My papa has a good camera, if the forger can develop the film."

"I'm certain he has the equipment." Cameron thought a moment. She didn't like further complications, but she supposed that went with the territory. "Now we need someone we can trust who isn't under scrutiny, someone who can deliver the photos and pick up the finished documents. That leaves out any foreigners and your family. But who?" She didn't like the idea that suddenly popped into her head. But it was all she could think of.

"Miss Hayes. . . ?"

"It is probably best I not say anything more, Sophia. I think that is how spies work, isn't it? The right hand not knowing what the left hand is doing? Anyway, just get me those photos tomorrow morning."

"So we are to become spies now?" Sophia asked with a worried look.

"Only in the best sense of the word." Cameron gave her an encouraging smile. How she wished she could have some of Johnny's cocky attitude now.

"I fear for you much." Sophia grasped Cameron's hands in hers. There was an intimacy in her eyes that had not been there in the past. They had suddenly gone beyond the employer-employee terms of their relationship. Cameron hoped they were now more friends than accomplices.

"Sophia, there is a saying, one that I used to bandy about much in my days of riding roughshod over anyone in order to get a story. It goes something like this, 'In order to make an omelet you must break some eggs.' Now I will probably find out what it feels like to be one of the eggs. We all will, I suppose. But this thing is more important than each of us as individuals. Oleg has known that all along. We are doing something that could really make a difference in this world. I accept the risks, as I know you and Oleg do. Let's just leave it at that, then."

Her eyes brimming with moisture, Sophia nodded, then, apparently unable to speak, threw her arms around Cameron, who returned the embrace, her own eyes feeling rather moist, as well.

HE LOOKED every bit like a physician making a house call with his black bag prominently in hand. His other hand clasped an umbrella over his head. Rain was falling in an unrelenting drizzle, further proof of his ruse—only a man who absolutely had to would have dared this weather. The streets were all but deserted of pedestrians, and the only moving vehicles besides a few automobiles were military trucks and vehicles. It was three in the afternoon and nearly dark.

Alex had chosen this time for his trek across town because the evening shadows would provide nice cover, but it was still too early for the air raids to start. He decided, as he splashed through the drenched streets, that it was an altogether peculiar circumstance that he was complicit in aiding the defection of a Russian citizen—he who had in essence defected *to* Russia three years ago. But then again, he would be the last person the NKVD would suspect of being involved in such activity.

Cameron had made the perfect choice in him as her accomplice. He was glad she had asked him, though she had done so with great reluctance. He reminded her that he also had close ties to Oleg and his family-by-marriage. He wasn't certain this idea of Oleg defecting in order to get his story out was the best plan, but it was an admirable plan. And when Alex realized Oleg was determined to go through with it no matter what, he knew he must help make it as successful, and safe, as possible. Of those involved, Alex was under the least scrutiny. He did have the usual NKVD tail, but it was slipshod at best. They simply did not have the stamina to keep up with a Russian doctor's demanding schedule.

This particular time Alex had lost his man after the first metro stop. It was obvious he was going to see a patient—a patient he had visited a few days ago. In fact, Alex had gone to the "patient" three days ago with Sophia's and Oleg's photographs. He now was going to pick up the finished travel documents.

It had all gone quite smoothly. When Alex returned to the hospital an hour later, he was proud of his part in the scheme. He was a little nervous carrying around the forged documents, but that was only natural Russian paranoia. Still, he could not help feeling relief when he handed the papers over to Dr. Fedorcenko, who would make the final delivery to his daughter Sophia.

Still, Alex made it clear he was available to help in any other way.

"Thank you, my friend," Yuri said as he tucked the papers carefully within his shirt. They were alone in a consulting room at the hospital. "But you have done much already."

"Everything is set, then?"

Yuri nodded but with reluctance.

"You still have misgivings?" Alex asked.

"I do not want to think what will happen if this fails. But"—he shook his head morosely—"if it succeeds, I will lose my little Sophia. I am torn, you see."

"At least she will have Andrei and Talia when they get to America."

"I must keep thinking of that. I'll envy Sophia that. Sometimes I miss my brother and sister and Talia tremendously. It has been twenty-three years since I last saw them, but we had such a bond, especially Andrei and Talia and I. If I let myself dwell on it, I still feel such a pain at the loss."

Alex well understood Yuri's emotions regarding his brother and sister who had defected to the States shortly after the Revolution. Alex did not know Yuri's sister, Mariana, or her husband, Daniel Trout, who lived in New York, but he was quite close to Yuri's brother, Andrei and his wife, Talia. They had been close friends of Alex and of his parents. Andrei had been instrumental in the Rostov family's journey toward God. And Andrei had stood by Alex during his difficulties three years ago. He, too, missed the big bear of a Russian.

"Maybe someday you can visit them. The war may bring new freedoms to this country," Alex offered.

"I have never been allowed to leave the country, not even for medical conferences and such. I can't imagine it ever happening. Nor can I imagine myself defecting. I feel I have work to do here, that in staying I may do some small good for my country. No, I must accept that when a loved one goes away, it is a permanent thing."

"I am so sorry, Yuri." Alex laid a comforting hand on Yuri's shoulder.

Yuri patted Alex's hand and gave him an appreciative glance. "God has given me the strength to bear it. For that I am thankful."

"It is good you have that, then."

"Do you truly think so?"

Alex smiled slightly, then turned and walked to the small window in the office. He thought about his many revelations during the tour of the Front. He wanted to casually shrug off Yuri's comment, but he could not do it; neither could he say for a certainty he was able to fully embrace his old faith. He opened his mouth to say as much to his friend, to perhaps even share some of the spiritual quandaries he had been considering. But the blare of the loudspeaker stopped him.

"Dr. Rostovscikov wanted in post-op immediately."

"We must talk sometime, Yuri," he merely said as he strode to the door. "Perhaps when all this with Sophia has been taken care of."

———

Sophia waited impatiently at the end of the street. The heavy rains had abated for the time being, but the clouds overhead were dark and heavy. Her impatience, however, did not spring from the inclement weather. Rather, it was because Oleg was late. He had not wanted her to come to his hiding place to get him. She did not understand why, because she had met him there twice already since their plan had been put into motion.

"I do not want to tempt fate," he had told her the last time she had seen him, two days ago, when they had made the final arrangements for their escape.

"We can trust our Lord," she had gently reminded him. "We need not be concerned with fate."

He had smiled then, and as always, the rare gesture was just a bit out of place among his darkly intense features. Yet that only made it more endearing, more appealing to Sophia. He took her into his arms and kissed her with the passion he had for all that he cared about intensely. His touch always made her feel vital, alive. She desperately needed that, especially now. She was not surprised when he uttered a similar sentiment.

"Sophia, I need you so!" he murmured into her ear. "Yet I fear I am being selfish letting you come with me."

"We cannot be parted again, Oleg. I could not bear it."

He brushed back a strand of her hair, damp now from being close to him. "I know," he breathed. "Nor could I. But still, you must not come back here. It is not a very clever hiding place, only a basement in a bombed-out building."

"But I have not been followed."

"Yes, but they will soon catch on. You will meet me tomorrow at the end of the street, two blocks over, by that little china shop."

And now she had been waiting a half hour past the appointed time. They had allowed an hour lead time before the eastbound train arrived at the Kazanskiy station, but if Oleg did not arrive soon, they would miss the train, the last until tomorrow. But each delay of their escape made them that much more vulnerable to discovery. Sophia knew Oleg was on "borrowed time," as she'd heard Americans put it.

For all she knew, he could have been arrested during the night. Or he could be ill, or perhaps hurt in last night's air raid, though this section of town had not been hit lately. With her mind whirling with fearsome possibilities, she decided she would give him another five minutes, then would go to the basement to look for him.

And then she saw him approach. Her heart skipped a beat as relief and joy washed over her. She wanted to run into his arms and hug and kiss him fiercely, but she could not cause a scene. With great restraint, she picked up her traveling satchel and met him.

"I'm sorry to be late," he said. "There were workmen inspecting the building. I had to wait until they were gone." His words were simple, matter-of-fact, but Sophia wondered what hid beneath them, the fear and tension he must have suffered as he waited in the building expecting at any moment to be found.

They had to hurry to the station, and Sophia feared in their haste they were not as careful as they should have been. But once at the station, they were easily lost in the crowds of refugees trying to leave Moscow for safer regions in the East. Still, Oleg's expression was more intense than usual. He kept looking around, his eyes stabbing their surroundings like daggers.

"Oleg, you must relax," she implored.

He only nodded, but she could see he was full of tension. She was, as well, and perhaps she also looked it, but they must make themselves appear to be normal travelers.

"This has been too easy," he muttered.

"That is good." But she didn't really feel her optimistic response. It had been easy, but she was certain she had not been followed. "I'm going to go buy a newspaper. Maybe that will help you relax."

"Sophia, no—"

But she had already turned, and a stream of people had come between them.

———

Oleg was about to go after her. This was no time to be separated. The train was due to arrive at any time.

Then he saw the uniformed police. Of course, there were always guards at the station, especially these days with so many citizens seeking transportation. Yet now there seemed to be more than usual. Worse than that, there were several men in black leather jackets. They had to be NKVD. Was this profusion of police just a coincidence? They could be looking for someone else.

Oleg knew he had to relax, had to act normal. He could just calmly catch up to Sophia—

Suddenly, as his gaze almost unconsciously scanned the crowd, he made eye contact with one of the NKVD agents. It was brief, but enough. Instinctively, Oleg spun around and started running. It was the worst thing he could do, he realized, but his only thought was to draw attention away from Sophia. He knew his ruse was over in that instant of eye contact, for he'd seen a flash of recognition in the agent's eyes. If the agent had not known Oleg specifically, he had known that look of fear in Oleg's eyes. The agent had known this was a fugitive.

"Stop!" yelled the agent.

Oleg crashed through the crowd, jostling and bumping anyone in his way. Someone stumbled to the ground, but Oleg did not pause. Others started screaming and yelling, making way as best they could for the police, who had joined the agent in the chase. The wail of the train whistle joined the noise of the mob and pierced through Oleg like the pain of regret. They would not board that train, their way to freedom.

He chanced only once a hurried look over his shoulder and caught a single final glimpse of Sophia staring at him in stark devastation.

———

Sophia's first instinct was to run after him, be with him no matter what. How foolish of her to have left him. For a newspaper! How could she have been so stupid? The one time he truly needed her support, her calming presence, and she had left him.

Her good sense prevailed over her instinct, leaving her to stand by helplessly and watch disaster strike. Another deeper instinct told her he was making a sacrifice in order to protect her, and she had to give that some meaning. So she watched her beloved being chased like an animal, watched as one leather-coated agent, a big brute of a man, tackled Oleg, the two sprawling out on the marble floor of the station. Oleg struggled against his captor until a huge fist smashed into his face and blood sprayed from Oleg's nose and mouth.

Sophia gasped, but no one seemed to notice. The crowd had all but swallowed her up.

The agent, now assisted by two others, hauled Oleg to his feet and cuffed his hands behind his back. They dragged him away, right past Sophia. Oleg did not spare her a single look. Her heart broke because she knew what ignoring her had cost him. She knew he longed for her comfort, her nearness if nothing else. It was costing her the same.

Miraculously, Oleg was not the only one to ignore her. The other guards and agents paid her no attention at all. That made her almost certain Oleg had been caught in a broader net, that they had not been specifically followed, otherwise she surely would have been sought, as well. Still, the result was the same. Their escape plot was foiled. Oleg was caught and gone from her.

Sophia turned and left the station, reaching the sidewalk just as the black NKVD vehicle with Oleg inside was pulling away. The rain had started again and splashed her in the face. Before she became soaked, she ducked beneath the eaves of a building. Only then did her mind calm enough to wonder what to do next. Her first thought was to go home, but that was on the other side of town, and by the time she got there, the police might have sorted out Oleg's identity and gone to the apartment, perhaps to arrest her, as well. Best she keep away from there for the time being. Of course, agents might also be at the Metropole waiting for her, but that was only a mile away. Certainly she could get there before the police. Anything she did now was dangerous, but she had to talk to someone she could trust. She could not think straight at the moment. She needed help.

49

CAMERON STARED at her plate of half-eaten food as she sat in the hotel dining room. There were about a dozen others dining, and the place was abuzz with several conversations, but she was sitting alone trying to distract herself by eating dinner. She was being quite unsuccessful at it because her stomach was in knots.

The eastbound train should have left by now. She had never felt more helpless. She had so wanted to see Oleg and Sophia safely to the station, but her presence would have been not only extraneous, but possibly dangerous, as well. In fact, she had done next to nothing in actual footwork in the escape scheme. But she had been instrumental in getting it off the ground. She had spurred Bob Wood into enlisting his contacts—the forger and also a sea captain in Vladivostok who would take Oleg and Sophia across the Bering Sea to Alaska. She had encouraged Oleg to take the chance.

In one sense, she had very little to do with the success of the plan, but she knew she'd have everything to do with its failure.

"Sweetheart, you look awful!" Johnny's chipper voice interrupted her thoughts. He sauntered toward her. "That's what you get for eating this hotel food. Now, I know a little place—"

"Not now, Johnny!" she snapped, then quickly relented. "I'm sorry. You didn't deserve that. I've just got a lot on my mind."

He slid into the seat opposite her. "I thought something was up these last couple of days—"

"Not here!" she said with a quick glance around.

"Doll, keep your cool." He grinned and chuckled as if she'd just cracked a joke. "Just smile and have a nice normal conversation with me, and for heaven's sake, don't keep looking around! So tell Uncle Johnny what's up."

"I can't."

"Now my feelings are truly hurt." Pausing, he grinned and laughed. "At least that little snip of a secretary of yours trusts me—"

"What do you mean?" Cameron gasped.

"Smile, baby, smile," he reminded her.

It wasn't easy, but she made her lips form a huge grin and even managed a chirruping giggle. Still smiling, she said, "What about Sophia?"

"She just waylaid me outside the hotel."

"Oh no!" And she kept grinning like a fool, despite the twisting of her stomach.

Johnny laughed again, then said, "Follow my lead, okay?" She nodded and he went on, "Hey, baby, let's go get some real food. I've got ration coupons burning a hole in my pocket."

"Sounds good, Johnny." She dropped her napkin on the table and rose.

First she had to fetch her coat from her room—it would definitely arouse suspicions if she rushed outside in the icy rain in only her dress. Five excruciating minutes later, they left the hotel arm in arm, strolling casually as if they had not a single care. At least outside they could talk more openly. They might be followed, but they could not be heard.

"Okay, Johnny, tell me. Now!"

He held an umbrella over their heads, and they kept walking. "I don't know much," he answered with a pointed frown. "But she called to me from the shadows halfway down the block from the hotel. I knew enough to be coy. I pretended to bend down to tie my shoe, and I don't think we were noticed. She said she was in trouble and needed to talk to you. I think she'd been waiting out front for some time. Poor girl was soaking wet. She was afraid to come directly to you. I told her to meet us at the Kuznetskiy Café, you know, the one near the Bolshoi Theater."

Cameron started to run a hand through her hair, forgetting her wool hat, which she nearly knocked off. Setting it straight, she took a deep, steadying breath. "Was she alone?"

"As far as I could see. But I tried not to look too closely at her hiding place. So what gives, Cameron? It sounds pretty serious."

She was reluctant to tell Johnny. He would think her a fool for trying to get Oleg out of the country. He'd never thought the story of the massacre should be broadcast in the first place. Yet Johnny, if he was nothing else, was the most resourceful person she knew. She had a sour feeling in the pit of her gut that she'd need someone like that now. In the few minutes it took to traverse the couple of blocks to the café, she told him all about the plan. When he refrained from even a hint of his usual sarcasm and did not reproach her in the slightest, she could have hugged him.

"That was a pretty brave thing you did," he said finally.

"I hardly did anything. And it looks like it's been botched anyway."

"Still, you did what you believed in." There was pride and conviction in his tone.

She was glad they reached the café just then so that she didn't have to respond. She knew she would have been able to reply to his jibes far easier than to his sincerity.

Before drawing near to the café entrance, they paused and waited a few moments. But there was no one suspicious hanging about outside. And it also appeared as if they had not been followed. Inside, Sophia was seated at a corner table. The place was deserted, and Cameron wondered if this was the best situation for a meeting. Yet there seemed to be no agents lurking about. They appeared in the clear for now.

Sophia's face was pale, and she was shivering as she greeted Cameron and Johnny with the merest twitch of her lips. It seemed she could not manage even a polite smile. Cameron slid into the seat beside her and took Sophia's hands into hers, while Johnny sat opposite them. The girl's hands were icy cold. Cameron took off her own gloves and gave them to Sophia.

"Maybe these will help a little," Cameron said. Sophia gratefully slipped on the dry woolen gloves, murmuring something about dropping hers at the station. "What happened?" Cameron asked softly, as gently as she could, ignoring her inner urge to scream her own anxiety.

"He was arrested at the station," Sophia answered, her voice as pale as her coloring, as if she could not bear even uttering the awful words.

"You were followed?"

"No, I don't think so. I believe it was a random thing. I had gone to buy a newspaper. I thought it might relax him. He was very nervous. He just looked suspicious, and I think the guards saw that. And he ran—to protect me, I am sure. To draw them away from me." Tears began to spill from her eyes. "I should never have left him, even for a minute!"

"Don't talk that way, Sophia. These things happen, that's all." She gave the girl's hand a reassuring squeeze and could still feel the icy-cold fingers through the fabric of the gloves. "Let's not waste time with blame, okay?" She was telling herself that as well as her secretary. Yet she could not keep from feeling responsible. Nor could she ignore the nagging inner suspicion that her efforts had not been entirely noble. She had *wanted* to get that story out. Not only for the vindication of murdered Jews, but she feared also for the professional coup it represented. Swallowing down the taste of gall rising in her throat, she looked at Johnny.

"She's right," he said to Sophia.

Though Cameron hadn't been expecting that kind of support, she was grateful for it.

"We gotta figure out how much hot water you are in—"

"I don't care about myself!" Sophia protested.

"Well, you'd better start to care for yourself," Johnny said firmly, "if you want to help your husband. It looks like you might be in the clear as far as today's events—wait a minute! Who has the forged papers?"

"I do," Sophia said. "I have both because I hadn't had time to give Oleg his."

"That's good. If Oleg had had yours on him, then the jig would be up for both of you."

"The 'jig'?" Sophia's brow creased in perplexity.

"Johnny, speak English so the poor girl can follow the conversation," Cameron said.

"Okay, first thing you gotta do is get rid of those papers. Where are they?" When she patted the satchel next to her, he added, "Give 'em to me, and I'll destroy them. I don't even want you to leave here with them. Next, and this'll be the hardest thing, you have to go about your life just like nothing has happened. The police will definitely question you, and you have to play dumb. You don't know anything! Understand?"

"But maybe if I told them he was trying to make his way back to his unit—"

"At the Kazan Station? They'll never believe it. There's nothing you can say that will help him—"

"Johnny!" Cameron thought he was being a bit harsh.

Gentling his tone, he went on, "Sophia, I think you know the kind of trouble your husband is in. I don't mean to be cruel, but I think I am speaking for him when I say the most important thing now is for you and your family to keep away from the repercussions of whatever happens to him. It's what he would want most, isn't it?"

She nodded, teary-eyed. She then sucked in a breath as she swiped a hand across her damp eyes. "Thank you, Mr. Shanahan, for your honesty. You are right, of course."

There was no smugness in his demeanor as he patted her hand. He did not like being right in this particular case.

"I completely agree with Johnny, Sophia, that you should distance yourself from the situation as much as possible," Cameron said. "But surely there is something I can do."

"No . . ."

"There must be something," Cameron insisted. She'd hated being so helpless before. Now was her chance to vindicate herself. "I know a few officials. I—"

"I don't think it would be good for you to get further involved," Sophia said with more resolve than she had yet displayed. "I just must have faith that God will protect him."

"That's well and good for you, Sophia. It is all you can do. But I may be able to help."

"You don't know Soviet ways." With a glance at Johnny, she added, "Mr. Shanahan helped me to remember . . ." Sophia's face darkened, and Cameron fully realized that little Sophia was well acquainted with those dastardly ways. Her father had been arrested for no good cause a mere nine years ago. Her husband's parents had both died in a Soviet gulag.

Cameron had known nothing but freedom her whole life—if one did not count her short stints in Russia. She had an academic idea of what Sophia meant, but it went no deeper than that, and it certainly did not penetrate her basic American arrogance—the sense that a person could do anything if she just put her mind to it.

"Sophia, I want you to go home," Cameron said. "Johnny, don't you think it is safe?"

"Just follow your usual routine," he said.

"But even the NKVD will understand your taking a couple of days off work when you learn of your husband's arrest," Cameron said, placing a comforting arm around the girl's shoulder. "In the meantime, I'll ask around—discreetly. I have a few friends."

Late the next morning Alex came by the hotel with the official news of Oleg's arrest. Official in the sense that his identity had been confirmed and he was being held as an escapee from a German POW camp. At the moment he wasn't being considered a deserter from his own unit, a crime for which he could have been executed on the spot. No one knew anything else. Sophia had been questioned by the police in her home, but no other threatening moves had been made against her.

Ten minutes after Alex departed, Cameron left the hotel, as well. She took the metro to Boris Tiulenev's office. He told his secretary, via the intercom, to let her in immediately. He was on the telephone, and he waved her to a seat.

The telephone conversation was in Russian, but Cameron's grasp of the language had been improving, and she could clearly tell it involved a government commissar attempting to strong-arm a factory owner into higher production. Nice old Uncle Boris was shouting into the receiver, his face turning a deep red, his eyebrows like storm clouds over his eyes. Finally he slammed down the receiver.

"All I hear are excuses!" he exclaimed. "Breakdowns, delayed shipments of raw materials, manpower shortages. Bah! Comrade Stalin has shot people for less failure—" He stopped suddenly and gasped. "Oh, my goodness! I am sorry. I didn't mean—"

"I didn't hear a thing, Colonel," Cameron quickly assured. Regardless, even if she wanted to tell her readers about executions of generals who lost battles and of officials who showed disloyalty by low production statistics, the censors wouldn't let it pass their scrutiny.

Regaining his composure, he said, "You are looking well. I am glad."

She had spoken to him once since the explosion and had tried to arrange a personal visit, but his hectic schedule had not permitted him the time.

"And you are looking harried, Colonel. Don't they ever give you a vacation?"

He laughed. "Vacation . . . this is an American concept that has not yet reached the Soviet Union."

"So what are all those dachas for in the country?"

"Most are now in German possession," he said grimly. "But I swear I will take one of your vacations as soon as this war is over. And believe me, by then the dachas will be back in our possession!"

"I have no doubt about that." But she tried to ignore the persistent image of the ravages she had seen on her tour of the Front.

"So, Camrushka, to what do I owe this surprise but most welcome visit?"

"I am sorry I didn't call first, but . . . well, you know about the phones." She shifted in her chair, beginning to feel an inkling of reticence. Was she doing the right thing? Should she heed Sophia's fears? But Boris Tiulenev was safe, a friend. "I need some help regarding a friend who is in trouble."

"Would it not be better for you to go to your embassy?"

"My friend is a Russian."

"I don't understand."

"For obvious reasons," she replied, "I won't burden you with too much detail until you decide if you'd like to hear more. Basically, my interpreter's husband has been arrested. He was a prisoner of war and escaped, but instead of returning directly to his unit he came to see his family in Moscow."

His brows bunched together in a deep frown. "This is a sad reality in times of war. I will tell you something few people know, and you must never repeat, but Comrade Stalin's own son was recently taken prisoner by the Germans. Stalin had the boy's wife arrested."

"Why?" gasped Cameron, nonplussed.

"It may keep the boy from revealing secrets to the enemy. It will keep him loyal to the Soviet government."

"That is terrible! Just terrible!" Cameron exclaimed, turning a bit red in the face herself. "What kind of loyalty is it if it's at gunpoint, so to speak? Those Russian boys couldn't help getting captured."

"That depends on one's viewpoint. Our leaders expect our men to fight to the death. If they let themselves get captured, perhaps they did not fight hard enough."

"Poppycock!" Cameron blinked and tried to rein in her temper. She wanted to ask for this man's help, not alienate him. "I am sorry, Colonel. But when I visited the Front, I saw just how hard your Russian soldiers did fight. Mr. Stalin has no reason to call into question the loyalty of any single one of them."

With a benevolent smile on his lips, Tiulenev nodded. "It is a hard thing to understand. It is hard for *me* to understand, and I live with it every day. It is the way of things here. We must accept it."

Cameron was growing tired of hearing how the way things were in Russia, but she forced calm into her reply. "My friend Oleg loves his country. I believe he would go out and fight again if given the chance."

"And he may do just that once the government determines that he has not been compromised by the enemy. In the meantime, Camrushka . . ." He sighed, but there was definite warning as he added, "You would do well not to get mixed up in the affairs of Russian citizens. Not only for your sake, but for the sake of your friend's family, as well. You would not want them all thrown into the gulag, now would you?"

"I feel so responsible—" She regretted the words the minute they were out.

"Why is that?"

"Oh . . . nothing specific." She suddenly felt an inner check. Yes, this was Uncle Boris, but he was still an important Soviet official himself.

"What is the boy's name?" Tiulenev asked.

Cameron should perhaps have found hope in his expression of interest, but she was checked again. She rose suddenly.

"I don't want to trouble you further, Colonel," she said, offering a hand to the man. "You have been so kind to see me."

Rising also, he took her hand, and his was warm, his grip firm. She'd been taught to trust such a handshake. She could not resist eye contact. His were steady, filled with concern.

"Cameron, please drop this matter. I cannot impress it upon you enough."

She nodded, thanked him again, and left. She wondered if Tiulenev had been as impotent to help in the matter of Semyon Luban. This was definitely not a good time to ask, but it did not bode well that the man had not even mentioned her earlier request. Not well at all.

Tiulenev returned to his chair, and it creaked as he eased himself into it.

His wretched back creaked, as well. The pain was with him constantly. This ancient chair did not help and neither did the stresses of life, so his doctor told him. And now another stress was heaped upon him. He had been good friends with Keagan Hayes. Why, the man had shared his last precious bottle of expensive twelve-year-old Scotch with him, and they had finished the whole bottle in one night, sharing their deepest secrets to each other, as well.

Tiulenev now feared his friend's daughter was heading into deep trouble, involving herself so closely with Russian citizens. Her desire to find a missing Russian—Luban, wasn't it?—was irresponsible enough. Then he had already heard that she had become quite friendly with a Russian doctor, probably as a result of that terrible accident that had almost killed her.

She was courting danger, and she was too *American* to realize it. She just did not understand.

The worst of it was that he knew she would not heed his warnings. That's the way these Americans were—brash, cocky, they called it. Stupid, he thought. But then they did not have to fear the same things as Russians feared.

He ran a hand through his thin hair. But what could he do? The wise thing would be to heed his own advice. But if he ever saw his friend Keagan again, how would he be able to face the man knowing he had silently stood by while his daughter walked over a cliff?

With sudden resolution, Tiulenev picked up the telephone receiver. In a few moments he had his desired party on the line. They exchanged a few initial pleasantries; then he launched into the purpose of his call.

"What do you know of the recent arrest of a young ex-POW named Oleg? I am sorry I have no surname." He waited a few moments, listening, then said, "My interest? Well . . . a friend of the family whom I happen to know asked me to make inquiries. No, I do not know the boy or his immediate family."

The colonel's heart sank as he felt himself become more and more deeply embroiled in a matter that should have been none of his business.

———

Two days later Cameron was in her room relaxing before the evening press conference when a boy came to her door with a note. She gave him a coin, sent him on his way, then opened the envelope.

The letter was written in Sophia's fine script.

Dear Miss Hayes,
It might be perhaps that you are in the mood to attend church this evening? Perhaps St. Mark's on Spasoglinishchevskiy Pereulok will be to your liking—sorry the street is not an easier one! You will take the Kitay-Gorod Metro, and it is a block from the station. There is an evening mass at eight.

That was all, no signature, no reasons for this peculiar request. Yes, Sophia had in the past taken Cameron on some sight-seeing excursions, but this did not have the sound of that, nor did she think at this juncture Sophia would be much interested in touring.

Glancing at her watch, Cameron saw it was already nearly eight. She'd never make it on time, but something told her that didn't matter, that she hadn't been invited to enjoy a worship service. Quickly, pausing only to burn the note in the bathroom sink, she grabbed her handbag and hurried out her door as she pulled on her coat.

Even hurrying, she did not arrive at the church until eight-thirty. It was a lovely domed building with a dark red and white façade. There was some attempt at camouflage, and no light showed from the black-out-shaded stained-glass windows. She stepped inside a darkened entry and carefully shut the outer doors before entering the main sanctuary. That kept any light in the sanctuary from spilling into the street. But actually, the sanctuary was fairly dark except for a few lighted candles at the altar. It was enough light to illuminate the magnificent iconostasis at the front of the church.

A priest was ministering to a few people kneeling at the altar. There were others milling about the pewless sanctuary, but it was clear the mass was over.

Cameron wondered if she had missed whatever it was she had been invited here to see. Then a soft voice spoke at her shoulder.

"Ah, Cameron, I am so glad you came."

CAMERON TURNED toward the sound and saw old Anna Yevnovona. She was wearing a long black wool coat and a bright blue scarf tied around her head. The woman looked remarkably like an ancient peasant now, little about her hinting at the nobility that must be in her blood. Except in those eyes. They sparkled, they glinted, they drew Cameron with their warmth. They impressed her with their hint of wisdom.

Cameron smiled. She was very glad to have a chance to meet this woman again. "I have learned never to pass up such a cryptic invitation."

"Yes, it was that, wasn't it? A bit like the old days it was . . ." A dreamy, faraway look dominated those eyes a moment; then the clear focus returned. "We felt such caution was necessary."

"I didn't think I was just being invited to attend church."

"No, but it is a lovely church, isn't it? I have not practiced the Orthodox faith in years, yet I am still awed by the splendor of their houses of worship. It reminds me of why the first Christian tsar chose Orthodoxy. Do you know the story?"

"I don't think so."

"In the tenth century, representatives of the major faiths—Islam, Judaism, Roman Christianity, and Byzantine Christianity—came to visit Tsar Vladimir in hopes of converting him. He seemed not concerned with the truth of the faith but rather which held more aesthetic appeal. He found the Jews were too austere, the Muslims too frenzied, and he beheld no 'glory' in the Roman faith. But he was most impressed with the pomp and grandeur of Byzantium, so he chose Orthodoxy for Russia." Her eyes skittered toward the front of the church and the heavily gilded altar with its rows of exquisite icons. "I have often wondered if that was the same way he chose his god."

"Weren't they the same thing?"

She smiled rather mysteriously. "We'll never know how his mind perceived it. I rather like the pretty *things* up there. But they have little to do with my God."

"Then what is the point of it all?"

"Good question, my dear. I'd have to give it some thought before attempting an answer. In the meantime, how about if we take a walk outside?"

"I'd like that."

A chill wind greeted them as they exited the church. Any moonlight there might have been was obliterated by clouds deepening the darkness. There were no streetlights, no headlights on vehicles, and certainly no glow of light from the surrounding buildings. Moscow must look like a great swath of black ink from the air. Unfortunately, that wouldn't fool the Germans. Air raids had been more and more frequent in the days since Cameron's return from the Front. The enemy was closing in on the city, tightening the noose. And yet here she and an old lady were strolling the streets as if it were a fine summer evening in middle America.

"Do you know why I wanted to see you, Cameron?" Anna asked after a few minutes of silence.

"Is it about Oleg's arrest? Is he okay?"

"We really don't know if he is or not. No one has seen him since the arrest." She was silent again.

Cameron knew nothing but lame words to speak, so she said nothing. Finally the woman continued. "Last night Sophia and her father and mother were taken to NKVD headquarters and interrogated."

"No! But Sophia said nothing about it when she came to work this morning."

"She feared she had troubled you too much already. Perhaps she is right." Anna sighed, and her brisk pace, incredible for an eighty-one-year-old woman, slowed. She looked up at Cameron. "I made her write you that note. I insisted on speaking with you. She argued with me—she has never argued with me, or anyone for that matter, in her life. When she didn't get her way about my going, she wanted to accompany me, but I thought it best if we met alone."

Truly baffled, Cameron said, "But I'm not sure why she would argue or why you would want to see me so much."

"Have you spoken to anyone about Oleg since you saw him or since his arrest?"

"Only to a couple people directly involved in the escape plan, and a colleague of mine, and Alex, and—" She gasped, bringing her hand to her lips. "Oh no! Two days ago I spoke to a friend, a man named Boris Tiulenev. He's a commissar in the defense industry. I thought he might help discover, if nothing else, what the police intended to do about Oleg. The colonel is a good man. I'm . . . well, I'm almost sure. But if Sophia and the others were questioned yesterday, that would be too coincidentally close to when I saw Boris. But I can't believe he would have informed."

Anna let out the kind of sigh that echoed every single year in which she had experienced life. "He might have thought he was doing you a favor. He might have simply made a casual mention of the situation, entirely innocently. I don't know. . . ."

"But it doesn't matter, does it?" Cameron practically groaned. "The result is the same. I am so sorry. I thought I could help."

"I know that, my dear. And it is possible your inquiries had nothing to do with what happened to Sophia and her parents. And thank God they have been released. But still I felt I should impress upon you how important it is not to stir things up further. Things work differently here in Russia than in America. Long years of repression have taught us the expediency of discretion. Maybe it is part cowardice on our part, but I also like to think of it as a means of survival. Cameron, you must not make any more inquiries—"

Suddenly the air-raid siren began its shrill blast. Cameron and Anna joined the growing throngs of people heading for the same metro station. The trains stopped a little ahead of their usual wartime schedule of ten o'clock. All the escalators were put in the "down" mode.

As they stepped onto an escalator, Anna fanned herself with her hand and giggled nervously. "I will never grow accustomed to all these modern contraptions."

It was indeed an awe-inspiring experience. Cameron had been on the subways of New York, but this was several notches beyond that. Thanks to natural Russian paranoia, the Moscow subway had been purposely built to be one of the deepest in the world, making it useful as a bomb shelter in times of war. The escalator, moving at incredible speed, slanted down hundreds of feet into the bowels of the earth. But this was only the beginning of the metro experience. The stations and platforms themselves were museum-worthy works of art. Lavish chandeliers, beautiful sculptures, intricate mosaics all breathtakingly extolled the Revolution, the Red Army, and the Soviet way of life. Cameron was especially impressed with the cleanliness of it all. No trash, no graffiti, as she'd seen in New York. She could philosophize about that, thinking that at least the citizens of New York had the freedom to defile their subway if they wished, risking only the mild punishment of a fine or such. She could wonder about the fear of a Russian citizen to even scratch a small "Ivan was here" on an obscure wall.

But Anna spoke, saving Cameron from further tedious mental exercise.

"I remember the first train I ever saw," Anna said. "I was sixteen. It wasn't a subway train, only the Pskov to St. Petersburg train. I thought it was like a hundred Siberian bears on the attack. I thought only the snow could stop it, but that beast plowed even through the snow! I was so afraid. Part of my fear might have been due to the fact that the train was taking me away from my dear village to be a servant in the house of a St. Petersburg prince."

"A servant? But I thought Sophia said you were of the nobility?"

"That was much later. I was a peasant, and I still am at heart."

They reached the end of the escalator, and Anna grasped Cameron's arm for support as the machine spit them most ungraciously onto the platform.

"Thank you, dear," Anna said, quickly regaining her balance.

"Did you live in St. Petersburg long?" Cameron asked as they found a place to settle in.

There were few benches and these were quickly occupied, so they joined the hundreds who reclined on the marble floor. Many had blankets, even mattresses, baskets of food, and other paraphernalia to make the duration of the raid endurable. Cameron and Anna tried to make themselves as comfortable as possible on the unquestionably beautiful but cold and hard marble.

"I lived in St. Petersburg—it will never be anything else to me—all my life from the age of sixteen," Anna finally answered. "I pray every day for my many friends still there, as they face the terrible German siege. I moved to Moscow with my family about eight years ago after my Yuri was released from the gulag. The government, perhaps to appease him, offered him this prestigious position as Chief of Staff at one of Russia's largest and finest hospitals." She smiled wryly. "Forgive me if I seem to brag. But I am proud of my son. Still, I suppose part of the reasoning behind the promotion was to remove him from the city in which he had lived all his life and where he had numerous friends and contacts. You see, to put him off-balance."

"Anna, may I ask you a somewhat dangerous question?" Anna gave a curious nod. "How do you feel about Russia after all that your family has been through?"

"I love Russia," Anna answered without hesitation. "I could have left. I could have escaped. I have a son and daughter in America who would take me in. I have thought about it, especially in those dark years when I feared even speaking the name of my God. I could give you some noble reason for my remaining and say that I felt I should stay in my country and work to keep faith and freedom alive. But in truth, I just never had the will to leave. It is my country, my home . . . my parents are buried here, as well as my two beloved husbands. It is hard to explain the draw of such things."

"The current religious freedom must be a great relief to you."

Anna shifted on the hard floor and tucked her coat more snugly around her knees. "I am not optimistic enough to feel anything close to relief." Pausing, she looked around.

They were talking softly, and there was no one close enough to hear their conversation, even if their English could be understood. But it was risky enough, Cameron realized, just to be conversing in a foreign language.

"Our leaders permit religion now because it benefits them. After the war . . . who knows? We have gone through many waves of acceptance and repression over the years—even in tsarist times non-Orthodox sects were heavily persecuted. In these Soviet times the leaders tried 're-education,' as they called it. Banning religious teaching in the schools, that sort of thing, replacing it with Communist indoctrination. When that didn't seem to work, they turned to physical persecution, imprisonment, and even some executions of those who attempted to practice their beliefs. Now they permit religious practices, and what has happened? The churches have filled! True, with mostly old people, but there are enough young among the worshipers that it must be alarming to the government. Where has all their 're-education' and persecution gone?"

"Nowhere, apparently," Cameron answered, though she knew it had been a rhetorical question.

Anna chuckled. "Exactly! Something that springs from the very depths of a man's soul cannot be easily killed."

Cameron thought of Alex. He said he'd lost his faith, yet even he had found himself praying when in an emotionally demanding situation.

"But God," Anna said, "both the concept and the reality, goes against everything that is holy—if I may use that term—to the Communist Manifesto. Thus the realm of God and the atheistic realm of Communism must be like two combatants struggling against each other throughout eternity." Anna shook her head grimly. "So forgive my absence of optimism about the recent changes. To those of us who believe, it matters little. We will continue to practice our faith whether free to do so or not."

"I admire your . . ." Cameron paused, searching for the right word.

"Stubbornness?" Anna supplied.

Cameron laughed. "That certainly is one way of putting it. I wonder if I would be so ambivalent about faith if I'd had to fight for it as you have."

"What is your religious background, Cameron? Of course, we in Russia believe all Americans are Christians." There was a definite touch of sarcasm to her final statement.

"They may claim to be, but I have a feeling many are like me, not knowing what to think and perhaps even a little embarrassed by too much Christian zealousness." Cameron felt compelled to offer a more personal insight, not because Anna expected it, though perhaps she did, but because the older woman's own openness made Cameron want to respond in kind. She added, "My mother is very religious, Anna. She goes to church every week and has even been known to go in the middle of the week! I think she prays and reads the Bible when she is alone. She is a weak person, at least from my perspective. She lets my father dominate her, even to the point where she allowed him to give all his daughters boys' names, which I know she hated. I've never seen her stand up to him. And to be honest, I have always believed her religion to be just another manifestation of that weakness."

"What is your father's religious preference?"

Cameron rolled her eyes. "He worships himself! He goes to church only for show, and then only on the big holidays. I would fall over in a faint if I ever saw him pray!"

"Hmm . . ." Anna rubbed her chin. "It must take a great deal of strength for your mother to so tenaciously practice her faith in the wake of that kind of attitude from her own husband."

Cameron just gaped at the woman's strange logic. Then it hit her as if one of the bombs falling overhead had taken a direct hit on her.

"I never thought of it like that!" she breathed. Her mother strong? The concept was staggering at the least. It totally knocked out of kilter the foundations of all Cameron had believed her entire life. Yet here was a woman, Anna Yevnovona, who, Cameron had no doubt, knew all about strength, and she was saying Cecilia Hayes might just be a strong person, as well. Incredible!

Cameron turned to Anna. "I am going to have to think about that one." She wagged her head, still bemused. Then she leaned her head back against the mosaic tiles of the wall. "Sometimes I feel as though I have been in Russia a hundred years because of all I have seen and learned, and all I have learned about myself, as well. I don't like a lot of it. Some of it scares me, and I definitely dislike *that* feeling!"

"Yes, change can be a frightening thing."

"I expect you have observed many changes, Anna."

"And lived through them!" She patted Cameron's arm. "As will you. Sometimes I felt the changes might indeed crush me, then I would remember one of my papa's favorite Bible passages. It says that a seed of grain planted into the earth must first die before it can bring forth fruit. That's what change does. It kills certain things in us so that something new may grow. My hope has always been that the new growth will be better than what came before."

"I'm afraid I am too much of a cynic to put a great deal of stock in that," Cameron said. "My immediate response to it is, 'What if something good is killed off instead?' "

"If you truly fear that, then I think you need not worry overmuch of the possibility. And—speaking of seeds!—God will honor even the tiniest seed of good like that. I am certain of it!"

How could Cameron deny the absolute glow about the old woman's face as she spoke? Cameron might not have enough faith herself to embrace the woman's optimism, yet she felt sure it was real. And a part of her was a little emptier knowing this and realizing she could not grasp hold of it herself just then.

LOZOVSKY'S BEARD bobbed up and down as he heaped on his usual palaver of ridiculous optimism at his regular press conference.

"I laugh at Hitler's speech!" he said, referring to a speech a few days earlier by the German leader announcing his *final* assault against Moscow. "He is desperate to do anything to appease his people and keep them fighting."

"What about Hitler's claim to have taken a half million prisoners in the Ukraine?" asked Shanahan.

"The battle in the Ukraine continues," Lozovsky hedged. "We must not risk the Soviet position by revealing figures prematurely."

"What about rumors that the Germans have broken through at Vyazma?" Levinson asked.

Cameron remembered that little town from her visit to the Front. It had been largely untouched by the summer campaigns. It was a hundred fifty miles from Moscow.

"The situation in the Vyazma area is a complex one," answered Lozovsky.

Shanahan leaned close to Cameron and whispered, "We all know in Russia that 'complex' means 'bad.' "

Could this announcement mean that the great victory at Yelnya had been for naught? What of the soldiers they had met at the Front, those smiling boys she had danced and laughed with? What of those cocky airmen? Were they dead now? Captured? All the blood that had been shed to retake that bit of land—had it been wasted?

By the end of the first week of October, no one was clear as to the gravity of the situation. No doubt only Stalin and his little war cabinet, consisting of Stalin, Beriya, Malenkov, Molotov, and Voroshilov, knew anything at all.

On the seventh, *Pravda* led with a story about women in the defense industry, hardly mentioning the situation at the Front, much less the precarious position of Moscow.

But the "rumor mill" worked overtime. This was the price of Soviet repression of the press. Reports of German tanks being spotted in a Moscow suburb were completely unfounded, but that did not curb the growing tension in the city. For a time, air raids over Moscow ceased, but that was no great cause for rejoicing because everyone guessed the reason was that the Luftwaffe was too heavily deployed elsewhere to spare bombers for Moscow.

Finally, the journalists learned that the Battle of Moscow, or Operation Typhoon, as it was called by the Germans, had been engaged. They were hardly surprised to hear that had occurred on October the second, several days *before* the actual announcement.

Lozovsky admitted dryly, "The Fascists have probably planned to lose several hundred thousand men in this offensive. They will achieve that aim!"

Then even the Russian press began to indicate alarm, calling the Russian people to vigilance, warning them against panic. And on October the twelfth *Pravda* actually admitted to a "terrible danger threatening the country." The panic grew like ripples in a pond, starting small, then building until the entire pond was consumed.

Air raids were stepped up, striking at irregular times, and factories were evacuated to the east so that war production would not be compromised. Many of the remaining factories were mined with explosives so that only a button needed to be pushed should the Germans break through, thus preventing vital industry from falling into the hands of the enemy. Word came that the German army had crossed the Volga at Kalinin, a hundred miles from Moscow, and that the vital Leningrad-Moscow railway had been cut off. No one had any reason not to believe the Battle of Moscow would not be another stunning German victory.

As the enemy pressed in, Alex was confronted with another concern. His friend Anatoly Bogorodsk waylaid him as he exited a ward of new surgical patients. Alex was harried, frayed, if the truth be told. He did not need a visit by even a friendly NKVD agent. He had known long before many others that the battle had intensified just by the huge influx of wounded he was seeing. Thousands of wounded were arriving at Moscow's hospitals daily.

"Hello, Anatoly. I didn't think you liked hospitals," Alex said. He kept walking, letting Bogorodsk catch up. He had fifty patients yet to see before he returned to surgery.

"This seems to be your new home, so how else am I to see you?" Bogorodsk smiled, but there was no warmth in his eyes.

"I'll wager this is not a social call."

"I am afraid not. If I had not been so busy myself, I would have come to you sooner, but—" He just shrugged. Everyone in Russia was busy these days, and it needed no explanation. He then sighed as if he was about to embark on a very odious task. "Aleksei, when was the last time you saw that American correspondent friend of yours?"

Alex scratched his head as if it was something so unimportant he couldn't be expected to have the information on demand. In fact, he remembered it quite well. It had been at the Metropole. There was a little band that night in the ballroom, and they had danced to Dorsey and Goodman tunes. He'd held her closer than the dancing required, and he could still remember the fragrance of roses in her hair. He remembered thinking that Shanahan was nowhere to be seen and feeling a crazy relief about that.

"Guess it was a couple of nights ago," he answered, glad the agent could not detect the sudden quickening of his pulse with the memory.

Anatoly took a small notebook from his pocket and flipped a couple of pages. "Two nights ago, Saturday. You dined and danced at the Metropole."

"Do you know what we ate or what we said?"

"We did not get close enough for that," the man answered earnestly, obviously missing the sarcasm in Alex's tone. "Did she say anything to you at that time about her contact with other Russian citizens?"

"No. What's this about?"

"You do not know that she has been in close contact with the family of her interpreter, Sophia Gorbenko?"

"No, I don't." They had, in fact, talked quite extensively about Oleg's arrest and her various encounters since. He had urged her to heed the warnings of Anna and Colonel Tiulenev. Could Anatoly know of all this, or even of Alex's visit to the forgers?

"It was you who recommended the Gorbenko girl to the job, was it not?" asked Bogorodsk crisply.

"Yes."

"Her father is your Chief of Staff?"

"Yes." Alex's mind raced, trying to figure out all the connections Anatoly could have made. "Look, Anatoly, I am very busy. What are you getting at?"

"The American is unwise to become involved with Russians, especially ones who are under the scrutiny of the police. But I am afraid I can do nothing to help her—"

"What do you mean by that?"

Anatoly cocked a brow. He was no dummy. Alex's sharp response was clearly not that of some casual acquaintance to the woman in question.

"Listen to me, and listen to me closely, Aleksei," the agent replied in a warning growl. "Earlier, I thought it was a lark to allow you latitude with the American. A bit of romance never hurt anyone. But things have changed. She has begun to overstep her bounds. I must warn you, Aleksei, do not see the American woman again, or you will risk your fate being wrapped up into hers."

Alex wanted that more than he would admit to himself but not in the way the agent intended. "What fate is that?" Alex forced out.

"She has not been playing by our rules, as the Americans themselves say. One can be deported for this offense."

"I should think with the Germans beating at Moscow's doors, you'd have more to be concerned with than the petty offenses of a foreigner."

"Internal security is always a primary concern of the Soviet Union. And foreigners, these days of all days, must not be dismissed lightly." Anatoly sighed, hardened edges softening once again with friendliness. "I understand that the woman is an American and cannot fully comprehend the dangers she is toying with. I do not believe she is a danger to national security. But . . . ah, Aleksei . . . if I don't do this job, someone with far less understanding will."

"Let me talk to her," Alex said.

"You must not. It has not been easy for you to attain the confidence of the Soviet government. You cannot jeopardize that by acting foolishly. Whatever happens to the woman is out of my hands. It is you I am now concerned with."

Alex chewed on that statement for the rest of the day. He would have left immediately to find Cameron, but he absolutely could not get away from the hospital. He cared deeply for Cameron, maybe too deeply, but he couldn't put her above his patients, not when dying men were practically piling up in the corridors.

Even if he could get away to see her, he'd have to do so discreetly. He had to assume Anatoly's warning meant that his NKVD shadows would now be far more vigilant than they had been in the past. Fortunately, as sinister as NKVD agents were, they still were fairly easy to lose. And in the chaos that Moscow was becoming, it would be only that much easier.

Luckily Cameron knew the place. The offices of *Izvestiya* were at the northeast corner of Pushkin Square, and the journalists had been given a tour of the Russian newspaper a couple of months ago.

The Square was about a quarter of a mile north of the hotel. At three in the afternoon, when Cameron arrived, it should have been a busy place, but everyone was getting out of the northern and western sectors of the city, where the Germans would make their initial assault. They were heading to the city center, which was now swarming with Muscovites, and the roads heading east and southeast were packed, as well. The Kazan train station, which served the Urals, was mobbed even more than usual, and this sector where Cameron now found herself was rather tame compared to what she had just left.

At any other time Cameron would have welcomed all the clandestine meetings she had been faced with lately, but she needed to keep near her phone because the foreign community had been put on alert to be prepared to leave at any moment, and there could be evacuation orders within the day. Not only that, but also she needed to be available to hear any breaking news. Regardless of her intrigues of late, she was still a reporter, and this could easily be the most thrilling and important time of her entire Russian assignment.

But the note she'd received a couple hours ago begged a response. It had been extremely cryptic. "Pushkin Square, three o'clock" was all it had said. She had no idea who it was from. The handwriting was not familiar. She had at first thought it might be from Anna. She would have liked to see the old woman again, even if she did talk a lot about religion. But the writing seemed more like a male hand, and it was almost illegible. Regardless of the sender, Cameron was not about to ignore it. Taking such risks had propelled her to where she was now in her profession, and she had no doubt of the risk she was taking meeting an unknown person. But she had been extremely careful coming, using some of the tricks she'd picked up from Sophia. She was all but certain she had not been followed.

At least the gathering darkness would give her some cover. And as she reached the great bronze statue of the Russian poet Alexander Pushkin, which graced the north end of the square, a light snow began to fall. It had been snowing all week, and the streets were slushy with the stuff. She paced about, beating her gloved hands together to keep them warm as the evening temperature dropped.

After a half hour, she began to wonder how long she should give her mysterious note-sender. She was bundled up warmly, but she was a Los Angeles girl, and October in Moscow was already far colder than she was accustomed to.

There were several passersby, but none took an interest in her. She assumed the person she was to meet must know her and thus she must know him. At any rate she could not stop everyone and ask if they were looking for her. She just had to be patient. A few minutes later another pedestrian approached. He was tall, but his face was shadowed by a fedora, pulled low over his face and by a wool neck scarf pulled high over his chin. He wore a wool overcoat. He slowed as he drew near, and then she saw the familiar face.

"Alex! So it was you. I am glad to see you, but—"

His lips twitched into a smile. "Sorry for all the mystery." He slipped his arm around hers. "Come, let's walk like a couple out for fresh air."

"Okay, but I am full of fresh air."

"Sorry I am late. An emergency came in. I feared I wouldn't be able to get away at all, and I worried about you freezing out here. Dr. Fedorcenko stepped in for me."

They walked for a couple of minutes. Cameron concentrated on keeping her teeth from chattering. They seemed to be alone except for the occasional passerby. She could see no sinister figures lurking about.

Finally Alex said, "I've been told not to see you anymore."

"What? By whom?"

"The NKVD. I told you I had a friend in the agency, didn't I? Well, he gave me a friendly warning. He indicated you were under their scrutiny and that any Russian associated with you could be dragged in, as well."

"And so the first thing you did was arrange to see me?" she said dryly, but with a hint of pleasure.

"Cameron, I don't intend to not see you anymore unless *you* tell me, and I'm not sure I'd listen even then." He paused, turned, and looked down at her. In a tenderly familiar way, he brushed away flakes of snow clinging to strands of her hair that had escaped the confines of her wool hat. "Whatever it is between you and the NKVD, I want to be in it with you."

"Alex, neither of us wanted anything permanent." She looked up into his intense gaze and forgot all her reasons for not wanting to make a commitment.

"We'll work that out later," he said dismissively, then grinned. "First, let's get the spooks off our backs."

"How do we do that?"

"I don't know. Come on, let's walk before the snow piles up on us."

She was oddly content to walk at his side. The city was literally about to go up in smoke, the police were nearly ready to deport her, but somehow she just couldn't get too worked up about it. She did not need a man, but there was something about this man that made her feel . . . was it stronger? More complete? His arm linked through hers felt so right.

"Well, I have backed off from my inquiries about Oleg," she offered.

"Yes, but those just seemed to unleash a raging bear, and getting him back under control is going to be like trying to stuff a storm into a bottle."

"I wonder if Oleg has told anyone about what he saw after he escaped?"

"I don't think it matters if he has. I doubt that what has happened has much to do with that. Oleg was a POW with the Germans for several weeks. He escaped and was found in Moscow not having dutifully reported to the authorities. Add to that the fact that both his parents were dissidents. The NKVD are notorious for jumping to obvious, however idiotic, conclusions. Compounding that is the fact that he met with a foreigner during that gap after his escape—"

"I don't know if they can prove that," Cameron put in hopefully.

"That is probably what has kept them at bay regarding any action against you—for now. If anyone saw you go to the Fedorcenko apartment and decides to inform—what am I saying? That doesn't even need to happen. If the police decide they just don't want you around, they can simply trump up something."

They had walked the length of the square. Cameron recalled that across the street there had once been a lovely convent after which the square had once been named. It had been demolished in 1935 and the Rossiya Theater built in its place. She wondered if the convent had been more appealing than the unimaginative façade of the Stalinist theater. She wondered, too, if any of it would survive the next few days. She still could not blot from her mind the images of demolished villages and towns she had seen—nothing was left of them but a memory, like the convent.

"Then there really is nothing to do," Cameron finally said. "Wait and see. The war is liable to intercede anyway, and that could work to my advantage as well as the NKVD's. But I don't like sitting still, sitting on my hands like this. There ought to be something that can be done for Oleg. Arrested for being a POW? It is outrageous!"

"Cameron, promise me—" He stopped walking again, faced her, placing his hands firmly on her shoulders so she was forced to look directly into his eyes. She trembled at the flicker of fire she saw in them. "Promise me that you will not do anything else to help Oleg."

"All right! I promise. I can't do anything anyway."

Then, much to her surprise, he leaned forward and kissed her. His lips were cold, as were hers, and they barely brushed hers, but enough heat was instantly ignited so that she would not have been surprised to find a puddle of melted snow at her feet.

"You'll be evacuated from Moscow soon," he said softly.

"And what about you?"

"I have to go wherever they tell me, where I am needed." He swallowed hard, his Adam's apple bobbing sharply under his scarf. "We won't lose touch with each other."

"No, we won't."

But they both knew how war was and what it could do. They knew that whatever they dared hope to have between them could go up in a literal puff of smoke. But neither said the words.

"How long do we have?" he breathed.

She noted his use of the word "we." How she wished she could spend her last days in Moscow only with him, ignoring the rest of the world. "The evacuation could happen any day, any moment."

He nodded. "If only . . ." But his words trailed away as he perhaps realized that he had almost voiced the innate hopelessness they were both feeling.

"Alex—"

"Cameron, I want to give you something," he said quickly as if to banish the dismal thoughts coming between them. "We may not be able to see each other for a while, and this will be just a small remembrance—"

"As if I'd forget!"

Smiling, he reached into his coat pocket. "I know. I thought it could provide a small connection. Here." He opened his hand to reveal an old key on a slightly tarnished gold chain. The key was of the kind used probably fifty years ago, like a skeleton key, only a bit smaller than the ones Cameron had seen before.

She took it reverently, as if it were a precious gem. "This must have some special significance," she said.

"It isn't much to look at, but it does have special meaning, to me at least. My mother wore this key around her neck until her death. It is the key to her house in Leningrad, the house where she lived until she married. She kept it because, as I think I have told you, she always hoped of returning to that house someday. I thought I might visit the house one day, but it hasn't been easy for me to get away."

She closed her hand around it as if it were a lifeline. "I'll treasure it, Alex."

"I know you don't wear jewelry—and this is hardly jewelry. You don't have to wear it—"

"I'd be honored to wear it." She reached up right then and placed it around her neck. The clasp worked remarkably well. Tucking it beneath the folds of her wool scarf, she said, "I know it didn't work out for your mother, but let's you and I make a promise that we will visit the house together when the war is over, when Leningrad is free again."

"That is my hope. That is why I wanted to give it to you. I can't go there now except with you."

"Oh, Alex—!"

But before she could finish, he took her in his arms, there in the middle of Moscow under a snowy sky with the faint sound of German artillery in the distance. He grasped her tightly and kissed her fiercely, and she responded with equal fierceness that seemed to encompass the fear that this could be the last embrace, the last kiss.

CAMERON SNIFFED smoke in the air. Bits of ash floated down from the sky along with the snow. Foreign diplomats and government officials were frantically burning important documents to keep them out of German hands, so many in fact that it left an actual haze over the city.

On that evening of October sixteenth, Cameron and several other correspondents had to push their way through the mobbed streets as they made their way to Spaso House, where they had been instructed to meet with only as much baggage as they could carry.

The evacuation of the foreign community had begun.

Despite Lozovsky's assurances that the Germans would never capture Moscow, *Pravda* had run an ominous headline: "The Mad Fascist Beast Is Rushing Toward Moscow." This ignited the already rumbling panic among the general population. After all, if the government, which normally kept everything a secret, was admitting to that much, then it must be bad indeed.

Already there was fierce fighting fifty miles northwest of Moscow. Civilians were called to volunteer for the "labor front." They were mostly women from factories who were taken several miles out of Moscow and put to work digging trenches. Sophia and her sister were among these. Cameron felt sick at the thought of little Sophia doing such backbreaking labor. But she had already been removed from her job as Cameron's interpreter. It had never actually been stated that the reason was because her loyalty was in question. She was just told one day that she could not work for the journalist. Cameron feared Sophia had joined the labor crew in a desperate attempt to prove her loyalty. And there was no ignoring that this was dangerous work, as it was very close to the German lines.

And now Cameron herself would be leaving Moscow, bound for Kuibyshev, some five hundred miles southeast of the Russian capital. She'd managed to reach Alex on the phone that morning with the news. He told her he would come to the station to see her off. He didn't bother to scold her for risking a phone call.

Cameron and the other correspondents were not far from the ambassador's residence when two Russian men joined the group and sidled up next to Cameron. There was no doubt they were NKVD.

"You would to please come with us, Miss Gayes?" one asked.

He looked like the same agent who had accosted her when she had first come to Moscow. That had turned out to be an innocuous experience. A quickly forming knot in her stomach told her this wasn't likely to turn out the same way.

"You're kidding, right?" she said with a scoffing laugh. "You've chosen a bad time."

"What's going on here?" Shanahan asked haughtily.

"We would to like just few minutes of your time, Miss Gayes," the agent said.

A couple of the other reporters tossed in their protests, but finally Cameron shrugged.

"Thanks, fellas, but I'm sure it's nothing. I'll be back before the train leaves." She turned to the agents. "I will, won't I?"

"Of course. Very minor matter," the agent replied. He didn't lie well. "A problem with your papers that must be cleared up before you leave."

"I'm going with you, Hayes," Shanahan said.

"It is not necessary—" the agent began.

But Johnny cut in sharply, "Forget it, buddy! I'm going." He turned to Levinson. "You let the ambassador know what is happening."

"Johnny, you are making far too big a deal of this, I am sure." Though Cameron's stomach twisted, logic told her even the police would not jeopardize her departure. They were as anxious as anyone to get the foreigners out of the city. It must be a small matter. Yet why even bother at all, especially now?

"I'm going, sweetheart. No arguments."

Johnny was firm, and to be honest, Cameron did think it was probably a good idea to have another American along. As a witness, if nothing else.

After leaving their baggage in the care of the other correspondents, Cameron, Johnny, and the two agents got into a car and inched through traffic to the Narkomindel. There, Cameron and Johnny were taken to a room, where they were told an agent would come in a few minutes to interview Cameron. The door shut and a lock turned.

Shanahan jumped up. "Hey!" He banged a fist against the door.

"Relax, Johnny," Cameron said, not feeling very relaxed herself. "Maybe the lock is just for our protection."

"Uh-huh. In case the Germans break through the lines?"

"Well, even if we don't make it out of Moscow, imagine the stories we'll get."

"I have no problem with being stuck in Moscow," Johnny assured. "But missing a train is not all you have to worry about."

They sat in two of several plain wooden chairs which, along with a small table, were the only furnishings in the room.

"I am worried," Cameron finally admitted. "But they can't imprison me. The worst that can happen is they'll deport me. But my parents do have connections in Washington. That's how my visa here was expedited in the first place, at least I'm pretty certain it was helped by a friend of my mother's in the State Department."

"So, you'd cry to your father for help?" Shanahan looked skeptical.

"I hope it doesn't come to that."

An hour passed, then another and another. Johnny banged on the door several more times and yelled. But they had been stashed in some out-of-the-way corner, and, Cameron had no doubt, they had been forgotten in the chaos of the evacuation. The time continued to drag on. Both "prisoners" were getting desperate to use a rest room, if nothing else. Johnny was getting hungry, as well. Cameron couldn't have eaten a thing.

Finally, the lock turned and the door opened. The man who entered was a balding, rumpled bureaucrat. He didn't look much like a police agent.

"My apologies!" he said without preamble. "So much is happening—"

"Yeah!" growled Johnny. "You picked a lousy time to detain us. And I want to know why!"

"I assure you, we had only intended this to be a brief interview. The agents who escorted you here were called away on some urgent matter and failed to inform the proper person of your presence. It is inexcusable, except by the present state of affairs in the city." He paused and shut the door but did not lock it. "My name is Major Smilga." He held out a hand.

Cameron and Shanahan ignored it. Cameron said, "What is this all about? We do have a train to catch."

"You will make your train," Smilga replied with rather ill-placed confidence, considering his foul-ups thus far. "I wanted only a brief interview. A few questions—"

"About what?" Cameron cut in, deciding that taking the offensive might be her best approach.

"Your interpreter, Sophia Gorbenko."

"And when, by the way, is she going to be restored to my employment? She is indispensable to me."

"At present, she has been reassigned to a new . . . ah . . . position. But another interpreter will be assigned you when you reach Kuibyshev. Please sit." Smilga motioned toward the chairs.

"I can stand, since this is to be a *short* interview," Cameron replied.

With a casual shrug, as if he was just as anxious as they to finish this thing, Smilga began, "You have met Sophia Gorbenko's husband, Oleg?"

Cameron felt as if the man had fired from a bazooka for his opening volley, but by force of will she kept her face expressionless. "What gives you that idea?"

"I am asking the questions," shot back Smilga with more force than his previous milquetoast approach.

"You just keep in mind," warned Shanahan, "that Miss Hayes is an American citizen with certain rights."

"Please, you must understand, I am not making any accusations against Miss Hayes. I am only attempting to sort out a matter involving a Russian, and I hoped she might be able to help."

"I am still not clear why Oleg Gorbenko was arrested," Cameron asked.

"So you do know him?"

"Only from a few minor references my interpreter has made about her husband," Cameron lied. "So why the arrest?"

"You are misinformed, Miss Hayes. The Gorbenko boy was not arrested."

Cameron cocked a brow. Either this man was lying as profusely as she, or someone was seriously misinformed. "What do you call it, then?"

"The boy was in a very agitated mental state," explained Smilga, now sounding like the benevolent benefactor. "He is merely being kept in a safe place for observation until his . . . ah . . . faculties stabilize. Hospitalized, you might say."

Cameron didn't believe the man for a minute, though his words, like all good lies, had the strength of being quite plausible, considering her own impressions of Oleg.

"What do you want from me?"

"Only your opinion as an objective observer, as to the boy's state. Perhaps some input as to things he may have said and as to his actions . . . that would help us to facilitate his recovery."

That was a lie if Cameron had ever heard any. "I am afraid, then, that I must disappoint you, since I never did meet him."

"Perhaps his wife might have mentioned something?"

"Nothing beyond his being a prisoner of war and her worry about him. She mentioned his arrest—that is, his *hospitalization*, is it not?"

Smilga nodded. "This is very disappointing. I had so hoped you could help."

"I wish I could help, too. As I said, Sophia is a fine girl and an outstanding employee."

Smilga moved to the door and opened it. "I will see to it that a car is brought around to take you to the train station. The train for Kuibyshev will not depart, I am told, until midnight."

———

Alex was frantic when he reached the Kazan Station and learned from the other correspondents that Cameron had been taken to the Narkomindel by two NKVD agents. He was almost as distraught when he heard that Shanahan had accompanied her. He should have been glad that she had a companion and a champion to assist her against the police. But why couldn't it have been someone else?

He choked back the unfamiliar and most unwelcome bile of jealousy to concentrate on far more important matters. What were the NKVD's intentions regarding Cameron? What could they do? What *would* they do? Was that evening in Pushkin Square to be the last time he would ever see her? His insides clenched at that thought. But it could very well be so. She could be summarily deported and not allowed back into the country. And he could very easily be denied an exit visa in order to go find her. But the question he could barely face was whether the bonds between them were strong enough to drive them to surmount the barriers the Russian government could place before them.

He put that question aside, perhaps in the same place he had stowed his jealousy, in order to face more tangible issues. What should he do now? His initial instinct was to storm the Narkomindel. But he knew that would not help. Therefore, it seemed the only sensible action left him was to wait at the station. The police weren't about to be responsible for making an American citizen miss the last chance to evacuate a nearly besieged city.

Alex paced the station, at least as much as the mobs of humanity allowed him movement on the packed platform. Then the boarding began of the last train to Kuibyshev. The foreigners piled into the cars along with hordes of other privileged Soviet citizens, mostly government officials. He thought that if the Germans dropped a bomb just then on the Kazan Station, they would have made a serious international impact. But no bombs fell. There had, in fact, for the last two days, been an almost eerie lull in the constant bombardment.

Alex assured the correspondents, who were almost as worried as he about their tardy comrades, that he would look out for them and make sure they found a way out of town in a timely fashion. Then the train pulled away.

Completely dejected, Alex slumped down on a bench and did the only thing he could think to do. He prayed. After a few minutes, feeling inexplicably better, he rose and left the station. He went to the Metropole and spoke to the manager, but Cameron had not come in. He then went to the American embassy. He spoke to the two attachés who had been left behind to finish burning papers and to close up the embassy. They knew nothing about Hayes or Shanahan.

He thought about camping out at the Metropole. But perhaps she had found another way out of the city and would not return to the hotel. Besides, Alex was not entirely his own man. The hospital was growing more and more shorthanded, as medical personnel were taken away to man frontline medical units. He had to return to work. Cameron would find a way to reach him.

He would—a slight smile bent his lips as the thought occurred to him—leave her in God's hands.

———

The traffic on the road to the station was incredible. Cameron had not thought there were this many vehicles in all of Russia. But there were not only motorized vehicles, but horse carts, and hand-drawn wagons, and people, people everywhere clogging the streets. The NKVD M–1 crept at little more than five miles per hour. Finally, Cameron and Johnny jumped out of the car and made their way on foot.

They reached Kazan Station at twelve-thirty. No one had to tell them they had missed the last train out. The thinning mob on the platform was the first indication. All the people who had been disappointed at the station had taken to the roads in a mass exodus, one way or another, from the city. If any of these people had heard Lozovsky's declaration that Moscow would not fall, they did not believe it. They were definitely fleeing a sinking ship.

Not knowing what else to do, they returned to the American embassy. Bob Wood was holding down the fort.

"What rotten luck!" he exclaimed when he heard their story.

"No worse, I suppose, than your being stuck here," offered Cameron.

"I volunteered. It's frightening, but a once-in-a-lifetime experience, I suppose, being present at the Battle of Moscow."

Cameron nodded with complete understanding. She wondered how much his staying had to do with the debacle of Oleg's escape. Bob had been devastated when he'd heard. But there was nothing to be done about it except move on. Maybe staying in Moscow till the end was his way of bonding himself closer to the Russian cause.

"Yeah," agreed Shanahan, "but it won't last. Our drivers said they would arrange transportation out of the city for us, maybe tomorrow. They will never let us stay where there is breaking news."

"Maybe we'll get lost in the shuffle," Cameron said hopefully.

"Not with our luck." Shanahan grimaced.

"Speaking of luck," said Wood, "there was someone here an hour or so ago asking after you, Cameron. Do you know a fellow, a Russian named Alex Rostov?"

"Yes!" Cameron brightened instantly. Her heart skipped a beat. "He was here?"

"Yes. He was quite frantic with worry over you."

"So he knows we missed the train?"

"Yes, and he knows about your little run-in with the NKVD. As I said, he was distraught."

"Distraught, eh?" Shanahan said with a cocked brow.

Cameron rolled her eyes but mostly to cover the bevy of emotions assailing her at that moment. "Well, that's understandable, isn't it? The city is being evacuated. The police drag me in. I mean anyone would be distressed to hear that about a friend. He was distressed over you, too, Shanahan."

"Oh, I'm sure he was in an absolute dither because *I* got arrested, then missed the last train away from a growing inferno," sneered Shanahan. "He was beside himself over *me*."

Cameron shook her head. "Really, Shanahan."

"The jerk's smitten with you, Hayes. As they say, wake up and smell the coffee."

"I *could* use a good cup of coffee," she hedged.

"There's a pot brewing in the other room," offered Wood.

Cameron took the cue and hurried from the room. Shanahan wasn't going to let her off that easily. He followed her.

"What're you gonna do?" he asked.

"Have a cup of joe."

"About the doc?"

Cameron grabbed a cup and filled it, but Shanahan intercepted it as she raised it to her lips. She released the mug into his hand, then poured herself another.

She savored a sip of the good black brew. "What is it to you, Johnny? I mean, what I do or don't do about Alex?"

"Hey, I'm just a concerned friend, that's all." He was not defensive. He was actually sincere.

"That's all?"

"Yeah."

She stared at him over the rim of her cup and realized that indeed was it. He was a concerned friend—a dear friend—but no more. It should have been more of a surprise than it was. But then she remembered his drunken words of love to her a few weeks ago. And she remembered Tatiana. She had pretty much postponed all her feelings about what had happened at the Front. But she was being forced to face them now.

Shanahan didn't love her. And Alex was *distraught* over her. No wonder she still wanted to dodge her feelings. It was simply all too much to take in. Especially since she had never wanted any such involvements. She'd done well all her life to keep all her relationships at arm's length. They only led to hurt. But now she could feel her protective walls cracking, and she wasn't sure she liked the feeling.

CAMERON WOKE with a jerk. She was perspiring from the tangled nightmares that had disturbed her sleep. Then she sat up in bed and quickly oriented herself. She and Shanahan had opted to spend the night at the embassy instead of returning to the hotel. The intermittent bombing in the night had kept her from seeking out Alex. The phones weren't working, so she couldn't call him. But she knew she must see him before she left Moscow. Her conflicted feelings aside, she owed him that much.

She slipped from her bed. She was fully clothed. In the bathroom, she splashed some cold water on her face and desperately wished she could brush her teeth. But presumably all her belongings were on their way to Kuibyshev. She went to Wood's office, and he was still hovering over the incinerator.

"Have you been at it all night?" she asked, pouring herself a cup of coffee from the pot he had moved closer at hand.

"I caught a couple of winks." He shoved another stack of papers into the fire.

"Where's Shanahan?"

"Still asleep."

"Any word from the Narkomindel?"

Wood shook his head. Cameron swallowed more coffee, then made a decision.

"Bob, may I use one of the embassy cars?"

"What for? Not to leave town, I hope. You can't do that without some sort of escort."

"I just need it for an hour. I have to run across town. The metro isn't running regularly anymore, and there are no taxis. But there's someone I must see—"

"Oh, the Rostov fellow, right?" Pausing in his task, Wood gave a morose shake of his head. "You are not getting mixed up with another Russian, are you? I would hope that after the experience with Oleg you'd have learned a lesson."

"I am not getting mixed up with anyone! But you said yourself that he was distraught. I can't reach him by phone, and I have to let him know I'm okay before I leave. It's only a matter of being considerate."

"Uh-huh." He stifled a smile. "Here—" He took a set of keys from his pocket. "But do be careful. There may be a lull in the air raids at the moment, but it won't last."

The embassy Packard was parked in the garage, and Cameron pulled out with some serious jerking. It had been a long time since she had driven a car. Even in Los Angeles she had used taxicabs more than her own vehicle. But her technique smoothed out as she progressed across town. The roads were not as clogged as they had been the previous day. But still there was much traffic. And other eerie scenes greeted her. She saw a man running down the street, a string of sausages circling his neck like a surreal string of pearls. On another block, a truck had overturned, and a mob was digging through the contents. Doors of abandoned shops were hanging open, and Cameron was certain there were looters carrying away merchandise. Where were the police? Had they abandoned the city, as well?

She pulled up across the street from the hospital and slammed on the brakes. She hadn't realized until then she had been driving so fast. She hurried into the huge building, and after spending several minutes asking around, finally located Alex. He was emerging from surgery wearing the green shirt and pants they called "scrubs" with a matching green cap still on his head and a face mask hanging around his neck. She couldn't believe how appealing he looked, even with bloodstains still on his shirt.

"Cameron, you're here!" he said, exclaiming the obvious.

"Missed my train, but I guess you know all about that."

"I'm so sorry." Was he? She couldn't tell.

An air-raid siren screeched outside, and Cameron was reminded of other matters beyond the stirring she felt in her body.

"You shouldn't have come here during an air raid," he said.

"I couldn't reach you by phone, and I thought you'd want to know I was okay. Anyway, there wasn't a raid when I left. Bob at the embassy loaned me his Packard, and I thought I could make it before anything happened."

"I guess there is no telling when the Germans will strike these days."

"Will the hospital be evacuated?" she asked.

"Some of the patients who could be moved already have been, but there are many who can't be moved."

"You'll stay with them."

"I have to come or go as I am told."

"As must I."

Sighing, he ran a hand through his pale hair, knocking off his cap, which fell to the floor. Ignoring that, he gazed at Cameron. "We knew this would happen."

"Yes."

"I'm just glad you are all right. I was worried, and I'll continue to worry until you are out of danger. . . ." He paused and smiled rather sheepishly. "I know that infuriates you, but I can't help it. That's how I am with my friends."

"Friends . . . yes." Her mouth went dry, and suddenly a fear gripped her. Their world was in complete upheaval, punctuated by the explosions outside from the renewed bombing. This was no time for declarations of anything. But she was torn between wanting to declare *everything* and a burning desire to run from it. His worry did infuriate her, but it touched her, as well. It also scared her to death, made her feel trapped, suffocated. Yes, they had made certain commitments that day on Pushkin Square, but even then neither had made that ultimate commitment.

"Where's Shanahan?" he asked suddenly.

"At the embassy. Why?"

"He took care of you—"

"I don't *need* to be taken care of!"

"Do you love him?"

She gaped, stunned, at the unexpected question. But she did not deny it. The question was like her escape hatch, and in her desperate confusion she grabbed at it. Hating herself for her silence, hating the fear suddenly gripping her.

A nurse rushed up to them. "Doctor, your patient is hemorrhaging."

"I have to go," he said, his voice hollow and cold.

She opened her mouth to speak, but the only words that came to her mind were "I love you!" And she couldn't bring herself to say them.

He disappeared through a door, and she watched, shaking inside and out. Turning, she retreated down the corridor.

What was wrong with her? She had never known this kind of fear. She heard the bombs outside. They were awfully close, but that barely fazed her. Could she face bombs easier than a declaration of love? She told herself that Alex had not declared his love, either. Then they were *both* enormous fools. Shanahan knew it. Even Bob Wood knew it. But she and Alex were too afraid to speak the words, not to mention making the commitment that went with those words. Would she spend her whole life running from love because her father had hurt her with his rejection? And Alex was little better, letting his fears of addiction stand in his way.

They were idiots! *She* was an idiot. And if it was because she felt trapped, it was not because of Alex. She had known almost from the first moment she'd spoken to him that he was not that sort of a man. If he worried about her, what was odd about that in the middle of a war? She worried about him, too.

As she exited the hospital, the ground shook under her feet. What was she doing out in the open during an air raid? She was definitely not thinking straight.

Turning sharply in order to return to the hospital and shelter, she heard the sound before she realized the nearness of the bomb. She saw the building across the street explode, and less than a split second later the impact reached her, knocking her down and throwing her several feet away. She banged her head on something, then all went black.

Alex was emerging from the recovery room after seeing that the nurse's excitement had been for nothing. The bleeding was no more than was to be expected. But she was a new girl, not even a trained nurse, and they were too shorthanded to quibble over such matters.

Suddenly the building shook with far more force that it had in previous bombings. Plaster cracked and snowed down on him as he stumbled against a wall. That was close! Had the enemy ceased to recognize the red cross painted on the hospital roof?

A few moments later, an orderly, jogging toward Alex, paused. "Doc, a bomb demolished a building right across the street! There was a car parked in front that was practically buried with debris."

"Oh no!" Alex breathed. Had Cameron had time to leave the hospital? Would she have been foolish enough to leave during an air raid? She said she had driven here. His stomach heaved. "Get help over there!" he shouted as he raced away.

Frantically, he shouted her name as he ran through the hospital to the exit. He knew she wouldn't respond. An ache inside told him she was not safely ensconced in the hospital air-raid shelter. Why would she have stayed? He had turned away from her, letting his fear and jealousy rule him for a moment that he now regretted.

Reaching the street, he was immediately arrested by the sight of the demolished office building across the street. And there was a car that looked like the ones used by the embassy. Little of it was visible under the bricks and debris that had fallen from the building, but the parts visible resembled the Packards he'd seen at the embassy.

Wildly he attacked the rubble, grabbing heavy bricks and tossing them aside. "Cameron!" he cried. "Are you in there?" Oh, God, please don't let her be in there. Don't let her be hurt! He hardly noticed how natural it was now for him to turn to God. But he had been doing so more and more often since that time at the Front. He hadn't questioned it, and he still did not question it. He'd never stopped needing God. That had not been the problem, anyway. Unlike Cameron, he understood the need for God just as he did the need for air. He did not feel less of a person or less of a man for it.

No, that had never been his particular stumbling block.

As he tore away at the rubble, his hands growing cut and bloodied, he murmured, "I know I'm not worthy. But, God, please hear my cry. Save her!"

He didn't care if she was spared only to give herself to Johnny Shanahan. Alex just wanted to see her alive again, to see her face. That would be enough.

"Do you need some help?" came a voice behind him.

It did not register with Alex that the voice had spoken in English, nor that it should have been familiar.

"Yes, she's in there. I've got to save her!"

"Alex . . ."

He stopped his desperate activity, but he continued to hold a brick he had been about to toss, afraid to turn, afraid to believe his prayers had been answered. She laid a hand on his shoulder, and the touch was very real and very warm and very alive. He dropped the brick and turned. In the next instant his arms were around her, and he was kissing her face, that dear face he'd been so sure he'd never see again like this.

"You're all right?" His eyes swept her with instinctive medical acuity.

"Yes. The blast knocked me unconscious for a few minutes. Bob's car fared a lot worse," she nodded toward the rubble.

"I was afraid—" But a knot made the words stick in his throat, so he just kept kissing her. It took a moment before he realized she was kissing him back with equal fervency.

Several moments passed, the only sounds being those of distant explosions. The planes had moved to strike new sectors. The ground still rumbled under their feet, but neither noticed. They only paused when a rescue crew bounded onto the scene. Then Alex nudged Cameron toward the hospital, and they ducked inside and found a secluded spot.

"I love you, Cameron!" he murmured.

"Wait a minute! I wanted to say it first," she said.

"What?" He was truly befuddled now.

"I love you." Her eyes glittered, glowed. He wondered why he had not seen it in them before. "You. . . ? What about Shanahan?" But he still was afraid to believe it.

She made a little snort. "Johnny is—was—just an infatuation. I was in awe more with what Johnny represented than with Johnny himself. But you . . ."

"Me?" he prompted when she hesitated.

"I don't know. I don't want to be in love. I don't want a relationship, a commitment. But it's stupid to run away from it when it is so obvious that even I finally saw it." Smiling, her eyes roved over him as if she'd also feared she had lost him. "Why us? I don't know. A hard, petulant reporter and an idealistic doctor? It doesn't make sense. Johnny and I made sense, but—"

"Hush," he breathed. "You've told me in the past that I analyze things too much. Don't you do it now. God answered my prayers and brought you back to me, and I am certain He brought us together. That is enough for me."

"God?"

He shrugged. "Don't you think I was praying my heart out when I thought you were in that car?"

"I guess even I would have prayed if I'd thought it was you."

He brought his hands to her face to draw her near, but she gasped.

"Alex, your hands!" She took his bloodied hands in hers and kissed them. "Your poor surgeon's hands."

"They'll heal." He drew her to him and kissed her again, long and languidly, as if they had nothing but time.

It was Cameron who finally burst that little bubble of false security. "Now what, Alex?"

"The end. They lived happily ever after."

"Don't joke. I have to leave. You have to stay. God only knows what's going to happen in between."

"That's good enough for me. Let's leave it in His hands."

"I'm not quite ready to do that," she said.

He felt a little twist of his stomach, but he shrugged off the tiny sensation of disquiet and said, "There's a chance I'll get to Kuibyshev eventually."

"Promise me we won't lose each other, you know, the way people get lost in wartime."

"I promise," he breathed with such confidence that she had to believe him.

PART VI

"*This will last out a night in Russia, when nights are longest there.*"

SHAKESPEARE
Measure for Measure

54

JACKIE DID NOT WANT to think of the place where she and Sam met as a *secret* place. It was in the middle of the UCLA campus—well, nearer to the edge among a clump of trees where there was seldom any traffic. At the moment there were about a half dozen students playing touch football fifty feet away. She and Sam had no secrets. They were friends, and they liked the solitude of the "trees," as they had come to call the little cove. They ate in public cafés now and then; they even went to a movie once in a while. All very open. Nothing in the world to hide.

"So your sister has gone all the way to the Philippines?" Sam asked when Jackie had filled him in on recent events.

"I was a bit shocked when she mentioned it, but after some thought, I decided perhaps it is a good move for her."

"So she can snag this lieutenant of hers?"

Jackie was taken aback by the edge to his tone. "Not exactly. They are already married," she answered defensively. "More so she can work things out with him, and with God, as well."

"I don't get it."

"It's complicated, but it made sense when she explained it. It is sort of like a paradox. She is afraid her motives for attaining faith might be to win Gary. But on the other hand . . ." Jackie paused and scratched her head. "Well, it did make sense before. But you don't agree, do you?"

"I guess I just keep seeing it from Gary's side," said Sam. They were sitting in the grass under a big oak tree whose leaves were changing

417

colors and falling to the ground. Sam picked up one fallen leaf and stared at it. He was clearly reluctant to offer his opinion on a matter that really didn't concern him.

"And what do you see?" Jackie prompted.

"It's really none of my business. I don't know these people."

"But I can tell you have something to say."

He gave her a smirk because she was right. "Okay. I know I'll regret poking my nose into this, but I was just thinking how, though I haven't met the man, this Gary sounds like a fellow to whom a relationship with a woman of his own faith is important."

Jackie nodded and Sam went on.

"I believe strongly in the sanctity of marriage, but what kind of marriage do they have? One, it seems, that is built entirely on lies. I know I said before it was best to let God do what He would with your sister, but that was before she tricked the guy into marriage. Forgive me if I sound harsh toward your sister. She may truly love him, but how will he ever trust her again?"

"That's why she's going to him, to try to build that trust again. Gary really didn't leave her. He had to go because of the army. He told her he felt honor bound to stand by his marriage vows."

"What a terrible way to build a marriage."

"Yes, I agree it is. But maybe it will work, as you suggested before. God will take the broken pieces and will build them into something good. Once even you seemed to think God might be putting them together."

"I don't believe I ever said that exactly," he protested. "I just thought it might be best for you to not get involved."

"You were right about that," she admitted.

He smiled, just a bit triumphantly. "And I should take my own advice."

"It's out of our hands anyway. But I am still confused by everything. I see what you mean doubting the wisdom of Gary getting involved with a woman who isn't a Christian. But what about the possibility of Blair finding God through it all?"

"Will Gary ever be certain her faith isn't just another act to keep him?"

"I guess they will have to trust it to God—"

He laughed. "Now you think of that!"

"I know, but I just couldn't keep my nose out of it. You should have seen how Blair was sliding off the edge. I think she might have considered suicide." Jackie took a breath and realized a lump of emotion was stuck in her throat. Tears filled her eyes. "I was so desperate for her. I prayed for her, and maybe I didn't wait for God, but I thought there was always the possibility that God wanted to use me—oh, Sam! Do you think I have ruined things again?" She sniffed loudly.

"No!" he relented. "I don't think you could ever ruin anything."

He gazed at her with an intensity in his eyes that made Jackie quiver inside. He reached out for her hand, and, as always, the warmth of his touch gave her a deep sense of security.

"I'm sorry for what I said. They are in God's hands, aren't they? God will take care of them."

"And He will take care of my blunders, too?" she asked tearfully.

"Always," he replied with assurance. He moved close to her and put an arm around her trembling shoulders.

She leaned nearer to him. They had never allowed themselves to be this close. Ignoring her racing heart, she told herself this was a brotherly act of comfort. She laid her head on his shoulder and felt his chin as it came down and rested in her hair. This was so much as it should be that she responded only with a contented sigh.

Sam kissed the top of her head. She sighed again.

A bouncing football intruded gradually into her contented senses. It was just part of the idyllic scene. Then came the *clomp, clomp* of heavy feet jogging across the grass.

"Sorry," a voice came.

Jackie turned casually toward the voice, which had come from behind. "Oh, that's okay." She honestly had forgotten, if she had given it a thought at all, that what she was doing might be wrong.

"Jackie!"

It was Jeffrey Meade. Sam's head jerked up, and his arm fell just as swiftly away from her. Guilt darkened his expression, and she would have been angry with this had she not been certain that the same look also marred her own face.

"Good grief, Jackie! What are you doing?" accused Jeffrey as he scooped the football into his hand.

"I . . . we . . ." she stammered but could manage nothing coherent. She felt guilty, as if she had been caught in some criminal act.

Sam looked very much the same, but he gathered his wits around himself much quicker.

"We're talking, if you don't mind," he said, and, to his credit, pride and even a touch of arrogance laced his tone.

"Talking, eh? I'll bet. And with a Jap, Jackie! I thought you had better sense than that."

Sam jumped up. "Take that back, Meade!" He literally got in Jeffrey's face, standing within two inches of the other young man's nose.

"Shut up, you!" Meade spat, then shoved at Sam and turned his back on him as if he were of less account than a bug in the grass. "Jackie, your parents are gonna croak when they see you've ruined yourself with this Jap—"

Sam grabbed Meade fiercely and spun him around. "Don't you talk that way to her! And if you start spreading lies about Jackie, I'll—"

"What're you gonna do, you yellow monkey?" sneered Jeffrey. "Now, get your puny face outta mine—"

Sam's fist cut off further comment as it smashed into Meade's face. Meade stumbled back and blood oozed from his nose. His hand shot to his face, and he touched the blood. He turned a little pale.

"Why, you . . . I ought to clobber you for this," Jeffrey threatened. "But you aren't worth it." He turned around and stalked away.

Jackie had watched the entire scene in stunned silence. She didn't know what dumbfounded her most, Sam's fierce defense of her honor, Jeffrey's incredible buffoonery, or the idea that her parents were very soon going to learn about Sam, and not from her. Pushing the last two issues from her mind, she decided to just focus on Sam. He was rubbing his bruised fist.

"I never hit a man before," he said in rather a dazed tone.

Rising, she took his hand. Yes, there were bruises already forming on the knuckles. She brought the damaged hand to her lips. But he jerked it away.

"Are you crazy?" he said sharply. "They're all watching."

Indeed, the group of flag football players was standing some distance away, and all were gazing in their direction.

A sudden smile twitched her lips. "You have just given the most popular and influential boy in school a bloody nose, and you are worried about me kissing your hand?"

"I don't want them to think ill of you."

"I don't care what they think." But she was remembering the momentary guilt and shame that had assailed her when Jeffrey first came up.

"Let's get out of here," he said. "But we shouldn't go together—"

"Stop it, Sam. Stop trying to protect me."

"This could ruin you!"

"Bah! I don't believe that for a minute."

It hit her with as much force as Sam's hand had connected with Jeffrey's nose. A strong, sudden urge to kiss Sam. And it wasn't because everyone was looking. It was because he had defended her and because he was focusing on her now a look of such amazing concern that it made her heart clench.

She restrained the urge, but she knew it was more for his sake than for hers, because he would have been mortified by the act.

"We are walking away from here together or not at all," she said stubbornly, trying to match the passion he had exhibited with his defense of her.

With a resigned shrug, he started walking and did nothing to stop her when she caught up with him and strode at his side.

When they were well out of sight of the others, he turned to her. "Jackie, we cannot see each other again."

"What!"

"Your parents will forbid it anyway."

"I don't care—"

"You do care what your parents think. You have worked all your life to please them." When she tried to protest, he shook his head. "In Oriental culture this is a good thing, honoring one's parents. I would not defy my parents, either, and I know they would disapprove as heartily as yours."

"By that thinking, we have already defied them."

"Not technically. We haven't lied to them. We just haven't told them, that's all."

"I didn't think you could be so devious, Sam Okuda!"

"Not devious. Just practical."

"Doesn't matter," she insisted. "We have done nothing wrong. What kind of world is it when two people of different races can't be friends?"

"It might be different if we were of the same sex."

"This is starting to sound like the Dark Ages! I will not—"

"It is the way it is. We must accept it."

She stared at him, unbelieving. "What about 'friends forever'?"

"We will always be friends."

"Poppycock! That's just another silly technicality."

He stopped walking. With incredible calm for a man who had just smashed the face of an adversary, he said, "I am going to my car now. Over there—" He jerked his head toward a distant parking lot. "You will go to the library. Over there—" He inclined his head in the opposite direction. "That is how it must be."

He started walking. She wanted to run after him, but she didn't. Something in her trusted him so implicitly, so strongly, that she could not force herself to fight the authority of his words. Sam always knew what he was about. His wisdom amazed her at times. She had to believe he now knew what he was doing. But she also had to believe that a Greater Power, a Greater Wisdom, would somehow make all this right.

After watching him for some time as he disappeared into the distance, Jackie turned. But she didn't go to the library. Instead, she went to the campus chapel. There she slipped into a pew and prayed for about an hour. She still had no answers when she left that place, but she felt better. And that was a good thing, too, because soon her world was about to take its first dip toward disaster.

————

It took a few days for news of her relationship with Sam to reach her father. Luckily, Keagan had been in Sacramento meeting with the governor for several days. But when he finally approached his daughter after his return home, there was a restraint to his demeanor. Jackie was the baby, and perhaps because of that, he had always treated her differently than the older girls. He was no less stern and demanding, but she did manage to get away with much more than her sisters.

Well, that wasn't exactly true, either. She had never tried to get away with anything. She had always done what was expected of her. It had garnered her little praise from her father, but it had bestowed upon her a kind of invisibility, so that she had seldom been yelled at or ridiculed.

When Keagan came to her room the evening after his return from the state capital, she braced herself for the full vent of his rage.

"Jackie, I heard some things from one of your classmates," he said evenly. His arms were crossed over his chest, and he looked imposing standing in her doorway, the red in his hair taking dominance over the subtler gray. His eyes, too, were especially vivid and portending.

"Yes. . . ?"

"You know what I am talking about?"

She nodded.

"I am very disappointed in you."

"Why, Daddy? I just don't understand. Sam is a friend—"

"A Japanese boy, right?"

"What does that matter?"

"I am not a bigot, but there are certain realities that can't be ignored. One is that a boy and a girl of differing races *cannot* be friends. To be honest, I am not certain a boy and girl of the same race can be just friends, not in the way you imply."

"That's ridiculous!"

"Watch your mouth, young lady!"

"I'm sorry, Daddy. But I just don't understand. We are friends, only friends. With all the unrest in the world today, it has to be a good thing for two races to come together in this way. It can only help."

"Listen to me, and listen closely. You want to bring racial harmony to this world? Then find a Jap—Japanese *girl* to befriend. Anything else is unacceptable—" He stopped suddenly and gasped a breath. His usually florid complexion paled slightly.

"Daddy, what's wrong?"

"Nothing. Just indigestion from that greasy rump roast Eleanor cooked tonight." He thumped his chest with his fist, took another breath, and continued. "Do you understand? You will not see that boy again."

"But, Daddy, he's a good friend—"

"Enough!" he boomed suddenly, losing all vestiges of calm. "You will not bring further shame to this family. If I hear you have defied me, I swear, I'll throw you out like I did your sister!"

He spun on his heel and stalked away.

In the middle of the night, Jackie awoke to the sounds of footsteps in the hall. Her mother opened her door.

"Jacqueline, your father is ill! I've had to call an ambulance."

Jackie grabbed her dressing gown and raced from her room behind her mother just as a siren could be heard outside. Within five minutes Keagan Hayes was being rushed away to the hospital. Cecilia rode in the ambulance, leaving Jackie to follow in the car.

It was a horrible night, sitting there in the hospital waiting room clutching her mother's hand and waiting for the announcement to come that her father had died. All she could think was that she had somehow been the cause of it because she had brought shame to the family.

But that didn't stop her from needing the comfort, the mere nearness, of her dearest friend. She thought of Sam constantly. When she slipped away downstairs to the hospital pay telephone, she felt a twinge of disloyalty, but it was simply asking too much of her to cut herself off from Sam so completely, especially now.

He came quickly to her. They sat in his car across the street from the hospital. She opened her mouth to tell him what she was feeling about her father, but a rush of tears superseded words.

He took her shaking, sobbing form into his arms, patting her head and cooing soothingly to her. Five minutes later she gathered enough control to speak, though her words were punctuated with sobs and sniffs.

"I g-gave him this heart attack!" she confessed. "H-He had a pain when he was yelling at me . . . b-because of . . ." But she couldn't admit the reason for the yelling. Sam would know anyway.

"Jackie, you didn't do this—"

"And now look. I'm defying him still. He's on his d-deathbed, and I couldn't . . . oh, Sam . . . I just needed you!"

"It's okay. I'm here."

"I made you defy your parents, too."

"Right now, that's not important." He brushed her tangled, damp hair from around her eyes. "Look at me. We are friends, Jackie. There's nothing anyone can do about that."

She sniffed loudly and fresh tears dripped from her eyes. "S-Sam . . . I'm s-so sorry . . . I think it's more than f-friendship. Sam . . . I think I love you!"

"Don't say that!" His own voice was strangled, as if he was on the verge of tears, as well.

"I can't help it! I am a terrible person. My father is dying, but I could only think of you, of how I needed you—"

"You need only God!" he cut in sharply. He let go of her and pushed himself up as close as possible to the door of the car.

"You know what I mean! God will always be in the middle of what we have. He has given me you. I am sure of it." She gazed at him. His Oriental features, hated by so many, seemed more obvious than ever, but she knew beyond all doubt now that she loved them as she loved the man behind them.

Sam shook his head at her words but without conviction. Jackie saw only his seemingly negative response. Had she been wrong then? Were his feelings not the same as hers? The thought of this devastated her, and new emotion assailed her. And this time she thought she would crumble because there were no arms reaching out to her. His body was pressed stiffly against the door.

Only for a moment. Then he reached out, and she melted to him, his strong arms holding her like a pillar.

"Sam . . . can you say it?" she breathed between sobs.

"Jackie . . ." He hesitated.

"Please!"

There was a long pause. She could feel the trembling of his arms around her. Then he spoke.

"I loved you from the beginning." His voice shook with its fervency. "From when you'd argue with our English professor, telling him about the love of God. You were so unafraid."

"I was s-scared stiff."

"Jackie, I love you so. But why do I feel like such a criminal for it?"

"No matter what anyone says, we are not criminals!"

"But we hide in the darkness of my car—"

"I don't care!"

"Can God possibly sanction this?"

"Yes!"

But despite her affirmation, new tears wracked her, and she didn't know where they were coming from. Her father might be dying, of course. She was in love with a man all of her society would shun. She had no idea what would come of any of it. She was afraid, unsure. She clung only to one certainty.

"Sam, say it once more."

"I love you, Jackie."

"I love you, Sam!"

And that seemed enough, for the moment at least.

55

On the outskirts of Moscow
November 1941

CAMERON TWISTED her head around to watch the city diminish behind them.

"Will we ever get back here?" she mused aloud.

"The better question is, will there be a city left to get back to?" Shanahan replied.

"I can't believe anything can destroy Moscow. Why, we have already heard rumors that the weather and the muddy roads have slowed the Germans."

" 'General Winter' will rise victorious!" Shanahan's tone suggested a slight sneer, but Cameron could see through that to the hope even he felt.

She'd sensed that same hope in the citizens of the capital, as well. It had begun with the news that Stalin had not fled Moscow. That brought a kind of sanity back to the remaining citizens of the wartorn city. Of course declaring martial law and handing out severe penalties for looting and even for rumor mongering also helped the capital to regain some of its lost footing.

As Cameron headed east out of the city in a convoy of supply trucks, she was torn in many directions. She was steamed with the Soviet authorities who would dictate her movements. It was not right that if she wanted to take the risk they should force her to leave. But news opportunities were not the only reason she desired to remain. She had taken a leap—a monumental leap for her—and declared her love to a man, only to be separated from him the very next day. She wanted to experience this new level of their relationship, but instead she was wrenched from it with only hastily spoken words to take with her.

Had they merely been words uttered out of the extremity of the situation they had been in? The classic wartime romance? She had not wanted romance, but she could not muster any regrets now that it had found her. She was already feeling empty without him and at the prospect of not having him around to talk to. She was missing the spark of his eyes, sometimes the color of a frozen river, other times the blue of a summer pond that you just wanted to dive into and absorb all the sweet warmth they held. And when that warmth permeated his easy smile, it made her tingle just to remember that.

How schoolgirlish, Hayes! she silently berated herself.

She had certainly never thought such things about Johnny. She took a covert look at Shanahan's eyes. No, they were just brown. She realized now it had not been his eyes or his smile that had appealed to her, but rather his prose. And though Johnny's talent was definitely an intricate part of him, it was not *him*. She had been in love with paper and words, not with the man. Yet even now that she could admit to her love for Alex, she knew she had lingering feelings for Shanahan. Respect, friendship, even a little awe. She loved him, too, but as he had once said, it was as a brother. She wondered if she could let go of even that for Alex's sake. She didn't think Alex was insecure in that way, yet he had obviously been a bit jealous of Shanahan.

Cameron tried not to think of giving up things for love. That had been one reason she had run from love for so long. Would Alex require such sacrifices of her? She licked her lips and tried to shake the unsettling thought from her head.

———

Factoring in bad roads, breakdowns, and general Russian inefficiency, it took a week to get to Kuibyshev. They were installed with other correspondents and foreigners at the Grand Hotel, a provincial wooden inn that was by far the best the town had to offer. Each floor had only two communal washrooms, one for males and one for females. Cameron found that the one for females had just one water faucet, and it gave only cold water. There was only one bathtub in the entire hotel, and it didn't work. But Cameron cared not for comforts, though as winter deepened, she could have wished for more consistent heat in her room. It helped that the room was tiny, since because of the scarcity of other foreign women, she had no roommate and thus was allotted the smallest room that could be found. Cameron also came to miss Sophia tremendously, especially after she was introduced to her new interpreter, Helga, a buxom middle-aged woman who, Cameron was certain, had to be an NKVD agent scarcely disguised by her narrow, suspicious eyes and impressively muscular arms.

Life in Kuibyshev quickly resumed the old Moscow patterns: combing of newspapers for material every morning, receiving Palgunov's daily communiqués, attending Lozovsky's uninformative press conferences, dealing with censors, and sending dispatches. But this town, though boasting to be the wartime capital of the Soviet Union, could not begin to measure up to Moscow in providing distractions. The Bolshoi Theater company had moved there and continued its regular program of performances, there was a cinema, and the relocated embassies tried to keep up their usual rounds of parties and receptions. But it wasn't the same, and Cameron could not believe she had complained about being bored in Moscow!

Of course it didn't help that Moscow was now where the action was on the news front. The biggest news was that two weeks after the panicked evacuation, the Russians still held their capital, despite the fact that the Germans had advanced to within fifty miles of the city, and in some places even closer.

On November seventh the Soviet Union celebrated the twenty-fourth anniversary of the Revolution. The correspondents gathered around the communal radio in the Grand's dining hall to hear Stalin's speech.

"I'd like to have been there to hear it in person," Cameron lamented.

"An impressive sight, I'm sure," said Donovan. "Uncle Joe, there, in Red Square surrounded by his troops, the cannon of battle booming in the background."

"Yeah, makes me tingle all over," groused Shanahan. He'd been taking the dreary atmosphere of Kuibyshev especially hard and had been more and more talking about getting reassigned; however, he continued to face the reality that there was little else happening in the world at the moment in regard to the war.

"I'm sure it will have a deep emotional impact on the Russian people," Cameron said.

"Any official words are emotional to them since they hear them so seldom," smirked Shanahan.

"Quiet, it's starting," someone said.

The radio made a few static noises; then the unmistakable voice of Stalin boomed forth. Shanahan's secretary interpreted the speech for the group. All the correspondents snickered when after several minutes of German baiting and Soviet glorification, Stalin claimed that since the beginning of the war, the Russians had lost 350,000 men in death; 378,000 were missing; and 1,020,000 were wounded; whereas the Germans had lost a total of over four and a half million men—dead, wounded, and captured!

"He must have got those cockeyed figures from Lozovsky," quipped Donovan.

"He sure didn't get them from Hitler." Shanahan shook his head. "The German figures are probably the reverse of that."

"Heaven only knows what the real figures are," said Cameron.

But the speech was stirring, no doubt about that. Cameron got goose bumps when he said, "Comrades, Red Army and Red Navy men, workers, men and women partisans! The whole world is looking upon you as the power capable of destroying the German robber hordes! The enslaved people of Europe are looking to you as their liberators. . . ."

The Soviet leader had to pause to allow for the booming applause to this statement.

"Be worthy of this great mission!" he continued. "The war you are waging is a war of liberation and is a just war. Death to the German invaders! Long live our glorious country, its freedom and independence. Onward to victory!"

The applause in Red Square was deafening, or Cameron was certain it would have been had she been in the midst of it and not stuck here in a dingy dining room hundreds of miles from all that mattered.

———

There was little time to listen to speeches at Alex's Moscow hospital. But he heard all about it from patients and staff. He was a Russian, even a member of the Party, but he could not be much stirred by Stalin's rousing platitudes. Cameron had called Alex an idealist, and he probably was compared to the journalist types like Shanahan, to whom she was accustomed, but he was too close to the ugliness of war to embrace the glorification of war that Stalin was selling.

Perhaps the real reason for his listless response to the speech was simply his utter fatigue. And for that reason he let Yuri talk him into taking a small tea break.

The two men drew tea from the samovar and sat in the shabby doctors' lounge. Alex was glad for this respite, not only for the rest it afforded, but also because he had been wanting to talk to Yuri for some time.

"I was thinking of specializing in plastic surgery after the war," Alex commented casually.

"I never realized that was an interest of yours." Yuri adjusted the nosepiece of his glasses as if to make sure he was speaking to the right person.

Alex laughed, or what passed for a laugh these weary days. "Not really, I suppose, but I'm thinking it would be a delightful change to do something that involves such exacting detail and care. I am quite sick of the assembly-line surgery I've been forced to do. I don't even see faces anymore, only abdomens, limbs, and chests."

"We have some fine plastic surgeons in this country. You would get excellent training."

"It's not as if I don't have far more pressing things in my future to consider," Alex mused. "I have been hoping for a chance to talk to you."

"What is it, Alex?"

"It's Cameron Hayes."

"Ah . . ." Yuri did not smile or offer any of the usual teasing responses, and for that Alex was grateful.

"We have finally accepted the fact that we love each other," Alex went on, but realizing that his statement came out rather laboriously, he added as brightly as he could, "We are very happy about it."

"I see."

Alex did not speak for a long time. He knew Yuri saw more than he was admitting to. And even Alex knew his weary tone was only partly due to his physical fatigue.

"I don't know what to make of it, Yuri," he said finally.

"Do you regret making the commitment?"

"No . . . yes . . . I don't think so. No," he said with more resolution, "regret isn't it at all. But what can come of it? She left before we could even attempt to test the waters of our newly declared feelings. In any case, what about later? She's going to want to leave Russia eventually. Will I be able to get out of the country? And if I could, what is there for me in the States? Would I give up medicine for her? Would she give up her country for me? I believe my love is real and worthy of sacrifice, yet what of the sacrifices I made to keep practicing medicine? I joined the Party to make it possible."

"I never could understand that," Yuri said. "I am not a member of the Party—"

"I had more to prove to the Soviet government. I wanted to give them every reason to accept me. That is one regret I do have. At the time I was so bitter, I didn't care much about one ideology or the other. But now, no matter what I do, I fear it will be a stigma hard to shake. Yet I was willing to take that risk because I thought I would perish if I could not practice medicine."

"Everyone changes, Alex."

"Are you saying, then, that I should do what I must to be with her?"

Yuri held up a hand in mild protest. "I would never presume to make such a statement! But tell me, do you plan to marry her?"

Alex snorted a dry laugh at this. "I think Cameron would run in the opposite direction if I proposed marriage at this stage. Before I met her, I didn't think I'd ever consider marriage, either. But now . . ." His words trailed away as he thought about his ultimate fantasy, a life with Cameron. Softly, as if broaching holy ground, he said, "Yes, I want to marry her."

"I am sure if you take it slowly, she will come around."

"That's not the only problem."

"You mean there are other problems besides her fear of marriage and your being a citizen of a police state while she isn't and can be deported at any moment?" Yuri allowed himself a wry smile.

"Yes, and it's quite ironic, too. At almost the same instant I was able to declare my love for her, I discovered that my faith in God is not as dead as I thought."

"Is that so?" Yuri's lips twitched as if he wanted to respond sedately; then suddenly he gave up and let his mouth follow the lead of his heart. He grinned.

"Of course, you knew it all along, didn't you?" Alex smiled, as well. Despite all the problems it raised, his renewed faith was the one bright spot in his life lately.

"It was only a matter of time," Yuri said, "based on when you would finally stop feeling the need to punish yourself."

"I suppose I am there with regard to God and also where my future with a woman is involved. Not wanting to drag a woman into my mixed-up life was a punishment, too."

"And now you are ready to do both."

"And Cameron is ready for neither."

"Perhaps it is that you both are just on slightly different schedules, as it were."

"I am afraid to hope for that."

"I had a discussion with my mother not long ago about Cameron."

"Really?" Alex cocked a brow and leaned forward. He had come to know that any insights of Anna Yevnovona's were worth listening to.

"She and Cameron were stuck in the metro during an air raid. They had quite a conversation. Did you know Cameron's mother is a woman of faith?"

"She had mentioned that, but mostly by way of attempting to show the drawbacks of faith."

"Yes, Mama mentioned that. But I have a little theory, Alex. I believe that the influences upon a person in childhood are strong, and even if they seem to stray for a time, they will be drawn back. Such was the case with my brother and me, you know. We both looked all around for our own way. Andrei tried to find it in the Revolution, and I sought it in social position and power. I suppose we had to look. But it was in the faith of our mother and father that we finally found peace."

Alex remembered that the big lumbering ex-Bolshevik he had known in the States had told him the same thing. Andrei Fedorcenko had been like a father to Alex after his own father had died, and his faith in God had deeply influenced Alex's Christian walk. He recalled clearly the pain on Andrei's face when Alex had slipped away into his dependency on drugs instead of turning to God. Andrei had been a pallbearer at the funerals of both Alex's parents. But it was at Alex's mother's funeral less than four years ago where Andrei had taken Alex into one of his breathtaking bear hugs and whispered into Alex's ear: " 'My son, forget not my law; but let thine heart keep my commandments: for length of days, and long life, and peace, shall they add to thee.' "

Alex had known the Scripture from Proverbs, but he had not quite understood Andrei's purpose in saying it just then, and still under the influence of drugs and bitterness, he had been in no proper frame of mind to question the man. But now it was clear the older man had been imploring him to cling to the faith of his parents.

Reverently, Alex now said to Andrei's brother, "The same thing has happened with me, hasn't it?"

"And it gives me great hope it will also happen to Cameron," said Yuri.

"But, Yuri, I don't think Cameron ever had that kind of faith in God to begin with." Pausing, he shook his head with self-pity. "A few weeks ago Cameron and I were perfect for each other. How quickly that seems to have changed."

"Earlier you said you didn't regret your love for her. Tell me, then, do you regret your renewed faith in God?" There was a hint of reproach in Yuri's tone.

Alex did not answer for a long time, but when he finally did, it was with assurance. "No, I don't regret it. And I don't regret my love for Cameron, yet they seem diametrically opposed."

"Only because you see but a portion of the whole picture," Yuri said. "God sees it all. And in His picture, perhaps Cameron is a great woman of faith. And you are both partners in Christ. If you feel what the two of you have together now is worth it, then give it time. See what God will do."

Alex nodded, not entirely convinced, but still he could not shake the sense he'd had for days now that his and Cameron's meeting was no accident. He believed it was good, right, the kind of thing only God could orchestrate. And he clung to that as hope.

————

A week after Stalin delivered his anniversary speech, Cameron received a cable from home. She read it and went pale.

"What's wrong?" asked Shanahan, who had gone with her to the cable office to send a dispatch.

"It's my father. He's had a heart attack."

"Is he alive?"

She nodded. "But it is still touch-and-go. My mother thinks I should come home."

"He'll be okay. The man is indestructible."

"That's what I always thought."

"What're you gonna do?"

"Take the first plane out of here."

Her words were so certain, not a hint of hesitation, yet indecision and doubt and fear ripped through her. Not over her need to go home. She and her father still had a huge gulf of hurt and anger between them, but she had no doubt that she needed to be with him now. He was her father. And if he was going to die, they had to patch things up between them.

Going home wasn't the question.

It was what she'd be leaving behind that gripped her with fear. There was no way she could see Alex again before leaving. They had not talked since the day they had spoken of their love. Letters were impossible and risky. He had been warned by the NKVD not to see her again. And that raised the greatest risk of her leaving the country. If the secret police had any doubts about her, this would be the perfect way to dispose of her, because it was completely in their power to issue her a reentry visa—or not issue one.

When she stepped on that plane, it was very likely she would never be able to set foot in Russia again.

She remembered Alex's promise that they would not lose each other, and she even now touched the key around her neck as tangible proof of that promise. But it seemed all was conspiring to separate them. And despite the most heartfelt promises, they were both completely powerless to halt the inevitable flow of events.

CAMERON WAS MET at the airport by Jackie. If she had been the crying kind, she would have shed a few tears at the reunion. As it was, Cameron's throat grew a bit tight, and she had to blink a couple of times before she felt steady again.

"Look at you!" Jackie exclaimed as they loaded Cameron's one small suitcase and typewriter case into the trunk of the family's Cadillac sedan. "You are a famous world traveler now. You must have wonderful stories."

"Indeed, look at me!" Cameron laughed. "I'm a wreck. I need a decent haircut. And what I wouldn't give for some lipstick. Blair would have a fit if she saw me—by the way, where is Blair? Somehow I thought she'd meet me, as well."

"I'll tell you all about Blair later. Are things so bad in Russia, then, that there's not even lipstick?"

"I ran out of lipstick a month ago. And a new tube would have taken so many precious ration coupons that I opted for soap and toilet paper instead. But I am so happy to be home I may even indulge in a visit to the beauty parlor. You can take me shopping, too, because I gave all my clothes and remaining toiletries to the Russian women who have been serving as interpreters and secretaries."

"Why would you do that?"

Cameron had almost forgotten that people in America could not possibly have any idea of the kinds of hardships being suffered now in Russia, and for that matter in other parts of Europe.

"They are short of everything in Russia," she explained. "I figured I could resupply myself here."

"This will be fun. I am so glad you are home!" exclaimed Jackie with a kind of buoyant, youthful enthusiasm Cameron had seldom seen in the last months. She noted Jackie was paler than normal and there was strain behind the front of enthusiasm, but as Jackie put an arm warmly around Cameron, she opted to ignore that for the time being.

They chatted constantly during the ride from the airport to the hospital where Cameron insisted on going first thing, even though Jackie hold her that their father's condition had stablized and he was getting stronger by the day. Cameron's most profound observation of her sister was that, while she herself felt like a completely different, changed person, Jackie seemed exactly as she had left her. Jackie had one year left of college and was still intent on being an elementary schoolteacher.

As Jackie drove, Cameron said, "Tell me about Blair."

Jackie let out a little groan. "Blair . . . oh, Blair. She's been gone for a while. Left town. I guess you didn't get the letter Mom sent about the wedding and then—"

"The wedding? Blair got married? I received no letter. Why didn't Mom cable me? That's the only reliable way of communicating lately."

"There was too much to say for a cable. And Mom didn't just want to give you a couple of lines—'Blair got married. Stop.' And that's it."

"I guess I can see that. So she got married and they moved away?"

Jackie hesitated and ran a hand through her hair as she gripped the steering wheel with her other hand. "It wasn't exactly like that . . . at first just her husband left. Well, he would have had to leave anyway because of the army assignment. But when he found out she had been lying to him—"

"Whoa, Jackie, this is confusing. Why don't you give it to me from the start?"

Jackie took a breath, then imparted as briefly and clearly as she possibly could the recent events in Blair's life. It was still rather complicated, but Cameron got the gist. Blair had messed up her life royally. In a whirlwind ceremony she had married a decent man whom she had apparently deceived into thinking she was the "girl-next-door" type. Cameron just shook her head, then reminded herself that her own life was in little better shape than Blair's.

"He left on assignment." Jackie finished with the most recent developments. "Blair started to hit bottom again with her drinking. Finally she snapped out of it and decided she had to go to him and try to work things out, to prove she really loved him. She made me promise not to tell anyone she was going until she was gone. She was afraid Dad might do something to stop her." Jackie gave an ironic shake of her head. "For a girl who was always saying her father didn't care about her, she was very concerned he might suddenly start to do so."

"Blair was never the most logical of women." So Blair finally broke away, Cameron mused to herself. But what a foolish thing to do not to tell anyone of her whereabouts—not even their mother. Poor Cecilia must be beside herself with worry.

"Mom and Dad did find out eventually—you can't go halfway around the world to the Philippines—"

"The Philippines! What in pete's sake is she doing there—oh, that must be where her husband was assigned? I do think that girl is off her nut. I thought she might have finally found her niche with that nightclub singing job. She really seemed to enjoy it from the sound of her letters. But then her letters, two in all, didn't say much. She never even spoke about this man she married."

"She wasn't happy at the nightclub, not really. She wasn't happy anywhere until she met Gary. But she lied to him and everything blew apart."

"You've heard nothing from her since she left?"

"Not a word. I'm just praying they have worked things out. Otherwise, she may be stranded there."

"Well, if he's a decent guy like you said, I'm sure he will help her. They are married—unless he's had it annulled."

"Not as far as I know."

"Whew!" Cameron laid her head back against the seat and wondered what she was coming home to. She had hoped this visit might be a bit of respite from the stresses of her Russian assignment. Instead, it appeared as if in addition to her father's illness, there were many other sources of turmoil.

They drove for a few minutes, and as Cameron saw they were nearing the hospital, she asked, "Is Dad able to have visitors?" She knew she was looking for a way out. She had traveled thousands of miles for this visit, but the nearer it came, the more second thoughts she was having.

"The nurses are very strict," answered Jackie. "But they will give you a few minutes after having traveled so far."

"That's good, then," Cameron said with resolution.

"You don't sound like you really mean it," said the ever intuitive Jackie.

"We didn't part on the best of terms, and I have not heard a word from him since I left. I can't help but fear the worst."

"But you came."

"Yes. Partly for Mom . . . though I suppose for him, too. I wouldn't want him to die with things as they were between us." Cameron looked at her sister, whose eyes were intent on the road. She thought it a bad sign that even Jackie did not offer assurances that their father had changed. "Despite everything, I never did hate him."

"None of us hate him," Jackie replied. "That's the worst part of it. All we really want is to love our daddy and for him to love us." Jackie's knuckles whitened as they gripped the wheel. Cameron noted that even as she kept her gaze focused ahead, her eyes seemed to glisten with moisture.

"What is it, Jackie?"

"I forgot that nothing much gets past you." Jackie bit her lip, then went on with resolve. "I've worried that I . . . well, that I might have caused Dad's heart attack."

"You? Jackie, you are the only daughter who *hasn't* given him grief."

"We had a big argument . . . just before . . ."

Cameron could not imagine anything Jackie would do that could upset anyone. It only proved what an insufferable man their father was. She laid a hand encouragingly on her sister's shoulder. "What did you fight about?"

Her voice trembling a bit, Jackie answered, "He'd heard some things about me and a friend—a Japanese friend."

"And Dad was upset about that? I didn't think even he could be so narrow-minded."

"Well . . . it's just that—that is, my friend is a boy, and Dad jumped to all sorts of completely unfounded and wrong conclusions."

"Oh, dear Jackie!" Cameron snaked an arm around her sister and gave her a tight, comforting squeeze. "Don't even think such a thing about your causing his illness. You know how Dad was—is! He pushes himself as hard as he pushes everyone else. He is a driven man. He probably yelled at a dozen people that day. You can't take it on yourself."

Jackie seemed on the verge of saying something else, but they came to their destination, and she was distracted in finding a parking place.

Finally Jackie eased the car to a stop at the curb. "Thanks, sis. I haven't been able to share that with anyone besides Sam. I really am glad you are home." She turned off the ignition. "The hospital is around the corner. This is as close as I can get."

"I can use some exercise after being on a plane for so many hours," assured Cameron.

But it was just a short walk, and as they climbed the hospital steps, Cameron was wishing it could have been a lot longer. She'd had the long flight to think about her father and what they might say to each other, but she had little on which to judge her father's possible reactions. Her mother had sent a few short cables to Russia, but they had, perhaps purposefully, said little about Keagan. And she had never received a single word from Keagan himself—and that was perhaps enough for her to think the worst. As for herself, she knew her anger had dulled. But she hadn't written her father to tell him so. Keagan had always left the impression that he believed apologies were for the weak. She truly believed that any act of contrition on her part would be thrown back in her face. Maybe a near-death experience had changed the man.

Thus Cameron had no idea what to expect when she saw her father. She was, however, much gratified by her mother's warm reception. In truth, Cameron had been almost as nervous about seeing her mother as she had been to see her father because she had done nothing regarding Semyon. She would have to face her mother's questions regarding that soon enough. In the meantime Cecilia, who was standing outside the room when Cameron and her sister approached, ran to her eldest daughter, threw her arms around her, kissed her, and wept. It was then that a few tears slipped past Cameron's defenses.

"You're here!" Cecilia breathed. "I didn't want to let myself hope— but you came! Thank God! You came!"

"I couldn't have done anything else." Cameron fought back tears even harder. She didn't want to be all red-eyed and trembly when she saw Keagan.

"I should have known better. I missed you so!"

It seemed an odd thing for her mother to say, considering that when Cameron had been home, she had not socialized with her mother all that often. Yet she did understand. She may not have seen her mother a lot when in Los Angeles, but there had been something about knowing she was close by—that's what Cameron had missed.

"How are you holding up, Mom?" she asked, mostly for something to say.

"Better now that he seems to be out of the woods—"

"Then he's okay?"

"The doctor says that if he makes some changes in his habits, he could live to a ripe old age. But . . . you know your father."

Yes, Cameron knew her father. He would do what he ruddy well pleased because of his unequivocal certainty that he was always right, so what he wanted must be right, as well.

"Can I see him?"

"There's a nurse in there now, and she told me to step outside. But when she is finished you can go on in."

Cameron licked her lips. "Will he see me? I mean, I don't want to cause undue stress to him."

"You have come all this way. Of course he'll see you!"

Cameron stared at her mother, a bit surprised at the force of her words. Was there something different about the woman, or was Cameron just seeing her through new eyes? Cameron had expected to find Cecilia unraveled by events, yet she appeared fairly calm and in control. Cameron thought again of what Anna Yevnovona had said about the strength of a woman who would adhere to her convictions in spite of her husband's disinterest. Had Cameron been so blind not to see it before?

"What is it?" Cecilia said, and Cameron realized she had been staring.

"Oh . . . nothing. Its just that I've been gone less than a year, but it seems so much longer."

"Yes." Cecilia took Cameron's hand. "I sense you've changed, Cameron—in a good way." Just then the nurse exited the room, and Cecilia said to her, "Nurse, my daughter has just arrived from Russia. May she see Mr. Hayes?"

"All the way from Russia!" the nurse exclaimed. "Whatever is all the way over there to make you leave your home?"

"Quite a bit," Cameron said simply. She was too nice to inquire if the nurse had been living in a cave to ask such a question. Didn't she read the newspapers?

"Well," the nurse said, "you may go in for just a few minutes."

440

"Shall I go with you?" asked Cecilia.

Cameron could not recall the last time she had leaned on her mother for support, but she was desperately grateful for it now. "Yes, Mom. Thank you."

Before Cameron opened the door, she gave a fleeting glance back at her sister. Jackie, who remained in the corridor, offered her an encouraging smile. Cameron opened the door and let her mother go first.

"Keagan dear, look who is here," Cecilia said sweetly.

"I'm not supposed to have any visitors but fam—" Keagan stopped suddenly as he caught sight of just who his visitor was.

His face became a mask that Cameron could not read. Only his eyes sparked a little, but that could mean anything.

"What're you doing here?" His tone was rough, but probably no more so than usual.

"I couldn't stay away when I heard you were ill," Cameron said, sounding so lame she herself could hardly stand it.

"Come to gloat, I suppose."

It was as if she hadn't been gone but a minute and the old battles were resumed without missing a beat.

"Keagan!" said Cecilia in such a soft voice that it was difficult, but not impossible, to read the warning in her tone.

"No, Dad," Cameron said steadily. All her previous tendency toward tears disappeared. "I just came, that's all."

"Well, I don't need you."

"I never thought you did," Cameron retorted, just barely controlling the anger that was perhaps not as dulled as she had thought. "You're my father, and when fathers are sick, daughters visit them."

"I disowned my daughter when she went to work for the enemy."

"That's ridiculous! Not even the correspondents themselves consider one another enemies. We work together. Sometimes we even help each other. You are a fool for hanging on to such a silly grudge."

"A fool, is it?" His voice rose.

Cecilia laid a hand on his shoulder. "Please take it easy, dear."

He shrugged her hand away. "Now that you've proven you can make it on your own, I'm a fool, eh?"

"Who says I've proven anything?"

"Oh, don't try to placate me! And please, no false modesty. You'll get your acclaim and glory for that weasel Arnett. To blazes with the *Journal*!"

"I don't know what you are talking about, but I do think I'd better leave. The nurse said not to get you excited—"

"Hang that blasted nurse and all her cohorts! I'll do as I please! And don't try to say you know nothing about the list I just saw."

"What list?"

"The nominees for the Pulitzer Prize, as if you didn't know."

Cameron felt the blood drain from her head as her knees grew weak. The Pulitzer Prize? She was a nominee? That couldn't be.

"I didn't know," she said weakly.

Keagan snorted. "A woman's not likely to win anyway."

She was absolutely nonplussed as she stared at him—torn between ecstasy at her good fortune and fury that she could not appreciate it because of her father.

"I . . . I'd better go," she stammered.

Cecilia glanced miserably between father and daughter. "Keagan," she finally said, "I am ashamed of you!"

Shocked even further than she thought she ever could be at her mother's words, Cameron followed her mother from the room.

Jackie drove them home. Cameron had an odd feeling as they drove up to the sprawling Beverly Hills house. It hadn't been home to her for a long time even before going to Russia, but she couldn't shake the strange sense of "coming home." Yet she thought it would have been an entirely different feeling if her father had been there.

Inside, the house was tastefully decorated in the latest styles. Cecilia, with little else to do with her life, redecorated every couple of years. This time around, it was airy with a strong influence of flowers, spring flowers in light refreshing colors. There were bowls of fresh flowers everywhere, because Cecilia's gardens were among the best in town. This late in the year, the floral arrangements leaned toward mums, but the Southern California climate produced a fine batch of fall roses that were in great abundance in the arrangements. The scent of fresh flowers was strong in the house.

"Eleanor said she would leave dinner warming for us," Cecilia said, leading the way to the kitchen.

"So old Eleanor is still here," commented Cameron. Eleanor had been the family cook since they had returned from Keagan's last assignment in Russia. Cameron remembered when there had been several servants working for the Hayes family. Now there was only the cook, the housekeeper, and the gardener, none of whom lived in any longer.

They found a lovely meal warming by the stove. A savory pot roast, parslied potatoes, green beans, and a wonderful Dutch apple pie. Though the correspondents in Russia had been far better fed than the average citizen, this was still a feast to Cameron.

She wanted to eat in the casual atmosphere of the kitchen, but Cecilia would not have them partake of Cameron's first meal at home anywhere but in the dining room. So they carried all the food and plates and flatware to the elegant cherrywood dining table that could seat twelve without its extensions. Cecilia switched on the chandelier, and the three women sat together at one end of the huge table.

They engaged in chitchat, as they had since leaving the hospital. No one yet had mentioned the scene in Keagan's room. Cameron wanted to forget it, though she couldn't. She wanted to believe it had been the fault of Keagan's medications, but she knew it wasn't. Nevertheless, she wasn't about to let her distress over her father inhibit her enjoyment of Eleanor's fabulous cooking. Cameron had not had food like this in months, and she wasn't about to let her father spoil that, too.

Cecilia must have felt the same way, because it was not until they had finished their pie and were lingering over a second cup of coffee that she broached the delicate subject—at least one of the delicate subjects hanging over them.

"I still can't believe your father's behavior," she said.

Cameron shrugged as if it wasn't as bad as it definitely was. "You know Dad. I thought the Russians could hold a grudge, but I'd not be surprised to learn that Dad taught them how."

"I know it hurt you, dear. Don't try to pretend it didn't."

"I guess it did hurt. I had gotten over the trouble we had before I left and just assumed Dad would have, too."

"Maybe if you had written him—"

"And why didn't he ever write me?"

Cecilia offered a pained, weak smile. "No sense in beating a dead horse, I suppose."

"It's hardly dead."

"What happened at the hospital?" Jackie asked. "I know it couldn't have been good from the way neither of you said anything."

Cameron gave her sister a brief synopsis of the disastrous visit.

"Someone ought to knock some sense into that man!" lamented Jackie.

"I thought the heart attack might have accomplished that," Cecilia said, "but I don't think it has done any good."

"I don't know how you have lived with him this long—" Cameron blurted, then regretted her words, deeming it an inappropriate time to voice such a sentiment in light of Keagan's serious illness.

Cecilia smiled. "Only by the grace of God."

"Okay, Mom, I want to know something. Did God make you stronger, or did He just make Dad more tolerable?" Cameron made no attempt to hide the challenge in her words.

Cecilia and Jackie exchanged a peculiar look.

"Well, what's wrong?" Cameron asked a bit defensively.

"It's just not often, Cameron, that you ask anything about God," said Cecilia.

Cameron shifted uneasily in her chair, wondering how she could retract what she had said. Yes, she had always been careful with her mother and her younger sister about avoiding spiritual issues. Her defenses were down.

Cecilia hurried on. "But since you asked, and before you take it back—" She grinned. "There is no doubt in my mind that God has made me stronger. I couldn't run away as you have, Cameron, so I depended upon God."

Cameron winced a little at her mother's words. "Mom, I always thought leaving, or running away as you put it, was a sign of strength. I thought maybe you were weaker because you stayed."

"I stayed because I had to. Keagan is my husband and your father, and there was never any question about leaving. . . ." Cecilia paused.

It seemed to Cameron that a little shadow passed over her mother's face. Yes, Cameron mused, of course her mother had thought about leaving, not only in Russia when there had been another man, but at other times, as well. "Sometimes I do think I have stayed because I am weak. God knows better than anyone just how weak a creature I am."

"No, Mama," Jackie said with firm conviction. "It has taken great strength to stay and guard our family bonds." She turned to her sister. "Cameron, that's what has kept this family together. It was always Mom. And if you think that is weakness—"

Cameron held up a yielding hand. "I know, Jackie." Then she laid a hand gently on her mother's arm. "I really had it wrong, didn't I? Anna was right."

"Anna?"

"A wise old woman I know in Russia. You would like her, Mom. She told me it must have taken great strength for you to hold to your religious convictions in spite of the lack of support from Dad." She was silent for a moment before adding, "Still, I don't understand how anyone who is strong enough should need God, or anything of the kind."

Cecilia placed her hand over her daughter's. "Yes, I can see how that would be a problem for you, Cameron. You are a very strong woman. I have always admired you for it."

"But. . . ?" Cameron prompted when her mother paused.

Cecilia gave her head a shake. A strand of her graying brown hair slipped from the confines of the bun in which she had it pinned. She is still a lovely woman, Cameron thought. In a way her delicate frailty reminded Cameron more of Sophia than of Cecilia's own daughters. She was almost insubstantial in appearance. But appearances could be deceiving.

"No, really, dear," Cecilia said, "there is no 'but.' I do so admire you, but—oh, I guess there is a 'but' "—she tittered self-consciously— "however, only a small one. It's just that nothing in life is ever as it seems. Often there is more than we expect, sometimes less. Strength is a wonderful thing, but it is not everything."

"I don't understand."

"I know. But you'll figure it out someday, and unfortunately, it is something you will have to sort out on your own. You must look outside yourself, though, to do it."

"To God?"

"If I told you 'yes' to that question, would that be enough?"

"I just don't see the need, Mom."

"My mother's heart hopes you never do find yourself in such a place that you see this need, because it could only be a very painful place. Yet that same heart in me hopes that you will, because it might be the only way you'll find God." She blinked as if she was fighting tears. "God knows what is best, and that's what I pray for you."

"You ought to pray for Dad, too."

"Oh, I do, Cameron. I pray for you both constantly." She paused, and a little, almost conspiratorial, smile quirked her lips. "But I confess

I pray for him just a little more! Forgive me for saying it, but I think he needs it more."

The sense of camaraderie Cameron suddenly felt made her say what she said next. She hadn't planned on telling anyone about Alex, not just yet at least.

"I've met someone in Russia—a man." Her voice was so soft as to be barely heard. But they had heard.

"Oh, Cameron, how wonderful!" exclaimed Jackie, ever the romantic.

"Well, I never dreamed, dear," said Cecilia. "Tell us all about him."

"He's a Russian doctor. He's . . ." She paused, suddenly feeling quite embarrassed because her cheeks felt hot. "He's quite special."

"A doctor! My, my. . . !" Jackie said with a teasing grin.

"A Russian citizen?" Cecilia's tone had changed, but Cameron didn't perceive it immediately.

"Yes on both counts," said Cameron.

"Shall I listen for wedding bells?" asked Jackie.

"We haven't talked about that. I . . . I don't know. I'm not sure what will happen. I'm not even certain I will get back into the country." All at once Cameron remembered why she had planned not to tell her family about Alex. There were too many uncertainties, and they would expect details she did not have.

"Why wouldn't they let you back in?" asked Jackie.

"It's complicated." Pausing, Cameron glanced at her mother, who had said little. It was then that she noted the shadow over the woman. She was staring into her cup of coffee. Her lips were quivering. "Mom? What's the matter?"

Sighing, Cecilia licked her lips. "Oh . . . nothing. I am suddenly very tired, that's all. I think I will go to bed." She rose. "Cameron, your old room is ready for you."

"Are you sure you're okay?"

"Yes . . . good night, girls."

Both sisters watched, stunned, as their mother exited. The change had been so sudden from the warmth they had only moments before been experiencing.

"Does she do that often?" Cameron asked after Cecilia was gone.

"No, but I guess Dad's illness and all is more difficult for her than she lets on."

Cameron sensed that her mother's startling change was not because of her husband. It seemed to be related more to Alex. Cameron had never given a thought as to how hearing about her relationship with Alex might affect her mother. Until now, she hadn't even drawn the obvious comparisons to Cecilia's own doomed Russian romance. A knot formed in Cameron's throat, and at the same moment she felt the weight of Alex's key around her neck. It was like hope and fear both clutching at her.

57

CAMERON SAW Max Arnett the next day. He confirmed the Pulitzer nomination, or at least that her article was being considered. He told her to keep in mind that it was an honor just to be nominated. She realized then she probably didn't have a chance of winning. But it *was* an honor to be nominated. The article in question was the one about the boys in the hospital. Shortly before the evacuation of Moscow, she had given it to Bob Wood at the embassy to try to get it out of the country. He had apparently been successful.

"It was a fine piece, Cameron," Arnett said proudly. "Several national papers picked it up. I have noticed a marked growth in your writing with each article I receive from you. They contain a richness that I am certain comes from deep inside you. You have grown since going overseas, haven't you?"

She nodded but found it difficult to speak. She should have been pleased to be having such a conversation with this man, but she simply could not keep from thinking how it would've been if it had been her own father instead expressing pride in her.

Finally, she said, "Max, I'll never be the same again. I know that. I have grown. How could I not after seeing all the heartache war brings? Sometimes I look longingly back to the days when I was such a brash young hack thinking only of the *story*. I have thought about the possibility of remaining here in the States, but I doubt it can ever really be the same here, either. I need to return to Russia, because for me that's moving forward."

"Have you doubts that will happen? I assure you, I want you to return."

She then told him about her little problems with the NKVD, and he assured her he would see that a reentry visa was issued. He wanted his best "man" in the Soviet Union, and she was it. He tried not to gloat too much about her successes, probably in view of her father's illness, but he made it clear he was pleased.

She asked his counsel about the Oleg Gorbenko situation, and he indicated to her that, though he was sorry for the young man who had been arrested because of it, it was probably for the best that nothing had come of the story.

"For now, at least," he added. "Unfortunately, the country isn't ready for such news."

"Since when do we fashion the news to suit the national mood?" she asked. "That's akin to what I have encountered in Russia."

He gave a woeful shake of his head. "You must know such things happen even where there is a free press. I do not call it censorship. I call it expediency. Beyond that, Cameron, this story your friend Gorbenko wants us to print would never be believed without strong confirmation."

"If I had proof. . . ?"

"To be honest, I don't know if even the personal presentation of Gorbenko would have mattered. Actual photographs would probably be the only thing that could be believed. Without that, I am afraid you have no story."

"I appreciate your candor, Max. To be honest, I hope and pray there never is proof of such horrible evil."

After the meeting with Max, Cameron went to the hospital, but her father was asleep and she tried not to feel relieved at this. The next time she visited him with her mother and Jackie, and he was on better behavior—civil, at least. Jackie and Cecilia did most of the talking, while Cameron was allowed to just sit quietly.

The best conversation she had with her father was when she told him about Colonel Tiulenev. Keagan actually relaxed a bit as he mused over "old times" and "the good old days." But Cameron could never really relax with her father because she never knew when the slip of a word or the mention of a taboo topic would send him on a tirade, which happened often when she saw him.

And so the days passed. She visited old friends at the *Journal* but spent most of her time with her mother and sister. They took her shopping, and she splurged on clothes as she never had before simply because the time spent with them was so much fun. They had lunch in their favorite old haunts. They talked about everything, though Cameron said little more about Alex, for each time he was mentioned, that dark mood descended over Cecilia. And much to Cameron's relief, Cecilia made no mention of her secret. Perhaps with Keagan lying ill in the hospital, she felt it would have been disloyal. Certainly Cameron did not bring up the subject.

Cameron marveled at the sunny November days and enjoyed the Southern California warmth as she never had before. She didn't mind at all the day it rained, which was little more than a mist compared to the drenching autumn rains in Russia. But oddly, Cameron experienced twinges of homesickness for that place thousands of miles away. She was forced to admit that part of her was there now in the form of Alex, and thus she would always have a strong connection to Russia.

She wondered when she would return. Her father was growing steadily stronger and would be released from the hospital in a few more days. Should she leave before he came home? She did not want to cause him stress, and the fact that he did speak to her occasionally at the hospital didn't mean they could maintain this attitude of guarded civility twenty-four hours a day in the same house. What if he had a relapse? What if he died? Somehow they had to make things right between them before she left.

That idea brought an ironic smile to her face. When had things ever been truly *right* between them? At the best of times they'd had little more than an armed truce. At the moment, however, that seemed the best she could hope for. Nevertheless, she went to the hospital every day. Cameron knew, though it was difficult to admit, that she wanted an amiable relationship with her father. She always had, but especially now when she understood better than ever that life was a fleeting thing.

She and her mother and Jackie spent a quiet Thanksgiving with

Keagan in the hospital. The visit was quiet in the sense that Keagan was silent and morose the entire time. He had badgered the doctor into releasing him for the holiday, but he'd developed chest pains the night before and he was forced to remain there for another week. If Cameron had anything to be thankful for that day, it was that Keagan was too depressed to needle his daughters.

After the women returned home, Jackie received a telephone call from one of her friends inviting her to a movie. Cameron and Cecilia went into the living room. Cecilia hoped to hear President Roosevelt's Thanksgiving speech on the radio, but apparently they had missed it. She left the radio softly broadcasting Glenn Miller and Tommy Dorsey tunes.

Cameron sat in the big easy chair, slipping off her shoes and tucking her feet up under her. She tried to relax, but it seemed with an evening alone together before them, anything could happen.

Cecilia sat on the sofa, her feet, clad in shoes, primly planted on the carpet. Her hands folded in her lap, she seemed to be listening to the music, but her mind was obviously far from Glenn Miller's swing version of "The Little Brown Jug."

"I've been thinking about Blair a lot today," Cecilia finally said. "She was always such a handful, but I do miss her. I wonder if she had anyone to spend the holiday with."

"Next time I see her, I'll wring her neck for not writing." Cameron's tone was more affectionate than truly angered. "Perhaps she and her husband are back together and all is blissful again for her."

"No . . . I think she would have written if there were good news. Her father and I were both very supportive of that marriage. I'm afraid she believes we think her a failure now that it fell apart. I fear, too, we won't hear from her until her life straightens out. *If* it straightens out." Cecilia's lips trembled over that final statement. She had been rather stoic all day, and Cameron had not considered what an emotional time this must be for a mother estranged from her child. "Cameron, do you think it is safe over there in the Philippines?"

"So far Japan hasn't made any overt moves toward the Philippines, but then, there is a strong American presence there." Cameron didn't like appearing to whitewash her response, because she had seen too much of that already in the States since her return. True, many Americans were seeing more and more the inevitability of war, but there was still a pervading sense of invincibility, especially where Japan was concerned. "But, Mom, you have to realize the Philippines are right in the middle of it all, and they are very strategic. Roosevelt is committed to avoiding war in the Pacific, but this oil embargo against Japan isn't helping the situation."

"Your father thought it wasn't a good sign when the old Prime Minister . . . what was his name?"

"Konoye."

"Yes . . . well, it wasn't good when he resigned. Keagan thinks the new man, Tojo, will lead Japan into war."

"There are many angles to consider," Cameron said. It was odd to have a political discussion with her mother, who seldom had shown an interest in such things before. But now world events were touching her personally. Cameron thought that might well be a mirror of the American people in general. The war was going to have to hit home, so to speak, before they offered their support. She hated the thought of idyllic America with its baseball games, state fairs, and boogie-woogie suffering the turmoil of war. Yet her time in Russia had convinced her that without America fully engaged in this war, Russia would fall along with the many other nations that had already fallen to Germany and Japan.

"Mom," she said after a long silence, "it would be good for you to at least mentally prepare yourself for war. We cannot stay out of it much longer."

A wistful smile played upon Cecilia's lips. "I thought having daughters would spare me seeing my sons off to war. But now you are in the middle of a war, and Blair well could be soon." She paused and the smile faded. "Must you return to Russia?"

"I thought you would want me to, after what you asked me to do last spring." Cameron stared into her lap and shifted uneasily. Yet she knew the time had come to confess her failure. "I haven't done much yet about finding him. It is not as easy as I thought it would be. But I am sorry. I feel so bad."

"I wasn't going to mention it," Cecilia replied. "Maybe it is for the best that nothing has come of it. I'd rather you stay home, away from that place that can so easily ruin lives."

"Mom, please try to understand. I have an important job in the Soviet Union. Sometimes it does drive me a little crazy because I feel as if I am just spinning my wheels in the mire of Soviet bureaucracy. But then there are those moments when I have a real breakthrough, and I know that's where I belong." She pointedly did not mention Alex.

"I suppose I understand." While Cameron had fidgeted a bit as she spoke, Cecilia was still and poised in her seat, a well-trained reserve. Only her eyes could not be controlled. In them was an anguish she could not hide. "It's not so much that. I am . . ." She paused and seemed to have to force herself to continue. "I'm just concerned about this Russian you are becoming involved with."

"I thought you didn't really approve—"

"You know it's not that. I'm sure he is a fine man. But can you blame me for not wanting to encourage you in this relationship? I can envision only heartache for you. I would have thought, especially after what I told you last spring, that you would have known better than to have let this happen to you." Her voice rose in a kind of desperate pleading. "That's the first rule of foreigners in Russia."

"I wasn't looking for this relationship." Cameron marveled that a moment ago they were having a simple political discussion. How quickly it had evolved into this! But then again, they could have avoided speaking their hearts for only so long. "What you told me has made me afraid, but what could I do? I have never known a man like Alex, and I have never felt this way about anyone. We are as different as two souls can be, but I feel so right with him. He is a remarkable man, and I know somehow, someway, we will beat all the *rules*."

"Or they will beat you."

"I won't let that happen." It was the first time Cameron really knew she would fight for Alex. It was the first time she truly realized she intended to spend the rest of her life with him.

"I know your situation is nothing like mine was, but I also know how easy it is in a place like Russia for people to become lost. There is so much that can come between you and your young man."

"We know that. But I love him," Cameron replied simply, though the word "love" was uttered with deep intensity.

Cecilia smiled. "I see you truly do. I saw it the first time you spoke of him."

"It scares me a little," Cameron admitted. "Both loving him like I do and the complications involved." Her lips twitched into a half smile. "See, I'm not as cocky as you feared."

"Perhaps love will be the key to your survival."

At the word "key," Cameron remembered Alex's gift. On impulse she loosened the chain from around her neck and handed it to her mother.

"Alex gave this to me. It was his mother's. It's the key to her home in Leningrad. She was forced to exile the country before the Great War, but she kept this always hoping to return. She died before she could fulfill that dream. I guess it is kind of a symbol to Alex and me that one day we will go and carry out his mother's wish. *Together*."

Cecilia turned the key over in her hand. "Now I know it is really love, for only true love can imbue such an old worn object with magic." She rose, went to Cameron, and replaced the chain around her daughter's neck. She kissed Cameron's cheek, wrapped her arms around her shoulders, and murmured, "Dear Lord, keep these two special children in your protective hand. Let no harm come to them; let no man come between them."

Cameron always used to feel awkward when her mother would pray for her like this, but now she didn't. It was oddly comforting.

58

KEAGAN HAYES was in a foul mood in those first days after coming home from the hospital. He was not a man accustomed to lounging about his house all day. In fact, now that Cameron thought about it, she had never known the man to take a vacation.

Twice Cameron found Eleanor, the cook, and Donna, the housekeeper, in tears after encountering the man. Once she even found old stoic Jiro, the gardener, cursing loudly to himself after a run-in with Keagan in the garden, a place Keagan had seldom graced with his presence in the past. Cameron herself avoided him whenever possible.

Jackie was taking midterms at school and had jumped ship altogether with the excuse that she was going to stay closer to UCLA with a girl friend to be near the library. Cecilia floated through the house like a pale wraith, making little noise and seeming to withdraw into herself. She doted upon Keagan as a dutiful wife but seemed distant from him even as she was tending him. Cameron wondered, however, if it had always been that way with her parents and she was only now noticing.

Two days after Keagan's release, Cameron had had a particularly tense run-in with her father, and she knew the time had come for her to leave. She hated conceding defeat regarding the man, but she could not take another minute of his cold snubbing or his harsh remarks when he did acknowledge her presence. The few civil conversations they had shared were simply not worth it.

On the evening following their argument she retreated to her room, where she spent the rest of the night working on her Russian journal. She wondered how she was going to muster the courage to tell her mother of her imminent departure—she, who had faced generals and commissars unflinchingly, quaked at doing what she knew would break her mother's heart.

Around eleven o'clock, Cameron discovered she needed a book she had seen in her father's study, and deeming it safe to go there since her father had gone to bed over an hour ago, Cameron emerged from her room.

The house was dark. The servants had gone. Only the ticking of the grandfather clock in the main parlor could be heard. The study was on the first floor toward the back of the house. Cameron opened the door and stepped inside.

Across the room moonlight spilled in through the large window behind the desk. It was the only light in the room, but it clearly illuminated a figure seated at the desk. His elbows were propped on the desktop, and his head was resting in his hands.

"Dad," Cameron said softly so as not to startle him.

His head jerked up, and in one single moment she saw her father as if with all masks removed. And what she saw stunned her, because in his eyes was something she could not have imagined ever seeing in Keagan—it was despair!

"What do you want?" he barked. The mask snapped visibly and almost audibly back into place even as he quickly scooped some papers from his desk and shoved them into a drawer.

Cameron, seldom one to keep away from where she was not welcome, strode into the room and slipped into the chair adjacent to the desk.

"I came to get a book," she said.

"Well, you won't find it sitting there."

"What's wrong, Dad? Are you okay?" She wondered if those papers he'd been looking at had caused his dismayed appearance or if it had been something else. But she wasn't on certain enough ground with her father to probe for too much detail.

"Do you know how sick I am of hearing that question?"

She nodded. "But it's hard to know what else to say to you."

"I don't want or need anyone to say any cursed thing!"

"Then what can I do for you, Dad?" She felt the fool for asking, but she could not shake away that brief glimpse of his vulnerability. In many ways Keagan had few redeemable qualities, but he was Cameron's father. She still remembered those happy days spent with him in Russia, and she knew that ever since then she had longed to have her father like that again. And now she was sucked in, as a fly is drawn to a spider's lethal web.

"I don't need a single thing, especially from you, you traitorous little chit!" he shot back, his words coming like a blow to her. "I never asked you to come here—"

"I came because Mom asked—"

"Then go annoy her. I don't want you."

"I can't believe that."

He snorted a dry laugh. "You think this broken-down heart of mine has made me soft? Well, think again, girl! I'll never forgive you for what you did, and your placating me now isn't gonna change that."

"What did I do, Dad, that was so awful?"

"You know exactly what you did."

"You forced me to quit."

They were both leaning forward now, and if the desk hadn't stood between them, they would have been nose to nose like two mad dogs. The silence that followed was charged with emotion. Cameron wondered at her stupidity for thinking things could be healed between them. The father she hoped for was an illusion, perhaps one that had never existed in the first place except in her imagination.

"I did no such thing," Keagan said finally. "You got huffy and quit without even giving me a chance." He paused, and the look on his face was far from vulnerable now. His green eyes flashed. "Then you had to stab me in the back by going to work for the *Globe*."

"I don't think that's it at all!" she retorted, letting her anger have full rein. "You are mad because I made a success of it. I made a success without you! Since I started working for the *Globe*, their sales have increased ten percent. That's why you're mad. You're my father, and you could have been proud, but you are too selfish, too self-involved for that." She jumped to her feet. "I was a fool for thinking I wanted a relationship with you. I'm surprised you had a heart attack. You haven't got a heart that I can see!"

"You had better leave," he said in a low, ominous voice.

Cameron gasped in a breath, on the verge of taking one final snipe at him. Nothing had changed between them. Nothing would ever change. Then all at once she remembered what Max Arnett and others had said about having seen growth in her. She knew that to be true. If nothing else, *she* had changed. She was not the same person she had been less than a year ago when she and her father had exchanged many of the very same verbal blows. Standing next to death, watching her friends suffer, confronting many wrenching complexities of life—all this must surely have given her some resource within to meet her father on a new level. Even if he was not able to stand upon a higher plane, she could.

All she had to do was conjure up that image of her father moments before steeped in despair. And more, all she had to do was remember that this was a man to be pitied, for even if he didn't realize it, his was an empty life—an emptiness of his own making.

Suddenly Cameron wanted to embrace him. Only his iron gaze, his set jaw, his clenched fists stopped her. Though she had changed, he had not.

"If that will make you happy, Dad," she said softly, "I'll be going tomorrow." It surprised her how abruptly her anger had dissipated. "I wish we could have talked more, that I could have told you about my experiences in Russia. Maybe I'll write you a letter if that would be okay with you."

He just gaped at her. She had never before seen such a look of bemusement on her father's face.

"I have no control over the U.S. Post Office," he sneered.

She left quietly, feeling crushed and broken inside. How could this man so easily reduce her to ashes? A few moments ago she'd felt so strong being magnanimous, reaching out to him in such a mature way. She'd even had a fleeting image of a tender reconciliation. But his rejection had more than ever leveled her, leaving her like the rubble after a bombing.

So much for all of her mother's prayers, she thought bitterly.

———

Cameron left home the next morning amid tears and lamentations from her mother. Her father did not show his face. Since her visa had been secured a couple of days after Thanksgiving, she was free to leave the country at any time.

Cecilia had begged Cameron to stay in L.A. until after Christmas. She knew this holiday would be even more dismal for Cecilia with both her daughters not only gone, but for all practical purposes estranged from their father. Cameron wondered if she should stay for her mother's sake. But Christmas was three weeks away! She was certain she had already pushed her father to the edge. If for no other reason than for his health, she decided it was better to go. Thus, she found a hotel room for her remaining days.

"Mother, I just don't want to risk upsetting Dad further." Cameron tried to reason with the woman. "Besides, my papers have come through, and I'm leaving day after tomorrow."

"I've lost both Blair and you . . ." Cecilia said miserably. "I fear Jacqueline will move away soon, too. I don't know what I'll do. But I don't worry only for myself. Cameron, you can't go like this with things as they are between you and your father. This estrangement will eat away at both of you until . . . oh, I don't know what, but it won't be good."

Cameron shook her head with apology to her mother. "I tried to mend it, but he wants no part of me."

"You just don't understand your father. He can't express his true feelings—"

"Come on, Mom! Don't defend him." Suddenly all the maturity she'd gained in the last year fled her, and she was a hurt child once more listening to her mother's lame defenses. Cameron saw in a painful flash the dynamic that had plagued her family for years. While Keagan had been in the hospital, she and her mother had had a strong relationship. But with Keagan back in the picture, back in control, Cecilia had returned to her place as an ineffectual mediator. She was both glue and catalyst, and successful as neither because she forever strad-dled middle ground, refusing to take a stand for either warring faction.

"Your father isn't perfect but—"

"He's so imperfect that you've been afraid for twenty-seven years to tell him about your child!" Cameron stopped abruptly, shocked at her words. How easy it was to slip back into old patterns. But she was determined not to do so, because if her new growth really counted, it was here with her family. That was the true test.

"I've ruined this family, I know." Cecilia wept.

"Oh no, Mom. None of it is your fault. What Jackie said before about you being the reason this family has stayed together as well as it has is true. I spoke out of turn because I am so frustrated with Dad. Please don't take this on yourself. I was wrong."

"I shouldn't defend him when I know he is wrong." Cecilia sniffed and dabbed at her tears with a hanky. "But you girls are grown, and soon Jacqueline will be gone. Then I will just have your father . . . so I must keep the peace with him. But I don't want to lose you in the process. I just don't know what to do."

Cameron gave in to the urge to hug her mother. Cecilia received her gratefully. Cameron was overwhelmed with pity for her mother, especially for her prospects of a future alone with Keagan. Contemptuously Cameron wondered what good Cecilia's prayers were to her mother. They didn't appear to be making her mother stronger, more confident, or even happier. Shouldn't they at least have done that? Shouldn't they have given Cecilia a modicum of happiness?

Cameron said good-bye to her mother there, not wanting to put her through another emotional parting.

———

Cameron was surprised that her mother was with Jackie when she showed up the morning of her departure to take her to the airport. After Cameron had checked in her luggage and verified her flight information, Cecilia drew Cameron apart from her sister for a private word. Cecilia had been weeping quietly on the drive, which was evidenced by her red-rimmed eyes. Cameron hoped there would not be an emotional scene.

"Cameron, I have something for you." Cecilia's tone was steadier than it had yet been. "I know a few days ago I said it was probably best not to find *him*." She didn't have to elaborate upon whom she meant. Cameron knew without asking. "One minute I think it is, and the next I don't, then I'm simply not certain either way. I'm sure the idea is farfetched, if not crazy and even impossible. Yet . . . lately I seem to be thinking of it constantly."

"Mom, I don't know myself. I feel your same confusion about this. But the sheer impossibility of the task may be the end of it. Last spring I was far too confident. Since then I've learned a bit. It's hard to get information about anything in that country, even innocuous matters. If I start asking about specific people . . ." She hesitated, remembering the trouble her questions about Oleg had caused. "It could be danger-ous."

"I don't want you to get in trouble or to jeopardize your job there, but—" Her beseeching eyes finished her thought.

"I don't think it would do any good," Cameron said. "And what if I did find them? What would you do, Mom? What of Dad?"

"I haven't a clue about what I'd do. I would just like to *know*, at the very least, if my child is alive."

"Mama . . ." Cameron drew an arm around her mother and hugged her close. "You can't torture yourself with this all over again—"

"I want to know!" Cecilia cut in sharply. Then she softened. "I need to know."

Cameron couldn't refuse her mother, despite the fact that she knew the request was an impossible one to fulfill. No doubt Cecilia knew that, as well. But she couldn't pass up this opportunity to have a trusted confidante search for her lost son.

"Okay, Mom, I'll do whatever I can."

Cecilia held out an envelope she had been holding. "These are Yakov's letters and a couple of photographs. Take them. Perhaps they will help you."

"You've kept these? In the house!"

"There are many hiding places in a house such as ours. Why would anyone have looked anyway?" Cecilia smiled faintly. "See if you can find your brother, Cameron. Then we'll decide what to do about it after that."

Cameron took the envelope and tucked it into her typewriter case. She was both anticipating and dreading looking inside the small packet, but she knew that when she did so, she ought to be alone. Whatever emotions the photos of her brother and the words of her brother's father might stir, they would be a private matter.

When her flight was called, Cameron hugged her mother and sister again, and they all promised to keep in contact, knowing that with a war touching nearly half the world it could be a difficult undertaking. Yet they promised, and it made them feel a little better about the parting.

As the plane winged its way over the Pacific Ocean, Cameron wondered what would become of them all. What if the war came to America? Would it tear them apart that much more? When would she see them again? And Blair, when would she see her?

And what of her father? She didn't want to think of him, nor of the sense of failure that gripped her when she did. She could hate him for that, but she didn't. Miserable fool that he was, he was still her father.

Cameron tried for the long hours of the flight to put these agonizing quandaries from her mind. She dozed off and on, but at each waking, her thoughts were plagued anew. She awoke in the wee hours of the final morning of the flight. It was one o'clock in the morning. The stewardess mentioned they were flying over Siberia. Soon she would be landing in Kuibyshev. There, it would be easy to forget all the pain carried from home. But she knew it wouldn't be right. Somehow she had to reach out to her father. It seemed that was a cog in her life that must be healed before anything else could be right.

On sudden impulse she took out her typewriter case from under the seat in front of her and propped it on her lap. Opening it, she took a sheet of paper and cranked it into the carriage. She had to move aside the packet from her mother, but she tried to push away the thoughts the package evoked. She had another purpose in mind just now. It had occurred to her that she and her father were writers. No wonder their conversations so often dissolved into chaos. Perhaps she could express herself to him better on paper. She began to type the date, then had to pause, figuring in the crossing of the International Dateline along with the early hour. Finally, her fingers pressed the keys.

December 7, 1941
Dear Dad,
  I am on a plane bound for the Soviet Union. I guess flying away so far from home, it is only natural that I become a bit pensive. The uncertainty of the future has loomed large in my thoughts. Your illness has made this seem even more important,

along with the current state of the world. Who knows where we will be tomorrow or the next day? Everything can change in . . . a heartbeat. It scares me, Dad. I know you taught me to be stronger than that, but I'm human. So are you. I know there is more to you than you try to present on the surface. I know you must be afraid sometimes, too. I think you are afraid of dying. I worry, too, that you will die, and it will be with words of anger hanging between us. Please, Dad, let us make things right between us! I love you, Daddy, and I know you love me. I will never understand why we struggle so against each other. I need you. I need you to be proud of me, I need your support. . . .

Cameron's fingers stopped, lingering on the keys. She wondered if she had the courage to send such a letter to her father. She doubted it. It was a risky thing exposing her weaknesses to him. He'd squashed her so often before. Suddenly she yanked the unfinished letter from the roller. She was about to crush it into a ball when she stopped once more. Instead, she folded the paper in half and slipped it under the packet from her mother.

Maybe someday she would be able to send it to her father. The world was changing. Anything could happen. There was a possibility that hard-nosed Keagan Hayes could change, as well. After all, Cameron had changed. She'd grown to the point where she could *think* of writing such a letter. Goodness, she'd even fallen in love, truly in love. She, who had once firmly declared herself not the marrying kind, was now considering sharing her life with a man. Wonders could happen.

Closing her typewriter case, she propped her elbows on it and rested her chin in her hands. She glanced out the small airplane window. Straining a bit, she tried to catch a glimpse of the snow-covered expanse that must lie below. But it reminded her only of how very far she was from home, and she decided not to give in to such weakness. She'd save worrying about her family for another time. There was too much beckoning her forward—a purpose, a task . . . and Alex. She knew that somehow she would draw courage from all that lay ahead to one day face what lay behind.